From one of the hottest new voices in paranormal romance comes a provocative new series—four spellbinding novels in four months—that will plunge readers into a world where vampires stalk the night and werewolves succumb to the tides of their desires with every full moon.

Meet Riley Jenson, a heroine unlike any other: a gorgeous werewolf with a touch of vampire in her blood. Each book will bring Riley face-to-face with some of the sexiest men in recent fiction—and launch her into a world of peril and pleasure that will leave readers panting for the next installment!

TEMPTING EVIL

finds Riley Jenson embarking on a new mission—and enjoying the attention of two irresistible men: Quinn, a sexy, inscrutable vamp, and Kellen, a gorgeous, grinning wolf. Caught between two lovers while hot on the trail of a killer, Riley's tempting fate—and loving every minute of it!

"Keri Arthur is one of the best supernatural romance writers in the world." —Harriet Klausner

"Strong, smart and capable, Riley will remind many of Anita Blake, Laurell K. Hamilton's kick-ass vampire hunter.... Fans of Anita Blake and Charlaine Harris's Sookie Stackhouse vampire series will be rewarded."
—*Publishers Weekly*

"A sexy and fast-paced novel aimed at the mature reader... The author excels at showing not just characters, but how they interact as a society.... The novel also rises above mere adult fantasy because the author carefully shows not just the juicy scenes, but their aftermath. This is not a novel where characters have sex and that's that; there are consequences and drawbacks to being a member of a race that simply can't deny sexual urges at certain times of the month. It may sound like great fun, but Arthur doesn't shy from the logical result of such behavior." —*Davis Enterprise*

"*Full Moon Rising* is the first book in a new paranormal series. It's sexy and exhilarating, with characters that revel in their sexuality and take it any time and any way they can get it.... It's provocative and edgy with enough heat to scorch the paper it's written on. It's a pleasure to see that within a genre that is getting crowded with uninspired and repetitive stories it is still possible for this author to create a unique and very strong heroine. For those who like Anita and Elena, the kick-ass and sensual Riley is worth a loud and satisfied howl. With books two and three already written and number four in the works, this will be a series to keep its readers hooked emotionally and sexually." —ARomanceReview.com

"As the trend toward bolder and sexier heroines heats up, Australian author Keri Arthur tosses her hat into the burgeoning ring with the first book in her new supernatural series, *Full Moon Rising*. Arthur creates a shadowy and believable world where werewolves, vampires and other supernatural creatures co-exist with humans, and where Riley and her kind are held hostage by the monthly lunar cycles—like wolves, their mating practices are uninhibited and definitely not monogamous. Arthur also cooks up a nicely paced *cloning* plot that Riley has barely begun to unravel by story's end—leaving the door wide open for all kinds of possibilities. *Full Moon Rising* definitely grabs the attention, and Keri Arthur is an author to watch." —BookLoons.com

"Unbridled lust and kick-ass action are the hallmarks of this first novel in a brand-new paranormal series.... 'Sizzling' is the only word to describe this heated, action-filled, suspenseful romantic drama...keeps readers on their toes in constant suspense...breathtakingly scorching. *Full Moon Rising* sets a high bar for what is now a much-anticipated new series." —CurledUp.com

ALSO BY KERI ARTHUR

Full Moon Rising
Kissing Sin

Tempting Evil

Keri Arthur

A DELL BOOK

TEMPTING EVIL

A Dell Book / March 2007

Published by
Bantam Dell
A Division of Random House, Inc.
New York, New York

This is a work of fiction. Names, characters, places, and incidents either
are the product of the author's imagination or are used fictitiously.
Any resemblance to actual persons, living or dead, events, or locales
is entirely coincidental.

Dell is a registered trademark of Random House, Inc., and the colophon
is a trademark of Random House, Inc.

ISBN 978-0-553-58847-7

Printed in the United States of America
Published simultaneously in Canada

www.bantamdell.com

OPM   10 9 8 7 6 5 4 3 2 1

Dedications for Tempting Evil:

I'd like to thank everyone at Bantam who made this
book possible—especially my editor, Anne,
and her assistant, Joshua.

I'd also like to add a special thanks to my agent,
Miriam, and to my crit group, the Lulus.

Tempting Evil

Chapter 1

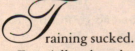raining sucked.

Especially when the main aim of that training was to make me something I'd once vowed never to become—a guardian for the Directorate of Other Races.

Becoming a guardian might have been inevitable, and I might have accepted it on some levels, but that didn't mean I had to be happy about the whole process.

Guardians were far more than just the specialized cops most humans thought them to be—they were judge, jury, and executioners. None of this legal crap the human cops were forced to put up with. Of course, the people in front of a guardian's metaphoric bullet were generally out-of-control psychos who totally *deserved* to die, but stalking the night with the aim of ending their undead lives still wasn't something that had reached my "to-do" list.

Even if my wolf soul sometimes hungered to hunt more than I might wish to acknowledge.

But if there was one thing worse than going through all the training that was involved in becoming a guardian, then it was training with my brother. I couldn't con him. Couldn't flirt or flash a bit of flesh to make him forget his train of thought. Couldn't moan that I'd had enough and that I couldn't go on, because he wasn't just my brother, but my twin.

He knew *exactly* what I could and couldn't do, because he could feel it. We mightn't share the telepathy of twins, but we knew when the other was hurting or in trouble.

And right now, Rhoan was fully aware of the fact that I was trying to pike. And he knew why.

I had a hot date with an even hotter werewolf.

In precisely one hour.

If I left now, I could get home and clean up before Kellen—the hot date in question—came by to pick me up. Any later, and he'd see me as the beaten-up scruff I usually was these days.

"Isn't Liander cooking you a roast this evening?" I said, casually waving the wooden baton I'd been given but had yet to use. Mainly because I didn't want to hit my brother.

He, however, didn't have the same problem, and the bruises littering my body proved it.

But then, he didn't really want me to be doing this. Didn't want me on the mission drawing inexorably closer.

"Yes." He continued to circle me, his pace as casual as his expression. I wasn't fooled. Couldn't be, when I could feel the tension in his body almost as well as I could feel it in mine. "But he has no intention of putting it on until I phone and tell him I'm on my way to his place."

"It's his birthday. You should be there to celebrate it with him rather than putting me through the wringer."

He shifted suddenly, stepping forward, the baton a pale blur as he lashed out at me. I ignored the step and the blow, holding still as the breeze of the baton's passing caressed the fingers of my left hand. He was only playing, and we both knew it.

I wouldn't even see his real move.

He grinned. "I'll be there as soon as this is over. And he did invite you along, remember."

"And spoil the private party you have planned?" My voice was dry. "I don't think so. Besides, *I'd* rather party with Kellen."

"Meaning Quinn is still out of the picture?"

"Not entirely." I shifted a little, keeping him in sight as he continued to circle. The padded green mats that covered the Directorate's sublevel training arena squeaked in protest under my bare feet.

"Your sweat is causing that," he commented. "But there's not nearly enough of it."

"Jesus, Rhoan, have a heart. I haven't seen Kellen for nearly a week. I want to play with *him,* not you."

He raised an eyebrow, a devilish glint in his silver eyes. "You get me on the mat, and I'll let you go."

"It's not *you* I want on the mat!"

"If you don't fight me, they'll make you fight Gautier. And I don't think either of us wants that."

"And if I do fight you, and do manage to bring you down, they're going to make me fight him, anyway."

Which pretty much sucked. I wasn't overly fond of vampires at the best of times, but some of them—like Quinn, who was in Sydney tending to his airline business, and Jack, my boss, and the man in charge of the whole guardian division—were decent people. Gautier was just a murdering freak. He might be a guardian, and he might not have done anything wrong just yet, but he *was* one of the bad guys. He was also a clone made for one specific purpose—to take over the Directorate. He hadn't made his move yet, but I had an odd premonition that he would, and soon.

Rhoan made another feint. This time the baton skimmed my knuckles, stinging but not breaking skin. I resisted the urge to shake the pain away and shifted my stance a little, readying for the real attack.

"So, what's happening between you and Quinn?"

Nothing had happened, and that was the whole problem. After making such a song and dance about me upholding my end of the deal we'd made, he'd basically played absent lover for the last few months. I blew out a frustrated breath, lifting the sweaty strands of hair from my forehead. "Can't we have this discussion after I play with Kellen?"

"No," he said, and blurred so fast that he literally disappeared from normal sight. And while I could have tracked his heat signature with the infrared of my vampire vision, I didn't actually need to, because my hearing and nose were wolf-sharp. Not only could I hear his light steps on the vinyl mats as he circled around me, but I could track the breeze of his spicy, leathery scent.

Both were now approaching from behind.

I dove out of the way, twisting around even as I hit the

mat, and lashed out with a foot. The blow connected hard and low against the back of his leg, and he grunted, his form reappearing as he stumbled and fought to remain standing.

I scrambled upright, and lunged toward him. I wasn't fast enough by half. He scooted well out of reach and shook his head. "You're not taking this seriously, Riley."

"Yes, I am." Just not as seriously as he'd like me to. Not this evening, anyway.

"Are you that desperate to fight Gautier?"

"No, but I *am* that desperate to see Kellen." Sexual frustration wasn't a good thing for anyone, but it was particularly bad for a werewolf. Sex was an ingrained part of our culture—we needed it as much as a vampire needed blood. And this goddamn training had been taking up so much of my free time that I hadn't even been able to get down to the Blue Moon for some action.

I blew out another breath, and tried to think calm thoughts. As much as I didn't want to hurt my brother, if that was the only way out of here, then I might have to try.

But if I *did* succeed in beating him, then Jack might take that as a sign I was ready for the big one. And part of me feared that—feared that no matter what Jack said, my brother was right when he said that I shouldn't be doing this. That I was never going to be ready for it, no matter how much training I got.

That I'd screw it all up, and put everyone's life in danger.

Not that Rhoan had *actually* said that last one. But as the time to infiltrate Deshon Starr's crime cartel drew nearer, it was in my thoughts more and more.

"It's a stupid rule, and you know it," I said eventually. "Fighting Gautier doesn't prove anything."

"He is the best at what he does. Fighting him makes guardians ready for what they may face out there."

"Difference is, I don't want to become a full-time guardian."

"You have no choice now, Riley."

I knew that, but that didn't mean I still couldn't rail against the prospect, even if my protests were only empty words. Hell, if Jack came up to me today and offered me the chance to walk away from becoming a guardian, I wouldn't, because there was no way in hell I'd walk away from the chance of making Deshon Starr pay. Not only because of what he'd done to me, but what he'd done to Misha, and to Kade's partner, and all those countless men and women still locked in breeding cells somewhere.

Not to mention all the things given life in his labs— abominations nature would never have created, creatures born for two purposes only. To kill as ordered, and to die as ordered.

A chill ran across my skin. I'd only come across a few of those creatures, but I had a bad, bad feeling that before this month was out, I'd see a whole lot more than I ever wanted to.

I licked my lips, and tried to concentrate on Rhoan. If I had to get him down on the mat to get out of here, then I would. I wanted, *needed,* to grab a little bit more of a normal life before the crap set in again.

Because it *was* coming. I could feel it.

A shadow flickered across one of the windows lining the wall to the right of Rhoan. Given it was nearly six, it was probably just a guardian getting himself ready for the evening's hunt. This arena was on sublevel 5, right next to the guardian sleeping quarters. Which, amusingly, did contain coffins. Some vamps just loved living up to human expectations, even if they weren't actually necessary.

Not that any humans ever came down here. That would be like leading a lamb into the midst of a hungry den of lions. To say it would get ugly very quickly would be an understatement. Guardians might be paid to protect humans, but they sure as hell weren't above snacking on the occasional one, either.

The shadow slipped past another window, and this time, Rhoan's gaze flickered in that direction. Only briefly, but that half-second gave me an idea.

I twisted, spinning and lashing out with one bare foot. My heel skimmed his stomach, forcing him backward. His baton arced around, his blow barely avoiding my shin, then he followed the impetus of the movement so that he was spinning and kicking in one smooth motion. His heel whistled mere inches from my nose, and probably would have connected if I hadn't leaned back.

He nodded approvingly. "Now, that's a little more like it."

I grunted, shifting my stance and throwing the baton from one hand to the other. The slap of wood against flesh echoed in the silence surrounding us, and tension ran across his shoulders. I held his gaze, then caught the baton left-handed and started to hit out. Only to pull the blow up short and let my gaze go beyond him.

"Hi, Jack."

Rhoan turned around, and, in that moment, I dropped and kicked his legs out from underneath him. He hit the mat with a loud splat, his surprised expression dissolving quickly into a bark of laughter.

"The oldest trick in the book, and I fell for it."

I grinned. "Old tricks sometimes have their uses."

"And I guess this means you're free to go." He held up a hand. "Help me up."

"I'm not that stupid, brother."

Amusement twinkled in his silvery eyes as he climbed to his feet. "Worth a try, I guess."

"So I can go?"

"That was the deal." He rose and walked across to the side of the arena to grab the towel he'd draped over the railing earlier. "But you're back here tomorrow morning at six sharp."

I groaned. "That's just plain mean."

He ran the towel across his spiky red hair, and even though I couldn't see his expression, I knew he was grinning. Sometimes my brother could be a real pain in the ass.

"Maybe next time you'll reconsider the option of cheating."

"It's not cheating if it works."

Though his smile still lingered, little of that amusement reached his eyes. He was worried, truly worried, about my part in the mission we'd soon embark on. He didn't want me to do this any more than I'd wanted him to become a guardian. But as he'd said to me all those years ago, some directions in life just had to be accepted.

"You're here to learn defense and offense," he said. "Inane tricks won't save your life."

"If they only save it once, then they're worth trying."

He shook his head. "I can see I'm not going to talk any sense into you until after the sexfest."

"Glad you finally caught the gist of my whole conversation for the last hour." I grinned. "And hey, look on the bright side: Liander's going to be mighty pleased to see you at a normal hour for a change."

He grunted. "Well, if he wasn't so damn clingy, he might see me early more often."

I raised my eyebrows at the annoyance in his tone. "He gives you free rein to be with who you want. I hardly call that clingy."

"I know, but—" He stopped and shrugged. "I don't know if I can give him what *he* wants. I don't know if I'll ever be able to."

Which was almost exactly what I'd said to Quinn two months ago. It was amazing how our love lives seemed to be following similar lines—although my reasons for saying those words to Quinn were entirely different than my brother's statement. Rhoan actually loved Liander. I couldn't say the same about Quinn. Hell, we barely even knew each other beyond the realms of sex.

And at least Liander had stuck with Rhoan, through good times and bad. Quinn had done a runner yet again, despite his declared intention of not letting me go until we'd fully explored this thing between us.

How he intended to do that from Sydney was anyone's guess. Maybe he'd simply decided I was just too much trouble and it was better to walk away. Though given we were sharing some mighty erotic dreams, I doubted walking away was a real option for either of us right now.

I touched a hand to my brother's arm, and squeezed lightly. "Liander loves you. And he'll wait for you."

Rhoan's gaze met mine. "I'm not sure I'm worth such devotion."

I raised my eyebrows. "I'm that devoted."

He flicked my cheek lightly. "Yeah, but you're my twin and my pack-mate. You have to be."

"True." I studied him for a moment, then said softly, "Just because our pack didn't love us doesn't mean we're unworthy of love."

How many times had he said that to me over the years? And yet now, when the crunch came for him, he wasn't truly ready to believe it himself.

His smile was sweet, but sort of sad. "The difference between you and me is the fact I don't want to settle down. At all. I want to be free to be with whomever I choose, whenever I choose."

"Whomever?" I interrupted, with more than a little annoyance in my voice. "Don't tell me you're still seeing Davern?"

Rhoan had the good grace to look uncomfortable. "Only when he's in town, and that's not often these days."

"But didn't you tell Liander you two were no longer an item?"

"Well, we aren't. We're more occasional lovers."

"A nitpicky difference Liander will *not* appreciate."

He shrugged. "Look, maybe my inability to commit is just a part of what I am."

I knew he was referring to his sexuality more than his being a guardian or a half-breed. And that angered me.

"Liander's just like you, and he wants to settle down. Don't start making excuses just because you're scared."

He raised his eyebrows, yet there was a keenness in his

silvery eyes that suggested I was right on the mark. "Scared?"

"Yeah. Settling down means making a commitment. And you don't want to commit to anyone because of what you *do,* not because of what you are. Admit that to yourself—and him—if nothing else."

"He deserves more than just a part-time partner."

"Maybe he does," I agreed, eliciting a startled response from Rhoan. "But neither you nor I have the right to decide that for him. It's his choice, his life."

He chuckled softly, then leaned forward and kissed my forehead. "You're pretty clever for a girl. And I hope you take note of that advice in your own life."

"Me? Take advice? It'll snow at Christmas before *that* ever happens." And given December was the first of the summer months here in Melbourne, something pretty disastrous would have to happen to the climate for that to occur. Though given the weird turns my life had been taking recently, snowing at Christmastime wasn't altogether beyond the realms of possibility.

Nor was me actually taking some of my own advice.

I gave him the baton, then shoved him gently toward the exit. "Go see him, and make sure you talk to him."

"You don't want me to walk you up to the change rooms?"

"Nah, I'll be all right." The arena was fully monitored by security whenever anyone was down here training, but I had no doubt Jack would also be around somewhere. He had a vested interest in keeping me safe and whole. Not only because he wanted me on this mission, but because he wanted me as a full-fledged guardian. "I'll see you here tomorrow morning."

He nodded, tossed the towel around his bare shoulders, and headed off whistling. Obviously, I wasn't the only one anticipating a good time tonight.

Grinning slightly, I headed down the other end of the arena where my towel and water bottle waited. I grabbed the towel and wrapped one end around my ponytail, squeezing the sweat from my hair before wiping the back of my neck and face. I might not have been fighting to full capacity tonight, but we'd still been training for a couple of hours and not only did my skin glimmer with heat, but my navy T-shirt was almost black with sweat. It was just as well I could shower here—with the way my luck had been running of late, Kellen would be waiting for me by the time I got home. And as much as most wolves preferred natural scent over synthetic, right now I was just a little *too* overwhelmingly natural.

I reached out to collect the water bottle, then froze as awareness surged, prickling like fire across my skin. Rhoan had left, but I was no longer alone in the arena.

My earlier intuition had been right—crap *had* been about to step back into my life.

And it came in the form of Gautier.

Towel still in hand, I casually turned around. He stood at the window end of the arena, a long, mean stick of man and muscle who smelled as bad as he looked.

"Still haven't managed to catch that shower, I see." It probably wasn't the wisest comment I'd ever made, but when it came to Gautier, I couldn't seem to keep my mouth shut.

It was a trait that was going to get me in trouble—if not tonight, then sometime in the future.

He crossed his arms and smiled. There was nothing

nice in that smile. Nothing sane in his flat brown eyes. "Still jumping mouth first into situations even the insane would think twice about, I see."

"It's a failing of mine." I idly began twirling the towel and wondered how long it would take security to react. And if Jack would *let* them react.

"So I've noticed."

He'd be hard-pressed not to when most of my mouth-first offenses of late involved him in some way. "What are you doing here, Gautier? Haven't you got bad guys to kill?"

"I have."

"Then why aren't you outside hunting, like the good little psycho you are?"

His sharklike smile sent a chill running up my spine, and in that moment I realized he *was* on the hunt.

For me.

Fuck.

Which didn't really fully encompass the shitload of trouble I'd landed in, but right then, it was the only word I could think of. And it was running over and over and over in my mind.

Along with the thought that I'd been set up. That this was what Jack had intended all the time when he'd arranged this training session.

Rhoan wouldn't have known. He would never have agreed to this. Never.

"So, you're here to put me through my paces, huh?"

His amusement rippled around me, as slimy as pond scum. "You catch on quick."

Not quick enough, apparently. I should have known

Jack was up to something. He'd been too jovial all day—
a sure sign the shit was about to hit the fan where I was
concerned.

But why would he put me up against Gautier so soon?
Hell, I'd only been training a couple of months. Most
would-be guardians had at least a year before they had
the pleasure of Gautier pulping them.

Maybe something had happened. Something that had
forced a revamp of the timetable.

Despite the situation, excitement trembled through
me. I wanted this ended. Wanted to get back to a normal
life—though given six months had now passed since I'd
first been injected with the experimental fertility drug,
normalcy might be a thing of the past. If that drug *was*
changing the very essence of what I was—as it had other
half-breeds—then those changes would soon start ap-
pearing.

Gautier began to stroll leisurely in my direction. I continued to twirl the towel, and watched him through
slightly narrowed eyes. I was never going to beat him,
and we both knew it, but I sure as hell was going to go
down fighting.

He stopped halfway down the arena. "You ready?"

I raised an eyebrow, feigning a confidence I didn't feel.
Which was pretty pointless, because he was a vampire,
and would know how accelerated my heart rate was.
Would know it was fear, rather than excitement.

But fear and I were old companions. It hadn't stopped
me before, and it wouldn't stop me now.

"Do you give all your targets a warning?"

"Yes."

The complete and utter stillness about him reminded

me of a snake about to strike. And it made me afraid, as no real snake ever had.

"And why would you do that?"

"Because tasting my prey's fear as I hunt them down is almost as heady as tasting blood." He paused to breathe deep. Rapture touched his flat eyes, and the chills running down my spine became a landslide. "I can taste your fear, Riley, and it is exquisite."

"You're sick. You know that, don't you?"

"But I'm very, very good at what I do."

The promise of death was in his eyes. And I knew that he and I would fight it out, for real and to the bitter end, sometime soon. Not here, not at the Directorate, but somewhere on his turf, on his terms.

Goose bumps ran across my skin, but I resisted the urge to rub my arms. Clairvoyance might be a latent skill coming to life, but it sure as hell was one I could do without.

Especially when it told me shit like that.

Gautier's fingers flexed, just the once, then he was gone from sight. His steps were featherlight on the matting, little more than whispers of air. I wished I could say the same about his scent. It was thick with the reek of death, so vile that it snatched my breath and made it hard to concentrate.

And if I didn't concentrate, this could go very, very badly.

Not that it wasn't going to, anyway.

I blinked, switching to the infrared of my vampire sight, and watched the heat of him draw closer. And closer. At the last possible moment, I flicked the towel forward, snapping the end across his stone-cold features, then I ran like hell out of his way.

He didn't give chase, simply stopped and raised a hand to his face. Though I'd been aiming for his eyes, the towel had actually snapped across his cheek, and hard enough to draw blood. It probably wasn't the wisest thing I'd ever done, but damned if the sight of his blood didn't cheer me up a little. I might get beaten senseless, but at least I'd managed to do the one thing no guardian had ever been able to do—draw blood from the great Gautier.

But then, few guardians would be insane enough to face Gautier armed with just a towel.

He ran a finger across the wound. Even from where I stood, I could see the blood sitting on his fingertip. His gaze met mine, and again I saw death.

For all of two seconds, I thought about running. Just getting the hell out of this arena and away from this psychopath. But if I did that, I'd be off the mission. And right now, I wanted that revenge more than I feared Gautier.

Gautier sucked the blood from his fingertip, then said, in a voice that was flat and yet oh so lethal, "For that, you will pay."

"Oh, I'm so scared." Which was nothing more than the truth. Anyone possessing the merest grain of sanity would *not* want to exchange places with me right now. Except maybe my brother.

I frowned at the thought. Rhoan would know what was happening—at the very least, he'd feel my fear. So why wasn't he here, watching if not intervening?

Gautier gave me the sort of smile a cat might give an

amusing mouse just before he ate it, then disappeared from sight again. I tracked him with infrared, waiting until he closed in, then threw the towel at his face even as I dropped, spun and lashed out with one foot, trying to bring him down. He avoided the towel and the kick, then his fist was arcing toward me. I dodged, felt the breeze of it scrape past my cheek, then dove forward, tackling him at knee height and bringing him down. As we both hit the matting, I landed a punch, kidney-high, before rolling to my feet and getting away. Close-in fighting with Gautier was something I was never going to win. I had to hit and run, hit and run, for as long as I could.

The bastard didn't even have the courtesy to grunt at the force of my blow. He climbed to his feet, his movements leisurely, calm. But there was murder in his eyes.

I wiped the sweat from my eyes, then flexed my fingers, trying to remain relaxed. He wouldn't kill me, not here. I had to believe that, if nothing else.

"Very good," Gautier said, his slimy, too-confident tones sending more chills up my spine. "There are very few who have managed what you just did."

I wondered if those few were still alive to speak about the experience. Knowing Gautier, probably not.

"I shall have to try a little harder, it seems," he added.

Oh, fuck.

The thought had barely entered my head when he was coming at me, a whirlwind of power and speed and sheer, bloody force. I weaved and dodged and blocked as best I could, throwing punches and kicks. But I was never going to beat him, and we were both too aware of that point. He might not be faster, but he was stronger and far more experienced.

Eventually, several blows got through my defense, leaving me winded, battered, more than a little bruised but somehow still upright. I kept blocking, kept fighting, then another blow came through, crashing against my chin, snapping my head back and sending me flying. Stars danced in front of my eyes, and the black peace of unconsciousness flirted with me. I shook my head, denying the call, and twisted in the air so that I landed catlike and on all fours. Saw, in a brief flash of awareness, my brother, his knuckles white with the force of his grip on the railing. Saw the four security guards holding him back. Saw Jack watching it all.

Then the air was screaming with the scent and force of Gautier's follow-up leap. If he pinned me, that would be the end of it. I rolled away and slashed sideways with my heel. The blow connected low down, against his ankle, and flesh and bone gave way under the power of it. He grunted, fury flashing across his dead features, then he spun and grabbed my leg even as I tried to scramble away.

A scream ran up my throat as he pulled me toward him, but I managed to push it down enough that it came out only as a slight gasp of fear. I twisted around, ignored the slivers of pain that ran up my leg, and kicked out with my free foot.

He laughed. *Laughed.*

Never a wise move when it came to dealing with werewolves—even if the odds *are* on your side. You might as well wave a red rag at a raging bull.

The anger that swept through me momentarily bolstered my reserves of strength. I called to the wolf within, and the power of the change swept around me, through me, tingling through vein and muscle and bone, blurring my vision, blurring the pain, the fury. Limbs shortened, shifted, rearranged, until what was lying on the mat was wolf, not human. It wasn't a move Gautier had expected, and just for an instant, he didn't actually react. I ripped my leg free of his grip, then leapt to my feet, launching at him rather than away. Teeth slashed, tearing through the flesh of his arm as easily as scissors through paper.

His blood spurted into my mouth, a foulness worse than even his scent. I coughed, spat out his taste, his flesh. Then his fist was in my side, burrowing deep. Something snapped within, and everything went red as the force of the blow battered me away from him. I shifted shape as I flew through the air, and hit the mat hard enough to knock the air from my lungs. Or maybe there wasn't any to begin with, because my lungs burned and I couldn't seem to get enough air no matter how much I gasped. All I could feel was pain and fear.

All I could hear was the wind of Gautier's approach.

"Stop." Jack's command barked across the arena.

Gautier didn't seem to hear. Or maybe he didn't want to hear, because suddenly he was beside me, his fist filling my vision as it hurtled toward my face. I curled into a ball, protecting myself the best I could, knowing it was never going to be enough.

"I said, stop!"

The blow never landed. After a few seconds, I opened an eye and saw Gautier still above me, his fist still clenched and so very close to my face. His arm quivered, as if he were fighting some restraining force, and not only was there sweat on his forehead, but fear in his eyes.

Jack had stopped the blow. Was holding him still now. Not physically, but through psychic means. Here, in this arena, in a building filled the psychic deadeners.

Which meant Jack was a whole lot more powerful, and a whole lot more deadly, than I'd ever presumed.

"Retreat, Gautier. Go to the med center and have those wounds looked at."

"This is not finished," Gautier hissed as he stepped away. "But we *will* finish it, believe me."

I didn't say anything, couldn't say anything. Just watched him hobble away as I kept on trying to get some air into my lungs.

The scent of spice and leather spun around me, then Rhoan was beside me, touching my face, my neck, his expression stricken.

"I'm okay. Really," I managed.

It came out hoarse, and didn't seem to convince my brother. "I'm going to kill—"

I touched a finger to his lips. "No." The bastard was mine, even if I had to do it from the shadows with a long-range rifle.

He caught my hand and held it against his heart. Its beat was rapid, fear filled. Just like mine. "He had no right—"

"I'm betting he had *every* right. I'm betting our dear boss had this planned all along. Help me up."

He did. Pain slithered through my torso, red pokers of agony that seemed to pierce far too many muscles. I hissed, and held on to my brother as the room spun briefly.

"You weren't ready—"

"Is anyone ever ready to fight Gautier?" Pain slithered across my jaw as I spoke. I winced and raised a hand to feel for damage. The whole left side of my face was swollen, and tender enough that even the lightest of touches hurt. I might be a wolf and heal extraordinarily fast, but there wasn't much I could do about bruises. I was going to be black and blue by the time I got home. So much for my fancy night out with Kellen.

Footsteps echoed in the brief silence, and I didn't need to smell his musky scent to know it was Jack approaching. Nor did Rhoan. Tension slithered through his body, and the anger I could almost taste sharpened abruptly. Before I could even open my mouth to warn Jack, Rhoan had turned and punched.

Jack caught the blow in his hand. Caught it and held it. Easily. As if all of Rhoan's strength and power was nothing more than that of a troublesome child.

"I have my reasons," he said, green eyes as intense as his soft voice. "Trust that I know what I'm doing."

Rhoan wrenched his fist free. "Gautier almost killed her!"

"I'm sure he would have loved to, but you're missing the point."

"The fact that you stopped him, despite all of the psychic deadeners in this place?" I rubbed at the ache in my side and wondered if I'd cracked a rib or something. It sure as hell felt like it. Changing shape might have healed any break, but it sure didn't stop the pain or the bruising. And it had totally wrecked my clothing. As I tied the end of my T-shirt together to stop my boobs from falling out, I added, "All that means is you've just warned Gautier how strong you truly are."

Amusement briefly touched the corners of his eyes. "Yes, but that's just a side benefit."

"Then what was the whole point?" Rhoan spat. "To beat her up when she wasn't even ready?"

Jack raised an eyebrow. "How many fully trained guardians have lasted ten minutes with Gautier?"

"Not many, but that—"

"One," Jack interrupted. "You. And Riley managed what even you couldn't. She marked Gautier, made him bleed."

"Which only succeeded in pissing him off," I muttered. "From now on, I'm going to have to watch my back."

"Even he won't dare go after you for several nights, and by then it won't matter because you'll be gone." He hesitated, lowering his voice a little as he added, "The time frame for the mission has been stepped forward."

So I was right. Something trembled through me, something that could have been excitement or fear, but more than likely was simply relief. No matter what direction my life was meant to go, it would be good to finally quit having to look over my shoulder all the time. I raised an eyebrow. "You've had a breakthrough?"

"Several."

"Riley isn't ready for this." Fury still filled Rhoan's soft tones, if not his expression.

"Will I ever be ready, at least in your opinion?" I touched a hand to his face and smiled. "We both know the answer would be no."

"You *shouldn't* be doing this."

"I *have* to do this. I may have been forced down this road, but I sure as hell intend to see it through now."

"But—"

"No," I cut in. "I won't change my mind, and I won't back down, no matter what I have to do or *who* I have to do. These bastards are going to pay for what they did to me."

His gaze searched mine, then he sighed and took my hand from his cheek, squeezing it lightly. "You really are a stubborn bitch."

"Much like my brother," I said dryly.

Rhoan smiled, but his gaze, when it shifted to Jack, was deadly. "If she gets hurt, or killed, I'm coming after you."

"As undoubtedly will she, if you get hurt or killed." Jack hesitated again, looking around. The only other people in the arena were the four guards down near the exit, but Jack wasn't into trusting anyone lately. Especially when we had no idea who else Gautier might be working with in the Directorate. "Report to Genoveve tomorrow at nine."

Genoveve was the lab that had been a major source of clones for several years—though it wasn't the lab that Gautier had come from. It had been purchased by Talon—one of Gautier's clone brothers, and a former mate of mine—some years ago so he could continue his cloning endeavors well away from the Government's prying eyes. We'd stopped that operation, as well as a crossbreeding operation, but we'd yet to find the main lab. That lab was still little more than a name—Libraska.

And the only person who apparently knew the location of that lab was Deshon Starr. Or rather, the shape-shifter who had taken over Starr's body and life.

"I thought Genoveve was being sold off by the Government?"

"It is, but we're still using it in the meantime."

"Then we're back into the fray as of tomorrow?"

"Yes." Jack glanced at Rhoan. "I've already called Liander. He'll be coming in with his full kit."

Given Liander was one of the top movie effects people in the country, that could only mean we'd be donning our disguises—and moving into our cover lives—from tomorrow. "Which means I'd better make the most of my time tonight." Bruises or no bruises.

"You'd better," Jack warned. "Because from tomorrow, there's to be no contact with *anyone* you're currently involved with."

I raised my eyebrows. Even *that* hurt. My sexfest wasn't looking good at *all*.

"Meaning Quinn's not in on this?"

"No."

Great. It meant I'd probably get harassed even more at night when he realized something was happening he wasn't involved with.

Rhoan lightly squeezed my arm. "You want an escort up to the change rooms this time?"

I nodded. No sense in chancing fate a second time.

We headed up several floors to the change rooms, where I admired the blooming, rainbow-colored range of bruises scattering my body before stepping under the shower to wash away the sweat and blood and the foul smell of Gautier from my skin and hair and mouth.

Luckily, I'd brought some extra clothes to change into after training, because the T-shirt and sweatpants weren't in a fit condition to be worn out in public.

Rhoan dropped me off at home, and I noted with some relief that Kellen's white BMW wasn't in sight. Maybe I had time yet to get myself into some semblance of working order. I climbed the stairs, but after hours of training and then fighting Gautier, the six flights just about did me in. I opened the door with a trembling hand, and discovered fate hadn't finished throwing curveballs my way yet.

Kellen stood at my door.

So did Quinn.

And neither man looked particularly happy to see the other.

Chapter 2

I blew out a breath and wished, just this once, that I could catch a break. I wanted to spend the night being wined, dined, pampered, and ravished, and not particularly in that order.

What I didn't need was having to deal with the annoyed sensibilities of two alpha males who hated each other.

Though as far as alphas went, you couldn't ask for two finer specimens. Neither man was particularly tall—Kellen was probably little more than an inch above my five seven, and Quinn maybe an inch more above that. Kellen was a lean and muscular brown wolf, though he was more chocolate in tone than the muddy coloring so often seen in the brown packs. His face was sharpish but handsome, his eyes the most delicious shade of gold-flecked green. And dressed as he was in the black tux, he looked absolutely scrumptious.

Quinn was just as athletic looking, but there was more of a sense of grace and controlled power in the way he moved. His dark blue sweater emphasized the width of his shoulders, while the tight fit of his jeans drew the eye to the long, strong length of his legs. His shoulder-length hair was night dark, and so thick, so lush, that my fingertips suddenly itched with the need to run through it. His skin was not the white of most vampires, but a soft, warm gold, simply because he could actually stand quite a lot of sunlight. His eyes were vast wells of darkness the unwary could easily get lost in, and he had the sort of looks even angels would be envious of. Not that he was in any way effeminate—just beautiful. Truly beautiful.

The stairwell door slammed shut against my back, knocking me into the half-lit hallway. It said a lot about the tension between the two of them that neither actually noticed my arrival until then.

"What the hell is *he* doing here?" they said in unison, each one pointing at the other.

I ignored the question and walked to the door. "Play nice, boys. I'm just not in the mood for petty fighting tonight."

"Then you should not have invited him." Kellen's voice was cold.

"I didn't. He just sort of pops in unannounced whenever he feels like it." I twisted the key in the lock and opened the door. "How do you two actually know each other?"

"He and my father are business rivals and old enemies."

"Mainly because your fucking father keeps trying to kill me off."

"My father would never—"

"Your father would and has."

If I wasn't so tired I might have laughed. The two of them sounded like a couple of squabbling teenagers. What made it even more laughable was the fact that one of them was actually well over twelve hundred years old and *should* have known better.

"Gentlemen," I interrupted, raising my voice a little to be heard over their arguing. "Can we take this inside?"

The old cow who owned the building would have a pink fit if she found a vampire and a werewolf arguing in the middle of her hall. And as much as I hated her and didn't mind giving her the odd bit of aggravation, something like this might tip her over the edge and us out of the apartment. And not only did I love the warehouse-style apartment and the big wide windows that gave such a feeling of freedom; I also loved the low rent.

I opened the door and ushered them both inside. Kellen walked over to the green sofa but didn't bother sitting down, while Quinn contented himself with leaning up against the wall near the TV. Both men had their arms crossed. Both still bristled with tension and anger.

So much for my much longed for evening filled with good food, good wine, and lots of sex.

I closed the door, threw my gym bag on the other sofa, and walked into the kitchen to get a beer. I had a feeling I was going to need it.

"So," I said, as I came back out. "To what do I owe the honor of this little visit, Quinn?"

The look he gave me could only be described as dark.

No surprise there, because that certainly seemed to be a favored expression when he was talking to me.

"We had a deal."

"Deal?" Kellen's gaze snapped to mine. "What sort of deal?"

"That he gets to see me solo when he's down in Melbourne." Trouble was, I'd only seen him once since we'd agreed to that deal. Most of our contact had come through dreams and, as good as they were, even I had to admit that wasn't enough.

"So you're *still* fucking him?" The annoyance deepened in Kellen's expression. "And here I was thinking you'd gained a little taste since Sydney."

"Apparently not." I took a swig of beer, felt the ice of it swirl all the way down. It felt good, but it certainly wasn't what I'd been looking forward to all day. "But who else I fuck is none of your business, anyway."

His gaze narrowed. Hardened. "You and I—"

"Are exploring options. Nothing more." I pointed a finger at Quinn. "If he were another werewolf, would you have any issue?"

"Yes."

"Why?"

"Because alphas do not easily share something that they consider theirs."

I snorted softly. "Then it seems like you two have something in common, despite the race differences."

"We have a date tonight," Kellen said, his voice like steel. "And we are already extremely late."

Like I didn't know that. "If you want to go on ahead, I'll meet you there."

He sent a dark glance Quinn's way and shook his head. "I can wait."

"Seems to me like he doesn't trust you," Quinn commented.

Yeah, it did. What pissed me off, though, was not so much Kellen's distrust, but the fact that it was Quinn pointing it out. "This from the man who thinks all wolves are whores?"

"I explained that—"

I held up a hand. I'd heard that particular song before, and didn't believe it now any more than I had before. "That's not the point here, anyway. After two months of no-shows, you can't just walk back into my life and expect me to drop everything."

"There are reasons—"

"There always are," I cut in dryly. "But that doesn't excuse bad manners."

"I tried to call. Your line was always busy."

"Being taken off the hook will do that to a phone. You could have left a message."

"Could have, but I didn't." He hesitated, and just for an instant, his frustration swirled around me, thick and sharp. But what made my breath catch and my soul tremble was the depth of loneliness that lay underneath that eddy of emotion. I recognized that loneliness. I had shared too many nights with it of late.

"I just thought it would be nice to drop in and see you," he continued softly.

Part of me wanted to melt into his arms. The harder part knew I couldn't afford to. Not until I truly knew why he was here.

"Meaning, of course, I have no life and just sit around waiting for you?"

"That's not what I meant—"

"It's hard for me to ever know what you mean when you never bother taking the time to explain."

"And when do you give me the time?" he retorted, his anger a hot wash of emotion that seared at my skin.

I rubbed at the ache beginning in my head, and suddenly felt wearier than I'd ever felt in my life. Why did this have to happen now?

"You at least owe me the courtesy of listening," Quinn continued.

"She doesn't owe you anything," Kellen cut in. "You are not wolf. You have no rights—"

Something inside me snapped. "You know what? *Neither* of you have any rights where I'm concerned. I'm not a prized bone that can be fought over and won." Even if my hormones were dancing with delight at the idea of having two gorgeous men fighting to win my affections. "Right now, I'm not in the mood to deal with this. Why don't you both just get the hell out?"

Kellen's expression became as dark as Quinn's. "But we have tickets—"

"I don't give a fuck about the tickets, or the premier or whatever else you have planned. I've had a shit of a day, and it only seems to be getting worse." I glanced across at Quinn. "Nor do I care why you're here. Just leave."

Quinn studied me for a moment, then asked, "Why? This is something that needs to be sorted out."

"No, it doesn't. Because I'm seeing you both, end of story. If either of you can't accept that, then walk away. I don't care." Which was a lie, but one I wasn't willing to admit. "Get out. Both of you."

Quinn studied me for several seconds, then turned and walked out. I glanced at Kellen. "And you."

"So you're serious?"

"Totally."

His expression was one of disbelief. I couldn't say I blamed him, and part of me was hoping he'd put up a fight, that he'd stay, and just hold me, comfort me.

But all he said was, "I'll call you."

"Do that."

He hesitated, his gaze sweeping me briefly, then he followed Quinn out the door. I closed my eyes against the sudden sting of tears. Not because the night I'd been so looking forward to had just been so thoroughly shot to pieces, but simply because neither of them had asked me if I was okay. Neither of them had even seemed to notice that I was battered and bruised. They'd been far too busy snarling at each other and trying to stake their claim to even notice something as obvious as my swollen jaw and cheek.

And yet both of them claimed to care for me.

I would have laughed at the irony if it wasn't so damn sad.

I scrubbed a hand across my eyes, then pushed away from the wall and headed into the bathroom. I lit a candle as the big old tub filled up, added some lemony-lime bath salts to the steaming water, then stripped and eased into the bath. Where I just relaxed, and tried to ignore the screaming frustration of my hormones.

I don't how long it was before I realized I was no

longer alone, but enough time had slipped by for the water to become tepid.

I opened my eyes. Kellen stood in the doorway, one shoulder resting against the frame, his expression a mix of fierce desire and even fiercer determination.

And he was holding the biggest bunch of red roses I'd ever seen.

Something inside me melted. Rejoiced.

"You really have to learn to lock your door when you have a bath," he said softly.

"But if I did, nice men bearing beautiful roses wouldn't wander in."

"Not only flowers," he said, and produced a small tube from behind his back. "But massage oil. I figure all those bruises meant a hard day at the office."

"And here I was thinking no one noticed."

"It took me a while." He placed the roses and the oil on the sink, then took off his jacket and rolled up his shirtsleeves before sitting on the edge of the bath. "I was too busy protecting my territory to even notice said territory was in pretty bad condition."

"I'm nobody's territory."

He smiled and dipped a hand in the water, touching my leg and gently running a finger up and down my thigh. Heat ignited low down, and trembled through the rest of me as furiously as a firestorm. My body might be battered and bruised, but everything else was in full working order.

"When you are with me, you're mine," he refuted softly. "And I'll fight all comers to reserve that right."

I raised an eyebrow. "Even vampires with a fierce right hook?"

"Even vampires. Though I cannot believe you're still with *that* particular vampire."

"I like him."

"Then I must accept him as competition. But don't expect me to be happy about it."

I smiled. "Asking *that* wouldn't be fair."

"No." His gaze rose to mine. The desire so evident in those mint green depths scorched deep. "I want you, Riley."

My name rolled off his tongue as sweetly as a lover's kiss, and my whole body seemed to hum in answer.

"I guess if you're gentle, we might be able to manage a kiss or two."

He reached between my feet and pulled out the bath plug, then turned on the hot water. "And a caress or two?"

I pursed my lips, as if considering a question there could only ever be one answer to. We both knew it. The smell of my arousal was as thick as his. "I suppose there's a few unbruised places to find."

His gaze drifted down, a slow perusal that was all-consuming. Heat prickled across my skin, and my nipples hardened, as if reaching for his caress. Bone-tired and body weary I might be, but I was also a wolf who hadn't had any sex for almost a week. And *that* ache took priority over all others.

"I can see one or two interesting possibilities," he murmured, leaning forward to replace the plug then turn off the tap. "Seeing it's such a big bath, do you mind if I join you?"

"Please do." It came out husky, thick with desire.

He smiled and rose, then unhurriedly began taking

off his clothes. I enjoyed the show, the gentle reveal of skin and muscle. The candle's dancing light lent a rich warmth to his chocolate-colored flesh, highlighting some areas of perfection while leaving others to shadow and imagination.

When he was fully naked, he stepped into the bath, but rather than lying beside me, as I'd expected, he lowered himself over me, using his elbows to keep his weight off me even though his body covered mine as completely as a blanket.

"Nice," he murmured, his breath whispering across my lips.

"Very." The heat of him washed over me, and the wet, raw scent of masculinity and desire had my heart racing so hard I swear it was going to tear out of my chest. I ran a hand down his muscular back, letting it rest on his rump and pushing him down lightly. The thick heat of him pressed in all the right places, and I sighed. "Very nice indeed."

The words had barely left my lips when his mouth claimed mine. He was a man who knew exactly what he wanted, exactly what *I* wanted, and his kiss reflected that. It was urgent, hungry, his mouth plundering as our tongues tangled, tasted, teased.

God, the man could kiss.

After what could have been hours, he groaned, an almost demanding sound that vibrated through my mouth. A sound I understood completely. Because, just like him, I wanted more than just his lips. I wanted him inside, deep inside, thrusting long and hard.

I moved my legs to give him greater access, then raised

my eyes to his. "If you want me so badly, why don't you take me?"

"Because I'm trying to be considerate of all those bruises." He pressed himself between my legs, sliding his cock back and forth, teasing, but not entering.

"I don't *want* consideration." But it came out a strangled sound as the heated tip of him began to slide inside.

"Then what do you want?" he murmured, withdrawing briefly. "This?" he added, sliding back inside again, harder and deeper this time.

Pleasure rippled through me, and I groaned. Heard his answering chuckle.

"I'll take that as a yes."

"Do," I gasped, and almost came as he rammed himself deep.

Then he began to move, to thrust, and I closed my eyes, savoring and enjoying the sensations flowing through me as the heat of him filled me and the cooling water lapped with ever more force across our skin.

He took his time, stroking slow but deep as he licked and nipped and kissed. Eventually the pressure began to build low in my stomach and fan through the rest of me, first in languorous waves, then quicker, faster, until it became a molten force that made me tremble, twitch, and groan. Had me wanting more, and yet not wanting it all to end so soon.

His breathing became as harsh as mine, his tempo more urgent. Water rocked over the bath's edge, splashing across the tiles, but right then, the only tide that mattered was the one of pleasure rising between us, and boy, was it rising. I shuddered, writhed, until my moans filled the night and it felt as if I was going to tear apart from the sheer force of enjoyment.

"Let go," he whispered, pressing butterfly kisses against my nose, my cheek, my lips as he thrust deep and hard inside me. "I want to hear it. Feel it."

As if his words were a trigger, my orgasm hit, and suddenly I was shuddering, squirming, my moans so loud they'd surely have to hear them in the apartment next door.

Then he was coming with me, his lips capturing mine as my body clenched around him, his kiss urgent as his body thrust and thrust, until there was nothing left but exhausted, joyous satisfaction.

For several minutes afterward we didn't move, just allowed the cooling water to wash the heat from our skin and our breathing to return to normal. Then he stirred and gave me a sweet, gentle kiss.

"Far better than attending a premier," he murmured. "Though I have to admit, I was intending to take you during the show."

I grinned. "Imagine the headlines that would have created, '*Son of billionaire thrown out of premier for indiscriminate sex.*'"

"Oh, there wasn't going to be anything indiscriminate about it—and we had a private box."

"I do like a man who thinks ahead."

"Rather than a man who thinks with his head?"

The cheeky twinkle in his eyes made me chuckle. I raised my hips and rubbed myself up and down his penis. He may have just reached the heights, but he was half ready to go again.

There were definite advantages to being a werewolf, and a revved-up sex drive was certainly one of them.

"Thinking with the lower head can sometimes have its advantages."

"Hmmm," he murmured, brushing my lips with another kiss. "Shall we retreat to your bed and discuss just what those advantages might be?"

"Most definitely."

So we did. And much enjoyable "discussion" was had.

It was only later, when I was lying warm and replete in the circle of his arms, that he asked the question I'd been waiting for all night.

"So, how did you get all the bruises?"

"Training." I yawned, fighting tiredness and the need to sleep, simply because the subject of my bruises would lead pretty neatly into the fact that I'd be disappearing for a while.

"Given the intensity of the bruising, I'd have to say it was more a beating."

"I'm a liaison. Given we have to work with guardians, we've got to know how to defend ourselves. As you can see, it gets pretty full-on."

His fingers were caressing my arm, not in a sexual way, but a caring, protective way. It made me feel warm and fuzzy inside—which wasn't something I'd really experienced before and I wasn't sure what to make of it. It wasn't love—I'd been there before, knew what it felt like, and this wasn't that. It was oddly different—safer, nicer.

"So, now that they've beaten you to a pulp, I'm gathering the training is over for the next year or so?"

"I'm afraid not." I looked up at him. "As of tomorrow,

I'm on a survival retreat. I won't be able to contact any-one."

Anger, and frustration, seared the depths of his beauti-ful green eyes. "At all?"

"I'm afraid not."

"For how long?"

I shrugged. "It depends on how well I cope." And how fast we brought down the bad guys.

His hand slid down my side and across my rump as he pulled me closer. "I've only just found you. I'm not too happy about having to let you go again."

Neither was I. But then, if turning my life upside down for several months meant actually getting my life back on track, I wasn't about to grumble. "Look at it this way—I'm going to be one frustrated wolf when I return, so you can be sure the reunion will be a good one."

He grinned. "Now that sounds a little more like it." He shifted slightly, turning onto his side. My head slipped from his chest to his arm, but it felt just as good resting there. "I'm guessing, then, that I'd better let you get some sleep."

I slid a leg over him and adjusted my position as I pressed him close. A shiver of delight ran across my skin as he sheathed himself inside. "I guess you should."

He did. But only after several more hours of loving.

Kellen left at seven. I grabbed some clothes then walked into the bathroom for a quick shower. Once dressed, I headed toward the kitchen to make myself breakfast. Only to discover Quinn sitting cross-legged and elegant in my living room.

I stopped short. He'd changed sometime during the night, because he was now wearing black on black. More than ever he looked like a dark angel—a sinfully sexy dark angel. "I really am going to have to start locking my front door."

"It wouldn't keep me out."

True. Once I'd invited him past the threshold of my home, there wasn't one damn thing I could do to stop him entering anytime he pleased, as often as he pleased.

I crossed my arms and stared at his beautiful but emotionless face.

"What do you want?"

He studied me for a moment, then said, "Would you like to have breakfast with me?"

Surprise rippled through me. Of all the questions I'd been expecting, that wasn't one of them. "Why?"

He raised an eyebrow. "You have to eat, don't you?"

"Yeah, but that's not what I mean."

He shrugged. "You told me two months ago that I needed to pamper you, romance you, to win your heart. Perhaps I've finally realized that was good advice."

"And perhaps tomorrow pigs might fly. Why are you really here, Quinn?"

He didn't react to my barb, and that was almost scary. Perhaps he really *was* trying to show me a different side of himself. And yet, instinct whispered all was not as it seemed, and I was never one to ignore instinct. It had saved my ass far too many times.

"I'm merely here to see you, and to have breakfast with you. Nothing more, nothing less."

"And I'm not on your menu? A quick snack on the side?"

Amusement glimmered briefly in the dark depths of his eyes. "It would be a bonus, but no." He hesitated, and the glimmer disappeared, lost to the sudden flash of annoyance. "I have attended to my blood needs, in much the same manner as you've attended to your own needs."

"I didn't ask Kellen back. He came of his own accord, bearing roses and an apology." I paused. "Have you even noticed my bruises?"

"Only a blind man could not."

"And you didn't think to comment—not even a simple 'gee, they look bad'?"

"Would they have felt any better if I had?"

They wouldn't, but I might have. "You know, for a very old vampire, you're sometimes awfully obtuse."

He shrugged. "Will you come to breakfast?"

"No." I spun on my heel and walked into the kitchen to flick on the kettle.

"Why not?"

Though I'd heard no movement, he was suddenly standing in the doorway, his arms crossed as he leaned casually against the door frame. His presence seemed to dominate the small kitchen in a way no bigger man could have. He was all dangerous energy and devastating masculinity, wrapped in an outer layer that was urbane and sophisticated. And I was as attracted to the power underneath as I was to the gorgeous outer wrapping.

I just didn't quite know what to do with the package as a whole. Or that I was entirely wise being in *any* sort of relationship with him. Two months ago I'd discovered that, for the first time in my life, I was fertile. Currently protected against pregnancy, but fertile all the same. The doctors were certain it wouldn't last, that my vampire genes would eventually assert themselves and I would once again become the werewolf equivalent of a mule, but it was a revelation that had changed my whole perspective when it came to Quinn. Yes, I wanted him. Fiercely. But I couldn't and wouldn't risk going exclusive with him. Not only because that might mean missing the wolf who was my destined soul mate, but for the simple fact that if the drug that had made me fertile didn't actually cause any other chemistry changes within me, then this might be my one and only chance to conceive. I'd wanted a family of my own all my life—wanted that whole white picket fence and two kids ideal—and I had no intention of missing the opportunity if it came along. And if ever there was a certainty in my life, then it was this—Quinn might be able to give me the white picket fence, but he could never give me a child. Never, ever.

Of course, he knew all this, just as I knew he wanted something more than what I was willing to offer. What that something was he wouldn't say—I wasn't even sure if he knew himself.

But why would he state that he had no intention of going anywhere until we'd explored this thing between us, then basically stay away for two months? Why show up again so suddenly? It didn't make sense—and everything this vampire did, he did with a purpose in mind.

His gaze touched mine, and those luscious dark eyes were rich with awareness and hunger. Hunger that was both sex *and* blood driven. Despite what he'd said about sating his needs earlier, his hunger was right here, burning between us, stronger, more alluring than ever before.

And it only intensified the feeling he was here for more than what he was saying.

"Answer the question, Riley," he said, voice soft yet holding a note that suggested it was almost a demand. "Why won't you have breakfast with me?"

"Because I have to leave for work very soon."

"Why?"

"Because I'm due to start at nine, and the goddamn train takes half an hour to get there on a Saturday."

The fact that Rhoan and Liander were picking me up here at eight-thirty was something he had no need to know. Though it did mean I'd have to get him out of my apartment before then. The minute he saw Liander, he'd know the mission to infiltrate Starr's cartel was on.

And he'd want in.

I turned away from him and grabbed a mug, then picked up the jar of instant coffee and dumped several spoonfuls into the mug. My preference ran to hazelnut espresso, but this was the best we had until payday. Rhoan had gone on one of his shopping sprees again, and left us with very little in the bank. I did have some very nice sweaters to show for it, though, which I suppose was something.

"Is Gautier the cause of those bruises?" Quinn asked.

"No."

"You lie, Riley."

I didn't say anything. There was no point.

"So you have passed the final step to become a guardian?"

I looked over my shoulder at him. "I've passed one test with him. The real fight with Gautier lies ahead."

Which was nothing but the truth, but he was staring like he knew something was up, that I wasn't telling him the *entire* truth.

Being a dhampire with strong psychic skills generally made me immune to the caress of a vampire's mind, but when it came to *this* vampire, there was no such protection. Not only had we shared blood, but we'd created a link that went far deeper than mere psychic touch. It was a link not affected by distance or the presence of psychic deadeners. A link that made him able to read my surface thoughts as easily as he drank blood.

Which was why my shields were currently up high. Whether it helped or not I had no idea, because I certainly wasn't going to risk reading him.

"Is it not usual for those who fight Gautier to be given leave? Why are you going in today?"

"Why are you so damn fixated on this?"

He shrugged. I wasn't for an instant believing the casualness behind the gesture. "I'm curious, that's all."

"Yes, it is unusual. But then, I'm not the usual guardian candidate, am I?"

"No, you are not."

I frowned at the edge in his voice, but the kettle chose that moment to whistle its readiness, and I turned away from him to pour my coffee.

Bad mistake.

Though my hormones quickly formed a differing opinion as his arms slid around my waist. "Why is it so hard to believe I am here to see you?" His lips brushed the side of my neck, sending a shimmer of delight right down to my toes.

But as much as my hormones had formed a cheer squad for some vampire loving, the itchy feeling he was here for more than just me wouldn't go away.

"Why did you suddenly show up on my doorstep after two months of no contact?"

"We had contact."

"One night in two months? Hardly enough loving to keep a gnat awake, let alone a werewolf."

"Running a multinational business sometimes takes more time than I would wish." He slid one of my top's shoestring straps off my shoulder. The brush of his lips against the flesh between my shoulder and neck felt like the touch of flame. "And our deal was you could be with others when I wasn't there. I'm sure you didn't go without."

"Oh, I didn't, trust me." I tried concentrating on making myself a coffee, but it was damnably hard when he was so close, so warm, and so very, very tempting. "And you're saying you had no time to even leave a message?"

"Why did I need to when we were sharing erotic dreams at night?" The second strap slid away with some help from his fingertips, then the top itself was being tugged down to expose my breasts. The warm air caressed my skin, as enticing as the man behind me.

"They were only dreams, Quinn. It would have been nice to have something with a little more substance."

"Which is what we now have."

His hand splayed across the flat of my stomach. Heat pooled under his fingertips, flared across my flesh like a flash fire. Lord, his touch was even more intense than I'd remembered.

His hands slid up to my breasts, pushing them together as he began to tease and pinch my engorged nipples. I squirmed against him, wariness momentarily forgotten as every inch of me vibrated with the hunger now flowing through my veins.

As if sensing the fall of reluctance, he began to kiss me, caress me, tease me, until tiny beads of perspiration covered my skin. Until every inch of me was trembling, and I was hovering on the edge of a climax, aching for the release he was keeping from me.

When his caress finally moved down, I groaned in relief. His fingers played around my thighs, close but not close enough to where I actually wanted them. *Needed them*. After a few more torturous moments, he hooked his thumbs under my panties and pushed them down my legs. I stepped free, then toed them to one side. He pushed up my skirt as I widened my stance, then his fingers were slipping through my slickness from behind, caressing and teasing until I was moaning from equal measures of pleasure and frustration. His soft chuckle whispered heat across the back of my neck, then his fingers were in me even as he pressed his thumb against my clit. As he began to stroke, inside and out, I shuddered, writhed, until it felt as if I was going to tear apart from the sheer force of pleasure.

And then he was in me, claiming me for real and in the most basic way possible. I groaned again as he gripped my hips, his fingers bruising as he held me still for too many seconds.

But oh, it was *so* glorious, just standing there, my body throbbing with need, his body deep inside mine, heavy and hot with the same sort of need. I loved the way he seemed to complete me. It had nothing to do with his size or his shape or anything physical, because I'd certainly been with men who outstripped him in all those areas.

This was far more—was almost as if when our flesh was joined, our spirits combined and danced as intimately as our bodies.

He began to move, not gently, but fiercely, urgently, and I was right there with him, wanting everything he could give me. The deep-down ache blossomed, spreading like wildfire across my skin, becoming a kaleidoscope of sensations that washed through every corner of my mind. I gasped, grabbing the bench for support as his movement grew faster, more urgent. Then everything broke, and I was unraveling, groaning with the intensity of the orgasm. He came with me, but it wasn't just his juices that flowed into me. So, too, did his mind.

And he was raiding my thoughts and my memories as fast as any thief fearing discovery.

Anger unlike anything I'd felt before surged through me, and without even thinking about it, I lowered my shields and let him have it with every ounce of psychic strength I had.

He made a gargled sound, then the force of my psychic punch wrenched his body from mine and he was flying through the door, out into the living room, where he landed with a thump on his back.

I re-shielded fast. Pain hit, but it might as well have been a leaf tossed on the wind, my anger was so strong. I grabbed my knickers and marched into the other room.

"You *bastard*!" I flung the panties at him, though why I had no real idea. It wasn't like it was a knife or a stake or anything *that* useful.

Which is probably just as well, because right then, I would have used either one of them.

He rubbed a hand across his eyes, then slowly raised

himself up on his elbows. "How the hell did you do that?"

"What the fuck does it matter, given what you just did?"

"If you'd tell me the truth for a change, I wouldn't have to resort to such measures!"

His voice was as loud and as angry as mine, but there was a tremor in his tones that suggested I *had* hurt him. Part of me was fiercely glad. Part of me hated it.

"I have a right to privacy. In my life, and in my thoughts."

"This is different."

"Why? Because you're a twelve-hundred-year-old vampire who no longer has to obey the rules?"

"And yet, for all my age, and for all my psychic skills and knowledge, you just ripped through my shields as if they were paper. And then you sent me flying. You couldn't have done that a few months ago."

A cold hard knot formed deep in the pit of my stomach. He was right. God help me, he was right. Even though Jack *had* been training me in the fine art of breaking through psychic shields over the last few months, I'd never managed to break through all *his* shields, no matter how hard I'd tried. And Quinn was far more powerful than Jack.

I licked my lips, and pushed the thoughts away. Now was not the time to think about the implications of his statement, or what it might mean to the future I so desperately wanted.

"Don't try changing the fucking subject."

He sighed, climbed a little unsteadily to his feet, and re-dressed himself. "I admitted to you months ago that I was, in part, using you. You were my quickest way of finding information about my missing friend—information that the Directorate, and my friendship with Director Hunter, wasn't providing. That hasn't changed—though the reason certainly has."

"So that's why you're back now?"

"Partially. Something changed yesterday afternoon. Something is happening. I can feel it."

He could feel it? How? We hadn't shared dreams in any way yesterday, so he couldn't have leeched information that way. And, usually, he could only catch my thoughts if he was physically near.

But maybe he had been. Maybe he'd been here in Melbourne all along, and just hadn't contacted me.

Bastard.

"So the real reason you came to my apartment last night was for a little extra information gathering? I bet it sucked having your grand plans foiled by Kellen's presence."

"It wasn't the only reason I was here last night. I did want to see you."

Yeah. Believing *that* big time. "How in the hell could you supposedly feel *anything* when we're supposedly only sharing erotic dreams and nothing more?"

He didn't answer. No surprise there. The bastard never answered questions that *really* mattered.

He walked toward me and held out my panties. I snatched them from his hand and threw them to the floor. And some childish part of me wanted to stomp all over them—or maybe it's just that I wanted to stomp all over Quinn, and with no hope of achieving that, they were the next best option.

"Was I ever anything more than just a convenient source of information?" I asked bitterly.

He reached out, his fingers briefly caressing my cheek with heat until I jerked away from his touch. His hand dropped back to his side, but the determination in his eyes said he was far from defeated.

"There has always been something more between us."

"Yeah, great sex."

"More than that. I care for you, Riley. Deeply."

I snorted softly. "You keep saying that, and yet you couldn't even be bothered coming to see me for the last two months. The only reason you're here now is the fact that you sensed something was happening with the case."

He studied me, arms crossed, face impassive. But there was nothing impassive in his eyes. Nothing impassive in the explosive swirl of emotion scorching my skin with heat.

"If it was your brother they'd snatched and killed, would you not do everything in your power to exact revenge? Even if that meant betraying someone you cared for greatly?"

"That's different—"

"No, it's fucking not! Henri was my brother in all but blood. I will not let these fools get away with his murder. I *will* have my revenge, no matter what I have to do!" He paused, then added softly, "Or who I have to hurt."

I held up my hands, not pushing him away but certainly ready to. "Don't touch me."

"This will not end here," he said flatly. "I won't let it."

"Right now, you have no goddamn choice. I want you to leave and I don't want you to come back and I don't want to see you again."

He snorted. "You'll see me, not only in your dreams, but on the mission. It starts today and I *will* be involved in it."

So he'd gotten that much from me. Bastard.

"Go," I said fiercely, "before you make me do something I might not regret."

He studied me for a moment, then spun on his heel and walked to the door. But he stopped with his hand on the knob, and looked over his shoulder at me. "I'll see you at the Directorate. And you had better tell Jack about that increase in power, or I will."

With that he left. The door slammed after him, the noise reverberating through the sudden silence. I closed my eyes and rubbed my temples for a moment, then turned and headed for the shower. And though I could wash the smell of him from my skin, there was no washing away the feel of him in my mind. No getting away from the huge sense of loss and betrayal.

And I hated that, hated that he'd reduced what was between us to that. Because he was right—there was something more, something that had the potential to be magical. Not soul-deep magical, perhaps, but still so very good. His actions might not have destroyed that, but I really didn't know if I would ever be able to get past them.

I lifted my face to the cooling water, letting it wash away the sting from my eyes. After a while, I got out and re-dressed, then headed into the kitchen to make myself another drink.

And it was there, while I was nursing the steaming mug of coffee, that I finally let myself think about the way I'd attacked Quinn.

I'd never had that sort of power before. Yeah, I rated extremely high in all the Directorate telepathic tests, but I'd never gotten anywhere near reading Quinn's surface thoughts before, let alone busting through any of his shields.

I had tonight, and with such power the force of it had blown him across the room.

Had anger allowed me to tap the reserves Jack kept insisting I had, but had never used? Or was this the first sign that the drug Talon had given me was finally beginning to affect my system?

I didn't know.

But I had a bad feeling I was going to find out, and all too soon.

Chapter 3

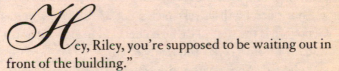

ey, Riley, you're supposed to be waiting out in front of the building."

Rhoan's cheerful voice rose out of the stillness, making me start. I glanced at the clock and realized that almost an hour had passed since Quinn had left.

"Sorry," I called, rinsing the mug under the tap as I tried to gather my composure.

Why I bothered I have no idea. He wasn't fooled any more than I would have been.

"What's wrong?" He stopped in the kitchen doorway, his cheerful expression fading quickly to one of concern. "Are you okay?"

"Just dandy, bro."

He frowned, then pulled me into his arms. For several minutes he didn't say anything, just held me. Comforted me.

"Quinn raided my thoughts during sex," I said eventually, my words muffled by his chest. "He knows we're going after Starr."

Tension slipped through his muscles, quick and sharp. "Bastard."

"Exactly what I said. Several times."

"I hope you made him pay."

I sniffed. "Yeah, I did." But who was going to be the real loser—him or me?

"Good." He released me and stepped back. "Have you warned Jack?"

I shook my head. "There's no need. Quinn's going to the Directorate. He never got deep enough to discover we were going to Genoveve."

"But once he discovers Jack's not at the Directorate, Genoveve is the first place he'll check." He glanced at his watch. "I'll ring Jack. You ready to go?"

I nodded. There was nothing to pack, nothing to take, because from here on in, I was going to become someone else.

"Then let's get out of here, just in case he decides to come back for a little more raiding."

I nodded, then suddenly remembered Liander. "I just have to get one thing."

I dashed into my bedroom to get Liander's birthday present, then we left. Once we'd gotten into Liander's van and had merged into the flow of Saturday-morning traffic, Rhoan called Jack. I leaned over the front passenger seat and plonked the present onto it.

"Hey, happy birthday, old man."

"Forty-nine is hardly old for a werewolf. And kindly

remember that you're going out with someone more than twelve hundred years old."

"Yeah well, that situation might have changed." Though I'd forced a cheerful note into my voice, Liander didn't appear any more fooled than my brother had been.

He gave me a concerned glance. "Are you okay?"

"Floating on happiness," I said dryly. Then waved at the present. "You can open it when we get to Genoveve."

"Or you could tell me now and save me the suspense."

"I don't think so."

He studied it for a second, then said, "It almost looks like a book."

It was—on the history of cinema effects. But I'd added a box of chocolates to fudge the shape a little. "You'll just have to wait and see."

"Bitch."

I grinned.

"Do a U-turn," Rhoan said, his hand momentarily over his cell phone. "Head for Chapel Street."

"Chapel Street?" I said, surprised. "What the hell is there, besides upmarket shops and trendy snobs?"

He waved a hand for me to shut up, so I returned my attention to Liander. In the sharp morning light, he was an almost icy silver. The only thing that lent him some warmth was the blue of his clothes and the matching streaks in his hair.

"Going for the winter look this week, are we?"

He gave me a smile that had all sorts of warning signals flashing. "Winter is very 'in' at the moment. But just wait until you see what I have planned for you."

"I think I should be afraid."

"Very. You are going to be extremely foxy."

My eyebrows rose. "Meaning I'm not now?"

"Darling, you're pretty but very underdone. A little time, care, and makeup certainly wouldn't go astray."

"That's a very backhanded compliment."

He grinned. "Sometimes the truth hurts."

"So can a smack in the head."

His grin widened and he shook his head. "You are so like your brother sometimes, it's scary."

I raised my eyebrows. "Rhoan's threatened to smack you?"

"Oh, many times." He gave me a glance that was pure mischief. "Trouble is, I enjoy it."

"I think that falls into the category of a little too much information at this hour of the morning."

"Gentle pain can be quite a turn-on if it's done right."

"Give me normal sex anytime." I pointed to the road ahead. "And if you don't concentrate, you're going to ram the back of that Ford."

He slammed on the brakes, throwing me backward. "If you'd stop yakking about sex, I *could* concentrate."

I shut up. After a few more ums and yeses, Rhoan hung up and glanced at me. "We're going to Chapel Street because Jack lives above a restaurant—he owns the building and leases out the restaurant section."

I frowned. "Is it safe going there?"

"Apparently only Director Hunter knows the address. A different address is used on files."

And Quinn would never get the address off Director Hunter. Not only was she older in vampire years—and therefore more powerful—but because he was honor bound to obey her. Or so Quinn had said when he'd briefly mentioned the vampire hierarchy system a few months ago.

"We're not going to get parking anywhere near that street at this hour," Liander commented.

"There's a multilevel parking lot behind the Jam Factory, which is just down the road from Jack's."

"Meaning we get to go shopping while we wait for Jack?" I glanced at my brother as I said it, but couldn't resist adding the barb. "Oh, that's right, you already have. That's why we have no money left."

"You got pretty sweaters, so don't bitch."

"I need to eat more than I need new sweaters."

"We have tin food."

"Spaghetti and baked beans just don't cut it after a few days."

He gave me an annoyed look. "You're beginning to take all the fun out of shopping."

Which was precisely the point of nagging. I grinned and looked away. We battled our way through the rush-hour traffic, getting there just after nine-thirty. Liander threw several large bags our way, then grabbed the remaining four himself. Jack was waiting in the shadows a few doors down from the Jam Factory complex, out of direct sunlight and well covered up. Age gave vampires a certain amount of immunity to the sun, so the older they were, the more they could walk in daylight. Quinn only had to avoid the hours between twelve and two. Jack, four hundred years younger, had tighter restrictions. He was probably pushing his limits right now.

We followed him to a small door to the right of an Italian restaurant, and up a set of stairs. His apartment was one long room—barring a doorway that led to what I presumed would be the bathroom and laundry—and surprisingly airy, with the front and back walls all windows. Though right now, awnings covered the back windows to stop direct sunlight. The color scheme and furnishings were very masculine, all blue colors, dark woods, and rich leather, and the walls were covered in what looked like prints from the old masters. Only they weren't prints, but real paintings. Given how old Jack was, that was more likely than it seemed.

"So," Jack said, as we dumped the bags on the floor near the table. "How did Quinn discover the mission timetable had been moved up?"

"Through me." I pulled out a chair and sat down at the table. "Apparently the fact we've shared blood has given him greater access to my mind—shields or no shields."

Jack raised his eyebrows. "If that were the case, he'd be here, not heading to Genoveve."

"You've got him under observation?" Rhoan asked.

Jack nodded. "We seconded several hawk-shifters from Overseas Operations recently to tail Gautier. One of them is currently on Quinn. He'd sense another vampire, even if we had a guardian who could go out in morning sunshine."

Which was why Jack was so determined to set up a daytime division, with me, Rhoan, Kade, and Liander all as its chief operatives. Right now, the Directorate was very limited in its operational times, and not all the bad guys did the nasty stuff during the night.

"Quinn can only read my thoughts during times of

stress or pleasure," I explained. "So right now, no matter how much he tries, he hasn't a hope of getting past my shield."

Which wasn't exactly the entire truth—he could actually touch my mind during sleep, as well. But I was pretty sure that was a connection that took both of us to form and went no deeper than a dream state.

And I have to say, the man gave amazing dream sex.

"We'd better hope he can't," Jack muttered. "Because I do not want him near this operation."

I raised my eyebrows. "Why?"

"Because he is only interested in revenge. We want to bring down the cartel's entire operation." He sat down on the chair nearest the com-unit and interlaced his fingers. "We had our first breakthrough about six weeks ago. You remember the letter Misha left you on his death?"

It was hard to forget, given the circumstances under which he'd died. A tremor ran through me. God, I still had nightmares about those watery spiders, and Misha being eaten alive from the inside. I licked my lips, and said, "He gave us the name of the fifth clone—Claudia Jones. But he didn't know the alias she worked under at the Directorate."

"We've since discovered she doesn't actually work for us—though she does visit several times a month."

The glint in his green eyes suggested amusement, but for the life of me, I couldn't see why. I mean, there were thousands of people who visited the Directorate every month, all of them for legitimate reasons.

"She's not one of Alan Brown's whores, is she?" Rhoan said, a note of incredulity in his voice.

"Yes."

I glanced at my brother. "How the hell did you jump to that conclusion?"

He just grinned and tapped the side of his head. "Brains, dear girl. Brains."

I snorted softly. "I wasn't aware that's where you kept your brains."

"Enough." Jack touched a button on the keyboard, and the com-screen sprang to life. On it was a picture of a white-haired, white-skinned woman. She was extremely pretty and yet oddly ethereal, and there was an unearthly sense of power in her luminous blue eyes. "This is Claudia Jones."

"She looks like I did—well, except for the eyes." I looked across at Liander. "When you made me up for the raid into Brown's office."

He nodded. "She seemed to be one of his regulars, so we thought it would be less suspicious if you looked like her."

"Of course, we weren't to know that she was Gautier's contact." Jack pressed another button, and the woman's picture gave way to porno—Brown fucking Jones in his office. As far as lovers went, the man had no finesse whatsoever—just got it out, shoved it in, and pumped away. Which was probably why he had to rely on prostitutes to relieve his sexual needs.

Jack froze the picture at the point of Brown getting his rocks off, and pointed to the screen. The image shimmered slightly as he touched it, then settled. "If you look at this hand, you'll notice her fingers have slipped under the desk. If I enhance the picture—" He did so, until the woman's hand dominated the screen. "You'll notice the silvery dot on the top of her index finger."

"And that is?"

"A microdot," Rhoan said. "Latest in storage media, and incredibly resilient."

Jack nodded. "The desk has a small hole drilled into it. The disk was placed into a container fitted into the hole."

"So Gautier just strolled in afterward and collected the container?" I asked, even as Jack dropped the close-up and sped up the film.

Brown did the dirty with the woman several more times, then both of them left. Nothing happened for a while, then Gautier wandered in, checking the office and walking past the desk in the process. He collected the container from the desk in a smooth, slick movement that would have been easy to miss, then left.

"So when Gautier sprung me and Quinn in Brown's office, he was actually going to collect a drop-off?"

"We think so."

"What made you suspect this was happening?" Liander asked. He was sitting on the arm of the sofa, behind Rhoan's chair.

"The fact that we could find no moles in the Directorate other than Gautier." He hesitated. "The only A.D. hiding secrets was Alan Brown, so we took the risk of reading him. You know he's being blackmailed?"

I nodded. Rhoan had told me that much ages ago.

"Gautier's behind it. Every Directorate decision is being relayed through Gautier to Deshon Starr. That madman knows what we're going to do before we even implement it."

"Which is why his cartel has managed to stay two steps ahead of the Directorate for so long."

Jack nodded again. "Of course, we then had to find

out how Gautier was passing the information, which meant watching his every move, not only within the Directorate, but on missions as well. Four nights after the incident we just watched, Gautier strolled into Brown's office, this time before Brown arrived with Jones, and even though he wasn't actually on watch that night. That's when we finally realized what was going on."

"And she retrieved the disk?"

"Yes. And undoubtedly passed on a detailed report of all the going-ons in the Directorate for the coming week."

"So how is Brown getting the information to Gautier? He couldn't risk being seen with him at the Directorate."

"No. But Brown likes the greyhounds, and is severely in debt to the bookies. Gautier meets him there every Wednesday night."

"Wednesday being the day the board generally meets," I muttered. They were organized, no doubt about that. But then, this mob had been operating for well over fifty years—though Starr's takeover had only been relatively recent.

"Have you pulled in the prostitute?" Rhoan asked, leaning back in his chair. "Questioned her?"

"No, though we did follow her. Brown drops her off in Fitzroy Street, St. Kilda. Five minutes after he's left, a limousine picks the woman up and drives her to a large house in Toorak."

"To another client?" Liander asked.

"No. She lives there."

I raised my eyebrows. "She's one hell of a prostitute if she can afford to live in Toorak."

Jack smiled. "She's not a prostitute at all." He pressed

another button, and the woman's picture reappeared. "She actually goes by the name of Dia Jones, and she does psychic readings for the rich and famous."

Surprise rippled through me. I mightn't read newspapers or watch the news much, but even I'd heard of Dia Jones. The woman's predictions were supposed to be deadly accurate and, last I'd heard, the waiting list to see her was over a year long. "Why in hell would a woman like that play prostitute for Deshon Starr?"

"If she is one of the clones, as Misha said, she may have no choice," Rhoan pointed out, then glanced at Jack. "And through her, Starr has a lot of access to the rich and famous, and possibly a lot of influence."

Jack nodded. "The house she lives in is owned by one of Starr's companies, and every weekend she goes to Starr's estate in Macedon. She's there the entire week before the full moon, and apparently there's also a lot of influential people in attendance at that time, too."

I remembered the estate I'd seen in one of the lab-made creatures' minds right before I'd killed him. That house had been large and surrounded by acres and acres of lush gardens. Only what roamed its grounds were not things of nature, but creatures whom evolution had little to do with—black ghosts who possessed little in the way of recognizable human features, blue things with rainbow wings and deadly claws. Demons and monsters and God knows what else. How did Deshon explain away his horrors?

"So," Liander asked. "This woman has wolf in her?"

"We don't know, but given all the cloning experiments at that time seemed to have involved werewolf genes, it wouldn't be beyond reason to think so."

"Then why Macedon? Isn't that a bit far out of the city to be running a crime syndicate?"

"In this day and age, no. Starr never actually leaves his estate, which is why we have never been able to pin any of his cartel's crimes on him."

"That and the fact the minds of his people are burned away before we can fully question them," Rhoan muttered.

"Sounds a nice type," Liander commented dryly.

"Oh, he's a charmer." Rhoan gave me a dark glance. "Which is why I don't want Riley in on this."

"Hey, I'm not the one who's planning to fuck the man, so stop worrying about me and start worrying about you."

"I'm not the one walking into this situation sans experience—"

"Enough," Jack said. "I need you both on this mission, and that's the end of it."

He pressed another button on the keyboard, and several more pictures came up, these taken at night and on the streets. They featured the same woman, only this time her pallid looks had given way to brown hair and soft makeup. In each picture she was talking to a different woman, and most of them were prostitutes if the clothing—or lack thereof—was anything to go by.

"A week before each full moon," Jack continued, "Dia apparently hits the streets for three nights on a recruitment drive. Last month, she signed up thirty women, though not all of them were prostitutes. She gives them cards, tells them to show up at a legitimate job-placement business the next day, where, after a background and physical check has been done, they're offered extremely large sums of money to provide sexual services for Starr's men during the full-moon phase. We gather some do stay beyond that two-week period, but most are returned unharmed to the streets the day after the full moon."

"Unharmed physically or mentally?" I asked.

Jack gave me one of his pleased-with-a-student smiles. "Physically, they're fine. But someone has shuffled through their memories, taking away the finer details."

"Meaning even if they were abused or hurt in the period they were there, they wouldn't remember it," Rhoan stated. "What about Starr? How does he pick his lovers?"

"From his security force." Jack hesitated. "We have someone in his estate already, and he's managed to uncover details about the firm Starr uses. That's how you're going in."

Rhoan frowned. "Who have you got in there? Gautier would have passed on Directorate photos, so Starr would recognize anyone we tried to get in there."

"But he doesn't know Kade. Starr has a passion for horses—he apparently doesn't ride them himself, just loves watching them run around with naked women on them."

"I'm betting the women aren't just riding them," Rhoan muttered. "From what I've heard, Starr loves watching others get it off. And the more dangerous the situation, the more he enjoys it."

Some people kept dogs as pets. Starr kept horses and lab-made nightmares, and, from the sound of it, combined the two interests sexually. It said an awful lot about the man. Or rather, his weirdness.

"Are the other horses shifters? Or just Kade?"

"Just Kade."

Then poor Kade. Having naked women riding around on his back was going to be mighty frustrating for the poor fellow.

"Tonight," Jack continued, "Director Hunter will place Rhoan's new identity in the security company's system and alter the memories of the three men who run the place. Tomorrow night, Kade will kill one of the current security force. Rhoan will, of course, be the recommended replacement."

"What about me?"

Jack glanced my way. "Dia began her recruitment drive last night."

I raised my eyebrows. "But the full moon is three weeks away, not two."

"Yes. And two nights ago, Dia left a message for Gautier saying the timetable has been stepped up to February fifth."

Which was one month away. "Do we know what timetable they're talking about?"

But even as I said it, I knew, if only because of the premonition I'd had earlier. Gautier would try to kill Jack that day.

Which is exactly what Jack said. "And while we have no idea why the timetable has been stepped up," he added, "it means we have less than a month to stop Starr."

"Is that going to be enough time?" Christ, Rhoan might know what he was doing, but I was a novice, and it would take me longer to uncover information for that reason alone.

"It's going to have to be." Jack reached past the computer and gave me a folder. "Your new identity."

I opened the folder and looked inside. "Poppy Burns?" I looked up at Jack. "Do I look like a Poppy to you?"

"You will by the time I've finished with you," Liander said, voice dry.

I poked my tongue out at him and kept on reading. Poppy apparently was the result of a horny werewolf and a human groupie encounter, with neither parent being intelligent enough to realize they were fertile at the time of their brief liaison. The mother didn't want the resulting child, didn't know where the father was, so poor Poppy was shoved onto various relatives until she ran away at fifteen. She'd had a multitude of jobs since then, but thanks to her temper and her attitude, hadn't been able to hold on to anything for very long. She supported herself in between with thieving and the occasional spot of prostitution. She'd gotten into Melbourne three days ago, after having ripped off the wrong house in Sydney and having the owners place a large reward for information on her whereabouts.

Charming. I'd just become a wanted criminal. "Poor Poppy's had a bitch of a life, hasn't she?"

Jack grinned. "Read that until you know her by heart." He hesitated. "And make sure you start reflecting her attitude."

I nodded. "I won't have a problem with that part of it."

"Which is why we put that in. Liander, you want to start in on her? Rhoan, here's your profile."

Liander grabbed my hand and led me into the bathroom. As he sat me down, I saw the scissors.

"How short are we going?" I said instantly.

"Very short."

"No," I said, my hands going to my hair. I loved it just the way it was—I could put up with it being dyed, but cut short? No way. I mean, I cut it to shoulder length every summer, but I didn't really consider *that* short. Not in the sense Liander was talking about, anyway.

He sighed. "Darling, your hair is luscious, I admit, but it is *so* out of fashion at the moment. Hell, even your brother has more style than you, and that's saying something."

"That's because my brother raids the bank account to go shopping, and I'm the one that worries about where the rent and food money is coming from."

"Yes, but lack of money doesn't excuse lack of style. I have been offering free haircuts for years."

"I *like* medium to long hair. Anything wrong with that?"

"Normally, no. But long hair doesn't suit the shoes you're stepping into. She's trendy. With it." He flicked the end of my hair. "This is not."

"I know, but—"

"Trust me," he said. "You'll look divine. And your hair will grow back, regardless."

I blew out a frustrated breath, but gave in to the inevitable. I was being ridiculous and I knew it. Besides, I wanted my life back, and if doing that meant cutting my hair extremely short, then surely that was a small price to pay. "If it doesn't look good, I'm going over to your place and destroying all your makeup."

He grinned. "Warning heeded. Now shut up and let the master create."

For the next three hours he had his wicked way with my looks, and I had to admit, the end result was startling. He'd dyed my skin a dark gold, covering the smattering of freckles scattered across my cheeks and shoulders, and giving me the rich glow of a sun worshipper. My hair was as short as I'd feared, the ends barely brushing the bottom of my ears, but had been layered so that it framed my face, giving me a cheeky, yet extremely sexy, look. He'd also streaked it with blond, which played amongst the natural gold highlights in my red hair and gave the overall effect of three-toned hair. Breathable, bright green contacts completed the transformation.

"Wow" was all I could manage to say. I didn't look like me, even though he hadn't changed all that much.

He gave me a pleased smile. "One more touch, and we're finished."

"And what's that?"

"Voice modulator."

"Ewww."

He smacked my shoulder. "Stop being a baby."

"Hey, it's not the inside of your cheek that thing is being shoved into it."

"I got hold of some of the smaller ones, just because I knew you'd whine." He showed me the round pieces of soft plastic. They were even thinner than the last ones we'd used, their thickness being little more than that of extremely fine paper. Width-wise, they were no bigger than a small coin. Once inserted, no one would feel they were there unless they were actually looking for the things—or I decided to deep-throat someone. *Not* an option considering where I was going.

"Open wide, darling."

"I bet you say that to all the men," I muttered, but did as he asked.

He inserted the small plastic chips in either side of my mouth, and it still felt like he was ripping out teeth rather than shoving plastic under my skin.

"Owww, owww, owww," I said, when I could. "You could at least use painkillers when you do that."

"Stop being such a baby. Besides, the surface of the modulators *are* covered with an analgesic and deaden the skin as they go in."

"Hate to tell you this, but it doesn't work."

"Trust me, this would be a whole lot more painful if it wasn't. Now, say something else so I know they're working properly."

"I hope one day someone does this to you, just so you can see it *is* painful, painkiller or no painkiller." My voice was several octaves lower, and rich with a huskiness that conjured long nights in smoke-filled rooms. A threat had never sounded so sexy, let me tell you.

"Very nice," he murmured, then bent and grabbed a backpack. "You wardrobe and worldly possessions."

"Joy." I unzipped the bag. Inside was jeans, tank tops, a pair of sneakers, a belt that had a real-looking spider as the buckle, a couple of sweaters, and one barely-there dress. All of them looked worse for wear, worn and wrinkled looking. Except for the underclothing, all of which was top shelf and extremely sexy.

"A female thief would at least ensure decent under-clothing, no matter what other state her clothes were in," Liander commented.

"But I'm not a very successful thief if this bag is all I have to show for it."

"Jack told me your cover had to leave Sydney in a hurry, and to pack accordingly. Why don't you change, then I can get on with transforming Rhoan."

"And just what are you going to do with Rhoan?"

"Brown on brown. Boringly so."

I raised an eyebrow. "If you're hoping boring will mean less appealing, I'm thinking it won't work."

He smiled. "No, but he hates boring, so it's a chance to get back at him a little."

I chuckled softly. After changing into the jeans and a dark-green tank top, I studied myself in the mirror. Someone remarkably younger, with a whole lot of sex appeal and attitude, stared back at me. Despite my original misgivings, I had to admit, it was a fantastic look. I leaned forward and kissed his cheek. "You do good work."

"I am the best at what I do," he said loftily, then grinned. "Go tell that loser brother of yours it's his turn."

I headed out, and even Jack did something of a double take. "Now, that's what I call smashing."

"I think I should be offended about all these sudden comments. It's only a hair and skin-color change. The rest is still me."

"Except for the voice," Rhoan said. "You could make a fortune on those phone-sex lines."

"We'll see who's laughing at whom when he finishes with you, smart-ass." I glanced at Jack as Rhoan headed off. "This look doesn't really match the type of person Dia seems to pick."

"As I said, she doesn't pick only prostitutes. Her other choices generally have good figures and looks, are clean disease-wise, and have a background that checks out—

someone who needs to make a lot of money and who doesn't mind spreading her legs to do it."

"And what if she doesn't notice me, or doesn't choose me?"

"Oh, she'll at least notice you."

I raised my eyebrows. "And how are you going to ensure that?"

He gave me one of his pleased smiles. "Tonight you're going to save Dia Jones's life."

"And of course," I said, voice dry, "she'll be so grateful, she'll beg me to come along to Starr's estate and shag the balls off his two lieutenants."

Jack grinned. "That's the plan."

"And if she decides not to follow your plan?"

"She will. Poppy is exactly what she's looking for— someone with no morals, who doesn't care what she does for cash."

Nothing like being confident in a plan. Maybe it was the pessimist in me, or maybe it was that pesky, emerging clairvoyance skill, but either way, I wasn't so sure everything would fall into place as neatly as Jack might wish. "And when I get to the estate?"

"Take a day or so to settle in—you'll be watched fairly closely in that period, at least, so don't try anything until you think you're in the clear."

"And when I think I am?"

"You attract the attention of Starr's lieutenants, and drag all the information out of their minds that you can."

It wasn't going to be that easy, and we both knew it. For a start, I was basically still a novice when it came to mind-reading, and my control wasn't always what it should be. Though given what I'd done to Quinn this morning, maybe that was more due to an increase in power than any lack in skill. Maybe I was having so much trouble simply because the power I was controlling was greater each time, and I hadn't the skill to realize it. "What if I can't read their minds?"

He raised an eyebrow. "What do you mean?"

"What I said. You may have been teaching me the finer points of telepathic control, but that doesn't mean I'll be able to break through their shields. They might even have electronic shields in place."

"Then you figure a way around either event."

Great. Thinking on my feet—or rather, my back. Just what I needed on top of trying to survive these lunatics. "How do I keep in contact?"

"You'll have a two-way com-link inserted—it'll also double as a tracker. And I'll be close enough that you can contact me telepathically, if needed."

"So if I get into trouble, I can call in the cavalry?"

"You can call. No guarantee we'll answer."

I snorted softly. I'd been with the Directorate long enough that I'd known the answer even before I asked the question. Jack wasn't going to risk the entire mission on getting me out if things went ass up, simply because Rhoan and Kade would still be in there. And unless those two also got into trouble, we were on our own as far as the Directorate was concerned.

"And with operative support like that, you wonder why I didn't want to become a guardian."

He chuckled. "Darlin', you might not have wanted to become one, but you'll be a better one than your brother."

"You can play that tune all you like, but you're not convincing me to sing along." Which was almost a rote protest by now, but I couldn't let Jack think he'd won my complete acceptance.

"We'll see." He handed me a couple of folders. "Study Poppy's profile, then look at the details Kade's been able to provide about Starr's estate."

I flipped through the second of the two folders. "There doesn't seem to be a lot."

"Because Kade only has access to the outside areas. Still, you need to know security and boundary details, as well as profiles of those who work in those areas."

"Because you never know who I might have to seduce for the good of the cause," I said dryly.

He grinned again, and slapped a hand on my shoulder. "Darlin', you're thinking so much like me it's almost scary."

"The day I think like you is the day I'll stand in front of a silver bullet." I waved the two folders. "If you want me to study these, you need not only to feed me, but supply me with caffeine."

"The pizza and coffee is already ordered." He glanced at his watch. "They should be here in ten minutes, and if you're not studying by then, you get nothing."

"Bastard."

"Totally. Go read."

I did.

The air in the tram was rich with the overwhelming scent of humanity. I hung out near the back door, desperately trying to get some of the fresh air coming in from the cracks of the bifold doors. I hated trams at the best of times. They were far worse than trains—smaller, more crowded—and always managed to give me that "penned-in" feeling.

I hitched the backpack into a more comfortable position on my shoulder, managing to hit the man standing beside me yet again. He swore, and I snarled right back. Poppy had attitude. Right now, in this stinking, humanity-soaked metal box on electric wheels, I was ready to give it.

I glanced at the windows, studying the night-flooded street, and noted with some relief that we were nearing my stop. Butterflies stirred in my stomach, but I beat them down ruthlessly. I couldn't afford butterflies, or fear, or anything else. For good or for bad, I was now on the path of no return. What might lie at the very end of that path, no one, not even me, was willing to guess. I could only hope it was a return to normal life.

I flicked the small, skin-toned disk that had been slotted under the skin behind my left ear, and said softly, "Carlisle Street," as I reached up to pull the cord. The buzzer sounded, letting the driver know someone wanted out at the next stop.

"She's near Luna Park." Jack's soft tone whispered out from the receiver that had been carefully placed into my right ear.

The tram lurched to a stop and the door swished open. I all but fell out, then sucked in several gulps of air. God, even fume-filled, this air felt like heaven in comparison to the tram.

"Your stray vamp on time?" I asked, as I headed up Carlisle Street toward the amusement park. Though the Government had made Luna Park a prostitute-free zone, many of them still plied their trade along the side street that ran the length of the park's rear.

"He'll be there in ten."

"You sure?"

"He wants to live, so yes."

I snorted softly. A vamp desperate to survive was more likely to run than risk the Directorate going back on its word. And knowing what I knew of the Directorate, that was an odds-on chance.

"And he's primed to attack, not kill?"

"He was warned."

"So what did he do to gain the Directorate's attention?"

"Killed a couple of humans." I could almost hear Jack's shrug. "Nothing too extraordinary."

Unless you were one of those humans. "So why wouldn't Dia be able to defend herself?"

"She abhors violence."

"And she works with Starr? That's highly unlikely, isn't it?"

"Given we know so little about her reasons for working with Starr, that's hard to say."

I fell silent as several packs of humans pushed past, then said, "Assure me again that these things in my ears won't be discovered once I'm in Starr's estate."

The last man of the last group gave me an odd look. I flipped him the finger.

"These are from Quinn's labs, and there is nothing out on the market like them. And certainly nothing that can trace them. You will have to be careful when and where you contact us, though, because the signal *can* be traced when in use."

"Kade didn't say anything about the electronic scanning situation."

"No. But then, he's basically restricted to the grounds and scanning would probably be done from inside."

"How did you get these things from Quinn without him demanding to be in on the mission?"

"We didn't ask. We took."

I raised my eyebrows. "When?"

"Two nights ago."

"And?"

"He came down to Melbourne almost immediately."

So he *had* been down here, just as I'd guessed. The bastard couldn't even give me one honest answer.

I was better off without him in my life. Truly.

So why did the thought of never seeing him again hurt so much? It wasn't as if I had a future with the man, for heaven's sake. A vampire could never be my soul mate.

"Then he suspected it was us?"

"His security was better than we thought."

I rolled my eyes. "How often have you told me never to underestimate the enemy?" I stopped at the streetlights and looked around. A tall brown-haired woman in pale gray stood near the park's famous laughing-mouth entrance. "Spotted my quarry. Try not to jabber in my ear for the next few minutes."

Jack's snort was loud enough to make me wince. "I have done this before, darlin'."

I grinned and crossed with the green light. A quick look at my watch said I had seven minutes to go.

I hitched my pack, took a deep breath, then slipped into Poppy, letting her identity, her attitudes, fill my surface thoughts. Then I strode directly toward Dia.

"Don't tell me the great Dia Jones has been reduced to hawking her wares on the streets," I said, voice low and sarcastic. "Always knew you were a fraud."

Her startled gaze swung around to mine, and in that minute I realized two things. The first was the fact that Dia Jones was completely blind. And second, the unearthly sense of power that had been evident in the photograph didn't even begin to do justice to the true power of her gaze. Even unfocused, her blue eyes were magnetic, unforgiving. All-seeing.

Which was an odd thing to think about a blind woman.

"Excuse me?" she said, voice soft yet hinting at ice.

Which suited the complexion that lay underneath the makeup.

"People like you make a living from ripping off the gullible. It disgusts me."

"And is a thief any better?"

I raised my eyebrows, wondering how she'd guessed. Wondering what else she'd guessed. "At least I don't make a living on the suffering of others."

She raised an eyebrow. "And you think I do?"

"Well, what else do you call feeding false hope to suckers?"

She regarded me for a moment, her luminous blue eyes seeming to see right through me. Those butterflies stirred again, though I had no idea why.

"And you do not believe in hope?"

I snorted. "Hope is a fool's desire. I deal with realities."

"Really?"

With a suddenness, and an accuracy, that surprised

me, she reached out and grabbed my hand. My instinctive response was to pull away, but I checked the strength of it almost immediately. Partly because I was curious about what she was doing, and partly because the minute her fingers touched mine, an odd sort of energy seemed to run over them. It felt like the power that caressed the air right before a summer storm.

She didn't say anything for several minutes, just gripped my fingers and frowned as the energy of her touch flowed between us. Then she sighed, and smiled as she released me.

"You will save us," she said softly.

Us? What the hell did she mean by that? Her and me? Did that mean she knew about the planned attack? Somehow, I didn't think so, but before I could ask what she actually meant, awareness surged, prickling like fire across my skin. With it came the stench of unwashed, unripe flesh.

Jack's stray vamp had shown up ahead of time.

And he'd brought a couple of friends along.

Chapter 4

There were three of them, all skinny excuses of flesh and bone. The vamp in the middle was the obvious leader—he was two steps ahead of his compatriots, and had one of those perpetual sneers so often found on those who think they're tougher than they truly are. His two mates were of Asian descent, though the blue eyes on one suggested there was something else in his mix.

"Well, well," the leader said casually, "look at what we got here, boys."

"Breakfast," blue eyes said, expression alight with anticipation.

I slipped off the backpack and placed it in Dia's hands. "You might have to hold this while I tend to this pond scum."

"But—"

I held up a finger, realized what I was doing, then touched her arm lightly and said, "It's okay."

She fell silent. While these three didn't look particularly old, they were still vampires, and I was going to need every ounce of concentration against them.

"In case you haven't noticed, little girl," the leader said, amusement rich in his harsh, annoying voice, "there's three of us, and only one of you."

"Unfair odds, I agree," I said. "You want me to keep one hand behind my back?"

They glanced at each other, then broke into laughter.

That's when I dropped my shields and hit the minds of the backup vamps, stripping through their meager shields and ordering them to run away, as far and as fast as they could. Their laughter stopped abruptly and their eyes went wide, the whites seeming to gleam brightly in the darkness. Then they turned and retreated into the night.

Even as they ran, pain lanced through my head, needle sharp and fiery hot. I wasn't entirely sure why, especially given I'd done similar things in the past and hadn't felt a reaction like this. But right then, I didn't have time to worry about it. Even as tears touched my eyes, the air stirred, brushing anger and the force of movement past my nose. I ducked away from the last vamp's fist, letting it skim past my cheek, then dropped and spun, kicking his legs out from underneath him. He grunted as his rump hit the ground, and his look of surprise might have been funny if it wasn't for the murderous expression that almost instantly followed.

He snarled, then scrambled to his feet and launched at me. I dodged, but his fingers caught my arm, his nails needle sharp and tearing into flesh. I yelped and he laughed, a sharp sound that was quickly cut off when my fist slammed into his mouth. He staggered backward, arms flailing, spitting out blood and teeth as he did so. I followed the force of my punch with another, this time chopping into his throat, crushing his larynx and dropping him to the ground. He didn't stay down, but scrambled on all fours toward Dia Jones. Blind or not, she seemed to sense his approach, because she gasped and backed away.

I grabbed his leg and dragged him away from her. He struggled like a madman, his kicks landing heavily on my already bloodied arm and bruising the hell out of my fingers. A growl of fury rumbled up my throat, and without thought, I dropped my shields again and let him have it. His mind fled before mine like a pebble before a landslide, and just as uselessly. Within seconds, I had him still and unmoving.

But, oh God, how it hurt.

I dropped to my knees and, for too many seconds, did nothing more than try to breathe as the pain in my head intensified, and all I could see were pinpoints of bright lights flashing before my eyes. They eased after a few seconds, but the pain didn't.

Why was this happening? When I'd controlled the two lab-made werecats in Moneisha, there'd been pain, but nothing as intense as this. Even when I'd attacked Quinn, there hadn't been a backlash like this—had there?

I frowned, and remembered the wash of pain that had briefly hit before I'd picked my panties up off the floor and stormed into the other room.

Maybe it was a simple matter of being too angry to even notice just how bad the pain actually was.

A hand touched my elbow, helped me to my feet.

"We must go," Dia said. "Before he recovers enough to attack again."

He wasn't going anywhere until I released him, but given the blinding pain, that was probably going to be sooner rather than later. I stumbled along after Dia, guided more by her touch and the sound of her footsteps than my own sight, which was at best blurry, and filled with heated white spots that danced about crazily. A situation that wasn't helped when the control I had on the vamp snapped. The pain of it rebounded through me, as sharp as glass. I gasped, stumbling and almost going down. Dia's grip tightened on my arm, and with almost inhuman strength, she kept me upright and kept me going.

Of course, Dia Jones wasn't exactly human, so inhuman strength wasn't exactly surprising. What I really wanted to know was how the hell she was moving so surely when she couldn't see and hadn't even a cane or a guide animal to help her.

A car loomed through the blurriness ahead. A man in a dark suit opened the rear door of a car that seemed to go on forever, then I was being shoved inside. I crawled across the soft leather, then leaned my head back against the thick seat cushioning and closed my eyes. Doors slammed shut, twin sounds that seemed to reverberate through the silence, through my head, then the car was moving.

Silence reigned for several minutes. I could feel Dia's

gaze on me—it was a weight that was at once both curious and cautious—but she didn't touch me. Of that, I was
glad. I had a feeling that she might learn far too many secrets if she did so right now.

"Telepathy is new to you, isn't it?" she said eventually.

I opened my eyes. Even though the limo was dark, the
glare of the streetlights as we passed them was a brightness that was hard to stand. My eyes watered, and the
ache in my head briefly intensified.

"What makes you think I'm telepathic?"

She smiled. "While I am not telepathic myself, I am
sensitive to the use of psychic power. Generally, it feels
like the caress of a warm summer breeze that swirls
across my skin—something I can sense but never catch."
She paused, tilting her head slightly to one side, her
amazing blue eyes seeming to follow even my slightest
movement. How was that possible? This woman *was*
blind—I was certain of that, if nothing else.

"With you tonight," she continued, "it was not a
breeze, but a cyclone. An overuse of power if ever I felt
one. Has no one ever taught you control?"

"I shield. I can protect myself. What else is there to
know?" And Jack *had* been coaching me, but I couldn't
exactly admit that.

"Power of any kind should be treated similar to an
onion. There may be many different layers, but you
should only ever strip away as many as you need to get
the job done." She smiled as she reached forward and
took a small cloth from a compartment under the seat
opposite, then handed it to me. "The only time problems
generally arise for the trained is when the power is still
new, or it increases in strength for some reason."

I wrapped the cloth around my bleeding arm. "How would either of those cause problems?"

She shrugged lightly. "You cannot control something when you do not know its boundaries."

That made sense. But was that what was actually happening? I'd been telepathic most of my life, and the last test done at the Directorate had not indicated any increase in psychic output.

Of course, those tests had been done several months ago. Who knew what the result would be now.

"But psychic strength doesn't alter." At least, it generally didn't with normal people. "You get what you're born with, don't you?"

"Sometimes. But puberty has been known to set off wild changes in psi-skills."

"Puberty? Do I sound like an adolescent to you?"

But even as I said the words, I had a feeling she'd hit the nail on the head. Thanks to the fertility drugs that had been forced into me by past mates, I'd recently begun menstruating for the first time in my life. Which in turn meant I *was* going through a form of puberty—if puberty was defined solely as going through the change and moving from a child's body to a woman's. *Not* that anyone would ever accuse me of having a child's body. I'd been D-cup since I was sixteen.

"No, you don't sound adolescent. But that doesn't alter the fact your power seems very uncontrolled. You are extremely lucky you caught those vamps unawares. Lucky, too, that none of them were particularly strong psychics."

"Why's that?" I rubbed a hand across my forehead. The needles were beginning to ease, but my brain still felt like it was on fire. If I didn't get some pain-relief tablets soon, I was going to have one doozy of a headache.

"Because by dropping your shields as totally as you did, you left yourself wide open for a counterattack."

"Oh." I hadn't even thought of that. Not when I'd attacked Quinn, and certainly not when I'd attacked those vamps. Quinn might have been too much of a gentleman to attack, but those vamps certainly could have.

She tilted her head to the side again. The brown hair fell to one side, revealing slivers of silver running underneath. She wasn't wearing a wig, because the silver and brown ran into each other. It was almost as if someone had dyed her hair but only done half a job. Odd, to say the least. "Did your parents not teach you to use your gift?"

I snorted softly. "My mother was a wolf groupie who considered the half-breed she gave birth to little more than an inconvenience to her sex life."

"And your father?"

"She never knew for sure who he was. I certainly don't."

"Sad."

"That's me," I said sarcastically. "A sad and sorry tale."

She smiled again. "Do you have a name?"

"Poppy Burns."

She raised an eyebrow. "Indeed? And what are you doing here in St. Kilda, Poppy Burns?"

Something in the way she said that had uneasiness stirring. I shrugged, and did my best to ignore those damned butterflies. "Looking for work, a place to stay. Usual shit."

"So where did you live before?"

"You're getting awfully nosy, aren't you?"

She shrugged. "Given what you said to me before those vamps showed up, I think I have the right to be nosy."

I sniffed, and didn't reply.

"And given your so bluntly put opinion of me," she continued, "why would you then go on and save me?"

"Who says I was saving you? Those stinkers had me in their sights just as much as you."

"Maybe."

"If we're going to be nosy, then tell me how you can be blind as a bat, and yet can walk around as well as any sighted person?"

She went still, and for a moment I thought I'd blown it.

"How do you know I'm blind?" The warmth that had been in her tones until now was replaced by cold steel, and a chill went down my spine.

It was a timely reminder that this woman—however nice she seemed—was one of the five clones and in league with the man I was trying to bring down.

"Easy. Though your gaze appears to look directly at people, there's no true life in your eyes, no response to the smaller movements people make, and no real response to facial expressions. It's like you can see, but only from a distance, so that up close things aren't clear."

Amusement warmed her expression. "You are very observant."

"You have to be when you live on the streets."

"True." She paused, considering me. "Are you after work now?"

I shrugged. "Depends what it is."

"You will earn more in two weeks than you could in a year of regular work."

"Lady, that sounds a little too good to be true. What's the catch?"

"You're being paid to have sex with strangers."

I raised an eyebrow. "And?"

"No 'and.' The resort is owned by my...employer."

Employer? Starr was more than just that. "So you're not just a scamming psychic? You're a pimp, as well?"

She stiffened ever so slightly. "I am *not* pimping you. I am simply offering you an opportunity to make a lot of money."

"Yeah. By having sex. It's called pimping, whether you like it or not."

I studied her for a moment, wondering how fine a line I should walk between reluctance and acceptance. But given Poppy's supposed history, she wasn't likely to be trusting *anyone* too quickly.

"This is one of those sex-slave scams they've been talking about in the papers lately, isn't it? You know, lure innocents with the enticement of money, then ship them off to parts unknown, to be held captive and abused. Well, I ain't interested, lady." I banged on the glass partition between us and the driver, wincing as the sound echoed through my head. "Hey, you, stop this crate and let me out."

"I promise, this is no scam."

"Yeah, right."

She reached into her pocket and drew out a business card. Only it wasn't from the employment agency Jack had mentioned, but one of her own cards. And it was her personal address, as well. "If you are interested in hearing more about the job, come and see me tomorrow."

I looked at her, then the card, and finally reached out to take it. "You never did answer my question, you know. About being blind."

She smiled again. "No. But perhaps I will later, if you accept the job."

"If that's supposed to be an enticement, it ain't working."

"If you want an enticement, then perhaps I can teach you to use your telepathy without dropping all your shields."

The car slid to a stop. I wrapped my fingers around the door handle but didn't open it. "And why would you be offering to do that?"

"Because you need it."

"And do you often run around offering psychic training to those who need it?"

"No." Her gaze came to mine. "Only to those who will save us."

"That's the second time you've said that, and it's no clearer now than it was before."

"I guess it isn't." Her gaze fell away as she leaned back in the seat. "I'll see you tomorrow."

It was a dismissal and a statement of fact, all in one. I frowned, but thrust open the door and climbed out. The night had grown colder in the brief time I'd been in the car, the breeze chill. Goose bumps ran across my skin. Thank God I wasn't actually sleeping on the streets tonight. I slammed the car door shut and watched Dia's black limo disappear into the night.

"So," I said, rubbing my bare arms as I looked around to see where I was. "You heard it all?"

"Yes. And I'm mighty disappointed you didn't tell me about the fluctuations in your telepathy strength."

"It's only just started happening, boss. With everything else that's been going on, it just slipped my mind."

"That's not good enough, Riley. We need to keep a close check on what is going on with your psi-abilities."

"So I'll try and remember to tell you the next time anything strange happens."

"Don't try. Do." He paused. "Why didn't you finish off those vamps?"

"You want them dead, you kill them."

"We have, but that's not the point."

No, the point was he wanted me to kill on order. I might have acknowledged the need to become a guardian—if only internally—but that didn't mean I had to happily dive straight into the killing bit.

"The card she gave me has her personal address, not that employment agency she and Starr have been using as a front." I looked left and right, then crossed the road, heading for the shops on the other side. Coffee and chocolate were in order—they might not actually ease the ache in my head, but they'd at least make me feel a little bit better.

"It's not a front, but a registered agency."

"Has she ever used her house before?"

"Given we've only been following her for six weeks, it's hard to say."

"So she could suspect something?"

"She didn't sound suspicious."

"No." I hesitated. "I've just got this feeling she knew more than what she was saying."

"She'd be naturally suspicious of anyone—which is why she does a check on them first."

"Maybe." I pushed open the door of the 7-Eleven and helped myself to coffee—they didn't have hazelnut, so I compensated with a hazelnut chocolate bar—then I headed around to grab some Panadol. Off-the-shelf painkillers mightn't be the strongest available, but they were better than nothing. Once I'd paid the man, I headed back out.

"What did you make of her saying, 'You will save us'?"

"A slip of the tongue, perhaps?"

"She didn't seem the sort to do anything by mistake." I sipped my coffee, wincing a little at its bitter taste. "There's something going on here that we don't understand."

"It's natural to feel that, given we know so little about her or her relationship with Starr." He paused. "But be careful all the same."

Like I wasn't going to be? "How thorough a background search did you do?"

"Very. We don't send people into dangerous situations willy-nilly, you know."

I grinned. "I'm mighty glad to hear that. So what now?"

"You go find a room at an appropriate hotel and catch some sleep."

"Then?"

"Then we see what tomorrow brings."

"Meaning, lots of things are happening, but you're not telling me just in case things go wrong on my end and I blab details."

He chuckled. "Rhoan's right. For a girl, you're pretty damn clever."

Meaning, as I'd suspected, he'd been watching and listening in to our training session. "If I was clever, I wouldn't be standing here on a deserted St. Kilda street, freezing my butt off, but in New York, or Paris, or even London—somewhere they couldn't give a damn about what my DNA could do for them."

"I'm not interested in your DNA."

"No, just what I could do for your new guardian squad," I replied dryly. "So how in the hell do I get to Dia's place from here?"

"Catch one of the trams that run along Malvern Road, and get off at Kooyong Road. Huntingfield is halfway between Malvern and Toorak."

"So either way I'm hiking."

"It won't kill you."

"Says the man who wasn't beaten to a pulp by Gautier yesterday."

"I feel obliged to point out that you weren't, either."

Only thanks to the fact he'd intervened. "Night, Jack."

"Night, Poppy."

I snorted and flicked the button behind my ear. The slight buzz of energy that had been teasing my lobes died, but the ache in my head didn't. I popped a couple of the Panadol, swilling them down with the bitter coffee, then munched on more chocolate to take away the aftertaste.

After strolling along for several blocks, I found a dingy-looking hotel that had rooms for rent at cheap rates. Just the sort of place someone like Poppy might settle for—though if I wasn't playing her part, I certainly wouldn't have gone near the place. The hotel sat next to a bar, so not only did it stink of sweaty humanity, but of booze as well. The raucous laughter coming from inside the bar suggested heavy patronage—which in turn meant little sleep. I blew out a breath, reminded myself it was only for one night, and headed inside.

The reek was worse within the four walls, and the rooms more dilapidated than the outside. The bed itself looked older than Methuselah, and had obviously seen more than a few couplings on it. I screwed up my nose and glanced at the floor. The carpet looked no better, but at least the floor didn't have a disastrous sag in it.

With a sigh, I hauled off the blankets—which at least looked and smelled clean—and made myself a bed on the floor. Then I stripped off, shifted shape to hurry along the already healing scratches on my arms, and settled down to sleep.

Surprisingly, and despite all the noise and odors, I *did* sleep, not waking until the hotel's manager banged on the door the following morning.

With a groan, I rolled onto my side and stared blearily at the clock on the bedside table above me. Eight. Time to get some breakfast and head on over to see Dia.

After stretching out the kinks and giving my face and arms a quick wash down with cold water, I dressed and headed back out to the street. Unfortunately, trams didn't run as regularly on a Sunday, so I grabbed a couple of McMuffins from McDonald's to munch on while I waited at the stop.

It was well after nine when I hit Toorak. I climbed off the tram at Kooyong Road and pressed the disk behind my ear.

"Heading for Dia's now."

"Keep the line open."

"Will do."

I strolled up Kooyong Road, admiring the million-dollar houses and wondering what it'd be like to live in a place that practically screamed money. Personally, I'd be afraid to move lest I break something.

Huntingfield Road came along, and I turned left onto it. Many of the houses here seemed more ornate, making me feel even more out of place. A feeling that grew when I stopped to press the intercom button to one side of the huge, wrought-iron gates that guarded Dia's house.

To say the place was amazing would be an understatement—though the house itself wasn't as ornate as some of its neighbors. It was an old, early-twentieth-century design that reminded me greatly of the grand old English mansions often shown on TV. Though this was painted a warm, soft gold, ivy crept over the brickwork and sprawled across the roof, giving the impression the house had been here forever. The lawn that stretched from the side gate to the porch was a rich carpet of green—so lush my feet suddenly itched with the need to run through it—and the pines that lined the boundary gave the whole property a feeling of isolation. I'd never been envious of anyone else's living conditions in my life, but I couldn't help thinking how amazing it would be to live in a place like this. A little bit of luxurious heaven, and yet with everything you could ever want or need within walking distance to your doorstep.

The intercom crackled, then Dia said, "Yes?"

"Poppy Burns, accepting your invitation."

"Ah. Good." The gates buzzed, then clicked open. "Come in."

I walked through the gates, and somehow resisted the urge to take off my shoes and run through the grass, instead following the herringbone-patterned brick path. Dia Jones opened the door as I approached. That surprised me. Surely someone who lived in a pad as plush as this would have a servant or two running around?

Her hair was no longer brown mixed with silver, just a pure whitish-silver, and with the long, flowing white dress she had on, she looked almost ethereal. Except for her eyes. They positively glowed with the power that shimmered across my skin like little zaps of lightning. I stopped, staring into her blind eyes, again struck by the sensation that this woman knew far more than we wanted her to.

"Come in, come in." Her smile was as charming as her voice was warm. "The house won't bite, and neither will I."

Obviously, she was taking my reluctance to enter for awe at her surroundings rather than her, and that was just fine by me. I stepped past her. The hallway beyond was huge, as was the chandelier that sprayed rainbows across the soft gold walls and carpets. A redwood sideboard was the only piece of furnishing in the entrance hall, and on it sat a vase filled with blood-red gladiolas. Two rooms led off the hall, and a staircase clad in a deeper gold carpet sat at the end, undoubtedly spiraling upward into more richness.

"Just head into the living room on your left," she said, as she closed the door.

The living room turned out to be another filled with

gold and creams. Though the room was huge, there wasn't a whole lot of furniture—just two large sofas, a marble coffee table, and a matching white marble fireplace. The chandelier that hung above all this elegance was smaller than the one in the entrance hall, but not by much. A bright, modernistic painting held pride of place above the fireplace, adding a much needed splash of color.

"Please, sit down." Dia waved a hand at one heavily brocaded sofa even as she felt for the sofa nearest her with the other. Odd, considering she'd seemed so sure of her movements last night.

I perched on the edge of the sofa, feeling more than a little out of place in all this richness. Which, given I'd had mates who were far wealthier than Dia, was weird. They'd never made me feel inadequate in any way when it came to money—or the lack of it—so why did this woman? Or did it have nothing to do wealth, and everything to do with the overwhelming sense of power I was getting from her?

But if she was so powerful, why was she doing Starr's bidding? It made no sense.

"I take it you are here about the job offer?"

I nodded. "The hotel I stayed in last night solidified the need for quick cash."

"And you wish to remain under the radar at the moment, thanks to the arrest warrant that's outstanding in Sydney?"

I gave her my best "outraged" look. Which, considering she was blind, was pretty dumb. But then, this woman was psychic, so who knew what other senses she relied on to help her "see"? "Is this what the invite was about? Hand me in and earn a quick couple of grand?"

Her smile was wry. "Look around you. I hardly think a mere couple of thousand is worth the effort of luring you here."

"Maybe that's how you got all this richness—trapping not only the suckers, but runaways."

"I always run background checks on people I'm about to employ. It's standard procedure."

"And having a warrant out on me makes me undesirable?" I snorted and thrust to my feet. "Your loss, lady."

I swung my pack over my shoulder and headed for the door—hoping all the while I wasn't about to blow it. But Poppy was the indignant type who fired at the drop of a hat, so anything else might have been seen as odd behavior.

"It wasn't the warrant that caused the problem," she said.

I stopped and looked around. She wasn't even looking at me, but staring instead somewhere to my left. It was almost as if she wasn't sure of my exact whereabouts, and again, that ran against everything I'd seen last night.

"Then what *is* the problem?"

"The fact that Poppy Burns doesn't actually exist."

Fuck. So much for Jack's clever paperwork. "I don't? Well, gee, thanks for the tip."

I forced my feet on. She hadn't locked the front door when I entered, so at least I could get out of the house. And it didn't matter if the gates *were* locked, because the fence was within a wolf's jumping range.

"I have a deal to offer you and the Directorate, Riley," she said softly.

"Stop," Jack said into my ear.

I mentally cursed him, but turned around and crossed my arms. Tension coiled through every muscle as I readied for action, readied to fight. Fight who, I had no idea, because Dia herself was offering no threat. No physical threat, anyway. "Why do you think I'm this Riley?"

"I touched your hand last night. It told me many secrets." She smiled. "You can drop the pretense. I know the truth."

How, when she hadn't actually read my mind? Did that mean her gift was some form of precognition that came online whenever she touched someone? "So why not mention something, then?"

"Because I had to make sure I was right, that I didn't have the wrong name."

Meaning not all her predictions came true? That admission had to be first in the world of psychics. "And this is important because?"

"Because Riley Jenson is the only person known to have either escaped or frustrated Deshon Starr's plans."

Her words did little to ease the tension running through my limbs, and if it wasn't for the fact that I could sense or smell no one else in the house, I might have run. Yes, I wanted an end to the madness, but that wasn't going to happen when I was standing here, far away from Starr.

"Ask her what she wants," Jack said.

If he'd been standing next to me rather than jabbering in my ear, I would have been tempted to kick him, boss or not. There were more important worries—like how much she might have told Starr, and whether or not Rhoan was in danger of discovery.

TEMPTING EVIL

"And what have you done with this knowledge?"

"Not gone to my would-be master, you can be sure of that." Her voice was dry, but there was something in the way her blind eyes flashed that had me believing her.

Which might just mean I was nothing more than a fool, and easily taken in by a bit of sincerity combined with contempt and anger.

"And why *wouldn't* you do that? He killed Misha for attempting to double-cross him. He'd do the same to you without a second thought."

"I know. But things cannot remain the way they are."

"What things?"

She gave me a cool smile. "Before we go into details, I need to know if the Directorate would be willing to deal."

"Yes," Jack and I said together. He added in my ear, "Depending, of course, on what she wants."

She raised a pale eyebrow. "You don't need to speak to your boss first?"

"I don't have to. I can hear him in my head." I was tempted to add, "and no, I'm not mad," but restrained the impulse. A, because she'd "seen" me in action last night, and B, because I actually think insanity had a lot to do with my current situation. After all, no one sane would willingly step into hell's den with the intent of fucking his lieutenants for information, no matter how pissed off and in need of revenge they were.

"Telepathy." She nodded. "A handy tool for those in your line of work, though I'm surprised they haven't taught you more control."

"We would have if we'd known it was needed." Jack's

voice was sarcastic. "But someone forgot to mention an apparent increase in power since our last lesson."

I ignored him. Anything I said was only going to count against me, anyway. "What sort of deal would you like to broker?"

She smiled and waved a hand to the sofa. "Please, come and sit down."

"I'm fine, thanks." Flight-or-fight mode was far easier standing up.

She raised her eyebrows again. "I sense distrust."

"That's because there is."

"Honest. I like that."

"And I'd like for you to quit fucking around and just get to the point."

She crossed one elegant leg over the other, and clasped her hands around her knees. "Okay. I want immunity from everything I have done on behalf of Starr."

"That depends greatly on what she wants to give us in return," Jack said.

"And?" I asked, sensing there was more to Dia's list of demands.

"He cannot know that I am helping you. Which means I will never testify against him."

She was more than a little naive if she thought Starr was ever going to reach the courts. The Directorate had the power to be judge, jury, and executioner, and it was a power they regularly abused. In my time with them, I'd seen a total of five cases make it to the human justice system—and only because those behind the deeds were partially human. Those with an ounce of human blood could claim the full protection of the courts and the law.

Nonhumans had no such rights. Which pretty much smacked of a legal form of racism, I'd always thought.

"Those terms I can live with," Jack said.

"Anything else?" I asked.

She paused. "I wish to continue living here. I want this house exempt when the Government sells off Starr's assets."

"No guarantee on that one," Jack said.

I repeated his statement, and she nodded. "I guess I can deal with that if it happens."

"And what do we get in return?"

She smiled, and waved at the sofa again. "Please. It is uncomfortable talking like this."

Why? Because her senses couldn't pinpoint me accurately from such a distance? I suspected that might be the case, which meant I was better off staying where I was.

"Go sit," Jack said, as if he was reading my mind. Which he wasn't, because I'd have at least felt it. Whether I could have actually stopped it was another matter entirely. Jack was not someone I ever wanted to test myself against for real. Though until yesterday, I'd never have thought I'd have the power to blow through Quinn's shields, either—even with the advantage of surprise.

I blew out a breath that did nothing to release the tension still riding my limbs, but did as I was told and walked across to the sofa.

"I gather from the profile set up for you that the Directorate knows about my recruitment drives for Starr?"

"Yes." I took off the backpack, and once again perched on the edge of the sofa.

"How?"

"Don't tell her about Gautier," Jack said. "Just in case."

Just in case? Just in case of what? Things go ass up? God, wasn't that a confidence builder! *Not* that I was expecting it all to go to plan—I mean, nothing else had over the last four months, so why would things change now?

I shrugged. "They didn't actually tell me. I just know you managed to catch their attention."

She nodded. Whether that meant she believed me or not was anyone's guess. "And they planned to get you into the mansion via this method?"

"Obviously."

"Then what?"

I studied her for a moment, still wary about providing information to someone who had yet to prove her worth. Or reliability. "You realize that if you double-cross the Directorate, they'll kill you as quickly and as surely as Starr."

"I have no intention of betraying the Directorate." Her bright gaze centered on mine briefly but oh so powerfully. "You are truly my only hope."

Even as goose bumps trembled across my skin, her gaze dropped from mine. She rubbed a hand down her thigh, then sighed. "Starr is not a fool. The women he brings in to service his men each month are strictly watched. They never move from the compound they are placed in. If it is your intention to gain enough information about Starr to bring him down, then you are tackling it from the wrong angle."

"All I need to do is catch his lieutenants in an unguarded moment and strip their minds of information."

It wasn't going to be that easy—I knew that, and Jack knew that. For a start, the minute either man realized what I was doing, I was dead meat. And while I might have strong telepathy skills, I wasn't as practiced in using them as I should be. Last night's attacks had proven that.

"But Starr's lieutenants do not use the women in the compound."

Well, shit. "Why not?"

She smiled. "If the Directorate has been following me, then they would know not all the women I recruit are prostitutes."

"Yeah, so?"

"So some of those who are not are recruited for the ring."

"The ring? As in, boxing ring?"

She shook her head. The chandelier's light caught the silken strips of her hair, turning them a molten silver. And in that instant, I realized just how similar she was to Misha, right down to her angular features. Odd, considering how dissimilar all the other clones were to each other.

"It is more a wrestling ring. Starr and his people enjoy watching women fight. The lucky winner gets to share beds with his lieutenants, Alden and Leo."

"Misha told us Alden and Leo go through women like sharks—that sex is a fix they must have every day. Does that mean the fights are a feature every day?"

She nodded. "Every evening. But the women are merely the encore to the main fight—Starr, as I'm sure you know, is homosexual. He makes his security forces fight, and takes the winner."

Something in the way she said that had my eyebrows rising. "Takes?"

She grimaced. "He prefers force. He likes the taste of fear."

If he tried to force my brother, Rhoan would have him for breakfast. He might not mind a bit of rough, but force was not something he tolerated—on himself or on others.

"Then none of these fights are serious?"

"Oh, they're serious. People do get hurt—broken bones and bleeding is something Starr insists on. Which is why most of those recruited for the ring are either shifters or weres. Healing is then not a problem."

Because shifters, like weres, were capable of healing when shifting. Of course, the fact that shifters generally thought themselves "superior" to weres in every way could make for some interesting times in the ring. Especially seeing most weres thought the same about shifters.

And really, the only real difference between any of us was the fact that weres were forced to shift with the full moon and shifters were not.

"You think this is the way I should go in?"

She nodded. "Those who fight in the ring have free run of the main house and grounds."

"And why would he give the fighters freedom and not the hookers? Surely he wouldn't trust them more?"

"No. But as a general rule, I've done a more intense background check on the fighters. And his halls are monitored by security twenty-four hours a day. He trusts them to keep an eye on what is going on."

"So it's just cameras?"

"And motion-sensing devices."

"Infrared?"

"Not yet in the house. There is infrared around the zoo, and I know he plans to install it elsewhere." She grimaced. "There was an attack by a rival recently that convinced him of the need. The vampire got very close."

"What happened to the vampire?" And was it perhaps *my* vampire? Though I guess that made no sense—if Quinn had known about Starr, he wouldn't have tried to ferret the information from my mind.

"The vampire was staked and left to the sun."

Definitely not Quinn, then. "Starr has a zoo?"

"Starr keeps a collection of nonhuman freaks." She shrugged. "It amuses his human guests."

I just bet it did. And it was a brilliant way to hide a growing force of specially bred assassins. "Isn't it a little dangerous to have humans around during the rising of the full moon?"

"Oh yes. But the moon dances provide good blackmail material, so Starr considers the risks well worth it." She smiled thinly. "What politician's family is going to raise a ruckus if their loved one dies in such a compromising position? Few, let me tell you."

I raised my eyebrows. "So it has happened?"

"Of course."

"Ask her if she'd be willing to name names?" Jack said. "We need to check what they might have been forced into doing before their deaths."

I repeated the question, and Dia nodded. "I will provide a full list of everyone who goes to Starr's dances."

I studied her for a moment, then said, "You're being awfully helpful, and I'd like to know why."

Her smile was tight. "Because when Misha died, Starr did something to me he should never have done."

I raised my eyebrows at the low fury in her voice. "And that was?"

Her gaze came to mine, and a chill ran across my skin. I'd never really understood the phrase "if looks could kill," but it became all too clear as I stared into Dia's unseeing eyes. The devil himself would have quailed at the depth of anger and hatred in her powerful gaze.

"Deshon Starr took my daughter away from me," she said softly. "And I will destroy him—and destroy his whole filthy organization—if it is the last thing I ever do."

"Has he killed her?" I asked, even as I wondered why I was feeling sorry for a woman who'd obviously allowed herself to be evil's pawn for a very long time.

Or was that being unfair? Misha had once told me that he had no choice in some of the things he did, simply because Starr was far more powerful and could control them all. Misha had skirmished from the edges, but he'd never managed to break free of the leash. Why would Dia, for all her abilities, have any more luck?

She closed her eyes and took a shuddering breath. "No. But he only allows me to see her on the weekends, and even then, only for several hours." Her gaze came to mine again, the vibrant depths dry but hinting at an agony I might never experience, but could certainly empathize with. "She's only six months old. She should be with her mother, not being raised in the cold, sterile environment of a lab."

"Like you were," I said softly, wondering if she meant the main lab—Libraska—or another one we didn't know about.

Her laugh was short, bitter. "Yeah, like me."

"And this lab is on his estate's grounds?"

She nodded. "It is a small research lab, nothing major." She paused, studying me. "I gather the Directorate knows about Libraska?"

"Yeah. What can you tell us about it?"

She shrugged. "Not a lot. Starr keeps that lab's location very secret. I'm not even sure Alden and Leo know."

I had to hope she was wrong, because otherwise we were up shit's creek. Rhoan hadn't inherited any psychic skills, so there wasn't a chance of him ever reading Starr's mind. And I certainly didn't want to try. I might have untapped depths of psi-power, but I wasn't about to test it on someone as unhinged as Starr. "Someone beside Starr must know. The lab has been around for over forty years."

She raised an eyebrow. "The Directorate knows more than I presumed."

I smiled thinly. "They always do." I crossed my arms and leaned on my knees. "So what are the chances of you drawing me a map of Starr's estate?"

She smiled. "Already done. It's yours the minute you agree to all my terms."

"I thought we had?"

"Not quite."

"Then what else do you want?" But even as I asked the question, I knew. She was a mother missing her child. It was natural she'd be top of the list.

"Before you take Starr out, I want my daughter out of there."

"That will warn him something is happening."

Her blue eyes bored into mine. Determined. Furious.

Scared. It was the last one that got to me. Made me trust her. She needed my help, and until I got her daughter out, I could at least depend on her to keep her end of the bargain.

"That is a risk you must take, because I will not help, otherwise. He has her wired—the minute he senses anything out of the ordinary, he will kill her. I will stay and help, if you insist, but she must be taken out of there, regardless of the cost."

"No," Jack said. "I will not risk the mission for the sake of a clone's child."

I didn't say anything. Couldn't say anything, because anger had become a block in my throat. Starr might be a bastard, but in many respects, so was Jack. For God's sake, it was a tiny *baby* we were talking about. It deserved a chance of life, no matter who its mother was.

And, of course, my own dodgy future with conception only made me all the more sympathetic—and Jack should have known me well enough to guess that.

I stared at Dia for a few seconds longer, then reached across the coffee table and squeezed her hand, just the once. Her answering smile was one of relief.

"Everything else we will agree to," I said, for Jack's benefit.

Dia nodded. "Then I will give you the plans to study, but destroy them afterward. The bus for our recruited fighters leaves the old St. Kilda train station at two this afternoon. A man named Roscoe will meet you."

I raised my eyebrows. "You're not going to be there tonight?"

She smiled thinly. "No. I have one more night of whore recruitment. But I will see you tomorrow."

"Why is he collecting so many women this time?"

She hesitated. "Because it is a gathering."

"A gathering?"

She nodded. "Every major person in his cartel will be there."

"Holy crap, we've hit the jackpot," Jack said. "This is fantastic!"

If it was so fantastic, why did I suddenly feel sick? Maybe because Starr wouldn't be taking such a risk unless the prize at the end of it was worth it. Or maybe it was simply a matter of the shark-infested pond I was diving into suddenly getting a whole lot more dangerous. And I wasn't sure if I was ready for a mission of that magnitude.

Not that I intended backing out. Even if Jack would let me back out.

"Why is he calling in his generals?"

"Because he plans his war against the other syndicates."

"In a month," I said, suddenly remembering Dia's message to Gautier. "When the Directorate lies in your control."

Her gaze swept me. "How did you guess?"

"Fledgling clairvoyance skills," I muttered, and rubbed a hand across my eyes. "We have to stop him."

"Yes." She hesitated. "Starr and his lieutenants have their very own, very secure floor under the mansion, and it is fitted with all the latest scanners. It is there he'll meet his people and plan his war. You will not get anywhere near it. Your best bet is the arena, winning the attentions of Alden and Leo, and reading their minds every night. If you can."

And that "if" seemed to be getting bigger and bigger every time I thought about it. I grabbed my backpack and stood up. "The plans?"

She rose and moved to the mantelpiece to pick up a notebook and several rolled-up sheets of paper. "Everything I know about security is in here." She handed me the book and the papers. "The other item is the contract you are supposed to have signed on recruitment. It's basically a work agreement and terms. The others will have read it."

"Then I'd better, too."

She nodded. "And in answer to your earlier question about my sight, I have assistance to help me see when I am outside the boundaries of this house."

I raised my eyebrows. "What type of assistance?"

"If you knew Misha as well as you have said, then you will know of the Fravardin."

I nodded. The Fravardin were guardian spirits Misha had met and enlisted when he'd been in the Middle East. "He never did tell me how he'd managed to get their services, though."

She smiled. "He saved them. Now they are indebted to him, and honor bound to following his wishes, even after his death."

One of his apparent wishes was the Fravardin protecting me, but I hadn't sensed the creatures, let alone met one face-to-face. If you could meet a spirit creature face-to-face, that was. "How is that related to your sight?"

"One of the Fravardin was placed in my service. Whenever I go beyond the four walls of this house, he is with me. I am able to connect through his mind and use his eyes."

I snorted softly. "So you were never in danger last night, even if those vamps hadn't been a setup?"

"No. The Fravardin would have taken care of any real threat."

Which was a warning as much as it was a statement. "Then why couldn't you use the Fravardin to take out Starr and rescue your daughter?"

"Because he is my eyes, and my bodyguard when required, but nothing more. Risa is my child, but she does not fall within his guardianship role."

"So they're sticklers for obeying Misha's wishes to the word?"

"Yes."

Then maybe I wouldn't feel the Fravardin's presence until my life was in danger. But how would it know if it wasn't around? And did I really want an answer to that, especially if it meant putting my life on the line to find out?

The answer was a resounding no.

"Why would Misha give you one of the Fravardin? I thought the five of you were less than friendly with each other."

She smiled. "That is true up to a point. But Misha and I shared more of a history than the others. I suppose you could say that he is my brother."

"You're his sister?" I said, incredulously. "But...aren't you all clones?"

She nodded. "Yes, but Misha and I are clones of siblings. Our original selves were born of a Helki mother and silver pack father, and were fraternal twins, born of the same mother and father. If a clone is capable of sibling love, then I guess we shared that. I miss him."

"So—" I paused, trying to gather my suddenly scattered thoughts. "If you're clones of siblings, does it mean that, like the originals, you are both able to shift shape?"

She raised a pale eyebrow. "What makes you ask that?"

"Simple curiosity." I'd wondered when I'd first found out about the Helkis and their shapeshifting abilities if Misha might have had another form—wondered whether the body he wore all the time was really his. Of course, he was dead and it really didn't matter anymore, but still, part of me wanted to know. Especially when his "sister" had the potential to either make or break our mission. My gaze went to her blue eyes—eyes that were so very different from his. Deliberately so, probably. "Misha told me that shapeshifting took a lot of power, and that the eyes were the hardest part to maintain. So which of you is closest to your real form, and how could he—and you—maintain the changes day in and day out?"

"Our changes are subtle, which is why we are able to maintain them so easily." She smiled, but it was a fleeting, almost sad thing. "Last night you saw our true hair color. Misha preferred to maintain silver hair rather than the mixed color, but he never changed his eye color. Like the original, he was born with silver eyes."

"And you?"

"Helki brown, ringed by blue."

"So why do you change it?"

"Because blue is more effective in my work." The bright depths of her eyes suddenly cleared of any emotion, and were all the more chilling because of it. "For Misha alone, I would have my revenge."

"Which is why Starr took Risa hostage."

"Yes."

"So why haven't you contacted the Directorate before now?"

"Because of Gautier. Because I did not know how much you knew about him, or how far his influence went." She snorted softly. "If I were to believe everything he said, he practically runs the place now."

That had my eyebrows rising. "I was given the impression that you and Gautier never met during your information exchanges."

"We don't."

"Then how have you talked to him?"

"Where else would I talk to him? At the estate, of course."

Chapter 5

*F*uck was the only word that came immediately to mind, and even that didn't really encompass the shitload of trouble that had just raised its ugly head. Or, given it was Gautier we were talking about, maybe that should have been its greasy, stinking, ugly head.

"Well, at least that explains where Gautier has disappeared to on the few occasions we've lost him," Jack commented. "But it doesn't change our plans. Liander's work is subtle, but good. I doubt he'd recognize either of you."

Maybe not by sight, but if I opened my mouth and started throwing barbs his way, like I normally did, he'd certainly suspect. There weren't many people as stupid as I tended to be when he was around.

"All you have to do," Jack continued, "is keep out of his way and keep your mouth shut. And that's an order, not a suggestion."

One I'd definitely try to obey. Gautier had already beaten up on me—I had no intention of giving him a second chance. Especially in a place where there was no one to save my ass at the last moment.

"So," I said to Dia, "how often does he appear there?"

She shrugged. "Only very occasionally. Starr does not wish him to be seen or recognized."

"He's a guardian—they work at night. I doubt any of Starr's regulars would recognize him."

Her smile was grim. "There are politicians who have access to files. Starr doesn't want to take the risk because he believes Gautier's position at the Directorate is unknown and safe."

Then yay us for keeping our knowledge of him a secret.

"Is he one of Starr's lovers?" Somehow, I just couldn't imagine Gautier being homosexual. Though I couldn't actually imagine him making love to women, either. He'd always seemed asexual to me.

"No. Starr uses him as an occasional form of punishment—do something seriously wrong, and you fight Gautier." She hesitated. "No one has ever beaten him."

No surprise there. The man was a stinking fighting machine. "Does he kill them?"

"Always. It is what he does."

Wasn't *that* the truth. "Is he expected anywhere near the place over the next couple of weeks?"

"Unless something dramatic happens, no. There's too many people going to be around. I doubt he'd take the chance of exposure."

Good. Because I didn't want to be anywhere near the

bastard, disguise or no. "Anything else I need to know before I board the bus this afternoon?"

She hesitated. "There will be eleven other women with you, all either shifters or weres. At least one of them is not who she pretends to be."

I raised my eyebrows. "Another plant?"

"No. She wants revenge."

Then maybe I could enlist her help sometime over the next few weeks. "Who?"

Dia smiled. "That I shall let you figure out yourself. I'd hate to influence your instincts."

"Meaning you're not entirely sure of your own guesses?"

"Meaning, I cannot say whether she will be a help or a hindrance to what either of us want."

Uh-huh. Typical psychic avoidance of the question if ever I'd heard it. "Why only twelve of us?"

"Because three women stayed on after the last moon dance."

"Why only three? I would have thought the money would be enticement enough to stay longer."

"I honestly don't know. Perhaps they simply wish to go home."

Or perhaps there was more going on behind the scenes than Dia was aware of. "Will it be safe to talk to you once you arrive at the estate?"

"In the house, no. As I said, there are voice monitors in the halls. But I will endeavor to be outside whenever possible. I have made it a habit to wander the grounds, so Starr will not think it unusual."

"There's nothing else?"

"Not that I can immediately think of."

"Good." I half held out my hand, then dropped it. Not because she couldn't see the action, but because she might do another reading. I had a feeling I wouldn't like what she might see. "I'll see you there, then."

She simply nodded. I flung the backpack over my shoulder and escorted myself out. I'd barely made it through the wrought-iron gates when a black van cruised up beside me, the side door opening even as I looked up.

"Get in," Jack ordered, both in my ear and out loud.

I did. As the van cruised on, Jack swiveled away from a bank of com-screens and monitors that lined one wall of the van and held out a hand. I gave him the notebook and contract.

"This is a bit of a risk, isn't it?" I plonked down on the other swivel chair and scanned the monitors. They were showing nothing more than fences, trees, and a long expanse of lawn.

"Dia knows who we are. And if what she said about Starr holding her daughter hostage is true, then he has no need to monitor her when she is not at the estate. Nor have we found any evidence of it."

Didn't mean there wasn't. If Starr knew about the Fravardin, what was to stop him creating similar creatures for his own use? I watched Jack flick through the notebook's pages, then asked, "Anything useful?"

He looked up, then gave me back the book. "Lots. Memorize it, then I can arrange to get the information to Kade and Rhoan."

I raised my eyebrows. "How? Neither of them are telepathic."

"No. But we currently have use of the seconded hawk-shifters, and only the fence line is fully monitored."

Which is basically what Dia had said. I nodded toward the monitors. "That the estate?"

"Yes. We're trying to get cameras closer to the house, but they're doing regular checks and it's making it extremely difficult."

I raised my eyebrows. "Stepping up security because he's called all his generals in?"

"I suspect so. After all, what better time would there be for another cartel to strike?"

"Given what Dia said about the vampire attack, he may be installing infrared, also." Which would put a serious dent in my nightly activities. I could shadow as well as any vampire, but infrared would pick up my heat trail.

"We're monitoring the infrared companies. So far, no order has been placed."

"What about the black market?"

"The devices can certainly be bought, but installation requires specialist knowledge, and there are only a dozen or so qualified people in Melbourne." He pointed to the notebook. "Start memorizing."

He went through the work agreement as I studied the notebook. Starr's estate consisted of over fifty acres of forest and paddocks. The house itself was a huge, square-shaped, double-story complex that featured not only a soccer-field-sized arena in the middle of the square, but an Olympic-sized pool and a huge gym complex. Set apart from the main building were several smaller ones, including quarters for security and the prostitutes. The barn and the zoo were on the opposite side of the complex to these. Behind them was a man-made lake apparently big enough to yacht on.

"Standard work agreement," Jack said, after a while.

"The only interesting point is agreeing to have your memories 'rearranged' when you leave."

"Which is what is happening to the whores."

He nodded and glanced at his watch. "We'll drop you off near the meeting point at one. That gives you an hour to read the rest of the notes as well as the contract."

So I read and memorized while he studied the banks of monitors. What he was looking for I had no idea, especially since there didn't seem to be a lot happening on them. At one, they dropped me off at a Kentucky Fried Chicken outlet. Obviously, he'd heard my stomach rumbling. Either that, or it was a last meal for the doomed. I grabbed a dinner for two—once again thanking my lucky stars that a werewolf's increased metabolic rate made it almost impossible for me to gain weight once I'd hit adulthood—then headed down to the meeting point to see who else might be waiting.

Three women were already there. Two were sullen excuses of womanhood, thin and rangy looking—in that long-distance-runner sort of way. The third was taller, broader, with spiky, bleached-blond hair and sharp blue eyes. She had tats up her arms and trouble written all over her sharp features. I would have categorized her as punk, except for the way she stood. It wasn't the typical, bite-me-or-fight-me stance that so many of the street kids in need of an attitude adjustment had, but rather that of someone who fought for a living. Light on her toes.

I gave her a nod, ignored the other two, and sat on a nearby brick fence to eat my chicken. Animosity rode the air, coming from the direction of the rangy chicks rather than the toey one, but neither of them said anything as other women began to roll up. By two, we had a full complement, and a good cross-reference of shapes, colors, and race. I didn't see another werewolf, but there were werecats, a bear-shifter, bird-shifters, and a sly-looking woman with red hair and reddish skin who surely had to be a werefox. The arena was going to be interesting, to say the least.

The bus rolled in about five minutes after the last woman had arrived, and a big man with slate gray hair climbed off. "Okay, ladies," he bellowed, in a drill sergeant tone. "When I read your name, you will board the bus."

He began snapping off names, and like obedient little soldiers, we rose and entered the bus. I hesitated on the top step, my gaze sweeping the semidarkness. There were plenty of empty seats, but most of the women already aboard had chosen to sit near the back. The bear-shifter sat about halfway down, her large frame barely squeezing into the seat. Her gaze, when it met mine, was challenging, as if daring me to sit with her, so I walked down the aisle and plonked down on the seat opposite hers.

"The little wolf is game," she said, her voice a rumble that seemed to come from somewhere deep. "Most of the others seemed a little afraid to come close."

"The wolf is only little compared to some." I made a show of looking her up and down. She was a big woman—in all ways—but the crow's-feet touching the corners of her brown eyes, along with the dimples in her cherub cheeks, suggested a good nature that was at odds with the attitude she was projecting and the fierce reputation bear-shifters had. "But with mitts like that, you can hardly blame them. I think they should be labeled an unfair advantage."

She laughed—a booming, merry sound that had me grinning. "You could be right there, wolf." She leaned forward and offered me one of her oversized paws. "Bernadine. Berna to my friends."

"Poppy." I grinned as her hand wrapped around mine. Though her grip was strong, it wasn't menacing or testing. A woman confident in her own strength and not needing to advertise the fact to others. "Pencil me in as a friend, Berna. I've got a feeling it could get dangerous to be considered anything else."

"And you might have that right, too, wolf." She grinned. "Sorry, but Poppy just doesn't seem to suit you."

"It's not a moniker I would have chosen, but my parents didn't exactly give me the choice." Nor did my goddamn boss.

The two sullen-looking women climbed on board, hesitating as I had on the top step as their gazes swept the bus. Both sneered when their gaze came to rest on me, then they turned as one and sat two seats in from the front of the bus.

Berna gave me an amused glance. "Are we taking bets on the fact that they're twins?"

"Twins don't echo each other's movements like those two do." Hell, my brother would kill me if I started parroting his movements like that. "The sync of those two is almost creepy."

"Which is why I bet twins. Separated at birth."

"Or they're just plain weird."

She chuckled. "I think we're all weird. After all, here

we are, sitting on a bus, waiting to be taken to God knows where."

"The money made me do it."

"Me, too. Have to wonder about some of the others, though."

Military guy climbed on at that point, cutting off the immediate chance to ask what she meant. As the doors swished shut, he said, "Okay, ladies, listen up." He waited until the slight murmur of conversation died, then continued, "As you will have noted in your contracts, the owner of the estate you are being driven to wishes to keep its location secret, so the windows will be blacked out in a moment and a curtain pulled across the front of the bus. The interior of the bus will be monitored, however, and anyone caught attempting to look out the windows will lose their position."

"I can't remember any mention of paranoia in the contract," I muttered.

Berna snorted softly. Military guy gave me a glare. "You have read and signed the contract, have you not?"

"I have."

"Then you will know backchat is not acceptable."

"And if you have read my file, you will know that is one of my more charming personality traits."

"Riley, shut the fuck up," Jack said into my ear. "You do not need to be shoved off the bus just yet."

I bit my bottom lip to restrain my grin and wished I could remind him that he was the one who'd made Poppy the mouth, not me.

Military guy's expression was less than happy. "Insolence may be good for the ring, but it will lose you money out of it."

"You'd dock my pay?"

"It was in the contract."

"Bugger. Guess I should have read it better."

His frown darkened, but his gaze moved on. Several of the woman sitting in the back of the bus shifted uncomfortably, and I wondered whether the cause was military guy's fearsome gaze or the realization they might have gotten themselves into more than they bargained for. Certainly I could "feel" concern in the air—and the mere fact that I was sensing *that* was a cause of concern for me. Since when had I been able to sense emotions? I'd always been able to sense Quinn's, true, but that was due to the extraordinary connection between us . . . wasn't it?

"Those of you who *have* read the contract"—the emphasis left me in no doubt to whom that particular comment was aimed at, but then, it didn't exactly take a rocket scientist to work that out—"will no doubt be aware that there is one final test on reaching the estate— an obstacle course. If you do not complete this course, you will fail and be returned to the pickup point. If you shift shape during the course, you will also fail."

"Why no shapeshifting?" I piped up.

He gave me a deadpan look. "Because that is the wishes of your new employer."

"So why employ shifters and weres if you don't want them to shift?"

"Why don't you just shut up before I stop this bus and boot you out?"

I shut up.

"Those who make it through the obstacle course will be prepared for the arena. It is hand-to-hand fighting, with some wooden weapons allowed. The winner gets a substantial monetary bonus, and will spend the night with my employer's lieutenants. This is not negotiable, and anyone uncomfortable with this can leave now."

He aimed that last bit at me, though why was anyone's guess. Poppy was supposed to be half-wolf, and wolves didn't place the same sort of emphasis on sex that many of the other races did. It was *just* sex, something to be shared and enjoyed rather than hidden behind closed doors and puritanical attitudes.

When I kept my mouth shut, he went on, "Any injuries received in the arena will be tended to by the contestant. Failure to show up in the arena due to injury will result in the loss of that night's pay."

These boys were all heart.

"There are two areas out of bounds for all contestants," military guy continued. "The zoo, which no one shall enter without proper guidance, and basement levels which contain my employer's personal quarters."

It also contained the small lab area, which meant getting to Dia's daughter without being seen was going to be doubly hard.

"Anyone found in my employer's quarters, for any reason beyond a personal invite, will be instantly dismissed."

No mention there of being returned home. I had a bad feeling that wasn't actually an option under those circumstances.

He glanced at his watch, then added, "We are now going to black out the bus. It'll take approximately one hour to get to the estate. Until then, please sit back and enjoy the ride."

I snorted softly as darkness fell within the bus. "Yeah,

I always enjoy riding into parts unknown in a pitch-black bus."

"And I came out of hibernation not so long ago, so black places are not on my list of favorite things at the moment."

I raised my eyebrows. "A bear who doesn't like the dark?"

"Oh, I have no problem with the dark, wolf. I just don't like being in it when there's no real need."

"So you sleep with the light on?"

She snorted. "Of course not. Nor do I make love with the light on. The wobbly bits look better in the dark."

I grinned. "And if you don't like the look of your partner, it's easier to imagine you're with someone else."

"Hell, yeah." She paused. "So what do you think this is really all about?"

I shrugged, and half-wondered why she was asking that question. I mean, she had no idea who was listening in or who I really was. For all she knew, I might be here to sort out any possible spies. But then, bear-shifters, for all their fearsome attitudes, also had a reputation for brutal honesty. Maybe she simply thought that because I was here, in the middle of the bus, I was trustworthy.

Or maybe *she* was the plant.

But for some reason, I thought not—and I have no idea why, other than the fact that I liked her. Considering my low batting average of late when it came to picking friends, I really should be taking *that* as a sign to be more cautious around her.

"I think we have a rich, eccentric recluse who likes to show off to his friends by throwing wild sex parties."

"But the arena? I like fighting, don't get me wrong,

but this seems a little more serious than the stuff I usually do."

"You fight for a living?"

"I'm a wrestler by trade."

Well, she certainly had the size for it. And though I'd never seen a bear-shifter in action, she probably had the speed, as well. Real bears could certainly move damn fast, for all their bulk. "There's a fair bit of money in that, isn't there?"

"If you're good. I don't make half as much as Ginny."

I frowned. "Who's Ginny?"

"The tat lady. You must have noticed her in the line earlier."

Ah—the light-on-her-toes woman. I'd been right. She did fight for a living. "So you know each other?"

"We work the same circuit."

Which could have meant anything from they were the best of friends to mortal enemies.

"You're both out of work at the moment, then?"

"No. But for me, this offer is just too good to refuse. It'll give me some decent fallback money. I might even be able to buy myself somewhere to live." She paused. In the brief silence, I heard the squeak of seats as the other women moved. None of them were talking. Maybe they were riveted by our conversation.

"So what were you up to when they recruited you, wolf?"

"I've only just come down from Sydney."

"Why?"

"Things got a little heated up there for me. Thought retreat was better than ending up sitting behind cell bars."

She didn't say anything, but there was suddenly a de-cided chill coming from her direction. "Anything major?"

"Just getting a little light-fingered in the wrong place."

"A thief."

She said it in a flat-toned, disapproving sort of way. Not surprising, given the brutally honest tendencies of her race. But her tone also suggested I'd just lost a poten-tial friend. That was sad, because I generally found it hard to make friends, and things had, up until that mo-ment, seemed hopeful.

"When I need to be." I shrugged. "A girl's got to live."

"A girl can get a regular job."

"I do. They always fire me."

"I'm not surprised if you're light-fingered."

I didn't say anything to that, and she lapsed into si-lence. The rest of the journey seemed to take forever, but eventually the blackout was lifted, revealing a long white driveway that was lined with elms. It led up to a white-pillared house that looked as if it belonged somewhere in the deep south of America—only it was far, far larger than any of those southern mansions. The "wows" that suddenly filled the bus were echoed by me, even though I'd already seen the floor plans. Obviously, crime paid *ex-tremely* well.

The bus didn't stop at the front of the place, but turned to the right and headed toward the rear. I studied the gardens and paddocks rather than craning my neck to view the building like everyone else, and managed to catch a glimpse of several bunkhouses, including one that was fenced by wire. The whorehouse, probably. And if you had to live in a whorehouse, then this was the type to go for. It was a miniature replica of the main house, with lush landscaping and its own small pool. Still, given the wire fencing and the cameras mounted on each corner, I was damn glad we hadn't followed our original plan. Getting out of that place on a regular basis would have been hell.

The bus came to a halt around the back of the house and military guy stood up. "As I read your name, you will leave the bus and walk over to the red door. From there, you will enter and complete the obstacle course. Depending on whether you pass or fail, you will either be led to your quarters or returned to the bus. Is that understood?"

We dutifully nodded, and he said, "Nerida Smith."

The fox-shifter stood and marched off the bus. As she neared the red door, it opened. She went through and the door closed behind her. Though I listened hard, I could hear no sound coming from behind the door. Whatever was happening inside was quiet. Either that, or the house was extremely well soundproofed.

The twins were next, then a dark-skinned woman who looked extremely fragile. About five seconds after she'd entered, I heard the screams—high and frightened. Military guy looked down at his folder and ran his pen across the page. Our first failure.

Ginny, the tat lady, was next, then Berna. "Good luck," I said, as she rose.

She gave me a tight sort of nod that spoke of nerves more than a reluctance to acknowledge me, and headed out of the bus. No screams came from either woman, which I guess meant they'd passed. A blonde went next, and she also failed.

"And the lucky last," he said eventually. "The mouthy werewolf."

I stood. "I guess you're meaning me."

He pointed toward the red door with his pen. "Let's see how sassy you get in there."

"Obstacle courses don't scare me."

His sudden grin held a decidedly nasty edge. "Oh, this one might."

And wasn't that something to look forward to. I jumped off the bus and headed for the door. "Going into the house," I murmured. "Turning off sound until I'm sure it's safe."

"Luck, Riley."

"Thanks."

I lightly pressed the com-link to switch it to off, then took a deep breath as the red door opened. The room inside was long and shadowed, and filled with varying stacks of boxes. I looked up as I went through the doorway, noting there was no door sensor on the inside of the frame. Meaning this particular exit was one way only. Cameras lined the roof at regular intervals, so someone was monitoring everything that happened between this door and the exit.

I wondered if they'd intervene if things got nasty.

The door began to swing shut automatically. I stopped on the small landing and sniffed the air. There was nothing more than age and dust to be smelled, but that didn't mean the room was empty. Awareness tingled across my senses, a warning that there were several other non-humans hiding within the maze of boxes—and one of them was a vampire.

The door clicked shut, then the lights went off, leaving a darkness that was blacker and thicker than night. I blinked, switching to the infrared of my vampire sight. An unfair advantage, but then, who said I had to play fair?

Whisper-soft steps rode the stillness. I glanced to my left—not because that was where the footsteps were coming from, but because someone was hiding there. I couldn't see them—they had to be hiding behind some sort of metal, because I wasn't seeing their heat signature. But their presence itched at my skin, as irritating as sand caught in a shoe.

I ignored the stairs, leapt over the railing, and dropped lightly to the floor. The footsteps stopped. For several seconds there was no sound other than the light rasp of my breathing. Then the red heat of a body flickered across the darkness, moving from one pile of boxes to another. Not the vampire, but some other nonhuman. I wasn't getting specifics, which made me wonder if they had some sort of psi-deadeners installed in the room.

I undid my buckle, then pulled the belt out from around my waist and held the two ends lightly in one hand. I didn't want either the people in this room, or those who were watching, to realize exactly what I could do, so using the spider-shaped buckle as a weapon might just deflect from the fact that I was faster and stronger than any half-breed should be.

I moved forward to the first line of boxes. Movement stirred the air, not footsteps but something else. Something that was arcing toward my head with deadly force. I dropped and lashed the buckle across the darkness. It hit something solid, and a man grunted. I followed the soft sound and dove forward, tackling the person I couldn't see with infrared at knee height and bringing him down. His head hit the concrete with a sizable crack, and he didn't move. And he still wasn't visible, even though he was solid to the touch. A spirit lizard, probably. The one I'd killed after he'd assassinated Roberta Whitby—the sister Starr had wanted out of the way—had been little more than an outline, a figure who had a basic shape but no distinct features.

I didn't bother checking whether he was okay—just felt along his arms until I found the weapon he'd been holding. Nunchakus. The bastard could have taken my head off—and it probably explained the screams I'd heard earlier. The two women had been caught un- awares by the black thing that had virtually no heat sig- nature and no smell.

After grabbing the weapon with my free hand, I moved back to the boxes and squatted down. Footsteps whispered across the silence again, this time from behind me. I padded forward, away from the steps, keeping low until I reached the end of the line of boxes. I felt for the top, noting that while it was high, it was still within my leap range, then threw the nunchakus as far and as high as I could. As they whirled through the air, I leapt on top of the box and made my way silently back along the top of them.

Tension filled the air, coming from the creature who was almost directly below me. The nunchakus hit some- thing with a god-awful clatter, but no one reacted. Then again, the two men left in the room were, at the very least, professionals, and not likely to be scared senseless by an unexpected noise. I waited, watching the heat of the man below me until he finally began to creep around the end of the box.

I unrolled the belt, flicking the buckle end toward the back of his head. It hit hard, and he went down the same way.

One to go.

And I couldn't see him. Or rather, couldn't see the heat of him. Either he was hiding behind something toward the end of the room, or, like the black thing I'd felled, he was somehow invisible to infrared.

I jumped back down to the floor and walked across to the wall. There was no sense in trying to be quiet, as the person ahead was some sort of vampire, and he'd hear the beat of my heart no matter how quiet the rest of me was. But with my back to the wall, at least I cut off one avenue of attack.

The air stirred, washing the faint stink of vampire across my nose. This one obviously washed more than Gautier, but I was betting the closer I got to him, the more he'd reek. One of these days the morons were going to wake up to the fact that their refusal to wash was making them easy prey for those of us who hunted by scent, and I'd be in serious trouble. Hell, the only reason I knew Gautier was around most times was thanks to his ungodly stink.

The stirring air told me that this vamp was on the move. I kept making my way along the wall, moving past the stacks of boxes as quickly as I could. The vampire was in the center aisle between the two rows, moving back as I moved forward. Tension rolled through me—not fear, just a need to get this over with.

His move, when it came, was quick. So quick I didn't

even see him, just got the faintest whiff of approaching death, then felt the force of his blow as it hit my chin. I reeled backward and half-fell, smashing my knee into concrete with enough force to bring on tears. Then he was on me, a whirlwind of strength and energy, his blows crashing into my body, my arms—anywhere and everywhere. After throwing up my right arm to block some of his punches, I flipped the belt buckle into my other palm and wrapped my fingers between the spider's metal legs, so that they stuck out like vicious little daggers. Then I punched hard and low. He obviously realized my intent, but he wasn't half as fast as he should have been. My blow drove deep into his dangly bits, and he dropped like a stone, wheezing for air and writhing in pain.

I took a shaky breath, then rose and replaced my belt. The lights came back on, and the door at the other end of the room clicked open. I remained near the wall until the last moment, just in case it was a trick, but no one jumped out at me.

I was barely out of the room when the stink of a vampire curled around me, so thick, so putrid, I gagged.

Only it wasn't just *any* vampire.

It was Gautier.

Chapter 6

I froze. What the hell was Gautier doing here? *How* had he gotten here? He might be a vampire by design rather than choice, but he was still restricted by the same rules all vampires faced. He wasn't old enough to be walking around in late-afternoon daylight—and though he could certainly move around in a blacked-out van like Jack did, there was no way on earth he could have gotten into one without being seen or tracked by those watching him.

And Jack would have warned me. He might have faith in Liander's skills, but he still would have told me Gautier was on the loose in the estate, simply because he knew Gautier was the one person who could blow the whole mission wide open.

My gaze rose to that of my nemesis, but those muddy brown depths held none of the hatred, none of the sick evil that was usually so evident in Gautier's gaze. This *wasn't* him, but yet another clone, one who shared his image *and* his smell. Relief swept through my system, leaving me momentarily shaking. Some guardian I was.

Not that I *was* one. Not a kill-on-order one, not yet.

"That almost has to be a record for going through the course," he said. "How did you sense the vampire?"

I sniffed, feigning a confidence I didn't feel. "His scent gave his position away."

"And the spirit lizard?"

"What the hell is a spirit lizard?" I knew, but Poppy wouldn't have, so the question had to be asked.

"The black creature who first attacked you. How'd you sense him?"

"The hiss of air as he whirled the nunchakus." I studied him for a moment. "You the guide to the next stage?"

His smile had a decidedly nasty edge. "And the bearer of the final set of rules."

"More rules? Haven't we enough already?"

"Babe, the boss is paying you extremely well for your services, so you'd better get used to doing what he wants."

I guess he had a point. I shrugged.

"You have two choices of clothing during your time here. The overalls that you will find in your wardrobe, or your skin."

I raised my eyebrows, though I was neither surprised nor particularly worried. "You mean run around naked?"

His glaze slid down my body, then came back up to rest on my tits. He grinned. "And those would look pretty damn special without the hindrance of a bra."

Yeah, and he wasn't getting his mitts anywhere near my D-cups. I might be a wolf, but I *did* have some taste—

and vamps who smelled worse than offal were definitely off my "to-do" list.

But I kept my mouth shut on that particular topic. Until I had more of a feel for who was who, it was better not to comment on anything, whether or not Poppy was a renowned mouth. He motioned me to follow him as he turned and headed for the door.

"Why the choice? Seeing we're getting paid big money to fight and have sex with your boss's lieutenants, I would have thought nakedness would have been a prerequisite. You know, a bit of viewing pleasure for those who can't touch."

He opened the door and ushered me into a long white hall. A polite stinker—not what I expected to find here. "Those who parade around in their skin are given the choice of saying no. Those who wear overalls aren't."

"That's not what military man said in the bus." Nor was it what Dia had suggested. But then, maybe she didn't socialize with the fighters, and therefore didn't know the entire truth. Which might also mean she didn't know the entire truth in other areas.

And wasn't that a fantastic thought?

He flashed me another nasty grin. "Didn't want you all leaving now, did we?"

"And the arena fighting is all naked?"

"And in mud." He hitched his pants in that way all men did when in the presence of a woman they were attracted to. "Very exciting."

"I bet," I said dryly.

We moved into another corridor, and from down the far end came raised voices. One of them was Berna's.

"Your quarters," he said. "You can pick who you wish to share with. We don't care."

"Cool."

"Dinner is at seven in the main dining room and is not optional. Other meals are." He stopped near the first door. "You are free to explore or use any of the facilities before and after the dinner show. Myself or one of the other guards will be here to escort you to the dining room at six forty-five. Don't be late."

"Or what?"

He gave me another nasty grin again, and I seriously had to resist the urge to smack it from his thin lips. "We'll dock your pay or punish you in other ways."

"What other ways?"

"You'll see an example tonight, over dinner." Anticipation gleamed in his eyes, giving me the bad feeling that it was something normal, sane people *wouldn't* like.

I nodded. After another look at my breasts, he spun around and left. I followed the sound of Berna's voice, passing several rooms that were already full, and stopped in the last doorway.

The bear-shifter stood in the middle of the room, her large paws on her larger hips, and her short dark hair fairly bristling with anger.

Nerida, the fox lady, stood in front of her, defiance written all over her red features. She was game, I had to give her that. Berna was twice her height and four times her girth.

"I got here first," she said. "The window is mine."

"I need fresh air or I snore. Believe me, if you cherish sleep, you would not want me snoring."

All this angst and noise over a damn window? "Really, ladies, this is easily settled."

Berna gave me a dark glance as I walked in. "We don't want thieves in this room."

"The thief doesn't steal from friends, and there are no other beds left anyway, so tough." I walked across to the bed in question and stripped off my coat. "To settle the argument, I'll take it."

Nerida glanced up at Berna, then the two of them stepped forward as one. Something about that itched at my senses. There was just a little too much precision in the way they did that—like it was a move they'd practiced more than once. Maybe Nerida was also a wrestler.

And maybe something else was going on.

Dia had mentioned that someone in this group wasn't who they pretended to be. Maybe there *was* more than just one pretender.

And why would they fake a fight? To make it seem they weren't friendly to watching eyes, perhaps? Now, why would they want something like that?

"I'm at least three times your girth, wolf, and probably twice as strong. I could thump you into the floor without even thinking."

"You could try," I said mildly. "I doubt you'd succeed."

She bristled. "That a challenge?"

I shrugged, and kicked off my shoes. Feigning disinterest when every sense I had was tuned on the both of them, waiting for a move. Any move. "Take it any damn way you please."

I half-turned, and that's when the fox sprung. I dropped, moving under her leap, then grabbed her and whirled her quickly around before letting go. I had no time to see if she'd hit the bed I'd been aiming for, because the air screamed with the warning of an approaching blow. I surged upright and caught Berna's fist in a two-handed grip. Held it and stopped it, even if the force of her blow sent shock waves up my arms and rattled my teeth.

"Looks don't always indicate strength," I said softly, as surprise flitted through her brown eyes. "Do not try and attack me like that again." I looked at Nerida, who'd landed beside the bed rather than on it and was currently rubbing her hip. "Either of you."

I pushed Berna backward and released her, then got back to the business of stripping off. "Do you know what's happened to our bags?"

"Coming once we've sorted sleeping positions out."

I glanced at her. "Which we have."

She sniffed. Whether that meant acceptance, or whether it meant I was going to have to turf her out of the bed when I got back was anyone's guess.

"Why are you stripping?" she asked.

"I'm going to explore."

"Trust a wolf to do the naked thing," Nerida said, contempt heavy in her voice.

"Better naked than having no choice."

"They're paying me to fight and fuck. They are not paying me enough to flaunt myself to all and sundry."

I couldn't see the difference and said as much.

She snorted. "That's because you're a wolf, and everyone knows wolves have no morals."

I raised my eyebrows. "So what's so moral about fighting and fucking for money?"

"Perhaps not a lot, but there are lines *some* of us won't cross. Werewolves don't seem to have *any* lines."

"And you've had how many years' experience with werewolves?"

She looked away and mumbled, "None."

I snorted. "One good thing about wolves is that they prefer to judge a person by their actions." I stripped off my knickers and dumped them with the rest of my clothes. "I'm off to explore."

Neither woman commented or offered to come along, for which I was extremely grateful. Not only did I plan to scout the house and grounds, but I also wanted to find me a stallion. And maybe even catch a little riding action.

The main house seemed a whole lot bigger in life than it had on the plans and, as Dia had warned, there were cameras everywhere. If the halls weren't darkened at night, then moving through them without being seen was going to be next to impossible.

After touring the rooms that were accessible, I glanced at my watch and was relieved to see I still had nearly two hours before I had to be back. I found a door that led outside and followed the white pebbled driveway around to the paddocks that housed the barns and the horses. There were several women out riding—some of them naked, some not—and men in dark uniforms hanging over the fence, wolf-whistling and throwing lewd suggestions at the women. Like that was attractive or something. I guess some men simply never grew up.

A crinkled, weather-worn man who had to be at least eighty came out of the barn as I approached. "You here to ride?"

I nodded and looked past him, searching the shadows for Kade. I couldn't see him immediately, but the barn was huge and he could be anywhere.

"You know the rules?"

Again I nodded. "We're allowed to ride anywhere, aren't we?"

"As long as you do your half hour in the front paddock for the boys, you can go where you like on the estate. Within the boundaries already outlined, of course."

Which meant we weren't likely to raise suspicions when we nicked off into the forest. Excellent. "And are we at least allowed a saddle blanket? Horse hair and nether regions are never a pleasant combination." And I knew *that* from experience.

He gave a short, sharp laugh. "You got that right, girlie." He reached behind the door, then handed me a blanket, girth, and halter. "Any one of them bad boys is yours."

I raised my eyebrows. "They're all stallions?"

"Mostly. The boss does sometimes bring in a mare in heat, just to watch the boys fight."

"Nasty."

He shrugged. "It's nature at its finest."

Or madness at its finest. "Thanks."

He nodded. "Just remember—you get hurt, we aren't responsible."

"Has anyone ever got hurt?" I asked, curious.

"Yes."

"So what happened to them?"

He shrugged. "Isn't my problem."

I very much suspected they weren't Starr's problem, either. Not after he'd tended to them in a less than conventional way. Like burying them. Dead people don't talk—unless, of course, they were vamps, and Starr was the type to stake first, ask questions later.

I flung the girth and blanket over my shoulder and walked into the shadowed barn. A careful study of the upper spaces of the barn didn't reveal any cameras or microphones. Maybe they figured nothing of interest would happen in the barn and hadn't bothered—and for that I was extremely grateful. It at least meant I could sneak in here after hours and not worry about anyone spotting me.

The air was rich with the scents of horse, hay, and shit, and as I moved down the aisle, heads swung my way, dark eyes gleaming intently in the muted light. They were all tall and strong looking, most of them chestnut or bay. And all of them reacted to my presence, either snorting in fear or backing away. Horses and wolves were never a good combination. Kade, a magnificent mahogany bay, was down the far end.

"Hey, big boy," I said, for the benefit of the stable hand cleaning the stall opposite. "Want to go for a ride?"

He stomped a foot and snorted, his velvet brown eyes seeming to gleam with anticipation. I grinned and opened the stall door, not bothering to lock it again because Kade wasn't going anywhere. I looped the halter over his nose and ears, threw the reins over his head, then tossed the blanket across his back. And noticed, when I was bending down to cinch up the girth, his erection.

"Someone's pleased to see me," I murmured, and had my rump nipped for my trouble. I chuckled, and hauled myself onto his back.

Kade was moving before I was fully settled, trotting back down the aisle and breaking into a canter once we'd reached the paddock. I moved in rhythm with his stride, enjoying the whip of wind across my skin and through my hair as much as the sensation of being a part of so much contained power. The bouncing boobs weren't so enjoyable—actually, they were downright painful—but I doubted the wolf whistlers hanging off the fences would care either way.

We did our allotted half hour, then cantered around the lake's shoreline before going into the trees, not stopping until we'd reached a small stream deep within the shadowed, green darkness.

I slid off his back and stepped back as the golden shimmer of shapeshifting appeared on his nose and quickly spread across the rest of his body. He was just as magnificent in human form as he was in horse, his mahogany skin, black hair, and velvet brown eyes a truly striking combination. And it wasn't only his coloring that was magnificent. He was built like a thoroughbred—broad shoulders, powerful chest, slim hips, and long, strong legs. I knew the power of those legs. Knew how hard and strong they could hold a person as he drove himself deep.

I wanted to feel that again.

Badly.

He stepped free of the blanket and girth, his gaze holding mine as he pulled the halter away from his neck.

"Do you know," he said, his voice deep and somewhat husky, "how long it has been since I've had a woman?"

I let my gaze slide down to the tent pole he had happening. "A while by the look of that."

"Three weeks," he murmured, as he moved toward me. "Three horrible, torturous weeks in which heaven was so close, and yet so far."

I grinned as he pressed a hand against my shoulder and pushed me backward, until my spine was pressed up against a tree. "I gather we're talking about the naked women riding you?"

There was only inches between us. The heat of him burned across my skin, and the air was deliciously filled with his musky odor and the rich scent of desire. It had me melting in an instant, and wanting him more than I'd wanted anyone for a while. Well, for at least the last twenty-four hours, and for wolf, that was a *long* time.

He raised a hand and brushed wispy strands of hair from my cheek. "I missed you."

His fingers trailed heat where they touched, and the longing already trembling inside became a symphony. I touched his chest and let my fingers explore the well-defined ridge of muscles that ran down his stomach. This man was hot in so many ways. "And I you."

The smile that tugged his lips went beyond sexy, and my hormones did an excited little jig. Of course, my hormones never needed much prompting.

His touch moved gently down my neck and sent my pulse tripping. Between his caress, the way his breath teased my lips, and the desire that singed my senses, I was pretty much in danger of internally combusting. But he didn't get on with it, just said, "You realize this first time will be fast. I need you too badly for it to be anything else."

"Fast is good." Right now, even *I* didn't want slow.

He smiled, then wrapped his arms around my body and crushed me close. His lips claimed mine and for several minutes, it felt like I was tasting heaven. And yet, despite the urgency that burned between us, our kiss was slow, and tender, and so very, very thorough.

But I could feel the tension in his broad shoulders. The hardness of his erection pressing against my stomach.

The quivering in his muscles as he restrained desire. It was too much. I didn't want his restraint. I wanted *him*. Wanted to feel the heat of him deep inside. Not in five minutes, not in two minutes. *Now*. And if he wasn't going to take any action, then I damn well would.

I slipped a hand between us and wrapped my fingers around his cock. His body reacted to my touch, seeming to jump with eagerness.

"Someone's anxious," he murmured, as I guided him to where it was warm and wet and ready.

"Very," I whispered. "So stop mucking around and get down to the serious stuff."

The words were barely out of my mouth and he was in me, driving hard and deep. Horse-shifters took after their animal counterparts when it came to the shape and size of their cock, and having him fill me so completely was an incredibly satisfying sensation.

His thick groan was a sound I echoed, especially when he began to move. His strokes were fierce, like he couldn't drive himself hard enough or deep enough. Or simply couldn't *get* enough—a feeling I understood completely. Sex with Kade was entirely different from sex with either Quinn or Kellen—not better, not worse, just different. And it wasn't something I was ready to give up in a hurry—no matter what the other two might wish.

I wrapped my legs around his hips and urged him deeper still, using the tree to support my back as he thrust and thrust, until it felt as if the rigid heat of him was trying to spear right through my spine.

My breathing sharpened as pleasure spiraled, and all too quickly my climax hit, the convulsions stealing my breath and tearing a strangled sound from my throat. He came a heartbeat later, his body slamming into mine, the force of it driving slivers of bark into my back.

At that moment in time, the slivers could have been daggers and I wouldn't have given a damn.

When the tremors eased, he leaned his sweaty forehead against mine, his breathing harsh, velvet eyes alive with amusement and desire.

"Well, that took a little of the edge off."

I grinned and ran a hand down his hot, sweaty cheek. "So there's energy left for a more timely seduction?"

"Hell, yeah." He kissed me fiercely, then added, "Did I mention I haven't had sex for three weeks?"

"It's a wonder the sperm factories didn't explode under the stress of all that production and no outlet."

He snorted. "Isn't that the truth."

I lowered my feet to the ground, and he stepped back. "How much time have you got?"

I glanced at my watch. "About three-quarters of an hour."

"Good." He took my hand, walked across to grab the saddle blanket, then led me to the water's edge. "Sit," he ordered, after spreading the blanket. "And I'll remove the bark you undoubtedly have in your back while I update you."

"Update being a new term for sex?" I said hopefully.

He grinned and slapped my butt. "Behave. We need to discuss business before we get down to more serious pleasure."

"And here I was thinking sex came first, second, and third in line for horse-shifters."

"When I'm not working, it does. You turning Jack on?"

"God, what a revolting thought."

He chuckled. "You know what I mean."

I did, and flicked the com-link into action. "Jack? I'm with Kade."

"About time you reported in. I was getting worried."

"I had to pass a few more tests, and that house is shored up tighter than a straight boy's ass at a gay bar."

He snorted. "You have such a lovely way with words."

"Blame my pack-mate for that one." Kade still wasn't aware that Rhoan was my brother—it was a secret we kept from all but a few. I folded my legs and sat cross-legged on the mat. Kade squatted behind me, filling my senses with his warm, musky scent.

"Has Rhoan reported in yet?"

I repeated the question and Kade shook his head. Not that I could actually see it, but right now all my senses were attuned to his every move, so the head shake was something I could "feel." Which maybe was something I should be scared about, because I wasn't emphatic, and I shouldn't be able to "feel" anything.

"It often takes several days for the new security officers to appear." His fingers skimmed my skin, sending little skitters of pleasure across my skin and stirring barely sated desire.

"Do they lose security personnel that often?" I asked.

"Yes, because part of their job is checking the zoo. Let me tell you, there's some very angry creatures penned in that area, and they often take it out on the guards."

No surprise, given the fact that being penned for any amount of time was enough to drive most nonhumans insane. There again, the nonhumans filling these particular pens were bred in a lab then locked in the zoo, so they probably wouldn't have had much of a grip on sanity to begin with. Not that Starr would care what his creations did as long as they killed on order.

"Did Kade get the floor plans I sent to him?" Jack asked.

Again I repeated the question, then winced as Kade pulled a sliver of wood from my skin.

"Yeah. Not that it'll do me much good. I have to stay outside—they'd pick me up as an unknown the minute I entered any of the buildings."

"So the cameras are monitored twenty-four hours a day?"

"Afraid so." He picked another bit of wood from my skin and flicked it away. It landed in the middle of the water and bobbled its way downstream. "Shift changes are seven in the morning and seven at night. You might have a few minutes' leeway there, but that's about it."

"Has he seen Starr about at all?"

I repeated Jack's question.

"I get the impression that except for mealtimes, he never moves from his bolt-hole."

"And there's been no mention of Libraska from anyone else?"

"None at all." He kissed my shoulder then sat down, his long, leanly muscled legs stretching out either side of me. "But there's been a lot of new arrivals in the last few days. Something is happening."

Jack snorted. "Starr is marshaling his forces for a war against the other cartels."

I repeated the comment, felt more than saw Kade's disagreement. Which was yet another worrying indication that the drug Talon had forced onto me was starting to affect my system.

Damn it, I didn't *want* any more psychic powers. And I definitely didn't want an increase in power in those that I did have. I was quite happy as I was, thank you very much.

But like so many other things in my life of late, I didn't appear to have much choice.

"I've studied the files and know most of Starr's generals by sight," Kade said. "A lot of the arrivals don't match what's in the files."

I frowned. "Maybe there's more generals than we know about."

"Or there's a whole lot more happening than we realize."

And wasn't that a pleasant thought. "Have you seen Dia Jones around?"

"The white psychic? Yeah. Pretty bit of tail, too."

"You seen her with a kid at all?"

He hesitated. "No. But word is Starr's holding her kid hostage for her good behavior."

So she was telling the truth there, too. "In the labs underground, apparently. You know anything about them?"

"Not really. I know they're on a lower level, but not the same one as Starr's. I also heard they have completely different access points and codes than Starr's quarters."

"Riley, why is this important?" Jack said. "You are not going after the kid. It'll jeopardize everything."

I ignored him. I was here, he was sitting in his van, and there wasn't a damn thing he could do to stop me now. And short of endangering Rhoan or Kade, I was going to do what I could to rescue that kid. "What about the scientists?"

"Six that I know of."

"You able to point them out?"

He pulled me back against him. The stallion was up and ready to go again, and I couldn't help grinning in anticipation.

"Why?" he asked.

"I need to get in there, which means I'll probably have to fuck one of them to get the information I need."

"Riley, I forbid you to do this."

"Bite me."

"Me or Jack?" Kade murmured, his teeth grazing my neck and sending shivers of delight skittering across my skin.

"Jack. And I'm not a fool, boss. I won't jeopardize the mission. I want Starr every bit as badly as you do."

He grunted. Whether that was agreement or merely the realization he couldn't actually stop me was anyone's guess.

"So, the scientists," I prompted.

"They're a pretty motley-looking lot," Kade answered.

"As long as they're male and therefore have a dick that takes over from the brain when confronted by a naked woman, I don't give a damn."

He chuckled, and slid his hands up to cup my breasts. "God, I do so love a werewolf's lack of inhibitions."

And I loved his touch. The way his large hands could cover and contain my breasts. The finesse of his clever fingers as they teased and pinched my engorged nipples. I leaned my head against his shoulder, closed my eyes, and simply enjoyed.

And it was in that moment I heard it. The snap of a twig, the gentle rustle of undergrowth. Someone was coming toward us.

I tensed and sat upright.

"What?" Kade asked immediately.

"Shift shape," I murmured as I scrambled to my feet. "Someone's approaching. Jack, I'm switching you off."

"Be caref—" His warning was cut off as I flicked the com-link. Kade shifted into horse form and moved away to graze while I stepped into the icy water and began scooping it up to wash away the evidence of lovemaking. Goose bumps fled across my skin, but the cause wasn't only the chilly water. The presence of the person approaching burned across my skin, as powerful as the electricity that ran before a summer storm. Unpleasant and yet, at the same time, exhilarating.

A man stepped through the trees to my right. He was thickset, broad shouldered, with golden skin and rippling muscles. His hair was a mane of darker gold, thick and lush, and his face was almost feline. His eyes, when he looked up, were tawny. Like a cat's.

He stopped, his eyes suddenly narrowing. The electricity in the air sharpened abruptly, rolling around me in waves that left me breathless, hot. But there was an undercurrent of brutality in what he was projecting, suggesting this man was into more than just vanilla sex.

"Who are you?" he said, voice harsh, rough. He moved his hand, and I noted the gun at his waist of his jeans.

"Poppy Burns. You?"

"And who is Poppy Burns when she's home?" he asked.

"I've been employed to fight in the arena. I came in today."

"Indeed?"

His gaze slid down my body, and moisture skated across my skin, tiny beads of perspiration that had nothing to do with fear and everything to do with arousal. My nipples hardened almost painfully and the throbbing, low-down ache got stronger, especially when his gaze seemed to linger on my hips and groin. As if, even from that distance, he could see the pooling desire. His gaze completed its erotic journey and rose to meet mine again. The lust so evident in those tawny depths just about melted my insides.

I might be wolf, and I might be so very easily attracted to a good-looking man, but what *this* particular man was projecting wasn't natural. It was too overwhelming. Not even a male werewolf using the full strength of his aura could create this sort of reaction in me. Not if I didn't want it to.

But I *had* reacted like this several times before—with Talon, who'd been lab-made by Starr's father. Obviously, given the heated desire boiling around me and his feline features, this man had werelion in him rather than lion-shifter. Shifters—even wolf-shifters—didn't possess this sort of aura. It only came with those who were forced to shift shape on the rise of the full moon. It was her gift to us, if you will.

Or curse, as many shifters *and* humans seemed to think.

Only I didn't actually think he was a part-breed, or even a clone like Talon, nor did I think he was a lab-born crossbreed. I think he was something else entirely—and someone I had been warned about. A human who, while still a fetus, had undergone several procedures that involved cross-planting DNA from shifters and weres to enhance reflexes and senses. According to Misha, the experiments started by Starr's predecessor had finally been successful, but one of the side effects was an overdeveloped sex drive and an aura to match. And given Starr's lieutenants were apparently the end result of such experiments, I was betting *this* man was one of them. There was too much authority in his expression, and in the way he stood, for him to be just another guard.

If it *was* Leo Moss, I had to tread carefully. Misha had warned that Moss and his counterpart, Alden Merle, weren't exactly chummy with sanity, and the last thing I wanted was to get in their bad books straightaway. But by the same token I didn't want to seem too submissive, if only because the unattainable often held the interest longer than the easily gained. I needed to hold their interest until either Rhoan or I got Libraska's location. Killing Starr and tearing down his cartel would be useless otherwise. Someone else would just step into the breach and keep producing nightmares.

The stranger walked toward me. I resisted the urge to step away. The nearer he got, the more my skin burned, and it wasn't just the intensity of his aura. There was madness in his eyes, in the very feel of him—as if his spirit, his soul, was infected with death and decay.

I licked my dry lips, saw his gaze follow the movement. Saw the flame of desire burn darker in his gaze. It was almost hypnotic, and it took a lot of effort to pull my gaze away, to look down.

Which is when I saw the fine down of hair covering his skin. It was silky, shiny, more like a small cat's than the coarser texture of a lion's coat. My fingers itched with the need to feel it, but I had to wonder if the hair covered *all* his bits. I wasn't into fuzzies when it came to *that*.

He stopped within arm's length. I crossed mine, feigning indifference when every inch of my skin trembled with desire and every sense was urging me to turn and run from this foul thing. "So who are you when you're home?"

A smile twisted his lush lips, but it held a hint of arrogance that provided a whole lot of reinforcement to my resistance of his aura. I might be a wolf and technically easy, but no one should ever think they could have me without at least a little effort involved.

"I'm the man you'll be spending the night with."

A shiver ran down my spine at the thought—even if that was what I was sent here to do. "Really? And why is that?"

"Because I want you."

"So? I can pick and choose who I wish to be with, and I see no reason to do so now when I haven't seen the other goods on offer." I let my gaze run down his length. If he wanted me now, it wasn't actually showing through his pants. But then, I fooled around with a stallion, so everyone was small in comparison.

"Have you read the small print on the contract?"

"Why does everyone keep asking me that?"

"Because if you had read it, you'd know it states that while it is mandatory the winner spends the night with Starr's lieutenants, said lieutenants can also choose to spend the night with someone other than the winner, and he or she will comply."

And Jack had said it was a standard contract. I'd like to see what he termed a nonstandard contract. "I think you people are making these things up as you go along."

He produced that arrogant smile again. "Then I shall have another copy of the contract delivered to you. I suggest you read it more thoroughly." He looked me up and down again, and again I reacted with the intensity of a bitch in heat. If he'd have dropped me to the ground and screwed me senseless right there and then, I wouldn't have cared. Kade might have, but not me.

Of course, my reaction afterward would be an entirely different matter. And one that would involve many showers and much soap.

But Moss didn't push the matter, just stepped back. The blast of his aura and lust abated, allowing me to breathe properly again.

"I shall have you brought to my rooms after dinner."

"Joy."

He raised an eyebrow. "Sassy. I like that."

"I couldn't give a damn what you like."

"Oh, you will. You surely will." He gave me a nod, then moved on, quickly disappearing into the trees.

I took a deep, relieved breath, then glanced around as Kade approached. "Wait here. I'm going to follow him."

"That's danger—"

"Is it usual for Moss to be roaming at this hour of the day?"

"Not that I know—"

"Then we need to know what he is up to."

I turned and walked into the trees. Moss's scent hung in the air, though it wasn't actually a smell as much as a teasing touch of heat, desire, and foulness. Now that I thought about it, the man didn't actually *have* a scent. Maybe it had been bred out of him.

I padded through the shadows, keeping close enough to follow his non-scent, to hear the soft crunch of leaves under his shoes. I was naked, my steps lighter, so hopefully I wasn't making enough noise for him to hear me. But given his senses were supposedly heightened, I had to be extra careful.

Especially since the forest itself was quiet. There were no bird calls, no fluttering of wings, not even the irritating songs of insects. I hadn't noticed it before, but then, I'd been wholly occupied with the prospect of satisfaction. Now, though, it struck me as odd. Eerily so.

We walked for a good ten minutes through the strange hush before I noticed the steps ahead had stopped. My heart just about leapt into my throat. God, had he heard me?

I paused in the shadow of a pine and listened intently. The only thing to be heard was the galloping of my heart. I took a deep breath, trying to calm my nerves, then slowly padded forward. The pines and gum trees seemed to close in, and the shadows thickened. Even the air seemed cooler, less welcoming.

His weird non-scent no longer rode the air, but the traces of Moss's passing—the faint disturbance of leaves and twigs—provided a tangible trail. At least it did until it disappeared.

I stopped and looked around. No smell, no trail, nowhere he could have gone.

The damn man had just vanished into thin air.

Chapter 7

Which was impossible, of course. If Moss had shifted shape, become a bird, I would have heard the flap of wings. The forest was too still, too quiet, and the sound would have carried. And if he'd become something else there would have been a trail to follow. Hell, even a vampire couldn't help leaving signs of his passing in the lush undergrowth of the forest floor. Not that a vampire could have disappeared like that in the middle of the day—unless, of course, he was some sort of day vampire, able to use the daylight to hide his form the same way a regular vampire can use the night and the shadows.

Even then, I should have been able to catch his non-scent on the still air.

So there had to be some other explanation. Like maybe a hidden entrance to underground hideouts. There hadn't been one on either the plans Jack had given me or the ones

Dia had drawn, but then, if Starr was so worried about security, he wouldn't have advertised the fact that his fox-hole had escape routes. Exits could become entrances to those with unsavory intent.

I let my gaze roam over the ground, but I couldn't immediately see anything that screamed "hidden entrance." Nor could I afford to waste time searching. Not now, in daylight. But it might be worth coming back tonight and checking it out more thoroughly. If I could escape Moss's clutches at a decent hour, that was.

I turned and retraced my steps. When I was well clear of the spot where Moss had disappeared, I hit the com-link.

"I just met Leo Moss."

"And?"

"He's madly in lust with me. I'll be spending tonight in his bed." Or wherever else it was he liked to have sex. It wouldn't be standard stuff, of that I was certain.

"Excellent. I wouldn't try reading his mind tonight, though. Scout out the situation, give it time, and let him feel relaxed around you."

"I wasn't intending to do anything until Rhoan got here." He was the experienced one, so everything I did I'd clear through him first. If that was possible. "Listen, has the Directorate got access to satellite scanning?"

"Yeah, why?"

"Because I followed Moss, and in the middle of the forest he simply disappeared. I'm thinking there might be a few tunnels under this joint."

"Makes sense that Starr would have escape routes. And we do scan this area every six months to record changes, but maybe the tunnels are a recent addition. I'll arrange for scanning in the next pass over."

"Good, but I might check it out later tonight anyway."

"Don't do anything to jeopardize your position."

"I'm not dumb."

"No, just inexperienced."

"This from the man who is constantly pushing me to be a guardian."

"Which is why I don't want to lose you just yet. Be careful, that's all I'm saying."

"I will. Talk to you later, boss." I pressed the com-link and loped the rest of the way to the clearing where Kade waited. Where, after a little discussion on what had happened, we filled in the remainder of the time sating his needs and mine.

The old man came out as I rode up to the stables. Kade stopped, and I slid off his back.

"Good ride?" he asked, accepting the reins from me.

I nodded, and patted Kade's sweaty shoulder. "This bad boy was horribly frisky. I think he needs to be ridden more often."

Kade snorted and stamped a foot, and I barely restrained my grin.

"You'll be back tomorrow, then?" the old guy asked.

"Yeah."

"I'll get security to notify us when you're headed this way, so we can have him ready for you."

"Thanks...have you got a name?"

"Tommy."

He thrust out a hand and I shook it. His fingers were rough, textured by time, grime, and probably years of hard work. He didn't seem the type to work for scum like

Starr, which was an odd thing to think about someone I'd barely met. For all I knew, Tommy could be Starr's uncle. "I'm Poppy. Thanks."

He took Kade inside, and I headed back to my room to clean up. Neither Berna nor Nerida were there, but my bag was sitting on my bed. A quick check revealed that my clothes and underclothes had disappeared, but all my toiletries remained. Grateful for small mercies, I headed into the bathroom to clean up. Surprise, surprise, there were cameras here, too. I couldn't see any microphones, though. Maybe they figured not a lot of nasty talk could happen in a bathroom—which only went to prove the installers were men. All women know just how nasty bathroom conversation can get—especially when it *centered* on men. Though, given the man behind this whole weird show wasn't exactly chummy with linear lines of thought, maybe he just didn't care.

By the time I got back to the bedroom, Berna and Nerida were both there, the still-clothed bear-shifter prowling the room like a caged animal and the overall-clad fox-shifter lounging on her bed, reading Cleo. The cream overalls were extremely tight and left very little to the imagination, making me wonder why she bothered. Hell, her breasts were so tightly packed they were stretching the material to the max, making the pocket—and the gray and white hanky sticking out of it—stand out like, well, dogs' balls. If she thought the overalls would draw less attention, she was seriously delirious.

Both of them were studiously ignoring me, so I returned the favor and headed over to my bed to open the window. Fresh air drifted in, touched by the coolness of the oncoming night. But aside from the snorting or stamping of horses and the occasional crunch of a guard's footsteps, very little noise carried on the breeze. All the normal dusk sounds—like the warbling of magpies or even the singing of crickets—was nonexistent here, and that one fact sent chills up my spine. Anything that scared insects senseless was something to worry about, in my estimation.

At six forty-four, Berna reluctantly began to strip. She seemed big in her clothes, but she was positively huge out of them. And none of it was fat. She was just large in every conceivable way—huge shoulders, brawny arms, melon breasts, big hips, and chunky, muscular thighs and shins. She pretty much looked as if she could snap someone in two without effort between those legs of hers, which made me wonder about her earlier statement that she wasn't a top wrestler. How could someone be built like that and *not* be one of the best?

It wasn't a question I had the chance to ask, because she'd barely finished stripping when our escort showed up. He gave us all a once-over, nodded in what I presumed was approval, then motioned us to follow him.

Which, of course, we did. The remaining women who'd been on the bus were already in the hallway and being guided away, and amongst them were two women I didn't recognize. Probably two of the three women who had remained from the last group.

We were escorted along until we'd reached one of the arena doors, which had been locked against my earlier explorations.

According to the plans, the arena was designed after the old Roman gladiatorial arenas, though on a far smaller scale. But as we walked into the room, I realized the plans gave no real indication of the sheer scale of the place. Not only did everything soar in this room, but everything seemed oversized, as if the whole intent was to make the room's occupants seem small by comparison. Which was probably the effect someone as warped as Starr would want. The ceiling arched so high above us that without the spotlights it would have been shrouded in darkness, and the statues of naked men and women that lined the wall were at least double the standard sizing. The arena walls were high enough to prevent most shifters and weres from leaping out, though it wouldn't have stopped winged shifters. The arena's center was sand, but studded posts stood at either end, the wood chipped and stained. By what, I just didn't want to know.

Tables and chairs lined three-quarters of the arena. A long table dominated the far end, the white tablecloths, gold settings, and grandiose, highly ornate chairs that looked like something out of the courts of kings. Starr's seating area, obviously.

Though he and his entourage weren't here yet, a lot of people were. There weren't many women, meaning the whores probably didn't rate an invite to this little shindig. Some of the men I knew from the files Jack had given me on known Starr associates, but there were many more I didn't recognize. Just as well Rhoan was coming in with the camera—I had a feeling there were a lot of wanted people in this room.

Of course, with so many people already here, the babble of voices and reek of aftershave and humanity was almost overwhelming. But it was the underlying scent, the base rawness of death and despair that seemed to be leaching from the sand itself that had trepidation stirring.

This room wasn't about fighting. Wasn't about enjoying a spectacle. It was about control. About destruction.

Of hope. Of humanity.

I didn't realize I'd stopped until Berna shoved me from behind.

"What the hell is wrong with you?" she said, voice low and annoyed.

"You're a bear-shifter—can't you smell it?"

"Misery," Nerida said softly, her sharp gaze briefly resting on mine. In the amber depths of her eyes, fear flickered. "This place is drenched in it."

"Weres," Berna said heavily, "are very strange people."

"No. It's just that dogs of all kinds have noses designed to trap smells, and certain emotions are accompanied by strong scents. Fear, for example." I glanced at her as our guide led us to a table near the wall and the stained post. "I would have thought a bear-shifter would know that, given your olfactory senses are as keen, if not keener, than a wolf's."

She shook her head. "That may be true, but we are attuned to physical scents and sounds more than emotional ones. The click of a gun being cocked one hundred feet away or the scent of a carcass two miles away, for instance. Emotions have no scent for us."

"So this arena doesn't worry you?"

"I'm being paid good money to fight in it." Her gaze came to mine. "So are you."

"I love a good fight as much as the next wolf, but this arena isn't just about fighting."

She raised an eyebrow. "If that turns out to be true, then maybe the three of us should plan a little bust-out."

"With cameras on every corner? They'd catch us inside

a minute." Though if I wanted to get out of this place, I'd damn well find a way, cameras or not. "And I'd be careful where you said that, because they have voice monitors as well as cameras in this joint."

She looked around as she sat down on the chair near the wall. "Really? Where?"

I nodded to the black dome above the table to our left. "That looks like a PTR-1043. It comes complete with sound and motion sensors." I grinned at their surprised looks, and embellished the truth with a little lie. "Fucked a home security guy for a while. He liked to go on about his hardware."

Nerida snorted. "As all men do."

"I'm gathering that's where you picked up the finer skills of a thief?" Berna asked.

I glanced at her. There was no animosity in her voice or on her features, yet I felt the wave of her disapproval all the same. "Yes."

She harrumphed and didn't add anything else, simply crossed her arms and stared out over the arena. Nerida looked at me for a few seconds longer, then said, "You don't seem like a thief to me."

That's because I wasn't, but if I was fooling Berna and everyone else, why wasn't I fooling the fox-shifter? What was she picking up that the others weren't? I forced a casual shrug. "And what does a thief look like?"

"Shifty. Desperate. You don't."

"Well, I'm not right now, am I?"

A set of trumpets blasted before she could answer, and an unseen announcer ordered us to rise. I ignored the speculation in Nerida's eyes, pushing to my feet as I glanced over to the main table. Starr, his lieutenants, and their hangers-on were entering the room like royalty. And considering at least one of them was a queen, maybe that was appropriate.

Starr himself wasn't the type of man who immediately drew the eye. He was on the small side, thin, with bristly brown hair and sallow-looking skin. Not that this was the real Starr—he'd been killed off some time ago and replaced by the shapeshifting son of the man who'd started the whole cloning nightmare. This Starr was flanked by his two lieutenants—Moss in front, Merle behind, both men naked from the waist up. Of the three, Merle was perhaps the most eye-catching. Not only did he have the build of an Adonis, but strong, almost feline features and the striped skin of a tiger. In any normal situation, I would have named him yummy and pounced. But knowing who he was, what he was, kind of killed desire.

Which wouldn't matter a damn if he had an aura as powerful as Moss's.

One of the accompanying guards pulled out the most ornate of the chairs. Starr didn't immediately sit, instead leaning his hands on the table as he skimmed his gaze across the crowd. He seemed to pause when he came to our table, and though we were far enough away that I couldn't even see the color of his eyes, a chill ran all the way down my spine. It was as if, in that brief moment, Starr sensed who I was.

I licked my lips, and clenched my hands against the sudden desire to run. This rush of fear was ridiculous. Starr *couldn't* know my real identity. I'd be dead, or locked up in one of his freak pens, if he did. His gaze lingered for several rapid heartbeats, then he leaned sideways and made a comment to Moss. When he finally moved on to

the remaining crowd, I sighed in relief. Not that it eased
the tension curling through my limbs any, because I had a
bad feeling I was going to get an introduction to that madman far sooner than I'd anticipated.

Once Starr had taken a seat, the rest of us were allowed
to. Waiters immediately appeared, plunking plates of veg-
etables and meats on the table.

As we ate, a solitary man walked onto the arena.
Spotlights followed his progress, shining across his hairless
cranium but throwing the rest of his body into shadow.
The babble of voices gave way to a weird mix of trepidation and excitement.

"Ladies and gentlemen." His voice seemed to echo
across the vast arena, and the clink of cutlery died.
"Tonight you will bear witness to the price of foolishness."

He made a sweeping motion with his hand, and part of
the wall on the far side of the arena began to slide up.
From it came two men and a woman. She was striking to
look at—white-blond hair, golden skin, big breasts, and
hourglass figure. The sort of woman who'd graced the
centerfolds of men's magazines year in and year out, almost since the birth of such things.

Though her hands were tied, her expression was defi-
ant, like she was sure this was nothing more than a minor
hiccup.

I was sure it wasn't.

The tension that had begun to ebb revved into high
gear again, and suddenly the food on my plate lost its taste.
I forced what I already had in my mouth down, then
pushed the rest away. I had no stomach left for food. No
stomach for whatever it was that was coming.

"This fighter, Janti Harvey, was caught in an off-limits

space. She was given the choice of being whipped for her mistake or facing the arena. She has chosen the arena."

Bad mistake. She had to be a shifter or were of some kind, so however bad the whipping was, for her it was a survivable punishment simply because shifting shape would heal the worst of the wounds. And okay, it wouldn't be pleasant and would probably haunt her nights, but that would surely be better than facing the unknown in the arena.

But as my gaze went to her face, I saw the arrogance. The confidence. Maybe this woman had been so successful in the arena she figured she could beat whatever foe they presented her with.

Obviously, no one had ever shown her the zoo or the creatures held prisoner within it.

"Bring down the cage," the announcer continued dramatically.

Both he and the woman looked up, so it was natural the rest of us would follow suit. From the shadows of the vaulted ceiling, a huge cage began to lower. It was made of some kind of shiny metal and looked very much like the top half of a fancy birdcage. It lowered to the wall and clicked into place with barely a whisper, covering the entire arena in a huge mesh of metal. Which was how they kept the bird-shifters in.

"Release her ropes."

The two guards did so, then quickly retreated. To anyone with an ounce of common sense, that would have been the first warning that things were going to get much worse. But the woman simply shook her hands and rolled her head.

I crossed my arms, somehow resisting the urge to stand

up and tell her to run. Because caged as she was, where could she actually run?

"Release her opposition for the fight." The words were barely out of his mouth and the announcer was beating a hasty retreat to the entrance he'd appeared from.

The woman began a series of warm-up exercises. Down the far end of the arena, doors slowly opened. Tension rolled through me, tightening already taut muscles to the point of pain.

I didn't know what was worse—sitting here waiting to see what would come out of those doors, or knowing there was nothing, absolutely nothing, I could do to stop the woman below from meeting her fate.

A fate she seemed so oblivious to.

The doors opened fully, and out of the shadows of the tunnel beyond stepped two thin, blue humanoids with butterfly wings folded at their backs. A murmur of approval ran across the crowd but stopped at our table. Nerida and Berna looked every bit as disturbed by events as I was.

The blue things halted just past the door and lightly fanned their wings. The lights caught the colors in the delicate, veillike membranes, making them gleam like a thousand different jewels. But the beauty of the wings was offset by the wicked claws that replaced the top half of their fingers. And by the barbs that lined their cocks.

The woman stretched her arms, wriggled her fingers. If she was alarmed by the fact she was outnumbered or that these things were naked and nasty looking in the equipment department, it didn't show. Confidence still held sway over her expression. But how long would it last once the blue things got moving?

One of them began to fan his wings harder and, with gentle grace, rose in the air. The other walked forward, his wings fanning slowly, barely even stirring the few pale wisps of hair that spotted his blue head.

She didn't wait for them to come to her, and attacked the man on the ground with a ferocity that was surprising. The blue thing was momentarily beaten backward by the force and speed of her blows, and yet, at the same time, seemed unworried by them. The second creature rose high, then with a flick of his wings dove downward. The air screamed with the force of his plummet, and the woman threw herself out of his path. Claws raked the air, missing her skin but snagging strands of gold. They glittered brightly under the spotlights as the creature soared upward again. The woman hit the sand and rolled to her feet in one smooth movement, but barely had time to turn around before the grounded creature was on her. His blows were a blur, fast and hard, and for every ten punches she blocked, five got through. No were or shifter, no matter how tough, could stand such a beating for long.

As her confidence gave way to desperation and her breath became little more than sobs of fear, the blue thing on the ground stepped back. The woman dropped to her knees, alternatively sucking in great gulps of air and crying. I wanted to jump up, to scream that it wasn't over, that those things hadn't finished with her yet, but I forced myself to remain still and watch events. I couldn't help her, and I couldn't risk drawing unwanted attention, so I really had no other choice.

The circling creature began to drop. Anticipation rode the air, thick and sharp. I looked across at the other tables.

Most were watching with avid fascination. Waiting for blood, wanting flesh to be rent and torn.

Bile rose, and it took every ounce of control I had not to throw up right there and then. At least the blue things were doing what they were bred to do—kill. The people watching had no such excuse. It made me hate them, made me want to throw them all into the arena and watch *them* scream and struggle against the blue things.

The stirring air must have warned the woman of the second creature's approach, because she suddenly gasped and threw herself to one side. Wicked claws rent her back as she rolled, and blood began to flow freely down her sides. A collective cheer went up in the arena, and some even began urging the creatures on.

The only table that was totally quiet was ours. Nerida wasn't even watching. Her eyes were closed and her whole body trembled—though I couldn't smell fear, so it was probably anger.

As one creature soared away, the other came in. This time the woman had no chance, and no time, to avoid the blows. Soon she wasn't even trying, just lying on the sand with her hands over her head, her whimpering lost to the whirring of wings, the thud of flesh against flesh and the cheers of the crowd.

After God knows how long, the other creature landed, and together the two of them dragged the bloodied woman over to the post. They pulled her upright and tied her chest-first against the wood.

And then, without ceremony, they butt-fucked her. She screamed, a sound so high and filled with agony that tears filled my eyes. I closed them, and covered my ears with my hands, but still her agony hit, battering my skin, my senses, reaching deep down to my soul, making me sicker than I ever thought possible.

They would pay for this. God help me, if it was the last thing I ever did, Starr, his lieutenants, and this whole perverted crowd would pay for what was being done here today. And the fact that I didn't even know this woman was inconsequential. No person—whether they be human, were, shifter, or whatever else there was—deserved to be treated like *this*.

Especially considering her only crime was trespassing. If she'd attempted to murder Starr, then maybe the brutality would be more understandable—still not acceptable, but at least understandable.

But there was no understanding this. It was just another pointer to the sickness of the mind controlling the cartel.

Eventually the creatures were sated and the woman dragged away. The announcer walked back onto the sand and introduced the next piece of entertainment—the evening's fight between two guards. I didn't watch any of it, just kept my gaze on the table. If I looked up, caught Starr's gaze, he'd see the need to kill, and that could be disastrous when the whole point of the scene with the woman was to bring fear, and cow those of us who were new.

After the fight, guards approached several tables, including ours. Berna raised an eyebrow as a guard motioned me to stand.

"Hang on. I thought if we were naked, we had freedom of choice."

I snorted. "Unless the boss's lieutenants decide they like the look of us. Apparently, it's in the small print."

"I read the small print. I can't remember that."

"Exactly what I said." My gaze went to the blood-soaked sand near the pole. "But I guess they figure they can pretty much do what they want while we're here."

Her expression suggested disagreement, but her gaze flicked to the camera and she didn't actually say anything. I followed the guard like the good little puppy I was pretending to be, but when he approached an elevator that wasn't on any plan I'd seen, I began to take a lot more interest. He shoved a key in the lock, then punched a code into the accompanying keypad, but his fingers were far too quick for me to see—let alone memorize—the numbers. The elevator doors opened and I was waved inside.

Though there were six buttons, only three had numbers. He punched sub-three and the doors closed. I casually looked up at the ceiling, checking for cameras and other security devices—particularly psychic deadeners. There was a security cam, which meant there was probably voice monitoring as well, but I couldn't see anything else. Not that that meant anything.

There was only one way to find out if I could do what I wanted to do. I lowered my shields a little, and felt for the guard's thoughts. His hunger and arousal hit like a club, and my body reacted as instinctively as ever. But below his hunger were his thoughts, and the ease with which I reached them surprised me. I would have thought anyone who knew the codes to any of Starr's private areas would have been either shielded or mind-blind.

Not that I was about to complain about the lack. I shuffled quickly but lightly through the guard's mind, picking up not only the code for the elevator, but general information like shift times and the fact that most of the security pool either visited the whores or played snooker in the

bunkhouse when not on duty. There was also some interesting impressions about the guy who was the head of
security—he was a tall, balding man with pockmarked
skin. According to *this* guard, he was also an all-talk, no-
skills fuckwit who liked taking the credit for other people's
work. Which just might mean he was ripe for a little werewolf action—and mind-reading. As head of security, he'd
surely know a whole lot more than this guard—and probably have access to the spare set of elevator keys. If there
was a spare set. This guard couldn't confirm that there was.

The elevator came to a stop. I withdrew from the
guard's mind, re-shielding quickly as the doors swished
open. Directly opposite was what I presumed was another
elevator, this one secured not only by a key and keypad,
but by a thumbprint scanner as well. The hallway to either
side was long and silent, with the only source of light coming from the elevator itself and two solitary light strips
down either end. Shadows haunted the space in between,
adding to the feeling of isolation.

"Mr. Moss waits for you down that end," the guard
said, pointing to the left. He had his hand on the elevator
door to prevent it from closing, which obviously meant he
wasn't coming with me.

"What's down that end?" I pointed to the right.

"Mr. Merle."

"They don't share quarters, then?"

The guard snorted. "They don't share much at all."

I raised an eyebrow. "Even women?"

"Especially women." He motioned down the hall again.
"You'd better move. He doesn't like to be kept waiting."

Tough was my instinctive response, but not one that was

wise given my mission was to seduce first, raid mind second. So I nodded to the guard and headed off into the shadows. My footsteps echoed across the silence, a sharp tattoo of noise that rebounded eerily down the long hall. I'm sure the whole setup was meant to be scary—to induce that whole walking-into-the-shadowy-unknown fear.

And it might have worked had it not been for the fact that I'd faced far worse in the last four months. Shadows and the unknown were easy by comparison.

The small light above the metal door flicked to green as I approached, and the door slid open. The room beyond was surprisingly welcoming. A solitary light lit one corner of the large room, giving the golden walls an even richer hue but leaving the rest of the room to the shadows. The furnishings were a mix of oak wood and claret-colored cushioning, and thick woolen rugs were scattered across the carpeted floor. A room that was comfortable and inviting was not something that I would have associated with Moss, but then, what did I know about the man other than the fact he was a psychopath with a hot and heavy aura?

Moss wasn't in the room, but something was. His scent was obscure, oddly hinting at earth and air. I stopped just behind one of the thickly padded sofas and let my gaze roam until I pinned his vague shape in the shadows. Another spirit lizard. Like the other versions I'd seen, this one also had suckered fingers and toes, so there was definitely gecko in their DNA mix somewhere. How "spirit" entered the equation was anyone's guess, but I figured it might have something to do with the fact that even in a room lit by the glow of a lamp, he was almost invisible.

Not that he was cloaking himself as a vampire might. He didn't need to. He was as naked as a newborn, and his skin was as black as the night. In the dusky light, he was little more than a black outline, a figure who had a basic shape but no distinct features. He didn't even have any noticeable type of genitalia—male *or* female—so why I kept thinking of it as a "he" I'm not sure. Maybe it was the shape of his face—there was something a little more masculine than feminine about it.

"So," I said brazenly, "what the hell are you? The welcome wagon?"

His thin lips curved into a smile. His eyes were blue—all blue. No white, no black pupil, just a dark, almost midnight blue. Pretty, but eerie. "Most first-time visitors feel fear when they first see me. Second-timers even more so."

I took the time to look him up and down again. "And what is there to fear?"

"Looks can be deceiving."

"Obviously." I let my gaze slide around the room. "Nice place—yours?"

He shook his head. "I am here to prepare you."

I raised an eyebrow. "For what?"

"Sex, of course."

My gaze jumped down his body. "With what?"

"With this." As he spoke, genitalia appeared, dropping down from inside of his body, finding shape and size between his legs. It was like watching a blow-up doll inflate and find form, only weirder.

"Interesting way to deal with the problem of getting kicked in the balls," I noted dryly.

He smiled. As he did so, spines appeared along his cock, flicking upright to reveal pointy ends.

"That," I added bluntly, "isn't coming anywhere near me."

"Yes, it is."

"You try, you die."

"You are here to do as you are told."

"No, I'm here to have sex with Moss. If he hasn't got the equipment to do the deed himself, then that's tough. I'm not fucking a cactus just so he can get his rocks off."

The black creature raised an eyebrow, and I would have sworn there was amusement in his eyes. Then all expression froze as his gaze moved beyond mine, and something inside me quailed.

"Interesting," a voice said from behind. "You do not fear the creature and the damage it could do."

A cold sensation ran down my spine. For several heartbeats, I couldn't move, could barely even breathe.

I didn't know the voice, but I didn't really need to. Not when his evil seemed to permeate the room, sucking away all the good air, leaving only foul.

The black creature mightn't have induced fear, but the man who stood behind me certainly did.

Because that man was Deshon Starr.

Chapter 8

I forced my feet to move, to turn around. Close up, Starr appeared even more inoffensive than he had from a distance. A weedy, nerdy type who looked as if he'd be more comfortable behind a desk and a computer rather than being the main power behind one of Melbourne's biggest crime cartels.

It was only when you met his gaze that you began to see the truth. There was no life in his eyes, no humanity. Just an endless arctic expanse of bloodshot blue.

Goose bumps skated across my skin, yet deep inside, recognition twitched. Something about those eyes reminded me of someone. Just who, I couldn't quite remember. Not yet.

And yet, there was no one in my life who caused the reaction Starr had—and surely they would have, no matter what form they were wearing. I mean, the outer layer might change, but the soul inside remained the same. And it was the evil that was this man's soul I could feel.

So why was this happening now, and not when I was with whoever he was in my life?

Did the reason have something to do with what Dia had mentioned earlier—that my so-called puberty was twisting and increasing my talents?

Like I needed *that* when I already had a drug running around in my system causing havoc.

Starr wasn't alone, and I thankfully averted my gaze. Anything was better than staring at evil incarnate for too long. The second man was Starr's other lieutenant, and Merle was every bit as impressive as he had been from a distance. I looked him up and down then raised an eyebrow. "Now, you I'd be willing to play with. Providing, of course, you have something resembling a regular dick."

The words were barely out of my mouth when his aura hit, every bit as heated and will-withering as Moss's. Sweat beaded my skin and rolled down my back, and the low-down ache of desire became so fierce it was positively painful. His smile was all arrogance.

"If I wanted you, I would have you," he said, voice soft, flat, yet filled with the confidence of a man who always got what he wanted.

And with an aura like *that,* I guess he always did.

His gaze skidded down my body, and the desire burning the air increased, until it felt like every inch of my skin was being flayed alive. My knees buckled under the pressure, and my butt hit the back of the sofa. It was the only reason I remained upright.

His gaze rose to mine again. "And I think I will."

He began to unbuckle his belt, and I wasn't sure if it was anticipation or fear that sent a tingle down my spine. Hell, the sex part didn't worry me, nor did having an audience. It was just *him*. There was something inherently sick about him, something wholly off-center that made a deep-down part of me shiver away from the thought of having him inside. And yet, that foulness held none of the intensity I'd sensed in Moss. Merle was survivable. I doubted Moss was.

"Merle, put it away," Starr snapped, even though Merle hadn't actually gotten it out yet. Thankfully.

But the force of Merle's aura died at the order, as suddenly as a switch being flicked. There had to be were in his mix.

"Where's Moss?" Starr continued, his gaze not leaving mine even though his question was obviously aimed at the spirit lizard.

"Greeting the new guards. He will be here soon."

My heart leapt at the mention of new guards. Did that mean Rhoan had arrived? God, I hoped so. I needed to see him. Needed to talk to him. Get reassurance and guidance and a great big hug.

"Tell him I wish to see him immediately on his return."

"Yes, sir."

Starr's gaze slid down my body. It wasn't a sexual look, more the sort of look one boxer might give another right before their bout. When his gaze returned to mine, it hinted at recognition, and that was a whole different class of scary.

"Do I know you?"

I resisted the urge to lick suddenly dry lips and shook

my head. "Unless you've been up to Sydney recently. I've only been in Melbourne for a few days."

"So why do I feel this sense of familiarity?"

"I can't say, sir."

His thin lips curved into what I presumed was a half-smile—though it very easily could have been a half-sneer. "Respectful to those of obviously greater power. I like that."

Right now, I liked that he liked. Anything was better than him mulling over the fact that he knew me. Because if he knew me, I obviously knew him. And for safety's sake, I had better find out how before he did.

I didn't say anything, and he continued to study me. My stomach turned faster than a washing machine on spin cycle, and was threatening to rise at the slightest provocation. Which was weird, because I'd always figured when I finally confronted the man who had chased me, abused me, injected me with crap, and tried to kill me, I'd feel anger—rage—more than anything else.

But I guess in imagining the whole scene, I'd forgotten one important point—Starr himself. Or rather, the fact that it had taken power, cunning, and sheer, bloody ruthlessness to take and hold control of the cartel.

"Are you from the red pack?"

Oh God…he *did* suspect. But how? Who was the man behind the mask, who was he in my life?

I forced a casual shrug. "I don't know. My mother was human, and never sure who my father was."

"You have the coloring of the red pack."

"She was Irish. I have her coloring."

"Ah. The offspring of a groupie."

I nodded. Wondered if he believed me. There was no

expression on his face, no flicker in his eyes, to indicate whether he did or didn't. Just the emotive swirl of evil sucking the very goodness from the air.

"We should talk some more," he said eventually.

My heart just about stopped. I might want to kill him, but I certainly didn't want to talk to him. Not now. Not later. Not anytime.

Even killing him wasn't an option right now, not only because of Merle and the black thing, but because Jack would kill *me* if I did anything before we'd discovered the location of the final lab.

"Talking is fine with me."

He smiled for real this time. It was the nastiest thing I've ever seen. "As if you even had the choice, my dear." His gaze moved to Merle. "Bring her in for brunch."

His words sent another shiver down my spine. I had a bad feeling Starr's idea of "brunch" was not toast and orange juice, but something a whole lot darker. Bloodier.

Merle nodded, and hitched his pants. "Is that all for now?"

Starr snorted and glanced back at me. "My assistant hungers. Prepare for a rough ride, my dear."

I arched an eyebrow. "And Mr. Moss?"

"Will undoubtedly be annoyed at missing the action." He glanced at Merle again. "Do not forget the whore bus."

He nodded. As Starr left, that switch went on again, drowning me in heat and desire. Merle held out a hand, and I went to him, my legs so wobbly it felt like they were about to give way at any moment.

His large hand wrapped around mine, his fingers

rough and burning hot. I shivered, and knew in that instant what Rhoan had been trying to tell me. It wasn't the sex that was the worry, it was this—the feeling that evil was about to invade, and somehow corrupt.

All I could do now was remind myself it was better *this* man than Moss.

Merle glanced over my head, and though he didn't say anything, the soft sound of footsteps indicated the spirit lizard was leaving.

His gaze came back to mine. In the tawny depths of his eyes, lust and insanity seemed to rage. Or maybe that was just my imagination—a natural result of the force of his aura combined with the base sense of his foulness that filled every quick intake of breath.

"We shall fuck here first." Merle tugged me around the sofa. "The scent of sex will inform Moss of what he has missed."

"That doesn't sound very friendly to me." The words came out breathless, sounding anticipatory when the opposite was true. The force of his aura might be such that my skin burned and I ached for sex, but part of me recoiled at the thought of spending *any* time with this man.

It was weird.

I was a *werewolf*. Sex was part of our psyche, part of our soul. Come full-moon time, I'd fuck the devil himself and wouldn't give a damn. So why this reluctance? Was it just the inherent sense of depravity I was picking up from Merle, or was it simply the fact that I was fucking him under orders from the Directorate, thereby taking one more step toward finally becoming a full guardian?

Was it a combination of both?

I didn't know.

What I *did* know was that I needed to talk to my brother. Desperately.

"Friendly is a matter of perspective." Merle pressed the hot ends of his fingers lightly against my chest and pushed me backward. I let myself fall onto the sofa, and watched as he stripped off his pants. Thankfully, his cock *was* standard stuff—no barbs, no furry stripes, just slightly less than regular-sized pinkish flesh. "He survives. That's friendly enough for anyone."

So the guard had been telling the truth when it came to the relationship between these two men. Interesting. But given my reaction to Moss, it definitely *wasn't* something I wanted to work with.

His gaze ran down my length, and an anticipatory grin split his lips. "I would fuck you for your looks alone, but it is a true bonus to do so first when Moss has chosen you."

He climbed on top, crouching on all fours over me. His aura revved up another notch, and suddenly it felt like I was drowning in a liquid that was all heat, all desire.

"Do not move. Do not talk."

Or what? I wanted to ask. But talking had become impossible under that wash of burning desire. All I wanted to do was obey. To feel him inside, foul or not. Passive wasn't much fun, but I guess fun wasn't the point of this whole thing. Not for me, anyway.

He thrust inside. With the force of his aura still assaulting my senses, the feeling of his flesh driving inside was such a relief a rumble of pleasure rolled up my throat. God, part of me was more than willing to be silent and still if it meant easing a little of the ache. And it didn't matter how bad his essence or how little I actually wanted him—my body screamed for the release only rigid flesh could bring.

Only it didn't get it.

It turned out Merle wasn't the caring, sharing type. He came far too quickly, leaving me aching with need and more than a little put out. A situation that was not improved when he dragged me up from the sofa then hauled me down the far end of the hallway to his own cold-feeling rooms. Where the whole process began again.

Frustrating, to say the least.

Especially since it pretty much set the tempo for the remainder of our time together. He used his aura like most men used foreplay, and while it made me ready for him, it also became incredibly boring—something I never thought I'd say about sex.

But then, I was never one for passiveness. I liked to get involved, to play and feel and taste. And occasionally, dominate.

Which meant, of course, I had to find something else to do while he got his trigger-happy rocks off. Short of throwing his dull ass off and finding a real lover, that was.

And really, there was only one avenue of exploration left—my senses.

Or rather, my psychic senses.

There were no cameras in Merle's room that I could see, and I hadn't felt the electronic buzz of deadeners anywhere within the mansion—even down here, in either Moss's or Merle's rooms. But Dia had mentioned their presence and I had no reason to doubt her. Besides,

I'd seen them in the arena, so they had to be elsewhere. And while I had read the guard's mind with ease, maybe all it meant was that the elevator somehow ran under the radar of the deadeners.

Or maybe my talents were.

The implications of which wasn't something I wanted to waste time thinking about, though I was more than willing to test the full extent of any supposed increase. I carefully slid aside one layer of shields, suddenly grateful for all the weeks of training Jack had been giving me. Dia might have exposed a weakness in my telepathy skills when it came to attack, but that wouldn't be a problem here as I had no intention of dropping all shield layers to attack Merle. I just wanted to test whether I could read his thoughts or not.

And I could.

Sort of. His thoughts were there, a distant blaze of color I could see but not quite touch.

But if I could see them, then surely I should be able to read them. I frowned and pressed a little harder. It felt like I was pushing through a wall of thick glue. Resistance dragged on every mental step, but it wasn't conscious resistance. Wasn't the sort of struggle that came from a telepath who realizes his mind is being invaded. Maybe Merle was too busy concentrating on satisfaction to grasp the fact his brain was being attacked. Or maybe my talents were simply slipping under his awareness in much the same manner as they were apparently slipping under the electronic deadeners.

But again, the whys of what was going on weren't important. Trying to reach and read Merle's thoughts was. The glue seemed to thicken near the center of the mental fence, and sweat broke out across my brow. My training with Jack had often left me mentally drained, but it had never left me physically exhausted, as this was threatening to. God, every ounce of strength I possessed was being channeled into trying to breach Merle's defenses, and my limbs were beginning to tremble with the effort. If I wasn't careful, he'd surely notice something other than sex was going on.

With the suddenness of a rubber band snapping, the glue gave way, leaving me mentally shaking but floating free in the rush of Merle's thoughts. Though rush was probably the wrong word to use—and if he was any indication, then men really *did* think of nothing more than reaching the big O during sex.

I moved carefully through his surface thoughts, past the gathering rush of satisfaction, into the darker areas of non-active thought. The bus Starr had mentioned earlier was indeed the one bringing in fresh bedding meat for the pleasure of Starr's guests. Who were, as I'd guessed earlier, both the "department heads" of his own organization and the various representatives from other cartels. Surprisingly, Starr had no intention of killing them. He was biding his time, waiting until he had gained enough trust to draw the true leaders of the other crime organizations into his nest. But he didn't intend just a mass murder, but a mass replacement. Starr was from the Helki pack, and many Helki wolves were also true shapeshifters—they could assume any human shape they desired. Starr would insert his own people as the head of these organizations, and the cartels wouldn't be any the wiser.

Merle's body began to grind harder against mine and

the fire of gathering ecstasy was greater in his mind—a warning I'd better hurry before awareness returned and he caught me in his thoughts.

I slipped a little deeper, trying to find mention of Dia's kid or even a location for the labs. Nothing. Either I wasn't deep enough or Merle was a linear-thinking guy. The sort who only contemplated the things he had to do in the immediate future—which is why I could get so much information on the bus and the other cartels. One thought linked to the other.

Merle began to jerk spasmodically as his orgasm hit, meaning I had to get out, pronto. I pulled back through the glue, the process seeming a little easier the second time around. Or maybe it was simply the fact I was leaving, not entering.

As I opened my eyes, a sharp ringing split the air, just about frightening the shit out of me. My heart seemed to leap up my throat, and I froze like a rabbit caught in a spotlight. Had someone somehow caught my psychic explorations?

Merle swore under his breath and climbed off, and I realized the ringing was a telephone, not an alarm of some sort. I blew out a relieved breath, then sat up and hugged my knees to my chest. Drawing deep breaths to ease the trembling that was part exhaustion, part fear, I looked around. And noticed, on the dresser near the bathroom doorway, a small set of keys.

The elevator I'd come down in had key locks. I had the code, so having the key was the next step forward. Whether the key that controlled the elevator was amongst those on the table was anyone's guess, but I had every intention of finding out. Of course, snatching those keys and getting them out without being caught wasn't going to be easy. Especially when I had no clothes and basically nowhere to hide the keys.

Well, there was *one* place. But shoving them up *there* wasn't exactly practical—and it would be more than a little noticeable given the maneuvering it would take.

Though cold steel was in some ways preferable to Merle's foul flesh.

Merle grunted and slammed down the phone. He didn't even look at me, just grabbed some clothes from the pile on a nearby chair and began dressing.

"Iktar," he said, as he pulled on his shirt.

A spirit lizard appeared in the doorway. Whether it was the same one that had been in Moss's room, or another, was anyone's guess. These things really did all look the same.

"Escort her back to the upper levels."

I shoved on my best outraged expression. "What? No 'thanks for the great time'? Not even a damn shower?"

He snorted as he swept up the keys I'd been eyeing and shoved them in his pocket. "No. Now get your butt out of here."

I flounced off the bed and out of the room—a fine piece of acting no one seemed to notice. The black thing led the way out of Merle's colorless rooms and down the sterile corridor, then key-coded the elevator. A soft chime indicated the elevator's arrival. As the doors opened, Merle stomped down the hall toward us, his expression dark as he stopped at the set of doors opposite. He inserted a key, then punched in a code and pressed his hand to the scanner pad. No bell chimed, but those doors opened to reveal, as I'd guessed earlier, another elevator.

More than that I had no chance to see as the spirit lizard all but pushed me inside our elevator.

My shoulder hit the wall with enough force to cause a grunt, but I quickly regained my balance and turned around. The spirit lizard pressed the ground-floor button, then turned to face me. Lust burned in his eyes, and his cock was out and erect.

I crossed my arms and feigned indifference. "Looks to me like the servant wants in on the action."

His smile was every bit as cold and as dangerous as Merle's or Starr's, but it was the astute glint in his eyes that made me think something was going on—something other than just the need for a bit of sexual relief.

"Which," he said, his soft tones barely audible over the hum of machinery as the elevator began to ascend, "I will get, or I shall inform my masters just what it was you were doing while you were being fucked."

Panic rose, swift and hard, but I forced myself to ignore it. If he'd been intending to report me, he would have done so by now. I clung to that belief, to the feeling that he wanted something more than sex, and said, "I have no idea what you are talking about."

His smile grew. As did his cock. A tremor ran down my spine. God help me, part of me wanted what he was offering. Wanted to feel his dangerous flesh inside.

Damn Merle and his selfishness.

"They can see, but not hear us, you know."

Like I was going to trust his word. I merely smiled.

"As long as this elevator is moving, they cannot hear conversation. The machinery interferes with the signal and they cannot fix it. And the guard who currently watches the monitors does not lip-read."

I still wasn't trusting him, so I simply asked, "And why are you telling me this?"

"Because I can taste the use of psychic power, as much as you might taste the scents carried by the wind. I know what you were up to."

Oh, fuck. I should have done as Jack asked, and scouted things out before going full steam ahead. What the hell was I going to do now? I glanced down at his cock. The thick spines lining it. Not fuck him, that was for sure.

"Yes," he continued, obviously catching my look if not the actual direction of my thoughts, "I can taste auras as well as telepathy."

My gaze rose to his. "You bring that near me, and I will kill you."

He raised an eyebrow. "And what makes you think you could get close enough to kill me before I rendered you unconscious?"

The mere fact I'd killed his like before—but that wasn't exactly something I could admit.

He glanced up at the floor indicator. "We have ten seconds left. I want you to meet me near the front of the zoo in half an hour. If you don't, I shall report your activities and you will be killed." His dark gaze met mine. "Deal?"

"I have a choice?"

He merely smiled and stepped away as the elevator stopped and the doors slid open. I walked out and headed back to my room. Berna and Nerida weren't in their beds, which given the ratio of men to women in the arena didn't entirely surprise me. And some men did prefer their bedmates at least willing rather than simply paid vessels of satisfaction. Though I guess that's exactly what those of us who were here as fighters were anyway—we just had a little more choice in the matter.

I hesitated near the foot of my bed, briefly consumed by the ache of tiredness. I wanted to sleep, to just lay down and forget Merle and Starr and every other weirdo in this godforsaken place. But sleep wasn't an option just yet, because I had a lizard to meet, a brother to find, and an ache to ease. I grabbed my toiletries bag and headed for the shower. A good scrub washed the smell and feel of Merle from my skin, but did nothing for the trepidation curling through my gut. I needed to talk to someone *now,* not later, and the only choice I had was Jack.

I headed outside, ensured no one was within listening distance, then lightly pressed the com-link. "Hey, boss, you awake?"

"About time you reported in," he growled. "I was starting to worry."

Yeah, he was so worried he'd sent in the rescue troops. Not. "You're the one who insisted on sending in the amateur. Don't whine at me if I don't do things the way you want them done."

He grunted. What that meant was anyone's guess. "What's happening?"

I headed up the small path that snaked around the building and on to the zoo. "Several things. Some good, some bad."

He sighed. "Tell me."

"Well, I've rubbed groins with Merle and made him a happy, happy man. And I've discovered that, with a little effort, I can slip through his thoughts, though I didn't dare go too deep tonight."

"Glad caution won out for a change." He paused. "So there weren't psi-deadeners in the lower areas?"

I hesitated, but the fact was, sooner or later he was going to have to know about my apparent ability to override the force of the deadeners. It might as well be sooner. And at least he couldn't rip me into the Directorate for more tests. "There are. My talents are apparently slipping under them."

"We noted a slight increase last time we tested, but it wouldn't have been powerful enough to slide past deadeners."

"Would it have been powerful enough to breach Quinn's defenses?"

He didn't say anything for a moment, then, "When did that happen?"

"Yesterday. I did catch him by surprise, mind."

"It shouldn't have mattered." Again the silence stretched a little, and if I didn't know better, I would have thought he was worried. "It's six months since you were given the ARC1-23. This could be the first sign that it *is* changing you."

"Or it could simply mean that Dia is right, and my talents are maturing thanks to the fact I'm finally menstruating." There was nothing like clinging to a forlorn hope until the very last moment, but what other choice did I have? I wanted to be normal—wanted to have a normal life. Well, as normal as a half-werewolf, half-vampire guardian could, anyway. I *didn't* want to be some freak monitored by the labs for every little outlandish change the drugs made. "Wolves do mature slower than humans. And remember, neither Rhoan nor I have any idea what our father was, besides a vampire. He could have been a hawk-shifter with massive psi-talents before his undeath, for all we know."

"There were indications of latent talents in all previous tests, I've told you that. But latent doesn't always mean those talents will develop."

"Maybe it's a result of the training you've been giving me."

"Two weeks ago you couldn't have broken through my full shields, let alone Quinn's. If that's what you did, then this is more than maturing talent. You'll have to come in for full tests once this mission is over."

I closed my eyes, blew out a breath. It did nothing to ease the deep rush of hatred and anger. The end of my life as I knew it was one step closer, and I had Starr and his fucking desire to not only build the perfect killing machine but take over the world—or at least the Melbourne section of it—to thank for it. If he'd been near me right then, I would have killed the bastard and been done with it, no matter what the consequences.

"I never wanted to be a guardian, Jack. You know that."

"There's only two places that can give you the sort of help you need to control the power you seem to be getting—us, or the military."

"I don't want anything to do with the military."

"Then my option is the lesser of two evils."

Which wasn't really saying much.

"What else happened?" he said.

I rubbed a hand across my eyes. "I've met Starr. He's not living on the same planet as you and me. You know that, don't you?"

"He may be insane, but he's also extremely clever. Remember that."

"I will." I hesitated. "He asked me if I was from the red pack. He seems to think he knows me."

Jack swore. "That's not good."

"Oh, it gets worse."

"How much worse?"

"I'm about to find out." I rounded the corner of the building and walked onto the soft grass. The night breeze stirred around me, filled with the scent of animals and captivity. Up until that moment, I would have sworn that captivity didn't have a smell, but there it was, filling the night with an odd sense of frustration, desperation, and hopelessness.

Odd that such things had aromas.

Odder still that I could smell them. I might have the nose of a wolf, but until that moment, fear, lust, and death were the strongest emotions I'd caught.

Though technically, death wasn't an emotion. Just a passing that lingered, a sadness staining the air.

"Merle and Moss have a spirit lizard houseboy. He's apparently sensitive to the use of psychic power."

"I take it he knows you were reading Merle and didn't report it?"

"Yes. But he did want a meet."

"Any chance it's just for sex?"

"If he's sensitive enough to catch auras, I have no doubt he's mightily aroused and needing relief. But there's no way known I'm going to be a good fuck-puppy when it comes to *him*."

"Riley—"

"His dick has spines, Jack."

"Oh."

"Oww is more like it." I grinned faintly. "But I think he wants a whole lot more than sex."

"It wouldn't hurt to have an ally in that place."

"If he can be trusted."

"Rely on your instincts. I do."

Only trouble was, my instincts had been wrong before. And this time, there was no one near to bail my butt out. "I'm heading to meet him now."

"Be careful. Keep the line open."

"Natch." I glanced up as high metal fences came into view. "I'm almost there."

"Just be prepared to kill him if things go wrong."

I didn't answer. If things went wrong, I'd do what I had to do to preserve the mission and keep everyone—including myself—safe. But killing wasn't something I wanted to become comfortable with—even if that's exactly what Jack wanted.

I walked up the small knoll and stopped. The zoo stretched before me, metal and wire entwined with desperation and anger. The things inside might be caged, but they certainly weren't accepting or passive. Which pretty much explained why so many guards went missing. Any misstep was taken as a chance of revenge.

I scanned the cages, taking in the array of creatures, then headed left, to what looked to be the main entrance. Cages containing blue creatures with wings gave way to spiny trolls which in turn gave way to fish people. Few of them slept. Most of them were awake and watching.

Their misery resonated deep in their eyes, deeper inside me. I hated it—hated that I was feeling it. I couldn't do anything for these things from nightmare and imagination. They'd been bred for death, and that's exactly what they'd get, whether from Starr or the Directorate. It wasn't fair, but life often wasn't.

I hated that, too.

Iktar stood, arms crossed, near the main gates. The light above the gates caressed him, making his skin glow blue-black and his eyes eerily luminescent. His cock was nowhere in sight.

Thankfully.

I stopped just beyond the pool of light. "Isn't this a little dangerous? They have cameras monitoring the zoo surrounds, don't they?"

He nodded. "And laser sensors. But whenever Moss and Merle take women, I am given time to come here."

My gaze went past him, and for the first time I noticed shadows in the shadows. More spirit lizards, and of both sexes. "For relief?"

"Yes." He smiled. "As you saw, I am incompatible with human flesh."

"And why would they give you time? You are nothing more than a weapon—a tool to be used—to them."

He smiled, but anger surged in his eyes. He hated captivity. Hated what he was doing and who he was forced to serve. This was no lab-born creature. He was something more. Something far more.

"They value my skills in protecting them when they are otherwise occupied," he answered steadily, voice devoid of the fury so evident in his eyes.

"So why does Moss use you to 'ready' his women?"

"Moss enjoys the taste of fear. I am not his only weapon to draw out such an emotion."

Meaning I had to be thankful Merle had stolen my "services." He might be a boring lover, but at least boring was survivable. While I didn't mind being tied or the occasional bit of spanking, if Moss had tried anything much nastier, I might have been tempted to knock his lights out. And that pretty much would have been the end for me and the mission.

"Those monitoring the cameras might think it a little suspicious that you're meeting me here, though."

"They would, if the camera was working. It isn't."

I raised my eyebrow. "Convenient."

"They are knocked out regularly. It is only a small inconvenience to Starr's people in the long term, but it does give us the means of a little revenge."

Meaning the guards—and the regularity with which they went missing. I shifted my stance and resisted the urge to demand such attacks stop immediately. Rhoan might be acting the part of a guard, but he was also a guardian, the best we had besides Gautier. If he could take on five vampires at the same time, he could handle these nightmares—at least long enough to get the hell away from them.

"What do you want of me, then?"

"I want to make a deal with whoever it is you're working for."

"Depends on what he's offering and what he wants," Jack said.

"What makes you think I'm working for someone?" I asked.

Iktar smiled. "Most women quail when presented with the sight of my genitals. You got ready to fight. That speaks of training. Whether military or something else, I don't care."

"I'm not military."

He shrugged. "As long as your people are willing to deal, it doesn't matter."

"So what do you want and what are you offering in return?"

"What I want is all my people out of here."

My gaze moved to the shadowy forms merged with the darkness. "Your people?"

He studied me for a moment, his featureless face expressionless, yet dark eyes somehow managing to be judgmental.

"How much do you know about Starr and his cartel?"

"I know what this zoo is," I said. "I know the origins of many of the creatures here."

That surprised him. "How?"

My smile was cold. "Let's just say I've had firsthand experience with Starr's objectives."

Some of the tension seemed to run from his shoulders. "Then you know of the labs."

"Yes."

"And you would also know that Starr gathers live samples for his DNA experiments."

"Yes."

He nodded, seemingly pleased. "Then you would not be surprised to discover that many of those behind us are not lab-born, but those collected as specimens."

I glanced at the creatures behind him again. "How did you all get here?"

His smile was grim. "The good thing about spirit lizards is that, aside from gender differences, we all look alike. We had hoped that replacing the lab-born and coming here would provide an easier escape. We were wrong."

My gaze returned to him. "And could you tell us the location of the labs?"

He shrugged. "The building we were kept in had no windows, and we were drugged before we were taken from that place. None of us have any idea where we were or how we got here—though I will say it didn't seem as if we were out for very long."

Not very long could have been ten minutes or ten hours. It all depended on your point of view. And surely if the labs were only ten minutes away, the Directorate would have noticed. They'd been watching the place for ages. "Then what are you offering in exchange for our help?"

"Whatever it is in my power to do."

Which really wasn't telling me much, as I had no idea what he could and couldn't do. I studied his featureless face for a second, then said, "If you are able to move around this place so freely, why haven't you done something to release your people?"

"Because we are booby-trapped."

I raised my eyebrows. "Booby-trapped?"

He stepped forward and held out his arm. "Feel."

I ran my fingers up his arm as directed. His flesh was cold and clammy, not unlike that of a frog. I repressed a tremor of revulsion and stopped my exploration when I hit something small and hard near his armpit. "What is it?"

"A bomb powerful enough to blow away half my body."

"Nasty." I let my hand drop and stepped back. I wasn't comfortable standing so close to him, and I had no idea why. Maybe it was just an itchy feeling that while this man might be telling the truth as far as what he wanted, he was about as trustworthy as a rattlesnake. That if he thought it would further his aims, his bid to freedom, he'd kill me quicker than I could blink. Or report me to Starr. "Have you all got one of those?"

"Only those of us he considers leaders."

"Why not just cut it out?"

"Because unless the main unit is destroyed, removing it will trigger the device. We discovered this the hard way."

I tried to ignore the image of splattered spirit lizard, and asked, "And the detonator? Where is it kept?"

"I'm not sure, but it would have to be in either Starr's rooms or the main security room. It needs to be destroyed before we can flee."

"Have you tried to get into either place?"

"I cannot."

"Why not?"

"I have access to Merle's and Moss's rooms and the upper levels. They would kill me instantly if they saw me anywhere else."

The main security room *was* in the upper level. But maybe Starr figured a spirit lizard heading there could only be up to no good. After all, if he trusted them, he wouldn't have booby-trapped them. "They'll kill me, too, if I go anywhere near either place."

He smiled. "But you have an invite to brunch tomorrow. That takes you deeper into his hole than I have ever been allowed."

"You know," Jack said into my ear, "the aim of an update is to actually report everything that has happened since the last update. What is it about that concept you cannot understand?"

I restrained my grin, and said to Iktar, "How about a trade?"

"Trade?"

"I'll try and get the detonator, if you try and snatch the keys Merle has for the elevator."

He considered me for a moment, then nodded. "It will be a risk, but I will try."

"Good. What does the detonator look like?"

"Like the controller of a game machine, with more buttons." His thin mouth twisted. "So he can kill us off one by one or all at once."

My gaze went back to the listening shadows. "What of the lab-born amongst you?"

"What of them?"

"They're programmed with a different kind of bomb, aren't they?"

Again surprise flitted through his eyes. "You know more than I realized. And yes, they are. But no one can do anything about the triggers in their DNA. They would rather die free, if that is to be their fate, than penned."

"And the other nightmares penned here?"

"They are not my problem."

Charity, thy name is Iktar. Not that I could blame him for looking after himself and his people before everyone else.

"Do we have a deal?" he said. "Will your people help mine escape this place?"

"If he upholds his end of the deal, we'll see his people relocated," Jack said. "I make no such promises about the lab-born amongst them."

"Deal," I said, and held out a hand.

Iktar looked at it, then back at me, and smiled grimly. "I will shake your hand, but know that if you and your people do not hold to your word, I will kill you."

My grin was nasty. "And if I get the slightest whiff of a double-cross, believe that I will kill every fucking one of you."

"That's my girl," Jack said approvingly.

I wished I could tell him to shove it, but with Iktar close that wasn't an option. "When do you want to meet again?"

"Given Merle was interrupted during his time with you, he will undoubtedly claim you again. I will signal you when I have the keys."

"It may take me a while to get the detonator." If indeed I could actually find it.

"That I understand."

I nodded and backed away, not turning my back to him until I was well down the hill. He looked a little amused at the precaution, but I didn't give a damn. Better safe than sorry, and I wasn't trusting that creature for an instant.

"Are you really going to let his people go?" I asked, when I was well out of earshot of the zoo.

"If he and his people prove to be no threat to society, yes. Do you trust him?"

"I think he's telling the truth as far as what he wants, but no, I don't trust him."

"Then be careful when dealing with him."

"Well, duh, wouldn't have thought of that."

He snorted. Not a nice sound in my ear. "Anything else I should know?"

"I want you to check a couple of people for me." I gave him Nerida's and Berna's full names. "Something about them just feels off."

"I'll let you know what we find."

"Is Rhoan in yet? I know new guards arrived this evening, but I'm not sure if he was one of them."

"He got onto the bus, but I can't tell you more because he hasn't yet contacted us."

"Talk to you later, then." I flicked off the link and stopped under the boughs of a leafy elm. The main house stood to my left. The stables to my right. I was bone tired, muscle weary, and the thought of slipping between the sheets to catch some sleep was more than a little enticing.

But so was the thought of easing the deep-down ache.

I wavered between the two desires, but in the end, horny won out over tiredness.

After wrapping the shadows around myself, I snuck toward the stables. They were dark, still. I switched to infrared, saw that there was nothing more than horses inside. The old guy wasn't about, and there were no guards. Still, I had to be careful. The last thing I needed to do was make anyone aware that there might be a horse-shifter spy amongst all the plain old horses in the stables.

I slipped inside the smaller door to the left of the main door and padded down the aisle. Though still covered in shadows, the horses snorted and shied away from my scent. The only one that showed any sort of interest was the only one *I* was interested in.

I slipped inside the stable and locked the door behind me. The golden haze of shifting swept across his body, then he was standing there, all mahogany magnificence looking good enough to eat.

A wicked grin curved his lush lips. "You have a lusty look in your eyes, my dear. Anything I can do to help you?"

"God, yes."

I took the few steps that separated us and he slid his hands around my waist, his touch possessive, almost demanding, as he pulled me closer still. His body felt like hot steel against mine, his erection even hotter where it pressed against my stomach. Flash fires of desire skittered across my already overheated skin, but I fought the instinct to simply take what I desired. There had been more than enough taking for one night. This time, desire needed to be shared.

"What I want," I said softly, wrapping a hand around his neck and pulling his mouth down toward mine, "is for you to caress me, tease me, cover me with your kisses and your scent, until we're both driven so wild with desire that we can't even think."

"I think I can manage that," he murmured, a second before my lips claimed his.

We kissed as only lovers who are familiar with each other's needs and desires could—deeply, intensely, thoroughly. Kissed until I couldn't breathe and my head was spinning and my body giddy with desire.

Then he moved on, tasting, teasing, his breath as soft and as sweet on my skin as the kisses he dropped down my neck and across each shoulder. And as his clever hands began to explore farther afield, I echoed his movements, running my fingers over his body, enjoying the ripple of muscle, the sensation of heated flesh against heated flesh. I breathed deep, letting the combination of musky desire and his more earthy scent fill my senses, my lungs, until the foul memory of Merle's body and scent had shattered and gone.

I let my hands slide farther down his stomach to stroke the long, glorious length of him. He groaned, thrusting into my touch. The heat burning between us became a furnace that made breathing even more difficult, and a primitive sense of power swept through me. This big, potent stallion was mine to do with as I pleased.

And right now, it pleased me to finally take what we both so desperately wanted.

As his cock slipped slowly inside, a moan escaped. I wasn't entirely sure if it was his or mine, and right then couldn't have given a damn, because he began to move and any attempt at thought and reason slipped beyond my grasp. All I could do was climb aboard and move with him, savoring and enjoying the sensations flowing through me.

This time, he took time, stroking deep as he licked and nipped and kissed. The pressure began to build low in my stomach, fanning through the rest of me in waves that built gradually but steadily, until they were a molten force that flowed across my skin, making me tremble, twitch, groan.

As that pressure threatened to blow me apart, his breathing became harsh, his tempo more urgent. His fierceness pushed into me into a place where only sensation existed, and then he pushed me beyond it.

He came with me, his lips capturing mine, kissing me urgently as his warmth spilled into me and his body went rigid against mine.

For several minutes we didn't move, just allowed the cool night air to wash the heat from our skin. Then he stirred, releasing my arms and giving me a sweet, gentle kiss.

"If that wasn't what you had in mind, give me a few minutes and I'm willing to try again."

I chuckled softly, and touched a hand to his sweaty cheek. "That was brilliant."

He raised an eyebrow, velvet brown eyes amused. "Does that mean there's no second round?"

"Did I say—"

I cut the rest of the sentence off as the squeak of a door opening cut across the stable's restless silence. Kade stepped back, the shifting haze scooting across his body until he was horse once more. He walked to the stable door and peered out. I kept in the shadow of his form, knowing that anyone but a vampire would have trouble sorting out the beat of Kade's heart from mine, the heat of his body from mine.

For several minutes, there was no sound, no movement, from the person who'd opened the door.

Then footsteps echoed, a whisper-soft tattoo of sound that had purpose, threat.

And they were bypassing all the stalls, coming directly toward us.

Chapter 9

I stepped back from the door and looked around for a weapon. A stupid reaction, really, when all the training I'd had over the last few months had made me as much of a weapon as anything made of steel or wood.

And there wasn't anything more dangerous than a water bucket in the stall, anyway.

I flexed my fingers, trying to ease the tension curling through my limbs as the footsteps drew closer. Kade flattened his ears and bared his teeth, yet his actions seemed to stem more from dislike than any attempt to attack.

The tingle of awareness suddenly caressing my senses told me why.

It wasn't a stranger, wasn't one of Starr's guards, who approached.

It was Quinn.

He stopped several paces short of the stall door. The

anger *I'd* felt at his actions earlier crashed through me again, and for several heartbeats it was all I could do not to burst through the door and attack him. Not that physically attacking him would do me any good, because he was stronger and faster, but I'd always been inclined to use my fists more than my psychic talents.

Besides, I was pretty sure the latter wouldn't be effective, no matter how much stronger they might have gotten. I'd caught him by surprise last time. There wouldn't be a second time. I was sure of that.

So I settled for stepping forward, keeping the door a barrier between us, and growling, "What the fuck are you doing here?"

He had his "vampires don't do emotion" face on and his smile was cold. I wasn't picking anything up from him along the sensory lines, which meant he had shields on high and his feelings locked down as tightly as his expression. "Did you think I would give up on my revenge so easily?"

I snorted. "I've experienced the lengths you'll go to for your revenge, so no. What I meant was, how did you get here?"

"On the bus."

"With Rhoan? Somehow I doubt he'd have allowed that."

"I said I was on the bus. I didn't say I was *in* the bus. One of the benefits of being an old vampire is the ability to slip past perception when I wish."

"Rhoan is a psi dead-zone. You couldn't have touched his mind and stopped him from sensing you."

"I didn't have to. I simply ceased to exist in any term the human mind recognizes."

I raised my eyebrows. "What the hell does that mean?"

"That there are more talents in this world than you and Jack and others know of. And it's also a reminder that when I crossed the lines between life and death, I not only inherited the talents of my maker, but I brought with me those talents I had in life."

"Humans don't have the sort of talent you just spoke about, and you told me you were human."

"I considered myself so."

"Meaning?"

"Meaning that I was raised human, but technically was only partially so."

"So the other half was . . . what?"

"Something that no longer exists."

I snorted softly. "And you wonder why no one is trusting you or being open with you at the moment? I mean, it's really hard to open up and give a direct answer, isn't it?"

Anger sparked deep in the dark depths of his eyes. "A fine statement considering the secrets you and Jack have kept. If you *had* confided in me more, I would not have been forced to such extremes."

Energy ran across my skin, and I knew without looking that Kade had once again shifted form and become human. The heat of him moved up behind me, a solid, comforting presence I was suddenly thankful for. Not because I was afraid of what Quinn would do, but rather, what I might do. I usually kept a fairly good leash on my temper, but right now, with everything that had happened and everything that was still left unsaid between us, those restraints were being tested to the limit.

Quinn might have betrayed my trust, but I didn't actually want to hurt him. And no matter how certain I was that I wouldn't be able to breach his defenses a second time, the mere fact that my psi-powers seemed to be developing at the rate of knots meant that if I *did* lash out again, it might be with more than I intended. Might do more damage than I intended. Not just to Quinn, but to Kade.

"Jack hasn't confided in you fully because of your single-minded determination to get revenge. There is more to bring down than just one man, you know."

"I realize that—"

"Do you?" I cut in. "So why tell me earlier that you will have your revenge, no matter the cost?"

"Jack would not have let me in on this section of the mission, no matter how big a team player I was, and we both know it." His gaze moved beyond me. "Though why the horse-shifter is considered more worthy is anyone's guess."

It was the sudden flash of vehemence in his eyes more than the slight edge in his voice that suggested he wasn't exactly talking about the mission, and a fresh wave of annoyance ran through me. This man was always judging me, always questioning my choices. Expecting me to rise to his standards, when his standards were totally alien to a werewolf's beliefs.

"Kade is here because he plays by the rules. In the field, and in the bedroom." At least he was willing to accept what I was, the way I was—and what I was willing to give. Probably because a stallion played along similar sexual lines as a werewolf. Quinn just wanted to play it his way, and given he was a vamp and I was a wolf intent on finding my soul mate, that wasn't ever going to happen.

Kade's big hands pressed warmth on either side of my hips. Before I realized what he was doing, he'd claimed me in the most basic way possible, slipping so very deep inside.

"Playing by the rules has its benefits," he said, his deep voice somehow managing to be both mocking and amused. "You should try it sometime. It feels extraordinarily good."

Annoyance ran through me at Kade's actions, yet part of me also wanted to stick it to Quinn, to play along with Kade and make Quinn even angrier.

But then, common sense isn't exactly my strong point when I'm pissed off at someone.

So instead of stepping away from Kade, as sanity suggested, I pressed back against him, thrusting him deeper still. Quinn's eyes narrowed dangerously. Though he wasn't close enough to the stable door to actually see what we were doing, he was a vampire and an empath. He not only would have heard the sudden leap of my pulse, but would have felt the heated rush of pleasure and annoyance.

I met his gaze, held it. Awareness burned deep in those obsidian depths, an awareness that bounced right back to me, making my heart stutter and causing goose bumps to tremble warmly across my skin. Kade might be the one who'd claimed me sexually, but truth be told, it was Quinn I wanted inside—attitude, anger, and all.

Not that wanting him would make me go any easier on him. Quite the opposite, in fact.

"What are you intending to do next?" I asked, as Kade

began to move ever so slightly, sending little quivers of pleasure shooting across my skin.

"I came here to inform you of my presence, and to get an update." His gaze was still on mine, and the awareness deep in his eyes had morphed into fierce desire.

The ever-pragmatic vampire might not approve of who was doing me, but he sure as hell was turned on by watching it. And who'd have guessed Quinn had leanings toward voyeurism?

"So you're not going to charge right in and kill Starr?"

"To do so might risk your safety, and Rhoan's. I have no wish to do that."

Meaning he had every wish to harm Kade. "In other words, you've realized it's not going to be as easy to get to Starr as it was to get onto his estate, and you'll bide your time until the chance appears."

"A very cynical statement."

"But a truthful one."

He paused for a second, his gaze filling me, consuming me, in a way that went way beyond anything physical. As if we were on the verge of sharing the best erotic dream ever, even though neither of us were asleep.

"Yes," he agreed softly, leaving me uncertain as to whether he was agreeing to the statement or the thought.

"If you didn't come here as a guard, you won't be able to move around freely." The words came out breathy, and it wasn't because of what Kade was doing. It was Quinn—the way our eyes connected, the way his thoughts seemed to be merging into mine, the sensation that we were becoming one in a way that went far beyond any sort of physical connection.

"The night is my servant." His soft words echoed

around me, through me, full of power, full of passion. Somehow, he used the night and connection he'd formed between us to enhance the growing sense of intimacy and arousal, and it was a connection I couldn't fight. Not that I really wanted to. I wanted to see where he would take this. How far he was willing to go.

"But the day isn't."

"Not yet, it's not."

The heat in his eyes would have melted steel, and I have never claimed to be that strong. My body was trembling under the force of it, and though I was vaguely aware of Kade's body moving in mine, all my senses were attuned to Quinn. To what was happening between us. To what was building between us.

"The day will never be yours, Quinn. You are a vampire, and that is a fact you can never escape."

We both knew I wasn't only referring to the day, and his smile was almost arrogant. But oh so sexy.

"Do not bet on that. I have been around a very long time, and I intend to be around for many more centuries yet. All things come to those who are willing to wait."

"Not all things can be claimed with time."

"But many things can be claimed with patience."

Sweat trickled down my forehead, tickling my cheeks. I wanted to swipe at it, but I couldn't seem to move, held in thrall by the furnace burning between us, by the sensations and desire tingling across my skin, across my senses. I licked my lips and somehow said, "Really? I haven't seen much evidence of patience lately."

"Perhaps not." He raised an eyebrow, his expression knowing, mocking. "But the real question is, would you like to see it now?"

"No." God, no.

His smile grew, and suddenly he was simply *there,* all around me, all through me, filling me with heat, filling me with passion. While it was Kade's cock that thrust deep inside, it wasn't Kade I could feel. Wasn't Kade I could smell. It was Quinn. All Quinn. He touched me, caressed me, claimed me. Perhaps not physically, but in a way that was total, absolute, and unlike anything I'd ever felt before. In reality our flesh might not be joined, but it didn't matter, because our spirits had combined and this dance went beyond intimacy, beyond mere pleasure.

It was all passion, heat, and intensity and I was drowning in it. Willingly. Wantonly. My heart pounded furiously, my body screamed for release, and every muscle, every fiber, felt so tightly strung that everything would surely break.

Then everything did break and it was such a sweet, glorious relief that I wept. His fingers touched my wrist, holding lightly, then his teeth grazed my skin. I jerked reflexively when they pierced my flesh, but the brief flare of pain quickly became something undeniably exquisite, and I came a second time.

As I remembered how to breathe again, I became aware of Kade, of his sated body still inside me. His sudden stillness, which was too unmoving to be natural. I glanced at Quinn, at his mocking, knowing expression, which was so at odds with the deeper depths of barely quenched desire in his dark eyes, then looked down at my wrists. At the two fast healing holes. Some of it, at least, had been real. I very much suspected that all of it had been, that he'd somehow crossed the boundaries of reality and imagination and merged the two.

I looked up at him again. Saw on the tip of one finger a droplet of water. A tear. My tear. He raised it to his mouth and slowly sipped it, and it was as if he were savoring the sweetest wine. Somehow, that one action seemed more intimate than anything he'd done in the last few minutes, as if he were drinking in my essence, my soul, making me his in ways I couldn't even begin to understand just yet. I crossed my arms to ward off the sudden chill.

"One day, you will be mine."

His rich voice was so soft, so sure. I licked my lips and tried to ignore the sensation that there was more going on here than I either realized or wanted. "You are not a wolf. We can never be what you wish us to be." Could never be what part of *me* wished we could be.

"Time will tell."

Yes, it would. And I had a feeling that only my death would dissuade him from his beliefs. But I didn't intend to die anytime soon, so my next bet was simply to ignore his statement, ignore my deep sense of uneasiness, and move on to other subjects.

"Horse-shifters can't be mind-read or mind-controlled. How are you holding Kade so still? How did you take control of him?"

"As I have repeatedly said, I am a very old vampire. And for a vampire, the older you are, the more power you have. Horse-shifters *are* difficult to read or control, but they are not impossible. No race or person is." He paused, his gaze sweeping the top half of me. "Except, perhaps, one."

I raised my eyebrows. "So are you telling me you can read Rhoan as well?"

"Two, then."

I let my gaze drift downward, and noted that he didn't have an erection. Either he wasn't turned on by what had happened between us, or Kade's release had somehow been his.

"There are more types of releases than mere physical," he said softly. "Emotional release is often far more satisfying."

He was reading my thoughts again, and though it should have pissed me off, it didn't. Right now, curiosity was stronger. I raised my eyebrows again. "So you're not standing there with a wet spot in your pants?"

Amusement touched his lush mouth, and made my hormones do their usual little dance. Sated they might be, but I was a wolf and it wouldn't have taken much to get them interested in another round.

"No, I am not," he said.

"Then how come all that affected me physically and not you?"

"Because you are not ready to step entirely beyond the physical." He paused. "You once said that it must be amazing to share sex with another telepath. What you just experienced was merely an appetizer."

"And I take it the appetizer is supposed to make me hunger for more?"

"Yes."

"Why? I mean, the appetizer was good, but I can get *that* sort of good from Kellen any day of the week."

Which actually wasn't true, but hey, it certainly never hurt to remind him that Kellen was on the scene and *was* a true rival. Because he was a wolf. Because he could give me what Quinn never could.

His gaze tightened imperceptibly and I resisted the temptation to smile.

"You will never achieve the sort of intimacy I'm talking about with Kellen."

"How the hell do you know that? You have no idea what goes on between Kellen and me."

"I know, because the sort of intimacy I'm talking about can only be achieved between telepaths."

"And why would that be?"

"Because dropping your shields so that spirits dance means you are placing yourself *completely* open to the other person. There are no secrets, no hiding, no lies. Just you, your lover, and the emotion and truths that lay between you." He hesitated, and I had a feeling he was about to add something else, then thought better of it. "It comes down to trust, complete trust."

"Which means we can *never* go any further than we already have, because I *don't* fully trust you." And probably never *would* after his stupid mind-raid for information.

He didn't say anything, just sort of glowered at me. I pulled away from Kade. He didn't move, didn't react. "Release him, Quinn."

The words were barely out of my mouth when Kade blinked, and a pleased smile stretched his lips. He stepped up beside me and put a proprietary arm around my shoulders. Which annoyed me almost as much as Quinn's continuing insistence I *would* play things his way. Eventually.

But before I could say anything, the main stable door cracked open and the cold night air filtered in again. Quinn disappeared in an instant, the night and darkness swallowing him whole. Kade stepped back, shifted shape once again, then pressed in beside me to peer over the stall door. I wrapped the shadows around myself and listened to the light puff of breathing that belonged to the person down the far end.

After a moment, footsteps echoed. Soft steps, neither hurried nor cautious, just a steady click of sound. I blinked. Those steps were from heels, high heels, not the work boots I'd seen the guards wearing. Whoever approached was female, not male. Not a guard. Someone else.

The night air stirred around me, bringing with it the teasing hints of jasmine and orange. And with those scents came the sense of something else—something not human, not even nonhuman, but something altogether different, altogether dangerous. A Fravardin. Tension slithered from my limbs. I flicked on the com-link so Jack could hear whatever was about to happen, then stepped up to the door and peered past Kade.

Dia walked toward us, her flowing white dress hugging her curvaceous figure and shining almost as brightly as her white hair in the shadowy darkness. Kade snorted softly, and it was an appreciative sound if ever I'd heard one.

Resisting the urge to smile, I let the shadows fall away from me and said, "You looking for me?"

She jumped, ever so slightly, then her powerful gaze centered on mine and again I was struck by the notion that this was not a woman you ever wanted to get on the wrong side of. And not just because of the unseen creature who gave her sight and kept her safe.

"Yes." She paused. "Why are you hiding in the stalls?"

"I'm in the stables because there's no one here at night, and in the stall in case a guard happens to walk by. And there's no microphones around here, so it's reasonably safe to report back to my boss. Why were you looking for me?"

"Because there have been changes since we last talked." She stopped several feet away, took a breath, then let it out slowly. "The timetable has been stepped up. He no longer plans to wait until Gautier has taken over the guardian division to attempt his cartel takeover."

We needed *that* like we needed a hole in the head. "What's happened?"

"He has been hosting not only his generals, but generals from some of the rival cartels. He has convinced them of his desire to work in unison with them to form an Australian-wide alliance that will profit all. The leaders of those cartels are coming here in two days' time for merger discussions."

Her information confirmed two things—that I'd read Merle's mind correctly, and that she was being as helpful as she could. "How many cartels are we talking about?"

"Three of the six."

"Half of them," Jack murmured. "It would be a damn good start to wiping out organized crime in Melbourne if we caught them all."

But it still left another three—and those three would undoubtedly step into the breach left by the other cartels' removal.

Still, taking half out was better than none.

"Two days doesn't give us a lot of time, especially since they are watching the new arrivals closely."

"I know, and I'm sorry, but there is nothing much I can do."

"Except give us information."

"Us?" She raised a pale eyebrow. "There is more than one of you here?"

I mentally cursed the slip of the tongue. I might believe Dia, might trust her desperation to get her child free, but that didn't mean she was playing on our side. If things went foul and if we were discovered, she'd do what she could to save herself and her child. Just like the spirit lizard. So I shrugged. "That's a metaphorical 'we,' not an actual one."

Her expression suggested she wasn't believing me. I really was going to have to get some lying lessons. "What information do you wish?"

"For starters, where does the second elevator on Moss's and Merle's floor lead to?"

She frowned. "What elevator?"

"You know, the one opposite the elevator the guards take the lieutenants' nightly toys down in."

Understanding flickered in her unseeing eyes. "That's no elevator, but doors that lead into Starr's rooms."

It was my turn to frown. "I saw Merle key it open. It looked like an elevator."

"It might at a quick glance, but it is similar to an air lock. One door must close before the other opens, and only after the right codes and scans are entered."

Confusion ran through me. I knew what I'd seen, and I'd seen an elevator, *not* a form of air lock. "So can you get in there?"

She shook her head, sending slivers of silver cascading across the night. Kade snorted softly again, his hooves barely missing my toes as he shifted. I elbowed him lightly to remind him that I was there, that he had to be careful no matter how attracted he suddenly was. He glanced at me, velvet eyes sparkling with amusement and interest.

"I have been there under escort, nothing more. Starr is not fool enough to trust me with such access," Dia said, bringing my attention back to her. "As far as I know, only Merle, Moss, and the head of security have access to that lock."

"Is the head of security a tall, balding man with severe acne scars?"

She nodded. "Henry Cartle is his name."

"Any chance of you getting me a security roster?"

She hesitated. "I'll try."

"Try hard, because I can't do this without help."

She stared at me for a moment, as if understanding what I wasn't saying more than what I was, then nodded. "Anything else?"

"What floor is the lab on?"

"The second floor."

"Riley, you are not going in to rescue that child."

I couldn't answer Jack, so I just ignored him. There wasn't anything he could do to stop me anyway, short of pulling me out, and we both knew he wasn't about to do that.

"And it has the same security precautions as the third floor?"

"Under no circumstances are you to go near that lab in an attempt to rescue the child. That is a direct order."

And I liked direct orders almost as much as I liked going to the dentist.

Dia nodded. "Entry is restricted to the scientists, Starr's lieutenants, and the head of security."

Meaning it might be easier to cozy up to one of the

scientists to get in there than risk security, Moss, or Merle. "Where are the scientists quartered?"

Jack swore loudly. "Jesus, Riley, are you listening to me?"

For an intelligent man, he was mighty slow in realizing I *wasn't*. I touched my ear, flicking off the com-link. Yelling would be next, and I didn't need that on top of the headache I already had.

"The scientists are the next building down from security."

"And does this Henry Cartle bunk with his men?"

"In the same building, but he has his own room."

Better and better. "What can you tell me about escape tunnels?"

She frowned. "I do not know what you mean."

"I was following Moss through the trees earlier today, and he simply disappeared. Unless he can shapeshift, there has to be an entrance to the lower levels in those woods."

"If there is, I do not know of it." She hesitated. "I will see what I can discover, though. Starr likes his future read when I am here."

I raised an eyebrow. "Meaning you not only see the future when you touch someone, but can ferret out the past?"

She shrugged elegantly. "Sometimes."

"And what did you see when you touched me? Past or future?"

"Future." She stared at me for several seconds, her blue eyes seeming to see right through me, down to my very soul. "It will be troubled, with many unwanted detours. Some dreams will be yours to take or forsake. Some have already slipped through your fingers."

Avoiding direct answers seemed to be catchy. "Psychic mumbo jumbo that could mean anything."

She shrugged again. "Because I touched you without a specific question in mind, I saw only generalities. If you wish a more detailed reading, then I suggest you see me after this is over and we are all safe."

"It's a date."

She smiled and glanced at her watch. "I must be going before suspicions are raised. I walk the grounds before lunch. Meet me tomorrow and I will tell you what I have discovered."

I nodded. She turned around and walked out. As the closing doors snatched away the filtering moonlight, Quinn reappeared. "What was that thing with her?"

"A Fravardin. It gives her sight and provides protection."

Energy rippled across my skin as Kade shifted shape. "Whatever it was, it had no emotion as we recognize it. It was little more than a vacuum of emptiness to my senses. She, however, was delicious." His warm gaze met mine. "I demand an introduction after all this is over."

"If we make it through this, you'll get it." I glanced at Quinn. "Given you keep reminding me how old you are, I'm surprised you didn't know what that creature was."

His lips twisted into a smile that was bitter. "There are many places on this earth I've yet to visit, many people I've yet to meet."

"That thing couldn't be classified as 'people.'"

"Just because it hasn't human form as we currently recognize it doesn't mean it can't be classed as an offshoot of humanity." There was a touch of censure in his voice, which was damn annoying considering he was the one who'd just called it a "thing." But given he seemed to be in an argumentative mood, there wasn't much point in saying anything. He continued, "Just as werewolves, shapeshifters, mermen, and the like cannot escape the reality that they are merely another branch of the well-spring from which humanity sprung."

"Werewolves, shapeshifters, and the like are not the ones you should be giving that lecture to," I reminded him tartly, "but rather those humans who hold themselves up as the pinnacle of development, and everyone else an oddity that should not exist."

He shrugged. "This is not the time for such a debate."

I snorted softly. "Yeah, that's why you're standing there throwing attitude my way—because you don't want to argue." I reached over the door and unlatched it. "I need to go find my brother before I'm tempted to get nasty."

"I shall accompany you." There was anger in Quinn's rich tones, but then, there often seemed to be when he was "talking" to me. "He needs to know I am here."

As did Jack, but given he was likely still ranting over my ignoring his orders, I had every intention of leaving Rhoan the task of informing our boss we had a fourth person on the ground.

I gave Kade a quick kiss good-bye, more to piss off a certain vampire than anything else, then headed out the stable doors. Quinn was little more than a shadow at my back, a presence I could feel but not see through normal vision. Hopefully, this meant no one else would see him, either.

"Unless they have infrared, they won't." His voice was

little more than a murmur that barely carried to my ears, but nevertheless brushed my senses as sensually as any summer breeze.

"They have infrared around the zoo and on the lower levels, so avoid those areas. And quit reading my mind."

"If you do not fully shield, I will continue to take it as an open invitation." Though I could not see his eyes, I could feel his gaze on me. "And in this place, it is *extremely* unwise—"

The rest of his words were cut off as an explosion ripped through the quiet night.

Chapter 10

The force of the blast sent hot air scurrying past my skin and rattled the nearby windows. A plume of flame reached skyward, fat fingers of yellow and orange that briefly illuminated the western edge of the house and the trees that grew nearby. These fiery fingers were accompanied by chunks of wood and concrete—weighty missiles that thudded to the ground with bone-jarring force. The spurt of flame died, becoming little more than a sullen orange glow that lit the night, but the acrid smell of smoke filled the air, mingling with screams that spoke of fear or pain or both.

I didn't even stop to think about what I was going to do or how safe it might be, just ran like hell around the side of the house. I wasn't the only one. Guards filled the night, pouring out of the buildings like a well-trained military force, some of them running for the end of the building, others forming a line to cordon off the area. Starr's men were efficient, you had to give them that. I kept the cloak of night wrapped around me as I slipped through the cordon and followed those heading for the explosion area. The closer I got to it, the more the air sizzled. Not just with heat, but with steam. The building's sprinklers, inside and out, were working, and the remaining flames were swiftly dying under the assault.

And the flames weren't the only things. The explosion had happened in the wing that housed the kitchen and dining areas and had basically blasted them apart. In normal circumstances it wouldn't have mattered, because most places who had live-in staff didn't often house them in the main building, let alone in the same area. But the staff here were. With the force of the explosion tearing apart the ground-floor level, the upper ones had no place to go but down.

I couldn't see any of the dead or dying in the black and burning rubble, but I could feel them. Their agony rode the night, surrounding me with the scent and despair of death, until every breath, every pore, was filled with it and it felt like I was drowning under the weight of it.

My stomach rolled, then rose. I spun away and bent over, losing what little dinner I'd eaten. A hand touched my back, and warmth spread like fire across the chill that was encasing me, holding it back if not totally erasing it.

"You are not an empath." Though I couldn't see him, his voice was next to my ear, indicating he was leaning close. "You should not be feeling what you are feeling."

His shadow-held fingers caught my hair, holding it away from my face. I sucked in a breath, battling the roiling in my stomach. "I'm a werewolf. Death is something we can smell."

"But you are not smelling this. You are feeling it, and that is completely different."

"I'm aware of that." Aware of the fact that he shouldn't be feeling what *I* was feeling. He might be an empath, but I had my emotions locked down as tightly as him. Or so I'd thought, up until then. I took another breath and carefully straightened. My stomach made threatening movements but didn't immediately rise. I closed my eyes and tried breathing through my mouth. It didn't seem to help. Death still rode the air, and its taste was foul. I swallowed heavily. "Can you read any of the guards? Do they know what has happened?"

He was silent for several minutes, but energy stirred across my skin, powerful enough to stand on end the hairs along my arms and neck.

"One of the guards reported the smell of gas several minutes before the explosion. They believe one or more of the stove jets may have been left on."

"So it was an accident?"

"It would appear that way."

I glanced in his direction. "Appear?"

"They are unsure where the spark that set off the explosion came from."

"It's a kitchen. They're full of pilot lights."

"True. Let's hope someone thinks to turn the gas off at the meter, or there will be more unpleasantness." He paused. "Is that one of Starr's lieutenants?"

I glanced down at the rubble. Moss was picking his way through the ruins, his hair and clothes disheveled and torn, his face scratched and bloody.

"Yeah, it's Moss. Damn shame he wasn't killed." I rubbed my arms. Though death still rode the night, the smell and taste of it was dying. Whether it actually was, or whether I was merely growing used to it was something I couldn't tell.

Quinn rubbed my back, sending warmth spinning across my skin. "He doesn't look all that happy."

With the last of the chills being chased away by his touch, I felt a little better. As long as I didn't see anything resembling mashed humanity in the ruins below, I'd be okay. I hoped. "I imagine barely escaping a gas explosion would do that to a person."

Amusement spun around me, as bright and as enticing as the first dance of sunshine that broke the hold of night. "This is more than that. Can you hear him?"

"Not from this distance." I frowned. "Why don't you just read his mind?"

"Some form of psi-deadener is blocking me. I could break through it easily enough, but it would warn him of my presence."

"Then let's get closer."

"Are you up to going closer?" His touch moved from my back to my arm, his fingers sliding down my arm and under my elbow. I wasn't wobbly enough to need support, but I wasn't going to fight it, either. Not when the warmth that flared out from his fingertips seemed to keep the horror at bay.

"As long as I keep upwind of the building, I should be fine." Though if I saw bodies, or bits of bodies, it would be a totally different story.

I'd seen death, in various incarnations, a few times over the years and it had never bothered me like this. I'd seen one wolf ripped apart by another, and hadn't felt sick, much less puked. I'd witnessed Misha being eaten from the inside out, and though I'd been both horrified and sickened, I hadn't come close to losing my stomach. But in all those times, I'd never *tasted* the death. Had never felt as if the souls of those who were dying or dead were invading me, filling me with their shock and anger and pain.

I wish I hadn't felt it tonight.

I swallowed heavily and forced my feet to move, keeping my gaze on Moss more than what he was walking through. Or by. He stopped to talk to several guards who were hovering near the far edge of the remains. Moisture from the nearby sprinklers danced around him, covering him in a fine haze of silver. He either didn't care or didn't notice, but there was something in his very stillness that was chilling. Deadly.

Merle might have felt foul, but he didn't scare me like Moss suddenly scared me. Just looking at him had trepidation running up and down my spine.

And I had to hope that the guard was right, that Moss and Merle *didn't* share, because there was no way on this earth I could cope with getting sexually close to that man.

So how did my brother deal with it? He regularly used sex to get information about targets—used it and enjoyed it, no matter what or who he was doing. Was it merely the fact I was psychic and he wasn't that gave him the advantage? If he'd been able to taste the foulness of the people involved, would he still be able to get intimate with them?

Somehow, I suspected the answer might be yes. Rhoan

had never cared who or how many, as long as *he* was enjoying himself.

I'd always been a little more fussy—despite what Quinn might think. Though I guess there were huge differences in what a werewolf termed fussy and what a vampire with human sensibilities might.

We circled the ruined sections of building, and began to edge closer to Moss and the guards, all the while keeping the shadows close and the breeze to our front so that it blew our scents away from, not toward, the men below.

"No, sir," the shorter of the two guards said, his tone all military preciseness. "I saw no movement in the kitchen."

"And yet you were the one who reported hearing steps?"

"Yes, sir."

"How long before the explosion was this?"

"Ten, maybe fifteen minutes, sir."

Moss swore and snapped his gaze to the second man. "And you?"

"I saw a heat signature in the kitchen, but by the time I got there, the person had left through the window."

"And you didn't give chase?"

"I saw no person, sir. Only a fox sniffing out the rubbish."

Something in me stilled. A fox? Nerida was a werefox, and even a vamp couldn't tell the difference between the heat signature of a real fox and that of a shapeshifter or werefox. He *should* have been able to sense the difference, but if he'd been more interested in getting back to bed, maybe he'd simply taken what he'd seen at face value.

And while I had no doubt that real foxes did scavenge around the bins here nightly, it just seemed a little too much of a coincidence that *this* fox was sighted so soon after the guard had sprung someone in the kitchen. Fact was, most real foxes would have scampered at the first hint of movement. They certainly wouldn't have stayed there scavenging as a vampire approached. Most wild ones feared the undead almost as much as most humans did.

But what would Nerida be doing in the kitchen? Had she been involved in the explosion or was it merely a coincidence? Why would *anyone* want to blow this section of the house up, anyway? There was little here but the kitchen and dining areas, and the staff who ran them.

So what was Moss doing here? How'd he get caught in the explosion when he was supposedly talking to the new intake of guards?

"I want you to do a walk around the area. See if you can spot that heat signature again."

The words were barely out of Moss's mouth when I was dragged back then forced up the slight knoll and into a knot of trees.

"Why the hell did you do that?" I asked, shaking free of both Quinn's grip and the shadows concealing my form as we stopped.

Quinn also stepped free of night's cloak, and a lot more elegantly than me. "He was about to switch to infrared. He would have spotted us in an instant."

"Given he wasn't even facing us, there was plenty of time to move."

"Maybe. Maybe not. Either way, it wasn't worth the risk of discovery." He paused, his gaze moving to the mess below us. "I think I'll follow Moss for a while. If you find Rhoan, let him know I am here, and that I will contact him later."

"If you kill Moss, they're going to know this place has been infiltrated."

His gaze flicked to mine, obsidian depths once again devoid of emotion. "I am not the amateur here."

He had a point, but it was an annoying one. "No, you're just the man hell-bent on revenge, regardless of the cost."

"I will not do anything to jeopardize you or Rhoan."

"That a promise?"

His hesitation was brief but nevertheless there. "Yes."

I studied him for a moment, weighing his words, hearing truth and yet not trusting it. "I don't know how much stock you vampires put in promises, but let me give one to you—if Rhoan gets hurt because your need for revenge overrides your vow, I'll make you pay for it."

He didn't say anything, just turned and walked down the hill, the shadows again taking him from sight as he neared the end of the trees.

I rubbed my head wearily, and let my gaze roam across the smoking mass of rubble and partial walls below. Moss was across the far side now, talking to other guards. The first two were walking around, heading my way as they scanned the area. Time to get moving, before I was spotted.

I padded through the trees, keeping to the deep shadows and away from the occasional flickers of moonlight. I didn't have the cloak of night wrapped around me because my head was beginning to pound, and it would take more energy to hold the shadows close than I really had right now. So hitting moonlight when my skin was basically lily white wouldn't be a good thing. As I drew away from the wreckage and closer to the whole sections of the house, I noticed a small gathering of people standing or kneeling in a group near the front of one of the main doors. A heartbeat later, a tingle of awareness ran across my skin, and my heart leapt with joy. My brother was amongst those below.

I stopped, my gaze searching the small crowd. I couldn't see anyone with red hair, and it took me a while to realize why. Rhoan didn't *have* red hair. Thanks to Liander's magic, he was now boring brown.

With that in mind, he wasn't hard to find. He was on the outskirts of the group, sitting on the ground, his clothes dusty and torn and a bloody cloth held to his head.

For the second time that night I reacted without thinking, and it took Rhoan looking up and minutely shaking his head to remember where I was and who we were supposed to be.

I slowed to walking speed and skirted the main group, pretending concern and offering words of encouragement to those being tended to before making my way toward him. His gaze met mine. His brown eyes might be alien, but his smile was all too familiar. So warm and welcoming. God, I was so happy to see him again, it was hard to restrain the urge to dance.

"Hey," he said, so softly it was little more than a stirring of air. "Glad to see you got here safely."

"And I'm glad to see you got out of that mess safely." I wanted to touch him, hug him, but that was impossible, so I simply kneeled beside him, my knees touching his thighs as I raised his hand to see the wound. It was nothing too bad, just a nasty jagged cut he could have easily healed by shifting shape. "Why haven't you fixed that?"

"Because my wolf is red, which is at odds with my new identity."

Of course. Stupid me. "So why were you even in the kitchen?"

"It's been a pretty rugged day, and none of us had much of a chance to eat." He shrugged. "Moss had arranged a meal in the kitchen, but luckily, he got a call about a possible intruder and split us up into groups to check out the different areas. I was in the outside group."

"Lucky you."

"Yeah." He touched my knee and squeezed it lightly. That one action suggested he'd been a lot closer to the blast than he was leading me to believe. "What's been happening with you? Besides pissing off Jack, that is."

I grinned slightly. "He should know me well enough to realize there's no way known I'd throw the baby out with the bathwater."

"Any attempt to rescue that child could be dangerous."

"I know that. I have to try, though."

He smiled. "I know that. Just don't attempt it too soon, or the whole mission could fall down around our ears."

I glanced around to ensure there still wasn't anyone within listening range. "That might still happen given certain time frames have been upped."

"Yeah, Jack mentioned that. Give me a hand up, and we'll talk as you help me to my quarters."

I rose and offered him my hand. "Have the medics seen you?"

"One of the lab boys declared I was fit enough to move. I've been ordered to clean up and get back to work within the hour."

He grabbed my hand. I hauled him easily to his feet, then tucked a shoulder under his and wrapped my arm around his waist. He didn't need the extra support—I could feel the strength in him and he wasn't the least bit shaky—but at least this way we could talk softly and take our time without raising suspicions in unwanted areas. "Nice of them to give you an hour."

"Yeah, they're all heart." His voice was dry. "So, what's been happening to you?"

"I've touched base with Merle, and learned I can read his thoughts."

"And?"

"And I now understand what you were trying to say when you asked me if I knew what I was doing."

He blew out a breath, and the sudden anguish that briefly flared in his eyes gave me some idea of what he'd been feeling over the last twenty-four hours. And it sure as hell was worse than anything I'd actually been going through. I hugged him close for a moment, letting him know without words that I was okay, that it wasn't really as bad as he'd been imagining.

"It's never pleasant the first time."

"Does it get any easier the twentieth? Fiftieth?"

"Yes, because we are wolves and sex is as important to us as air itself. You'll learn to switch off and just enjoy the moment, if not the person." His gaze met mine. "But that's easy for me to say when I'm not psychic and cannot ever feel things as deeply—or as intimately—as you do."

Some of the tension that had been with me for hours slithered away. He understood *exactly* what I was feeling, without my having to say a word. But then, if my twin didn't, who would? "It's not the sex itself that worries me. Hell, I was with Talon for ages and I can't ever say that I actually liked him. With Merle, it was different. It felt like his foulness was invading my very essence. But Moss felt a hundred times worse, and if they all felt like that, I just couldn't do it. Jack's telling me I have no choice but—"

"You'll always have at least one choice, even if you are forced into the system. You don't have to fuck them, sis. Not when you have the psychic strength to make them believe anything you want them to believe."

I blinked, and something that was either relief or joy or a mix of both ran through me. Goddamn it, he was right. Even if I was forced into the system, I *didn't* have to play it entirely Jack's way. It didn't matter whether the seduction was real or not, because that wasn't the point. Getting information *was,* and Jack couldn't complain as long as I was doing that.

Of course, Jack didn't just want me as an information gatherer, but as a full guardian—a hunter *and* a killer—but that was a whole different fight. And it certainly wasn't a place I was willing to go or even compromise on, even if he did drag me into the ranks.

I leaned forward and kissed Rhoan's cheek. "Thank you for clearing muddy thoughts."

He grinned. "Isn't that what big brothers are for?"

I smiled. He'd come howling into the world a whole

two minutes before me. "That and rescuing little sisters when they bite off more than they can chew."

"Which thankfully hasn't happened in a while. Anything else I need to know about?"

I told him about the spirit-lizard, then about Quinn's presence. He swore under his breath. "Jack's not going to be happy."

"Which is why I thought I'd leave it to you to tell him."

His brown eyes glimmered with amusement. "Coward."

"Yep." I looked up and noted that we were drawing closer to the guards' quarters. I needed to ask my questions before we ran out of time. "Did you see or feel anything unusual when you were scouting around the outside of the kitchen?"

He smiled. "I've a feeling you already know the answer." He reached into his pocket and withdrew a piece of cloth. "I saw a shifter pretending to nose through the rubbish. The minute I approached she ran, but I found this in amongst the rubbish. I think it must have dropped from a pocket during her original shapeshift."

"You didn't give chase?"

"I had no chance."

He handed me the cloth, which turned out to be a gray and white handkerchief. Just like the one that had been tucked into Nerida's breast pocket.

"It had a musky, feminine scent, but there was little in the way of perfume," he continued. "Given what it's been through recently, it now probably smells of nothing more than me and smoke."

I sniffed it. He was right. "One of my roommates is a

werefox, and happened to be wearing a hanky like this earlier. I might go check if she still is."

"Be careful with her. Foxes are as slippery as snakes."

"Or as cunning as foxes." He groaned at my admittedly bad pun, and I grinned. "So you think this werefox might have had something to do with the blast?"

"I have no idea, but she's certainly worth questioning. Just don't get caught doing so by the wrong people."

"I won't." I stopped as we neared the gate leading into the guards' quarters. There was a guard watching us, but the mere fact I couldn't read him said he was human. He wouldn't hear what we were saying as long as we went no closer. "One thing you do need to know—there's three underground floors that aren't on the plans. I have no idea what's on the first level, but there's a small research lab on sub-two, and Merle, Moss, and Starr have quarters on sub-three."

He nodded. "They told us that during briefing. Warned us that no one but the head of security and assigned guards went down there."

"Did they mention the fact there's an escape tunnel leading from one of the sublevel floors out into the forest?" When he shook his head, I continued, "And there's also what looks to be a second elevator on the third level that no one else seems to be aware of."

"So how come you know about it?"

"I saw Merle key it open. When I asked Dia about it, she said it was a type of air lock provided for Starr's protection."

"But you don't believe she's telling the truth?"

"Oh, I believe she believes that's what it is. I just don't believe it *is* that."

"So the levels could go lower?"

"Why else would they have a secret elevator? If it went back up to the other levels, surely others would know about it?"

"It's a lead worth following. Though unless I can attract Starr's attention, I won't be the one following it."

A shiver ran down my spine. "Be careful with him. He doesn't walk in the same sane world as you and me."

"That's a given." He squeezed my shoulder then stepped away from my hold. "Keep in touch."

"I will. Just promise to be careful around your target. I have a bad feeling about him."

"That's because he's a bad man." He gave me a lopsided grin. "It's part of my job to associate with, and then destroy, bad men."

"But this bad man seems to think he knows me, disguise or no. He's in our life somehow, and the slightest slip could tip him off as to who we really are."

"Warning heeded." He glanced briefly at the watching guard, then leaned forward to kiss my cheek. "Don't play with our friendly neighborhood stallion too much. You have got a job to do here, you know."

I gave him a light whack on the arm before he could jump away. He chuckled softly, gave me a wink, then walked off. I watched him until he was inside, then turned and headed for my own quarters.

The fighters' quarters were full, and most of the women were asleep. One or two were staring out the windows or chatting amongst themselves, but for the most part, silence reigned.

Berna was in bed and, as she'd warned earlier, snoring heavily enough to wake the dead. Or undead, as the case around here might be. Nerida wasn't in the room, and her toiletries bag was missing from the bedside table where she'd placed it earlier. But the sound of running water was coming from the bathroom.

Perfect. Just perfect.

I collected my still-damp towel and soap, and headed to the bathroom. The water flicked off as I entered.

"Hey," Nerida said, "throw me the spare towel that's sitting near the basin, will you?"

I quietly shut the door, dumped my towel and soap in a nearby stall, then moved over to grab Nerida's towel. "Catch," I said, and tossed it high, not over the door but at the camera in the corner above it. I might never have been tall enough to be a basketball player, but I was a pretty handy shot at goal. The towel landed precisely where I wanted it—catching the body of the camera and draping down over the edge of the lens. With the camera now covered and sound not an issue—thanks to the fact there were no microphones in the bathroom—I stepped forward, raised a foot, and kicked open the door.

"You stupid bit—" The rest of Nerida's curse was lost as the door slammed back against the stall wall.

She spun around, a look of shock and perhaps a little fear etching her features. I gave her no time to react any more than that, simply wrapped a hand around her throat and slammed her back against the wall.

She grunted—a sound that was strained and angry all at once. The fear, if it had been fear I'd seen, was gone. And that in itself suggested this woman was more than what she was pretending. Anyone with any sense feared a werewolf when they were angry. That she didn't meant she could defend herself when she wanted—or she had other sources of protection I wasn't aware of.

Even as the thought crossed my mind, awareness tingled across my senses. I ducked instantly, and a fist the size of a shovel skimmed across the top of my head. I squeezed Nerida's neck harder, making her gasp, even as I lashed out backward with a bare foot. I connected with flesh, felt the blow sink deep enough to hit bone, and got a grunt in response.

"I'll break her fucking neck if you don't stop, Berna. I swear to God I will."

"Release her, then." Berna's words were as quiet as mine, but filled with the restrained promise of violence.

"Release someone who's just killed at least ten people? I hardly think so."

I twisted around to check on Berna, but didn't ease the force of my grip around Nerida's neck. The werefox was huffing, her face darkening with her battle to breathe, but I didn't damn well care. Everything I'd smelled, everything I'd felt, when I first walked up to the blast area had come back with a rush, and the dead and dying who'd filled me with their pain wanted revenge. And my fingers—my whole arm—were shaking with the effort *not* to squeeze that little bit tighter. To kill her, and let the dead have her.

Berna's brown eyes narrowed a little. Bear-shifters might have the rep for honesty, but I had a feeling I'd be getting anything but that from *this* bear-shifter. At least for the immediate future.

"Don't speak rubbish, wolf. She was with one of the people from the arena for hours, then she came here. She didn't have anything to do with that explosion."

"Hard to believe when she was actually spotted not once, but twice. And if you don't step back this instant, she's one dead werefox." I squeezed a little harder, just to emphasize my seriousness, and Nerida made an odd gargling sound. I eased up immediately. I didn't actually want to kill her, no matter what the remnants of the dead might be urging.

Berna raised her hands and stepped back. "Okay, okay, just let her breathe."

I loosened my grip a little more, and Nerida's entire body shook as she sucked in great gulps of air. Guilt ran through me, but the dead were having none of that and quickly swatted it away.

And the fact that I could feel them, knew that they were all around me, demanding revenge, was terrifying. Empathy was one thing—but empathy with the dead? What the hell kind of talent was that?

Not one that I wanted, that was for sure.

"Now, just let her go," Berna continued, in that same quiet tone. Like she was dealing with a psycho ready to explode. And if that impression meant they were less likely to try a concerted attack, then I was happy to keep reinforcing it. "And we'll talk about this like civilized human beings."

"Which none of us are." I shook Nerida a little. "Why did you blow up the kitchen area?"

"I didn—"

"You were *seen*," I cut in. "In your fox form, twice, by guards."

"There are tons of foxes running wild," Berna said patiently. "That doesn't mean squat."

I let the handkerchief unfold and held it up so both

could see. "How many foxes run around with a gray and white hanky in their pockets? A handkerchief that held a feminine scent the match of Nerida's—at least until the guard holding it was caught in the explosion."

Berna swore. Nerida didn't say anything, just stared at me with small green eyes that spoke of death. I snorted softly. "I don't fear the death you're threatening, fox, because the dead are all around us. And they are demanding satisfaction."

That got a reaction. Finally, something more than anger sparked in those beady green eyes. "What do you mean?"

"I mean, unless you start telling the truth, I'm going to give the dead what they want. You."

"You can't—"

"I can. Or I could report you to the guards and let them give you to those blue things in the arena."

She shuddered. "No. Please, I'll talk."

"I want truth, not lies." I glanced back at Berna. "I want to know why you're both here and why you blasted the kitchen."

"Then what? You'll go to the guards anyway. We lose either way, wolf."

"Not if you tell me the truth."

"And trust the word of a thief?" Berna snorted softly. "I think not."

I glanced at the covered camera, then back to Nerida. "The guards will undoubtedly be here soon to unfoul the camera. It's your choice—trust me, and tell me what is going on, or I'll hand my discoveries over to the guards and let them make of it what they will."

Indecision shone in her eyes. She didn't want to trust

me—neither of them did. But we'd all seen what had happened to anyone who went against Starr's rule, and that was far worse than anything I might do.

"Okay, okay," she said, voice hoarse.

I glanced at Berna as footsteps echoed in the hallway. "And you?"

"I will talk."

"And not attack?"

She grinned. It wasn't a pleasant grin. "Not immediately. But I would suggest you sleep lightly."

That threat could at least be dealt with later. I released Nerida and she collapsed to the ground, alternatively coughing and sucking in air. I stepped past her, past Berna, and into the other stall, slipping the handkerchief under my towel before quickly turning on the water. As I stepped under it, I switched on the com-link. The door opened and the guard stepped in, I put on my best confused expression as I stepped out of the water and grabbed my towel.

"What the hell is going on?" The scowling guard looked me up and down, then shifted his gaze to Berna, who hadn't moved.

"Anxiety attack," she said. "Sometimes happens to foxes in enclosed spaces."

"Why is that towel up there, then?" He waved irritably at the camera.

"I meant to toss it over the stall door and threw too high." I shrugged.

He grunted, and pointed to Berna. "You, get that down immediately."

Berna obeyed.

"All of you, you've got ten minutes. Finish whatever it is you're doing and get back to your room."

The guard gave us all another once-over, like he suspected there was more going on than what was being said, then grunted and spun on his heel. I waited until he was out of earshot, then crossed my arms and leaned against the door frame. I couldn't physically see Nerida from where I was standing, but her image was crystal clear in the mirror—which was why I'd chosen this stall.

"You heard the man—we've got ten minutes. Tell me a little story."

Nerida leaned her head back against the tiled wall. The red marks around her neck were very evident, and this time not even the dead could hold back the guilt.

"I didn't mean for the explosion to be so big."

"You put gas and flame together, and the end result is usually a big explosion."

She grimaced and ran a hand through her damp hair. "Yeah. But I didn't mean for it to bring down the floors above. I just wanted it to be big enough to kill a man."

"What man?" But even as I asked the question, I knew.

"Leo Moss." She spat the name like it was a curse, and even though I was viewing her through a mirror, it was very evident that the complete and utter hatred she had for the man verged on madness.

"Why?"

"Because he and Merle killed my father and destroyed my family." Her gaze met mine in the mirror. "I will kill them both. Have no doubt of that."

I didn't doubt her vow. I just didn't think she had the

strength to do it. I glanced at Berna. "And your part in this whole little revenge scheme?"

The bear-shifter shrugged. "I came here in the hope of keeping her alive. We've been friends a long time."

"If these are those two women you asked me about," Jack said, voice like a scratch of anger in my ear—was I ever going to get a dressing-down when this mission was over!—"prelim searches have revealed they had military time together, in the ranger division. Left four years ago, and the trail runs a little cold after that."

"Friends don't usually go to such lengths—unless they've sworn an oath to protect each other." Or were lovers. I paused, then aimed the second question at both Jack and Berna. "How far would you go?"

"Until we know more about these two," Jack said, "you say nothing of your reasons for being there."

Which was going to be damn difficult, considering they already had their suspicions about my identity after I'd challenged them both over the bed.

"She saved my life." Berna hesitated, then added, "And I will go as far as I am required to uphold my vow and return the favor."

Which was a very military sentiment. It also explained why they'd moved as one when they'd threatened me earlier. "How did Moss and Merle wipe out your family, Nerida, and how did you uncover information about this place? It's not exactly on any known map."

The bear-shifter's eyes narrowed slightly. "What does either of those matter to a thief?"

I smiled coldly. "I have my own reasons for being here, and they aren't so very different from yours."

"I knew you weren't what you were pretending to be," Nerida muttered, as she pushed to her feet.

I straightened a little, watching them both warily. "Answer the question."

"My family ran a shipping business. When my father refused to sell, Merle arranged to have him arrested. Moss then killed my mother and my sister." She paused. Her gaze became haunted, and her struggle with a grief that was obviously still too raw, too close to the surface, was evident. I wondered how long ago it had all happened. "He has the aura of a were and a taste for pain. He used my family until their injuries were too great, and then he left them to die. Only they didn't die soon enough, and I found them. That's how I know who it was. That's when I made my vow."

I glanced at Berna to confirm the statement, and it was in that moment Nerida attacked. She was fast, with the skills of a fully trained soldier to back her up, and for several seconds it was all I could do to simply block and survive, let alone counterattack. Granted, she was no Gautier, but then, this wasn't a wide arena but a shower stall with next to no room to move. And I was in it while she wasn't.

I ducked several whistle-fast blows, caught another in my fist, and missed the one aimed at my stomach. Her fist sunk deep and my breath left in a whoosh. I had no choice but to ignore the burning sensation in my gut as I ducked and weaved and was gradually driven back farther into the stall.

Then lights went out. Berna, probably. And though she was undoubtedly trying to stop the monitoring guards from seeing what was going on, she'd unknowingly given me an advantage. Night was my friend, not theirs. I switched to infrared, dropped underneath another one-two series of blows, then came up fast and pushed her backward, as hard as I could. As the werefox staggered backward and tried to catch her balance, I wrapped the shadows around myself then leapt upward. Wolves could leap extremely high—vampires even higher. I had the skills of both at my call, and landed with little effort on the thin edge of the stall wall. I took a moment to balance, then quietly stepped onto the top of the next stall, then the next, before easing lightly back down to the floor.

"Where the fuck has she gone?" There was a thump and a rattle as Nerida's fist hit the wall. "She's disappeared."

"That's impossible. She's probably just cowering in a corner." Exasperation edged Berna's voice. Maybe she was getting a little tired of her friend's actions.

And I had to wonder why they were wasting time thumping the walls rather than using their olfactory senses—hell, given I'd been with Kade in the hay and had then been surrounded in smoke and death, I'd have to be leaving one hell of a scent trail.

But I wasn't about to give either of them time to remember that option. Nor did I have much time left to contain them, as the scowling guard was probably already on his way back down.

Berna bent over and peered into the stall. I padded over, shook off the shadows, then grabbed a fistful of her short hair, yanking her back and up before thrusting her hard into the stall. She collided with Nerida and both hit the back wall, and there was a crack loud enough to suggest broken bones. They went down in a heap and stayed there. But the heated looks being flung my way suggested it wasn't because they were too hurt to move, but rather because any good soldier knows when to retreat in order to fight another day.

I crossed my arms and resumed questioning. "How did you set the gas off?"

Nerida swore as she pulled her leg out from under Berna's rump. "Small incendiary device we snuck in."

I wasn't going to ask how they'd managed that, because given all the bags had been thoroughly searched, there was really only one place they could have hidden it. And I was mighty surprised Starr hadn't brought in measures to cater for such occurrences. Hell, I knew for a fact many of the cartel employed female assassins. A good amount of Directorate time was spent hunting down the bitches after they'd completed their bloody deeds.

"And you didn't ever stop to consider who else might be in the way of the explosion?"

Nerida's gaze met mine. "Not once I saw Moss."

Insane with revenge and blind because of it. Great. "And have you ever stopped to consider that the picture is way bigger than the piece you're concentrating on?"

"No."

"Then I suggest you fucking start, before you end up on the wrong end of someone else's revenge." I flicked on the light. "Moss, Merle, and Starr have destroyed more lives than you could ever imagine. Stop being so blinkered, start seeing what is really going on, and for God's sake don't blow anything else up. Or I'll have you taken out so fast your heads will spin."

I glanced down the corridor to see the guard headed

our way again. And he looked even unhappier than he had the last time.

I leaned forward and grabbed my towel, soap, and the handkerchief. "Now, if you don't mind, ladies, I need to complete my shower."

I flung the towel over my shoulder and headed for the shower stall Nerida had originally used. It had a good line of sight via the mirrors, and while I needed to get clean, I wasn't fool enough to turn my back on either of them.

The guard stalked in as I stepped under the water. "What the hell is going on here?"

"Just a little disagreement," Berna muttered. "Nothing to worry about."

"It is when I'm wasting time coming down here to sort it out. You two, back to the rooms now. And you in the shower, hurry up."

Though the heat of the water did a lot to wash the smell of death from my skin, I didn't want to linger too long. That would only piss off the guard more and maybe bring our little scuffle to the attention of those higher up. So I washed and dried and meekly made my way back to my bed.

"No more," the guard said from the doorway, once I was settled, "or I'll report all of you."

I resisted the impulse to snap that we weren't kiddies— mainly because that impression was far better than the real reasons for the fight.

I waited until the guard had gone, then reached my hand under my wet towel and grabbed the handkerchief. "You dropped this earlier," I said, and tossed the scrap of cloth across to Nerida. "Don't do it again."

"Oh, I won't. You can be sure of that."

Meaning next time she would ensure there were no telltale signs left behind. I blew out a breath and laced my fingers across my belly. After a while, their breathing grew slower—or in Berna's case, noisier—indicating they were slipping into sleep. Whether they actually were, or whether they were foxing, I couldn't say. But I wasn't about to let the desire to sleep overwhelm me, not with Berna's threat hanging over my head.

I flipped off the sheets and headed out the door.

Voices and the growl of machinery rode the night, and lights now lit the far end of the house. Starr wasn't wasting time getting down to repairs, it seemed.

I headed in the opposite direction, getting as far away from the sounds and the smells as I could. But even deep in the trees, where the moonlight failed to pierce the thick canopy of leaves, the dead were with me.

And they wanted their revenge.

Chapter 11

I woke with a start, and to the realization I was not alone. I twisted around sharply. Quinn sat two feet away, his expression thoughtful as he leaned back against the gnarled trunk of an old pine, his arms crossed across his chest and long legs stretched out in front of him. He seemed little more than a shadow of the pine, even though the sun was still too low to cast such things this deep in the trees.

I rubbed my eyes and struggled into a sitting position. "What time is it?"

He glanced down at his watch. "Just after seven."

No wonder I felt like shit. I'd only had five hours' sleep, and after the last few fun-filled days, that just wasn't enough. "Why did you wake me?"

"I didn't. I was merely watching you."

Something had woken me, but I let the matter slip and raised an eyebrow. "I'm not that interesting when I sleep."

"Perhaps not, but you were at least quiet. A rare thing, I'm discovering."

I picked up a twig and flicked it at him. He smiled, and it rose to his eyes, briefly warming the night dark depths. Something deep inside sighed in pleasure. "Did you uncover anything interesting last night while following Moss?"

"Nothing other than the fact that he and Merle do not see eye to eye. You?"

I shrugged and told him about Nerida's mad quest.

"So you've warned her off?"

"Yes." I hesitated, then added, "But there's still a problem."

"What?"

"The dead want revenge." I paused again, mainly because I didn't want to sound like an idiot. But if there was one person who could help me understand what was going on, then surely it was Quinn. He was an empath *and* one of the dead. "I could feel them all around me last night, feel their anger and their need to get back at her."

He raised an eyebrow. "Empathy with the truly dead? An interesting path for a developing talent to take."

"It's not interesting, it's freaky." I drew my knees up and wrapped my arms around them. "How is something like that even possible?"

"Many clairvoyants are able to see, and converse, with shades or spirits."

"But I didn't converse with them or see them. I could just feel them—or rather, their emotions."

"Maybe the rest is yet to come. But you have always had

empathy with the dead—how else would you have been able to sense my emotions so often?"

I wanted to argue that *that* was different, because he had flesh and a heartbeat—however slow it might be—so, technically, he wasn't dead *dead*. But what was the point? I *had* always been able to sense his emotions. And sometimes even Jack's. How else would that have been possible if it wasn't some twisted form of empathy with the dead? And surely it wasn't a huge step from reading the undead to reading the dead.

I rubbed my arms lightly against a sudden chill. Trust me to develop a talent that held no earthly value and was as scary as hell. "Thing is, this empathy is extending. I'm beginning to sense the emotions of some flesh-and-blood people."

"If that's the case, and this is the first sign that the ARC1-23 is having an effect, then you should not be here. You should be back at the Directorate, being tested and watched."

My gaze met his. "I'm not walking away from this mission. I want to be a part of Starr's downfall."

"Why? What is so important about it that you risk your life, or at the very least, your future?"

"Starr kidnapped me, abused me, and most importantly, he murdered a friend. And for all that, he will pay."

"So this Nerida is not the only one on a quest for revenge?"

I smiled grimly. "This question coming from a man who has spent how many years and wasted how many lives seeking his own revenge?"

He smiled his sexy smile, and desire prickled across my skin. The moon heat might be a few weeks off yet, but being in the presence of this vampire always made me feel like the moon was full and ripe. I wanted him, always wanted him, no matter how angry or just plain pissed off with him I might be. And in a totally different way from how I wanted Kellen or even Kade. This was deeper. Way deeper.

How much deeper was something I might never find out, given his problems with the werewolf lifestyle, and my own determination to find my werewolf soul mate.

"I guess I should not throw stones," he agreed.

"No, you should not." I stretched out my legs. "So why are you here? Really?"

"I want you to show me the section of the forest where Moss disappeared. I'll try and find the tunnel entrance, if there is one."

I frowned. "Your infrared can't see past soil, can it?"

"No, but if there is an entrance, there will be other indicators, even if it is something as simple as an area of grass trampled down."

I nodded. "Jack knows you're here. He isn't happy." Which was the understatement of the century. After he'd spent ten minutes telling me off for continuing to ignore direct orders, I'd innocently mentioned Quinn and had learned the hard way my dear brother hadn't gotten around to telling Jack about his presence here. Meaning I'd been on the receiving end of yet another tirade. Was it any wonder I still had a headache?

What I needed was coffee. Buckets of it. And a big, hearty breakfast. Both of which might be difficult to get considering Nerida blew the kitchen apart last night.

"I'm here to help, not hinder, your mission," Quinn

said. "I will not take out Starr until you have all the information you require about his organization and the labs."

"Well, actions speak louder than words, so I'm not believing until I actually start seeing evidence of your restraint." I pushed to my feet. "I'll take you to the place Moss disappeared. They want us to do some fight training this morning, then I have a brunch meeting with Starr."

He fell in step beside me. "Why do you have a meeting with Starr?"

"Because he's fascinated with my unusual beauty." Just saying those words had me grinning. Anyone who knew me would certainly class me as unusual—or, more likely, just plain weird. But men usually only considered me a beauty after the intake of several glasses of booze. Not that I was ugly by any stretch—just an ordinary girl with a good figure and big tits.

Which I supposed was the only thing some guys worried about.

"Well, it was your hair I noticed first." His fingers briefly touched my hair—a featherlight caress that shimmered right down to my toes. "It was so long, and such a glorious color. It's a shame you cut it so short, even if it suits you."

I raised an eyebrow. "I cut it to shoulder length only a few months ago. You said you liked it. Or was that another lie?"

"No lie. But this is even shorter. It's a shame."

Hard to disagree when he was basically echoing my own comments to Liander. "So that comment you made about me not being as flat as most werewolves did not come from observation?"

He smiled. "Okay, so maybe there was just a little observation. But I'm hetero and Starr is not." Despite the amusement touching his lips, concern gleamed in the dark depths of his eyes—which shouldn't have surprised me as much as it did. I knew he cared, but it was often hard to remember when he was continually stabbing away at my heritage. "We are talking about a man who has made a concerted effort to get you into his labs. Is it wise to get so close? I thought that was Rhoan's job?"

"It is, but saying no wasn't an option."

He glanced at me again, and the worry was deeper. My daft hormones did an excited little shuffle. Nothing like a man worrying about my safety to get them zooming along excitedly.

"I have noticed this place is run like a dictatorship."

"You should have seen last night's dinner entertainment. If that didn't turn people off thoughts of rebellion, I don't know what would." I hesitated. "What do you plan to do if you find the tunnel?"

"Explore it, of course."

"It might have infrared sensors."

"It might, it might not." He shrugged.

Meaning, of course, he was well able to take care of any resulting guard dispatch. Given the little I'd seen of his skills, he was probably right. "And if you can't find the tunnel?"

"Then I shall dig myself a nice little ditch, cover myself in soil, and wait out the noon hours."

I raised my eyebrows. "Is that where the legend of vampires and coffins comes from?"

A smile touched his lips. "In itself, no. The world was

not always as densely populated as it is today, and protection in the form of housing was not always easy to find. Soil, on the other hand, is readily available in all lands, at all times."

"Does it have to be a particular depth?"

"No. One or two inches is sufficient. Though it is not unusual for the newly turned to panic and go as deep as they can. And, of course, the tombs and graves of the recently dead are often the easiest place to borrow."

I chuckled softly. "Hence the legend."

"Yes."

The brief spark of amusement in his eyes died a little, replaced by the thoughtfulness I'd seen earlier. But again, whatever his thoughts were, he was keeping them well and truly to himself. Which was a nice change, and yet also a little alarming. I had a feeling those thoughts were about me—us—and part of me itched to ask. But the sane part knew it was better not to. However much this vampire irritated the hell out of me, he was at least still in my life, still by my side. No matter how much I might have told him to leave if he could not accept my nature and beliefs, I didn't actually *want* him to go.

Because he was right. There *was* something good between us, something that was worth taking the time to explore. I was willing, as long as it was an open relationship. Maybe he was beginning to see the benefits of such a deal, as well.

Besides, it wasn't as if we actually knew much of each other beyond the realms of sex. It might actually turn out that we were totally incompatible outside the bedroom. Hell, I hadn't wanted Talon in my life on a regular basis, but we sure as hell had a good time sexually. Of course, he'd turned out to be a sick psycho. Maybe Quinn would, too. Who really knew?

Only time would tell and the reality was, we hadn't had a lot of that so far.

I glanced ahead and saw that we were near the clearing where Moss had done his invisible trick. I stopped in the shadows of some gum trees and waved a hand around. "It happened here, somewhere."

His gaze scanned the area, then came back to mine. "You be careful."

"You, too." I paused, suddenly feeling awkward and having no idea why. "I'll talk to you tonight."

He nodded. But as I turned to retreat, his fingers slipped down my arm and caught my wrist. "Make sure you use full shields," he said softly. "Remember what Misha said about Starr. If I can read your surface thoughts, then it is most likely Starr can. You cannot afford the slightest mistake while in his presence, or the game will be up and we'll all be in danger."

God, didn't he think I knew that already? Stating the obvious would only succeed in making me even more jittery.

He released my hand, his fingers sliding over mine almost sensually. I turned and walked away. But I could feel his gaze, a heat that was centered in the middle of my back before flooding across my skin in waves. The vampire wanted me, and his desire was every bit as powerful, every bit as alluring, as a wolf.

Which he wasn't, so I shouldn't be feeling what I was feeling. Unless I'd somehow become even more attuned to him.

But I resisted the temptation to turn around and ask

him what the hell was going on—or more precisely, what he'd done. I had training and a brunch to attend, and right now, they had to take precedence over emerging metaphysical and sexual connections.

*T*raining for Starr's arena was a whole lot easier than training with my brother. Most of the women who'd been brought in were shifters of some variety, and therefore had strength and speed. While many didn't have any actual fighting skills, it really didn't matter because it was mainly wrestling, and in mud at that.

Skill wasn't a prerequisite. Good balance and intuitiveness was. The trainers matched us according to weight and height, which meant that at least in the initial rounds, I avoided both Berna and Nerida—who still managed to scowl at me down the length of the arena.

We practiced for two hours, and damn if it wasn't fun. In fact, if I'd been training with men rather than women, it could have been erotic. I've never mucked around in mud before, but the sensation of hands and bodies sliding across mud-lathered skin was sensual, to say the least. I made a mental note to try this with a more suitable partner, and kept on fighting and following instructions. Afterward, we were escorted to the showers. The rest of the women were then taken to breakfast, while I was herded from the pack and escorted to the private elevator.

Which was more than enough time to realize my guard definitely didn't believe in regular showers. Needing something to distract my nose from the overwhelming odor of stale, sweaty human, I lowered my shields a little and tried reading him. His thoughts were all over the place—one minute he was thinking about his night with one of the hookers, the next wondering what the powers that be were going to do about breakfast, because he was mighty hungry and hadn't signed on to this crummy outfit to starve. And in between, he admired my tits and wondered if it was the red hair that was turning him off.

Not one of Starr's great thinkers, obviously.

I re-shielded and glanced up at the ceiling. There were definitely monitors up there, and I had no doubt the psi-deadeners were present, too. So how come I was slipping past them?

Granted, it wasn't as if there weren't precedents for such events—Jack had proven it was more than possible a few days ago when he'd stopped Gautier's attack on me. I wouldn't have put my developing talent in the same league as Jack's, let alone Quinn's, but maybe it was. Maybe it wasn't *just* the onset of menstruation affecting my telepathy, but the ARC1-23 drug as well.

So what else was happening inside of me?

Part of me thought it might be better if I *didn't* know. Because in not knowing, I could still believe there was the chance of a normal life—even if that chance was disappearing faster than water down a drain.

Yet I had to acknowledge that ignorance *wasn't* bliss. I *had* to know what was going on, if only so I could plan a new future. To do that, I had to tell Jack everything. He needed to know, because I needed to learn control. I'd been at the Directorate long enough to know that anything else could be dangerous.

The elevator finally arrived and the guard shuffled me inside. I watched the numbers slide by, wondering who would meet me—Moss or Merle.

It turned out to be neither.

As the elevator bumped to a halt and the doors slid open, Starr himself was standing there.

Again the sense of something depraved, something so evil it was beyond contemplation, swamped me. My insides froze in terror, and for several seconds, even breathing had become a luxury I couldn't afford. Because to breathe, I'd have to inhale the scent of him, and even *that* felt like poison.

"Sir," the guard said, as he straightened slightly. "Poppy Burns, as you requested, sir."

"Thank you, Tarrent." Though Starr spoke to the guard, his gaze was on mine. In those bloodshot blue depths, I saw my death. Or at least, the specter of it if I twitched so much as a fingertip the wrong way. "Follow me, my dear."

He turned around and walked across to the other doorway, providing me with the perfect target, the perfect moment. And it was tempting, so very tempting. My fingers twitched, and the urge to grab the guard's gun and shoot the hell out of Starr, to splatter his brains across the walls and bring to an end his bloody reign, was fierce. But the mere fact that he'd offered such a target had warning bells ringing.

Only a man who felt very secure about his safety measures would do such a thing. I flexed my fingers, vaguely hoping it would ease some of the tension running through my limbs, and forced my feet forward, past the guard and into the hall.

Only to discover Moss and Merle waiting in the shadows, both of them armed. I wouldn't have gotten past cocking the weapon, let alone firing a shot. They would have splattered *me* across the walls, not the other way around.

I stopped. The elevator doors closed and darkness settled in. I didn't bother switching to infrared. Moss's and Merle's inherent corruption stung the air, and though their scents paled compared to the man in front of us, the smell of them was still so thick and foul it quickly seemed to clog my throat. I certainly didn't need to see them to know where they were.

The doors to the second elevator swished open. Starr stepped inside and we followed. It wasn't a tight squeeze and yet, as the doors slid closed again, panic surged. Suddenly I felt caged. Trapped.

Sweat began to trickle down my forehead. I licked my lips and tried to get a grip. I'd been in far worse situations—though right now, I was hard-pressed to think of one of them.

I glanced around. Met Merle's gaze, and saw the heat there. Iktar was right—Merle hadn't yet finished with me. I wasn't sure whether to be happy or sad about that, though he was definitely the safer option of the two hetero men. The vibes I was picking up from Moss suggested anger—deep anger—over the events of the previous night.

I swiped at the moisture running down my hairline and silently prayed Starr would either open the second door or get this elevator moving.

He did the former rather than the latter, and as the metal doors swished open, I got my first glimpse of the room beyond. It was like stepping back into time and coming out in the Middle Ages, in one of those vast, lush banquet halls so often seen in movies. A large wooden table, complete with rough-hewn, high-backed wooden chairs, dominated the far end, and behind that, lush wall hangings that depicted images of beauty and brutality. The rest of the concrete walls were brown, painted so that they resembled wood planking. A small arena of sorts lay in the middle of the room, though its base was rushes rather than the sand of the bigger arena upstairs. Scattered cushions and heavily padded benches were strewn haphazardly around the rest of the room. Heavy metal sconces lined the painted walls, these so laden with wax it was easy to believe centuries of candlesticks might have burned there. The candles were the only source of light, and the flickering amber glow added to the brooding, old-style atmosphere.

It should have been inviting, if perhaps a little mysterious, but it was neither. The smell of death rode the air and, as my gaze skirted the room, the faces of those who had died here seemed to step out of the shadows, filling me with their despair, their anger.

I stumbled under the weight of it, and would have fallen if Merle hadn't grabbed my arm. The sick heat of him ran across my skin, overrunning all other sensation. When I looked up, the wraiths had gone. Maybe they were never there. Maybe it was just my imagination, my fear.

Maybe.

I swallowed heavily and wrenched my arm from Merle's grasp. He chuckled, a heavy sound that itched at my skin. "You won't be pulling away like that later. You'll be begging."

"Yeah, that you've somehow learned some technique overnight." The words were out before I could stop them, and Merle's face darkened. Even more so when Moss chuckled softly.

"The wolf has spunk," he said. "Perhaps I might have to steal her back. Sounds as if she'd appreciate a man with a little more style."

"What I have claimed you cannot have," Merle growled. "You had your opportunity. You were too busy looking for new talent in the recruits."

Moss's face went red, and little veins began to stand out in his forehead. "I am not the ass-lover amongst us—"

"No," Starr interrupted calmly, "I am. And if you two can't shut up, kindly remember that I am not overly fussy about my partners being willing and that I am more than ready to try someone I have until now considered off-limits."

As threats went, it was pretty darn efficient. The two men continued to scowl at each other, but otherwise fell silent. But they'd obviously been around Starr a long time, and would have had plenty of firsthand experience about how ugly he could get. And how far he would go.

Starr walked across to the table and took the middle seat. Moss headed left, while Merle motioned me to the right. Lucky me got to sit between death and his right-hand man. Not a place someone with a stomach as fragile as mine was feeling right now should really be.

As I pulled the chair up closer to the table, I looked up at the ceiling then around the walls again. There were no monitors to be seen, but there were guards hiding in the shadows. Surprisingly, they weren't Iktar's kin, but gray things with scaly skin and human extremities. They were armed—candlelight flickered across the barrels of the guns they held inhumanly still.

And they were watching me with that same unnerving stillness. One wrong move, one nod from Starr, and I was one splattered puppy, of that I had no doubt.

Starr clapped his hands, the sudden sound making me jump. Well-built men wearing skimpy thongs and little else appeared, all carrying either wine or food. It was a decadence I would normally have enjoyed, except for the fact Starr was so close. He watched them appreciatively for several seconds, then turned in his seat so he could look at me. And he wasn't looking at me appreciatively—far from it.

A chill ran down my spine. This man suspected I was not who I was pretending to be, and I had no idea why.

"So tell me a little more about yourself."

I shrugged, wishing like hell I had a coffee to hang on to, and yet at the same time, glad I didn't. My hands were trembling so much I probably would have scalded myself. "I'm sure you've read my file."

"I have, but it's all dry details. I'm sure there is more to you than that."

"And I assure you, there's not." I shoved my hands under my knees and let my gaze drift to the nearest waiter. I just couldn't look at Starr for very long without my stomach turning at the vileness of his aura. At the deadness in his eyes. "The life of a thief is not very exciting."

"These people you stole the jewelry off—Jamieson was their name, wasn't it?"

I shrugged again, and did my best to ignore the sick trembling in my limbs. Sitting on my hands helped them, but it didn't do much for the rest of me. "I have no idea. I don't study the people before a job. I just study the house."

"And the jewels? Who was your fence?"

Fucked if I knew. If it had been in the files, then I'd

managed to skip that section of it. I glanced at him briefly. "Who said I've fenced them yet? Maybe they're a little too hot right now."

He grinned. He had an awful lot of teeth, many of them pointy. And not just the canines. "A nice safe answer."

"The truth always is." I thanked a dark-skinned man as he placed a platter of meats and bread in front of me. His gaze met mine, and the warm brown depths were haunted. This man might not be physically dead, but deep down where it really counted, only ice existed. Everything else had been ripped away by the perversity of the man beside me.

I blinked at the sudden insight, and had to clench my hands against the urge to reach out and touch him—reassure him—either physically or psychically. There was nothing I could do for this man, nothing I could do for the others in this room. Nothing other than destroy the foul thing who had ripped away their self-respect. Their humanity.

"But how do I know you are telling the truth?" Starr said.

My nerves were so bad I jumped at the sudden sound of his voice.

"You don't." I reached forward and plucked a slice of beef from the platter. "I don't have the jewels with me, so there is no way I can prove anything right now."

The beef was butter-tender, but it tasted as dry as sawdust. I swallowed with some difficulty, and reached for a glass of wine to wash the taste away.

"How very true. Unless, of course, you have a psychic at your disposal."

He clapped his hands a second time. The elevator doors slid open, revealing Dia and a guard. At least she hadn't lied about that. Which maybe meant she was playing this whole thing *completely* straight. Maybe it was just my suspicious nature suggesting otherwise.

She stopped in front of the table. Her stance was neither compliant nor aggressive, but somewhere between the two. "You called for me?"

She wasn't looking at me, wasn't looking at anyone except Starr. Never turn your back on a tiger snake in mating season, my brother had once warned me. Obviously, someone had told Dia the same thing.

"I want you to read this woman." Starr's hand came down on my forearm. It was only a brief touch, but even so, his flesh burned mine, leaving red marks long after his fingers had gone.

Dia nodded and glanced at me. Despite her stance, her expression was serene, businesslike. "Hold out your hand."

Given I had little other choice, I obeyed. Her cool fingers wrapped around mine, and electricity leapt from her fingers to mine, tingling warmly across my skin. Something flickered in her unseeing eyes, and just for a moment, there was a tightening around her eyes and mouth. What that meant I had no idea, but I sure as hell planned to ask her later.

"I see much anger in this one." She hesitated. "She has already fought with several of the women. She will fight with others before her time here is over. Rebellion is part of her nature."

"A given, seeing she's here as an arena whore," Starr snapped. "Tell me who and what she is."

Tension ran through me. If his instincts were suggesting I was a fake, why wasn't he just getting rid of me? Doing this made no sense. But then, when did psychos ever play by the rules of the sane?

Dia's fingers briefly tightened against mine, as if in reassurance, then she said, "She is a wolf who has been rejected by kin. She has fought to survive, and will continue to fight through the many life changes that are on the horizon. Her path will not be easy."

"The who, Dia. Stop hedging."

Dia hesitated, and for a moment I was so sure she was going to give me up that my heart lodged somewhere in my throat and every muscle twitched with readiness to leap from the chair.

"She is who she says she is," Dia said softly. "A no-good lying thief. Lock up your valuables, Merle. She has already noted the gold watch resting on your side table."

Starr laughed. It was an uncomfortable sound that itched at my ears. "Then the thief has taste problems. That watch is gaudiness at its worse."

"But it would have a good street value." Dia dropped my hand and stepped back. With her touch gone, the tingling sensation of electricity quickly died. I wasn't sure whether to be happy or sorry about that. At least her touch offered warmth in a room that was so, so cold.

She rubbed her forehead wearily and looked at Starr. "Is that all?"

"For now. I will have my reading later. After we go for our little walk."

Though her expression didn't change, a wave of anger and hatred rolled across my skin, drowning my senses for too many seconds. Dia wasn't playing games—not with me, anyway. And she would do anything to get her child free *and* destroy this man.

She nodded and walked back to the door. Once she'd gone, Starr looked my way. "Perhaps we should have some entertainment while we eat?"

Though it was phrased as a question, he didn't wait for an answer, simply clapped his hands again. Talk about taking the role of a king to the extreme. The curtains on the door to our left swept open and two men entered. The first was a black giant, so tall he had to bend almost at the waist to get through the doorway. And he was big width-wise, too, with hands and feet the size of paddles, thighs thick enough to support a jetty, and shoulders that just seemed endless. Unfortunately, the old saying of big hands, big dick didn't apply here. My thumb would have been bigger than his appendage. Maybe that was the reason for all the muscles—maybe he got tired of the jokes.

The second man, though not small, almost seemed dwarfed by comparison. He was lean but muscular, a man who walked light and with understated power, like that of a predator on the hunt. His brown skin glowed like dark honey in the subdued lighting, and his expression was that of a man confident in his own strength, his own power... Shock rolled through me as he drew closer.

This wasn't a stranger. It was my brother.

My stomach sunk to a new low, and fear—sick fear—ran through me. Why was he here? Was it merely a coincidence, or did Starr suspect not only who I was, but who Rhoan was? If so, how? Who was this man in our lives that he suspected us instantly?

And if he *did* suspect us, why the hell was he stringing this out?

Did he want to see how far he could push it before we broke cover?

I tore my gaze away from Rhoan to look at Starr. The hints of self-satisfaction and anticipation in his expression suggested the answer to *that* particular question was yes. He intended to push and push and push until one of us broke and admitted the truth he suspected. Which meant, from here on in, we would be totally supervised.

Or maybe we had *always* been supervised. Maybe that was the only reason Moss had made his appearance in the forest in the first place.

We had to get *out*. Somehow, we had to get out of here. The mission and revenge and Jack's plans could be damned. None of those were worth the weight of Rhoan's death or mine.

My gaze went back to my brother as he and the giant walked closer. Sitting there, doing nothing, holding in my reaction, my dread, was the hardest thing I'd ever done in my life. I'd been trained to fight and defend, not sit around and role-play. And while I could sometimes act with the best of them, this was different. This was our lives. And I was afraid that I would be the first to give something away, that I'd betray Rhoan and get us both killed.

My brother stepped out of the giant's shadow, and his gaze met mine briefly. Though his expression didn't flicker, I felt his unease like it was my own. Rhoan might be mind-blind, and therefore unreadable via psychic means, but that had never stopped me from sensing his presence or knowing what he was feeling. Or him sensing the same in me. We were twins. Our bond went deeper than mere flesh and bone and mind. We were two halves of a whole.

And any man who took me on as a life-mate would

have to accept that my brother would always be an intense part of my life. Though that would only matter if we both survived this hellhole.

The two of them stopped in front of the table, but only the black man bowed. Now that he was closer, I could see the scars littering his arms, chest, and stomach. This man was a veteran of the arena. Which, in turn, meant he was an extremely good fighter.

So was my brother, but this giant had the advantage of reach and sheer damn size. And those would matter, as Rhoan couldn't afford to use his vampire-gifted strengths. He had to play it strictly as a wolf.

I pushed my plate away and leaned back in my seat. If I ate any more I'd lose my stomach. Which might delay things for a minute or two, but not stop. The gleam in Starr's eyes suggested nothing short of *his* death would stop this game unfolding.

And if not for the guns trained on me, and the closeness of Merle, I might have considered that option.

Starr looked at me, eyebrow raised. "Lost your appetite for any reason, my dear?"

"Yeah. I saw your idea of entertainment last night. I'm not up to seeing someone else beaten up and then buttfucked until they're almost dead." I let my gaze roll down the giant's body. "Though one of them doesn't look as if he's got a dick, let alone spines."

The giant snarled, and Starr laughed. "Perhaps I should let him show you just how well a little man can use his weapon."

I met Starr's gaze evenly. "You let him anywhere near me, and I'll kick him in his unseen goolies, bring him back to a manageable height, then take him out."

He raised an eyebrow, his expression mocking. "I know wolves—or even part wolves—are strong, but are you seriously trying to tell me you think you could take the giant out?"

"Have you ever been kicked in the goolies?"

"No, but—"

"Would you like to be? Just to experience how well it can nullify a man?"

He laughed again. The sound sent another round of chills down my spine. "You have attitude. I like that."

So if he was liking it so much, why was he looking at me like a cat who'd just spotted a tasty mouse? And why did all the sickos of this world always have to look at me like that? First Gautier, now Starr. Or was it simply an inherited look? After all, they did share the same gene pool, even if Gautier was conceived in a tube and Starr in the womb.

"Would you like to fight him, then?"

"I may have a big mouth, but I am not a fool." Sarcasm edged my voice. "So no. Especially when he's been warned of my intentions."

"Shame." Starr glanced at the two men. "Proceed."

And just like that, the fight began. The black giant was fast, his huge fists a blur of power that could easily have smashed Rhoan across the room if they'd gotten anywhere near him. Which they didn't. Even relying only on wolf skills, my brother was fast enough to avoid the blows. He wasn't replying with any of his own just yet, merely sitting back, watching the giant and biding his time.

A tingle ran across my skin, and I knew without looking that Starr was watching me again. I forced myself to lean back, to pretend disinterest when all I wanted to do was cheer Rhoan on. I picked up my glass, and slowly sipped at the cool, bitter wine. Or maybe it was sweet, and it was just my taste buds that were off, frozen by the fear that was continuously building deep inside. "If this is your idea of breakfast entertainment, I sure as hell don't want a dinner invitation."

"If I want you here, you will be here." Starr's voice was mild, and yet still managed to be menacing. "Just as if I wanted you to watch that fight, you would."

I looked at him. "Short of hog-tying me and forcing my eyelids open, that's not possible."

"Anything is possible when you put your mind to it, my dear."

Even as he said the words, a scratchy, burning tingle began to buzz the edges of my thoughts and his bloodshot gaze seemed to grow, until it consumed my entire vision.

He was trying to get a mind-lock on me, trying to read me.

I threw as much energy as I could into my mind-shields, and tried to ignore the terror threatening to swamp me. Luckily, he wasn't a vampire, and wouldn't hear the rapid pounding of my pulse. But he—or the man who'd taken over Starr's identity—*was* a wolf. And he would smell my fear, if nothing else.

But maybe that was a good thing. Only a fool *wouldn't* be afraid in this sort of situation, no matter how big a front they were putting on.

The buzzing got stronger, sending tiny reverberations of sick-feeling energy down my spine. Under normal circumstances I wouldn't have worried—I worked with vampires, and knew from experience they couldn't break my barriers. But this situation—and this man—wasn't normal by *any* standards. I had no idea if my shields were strong enough to stand up to such a concerted assault, simply because I'd never really been tested that way. Gautier tried just about every time he saw me, but it was almost a habit these days—something he did more to piss me off. He didn't have the strength of mind to get past my shields and we both knew it.

Starr, however, was an entirely different matter.

The assault continued to grow, until my entire body seemed to hum with the force of his energy. It was a horrible sensation—like having my hand wrapped around an electric fence, only the energy flowing through muscle and nerve was fetid rather than clean. Sweat began to dribble down my hairline, and deep behind my eyes, an ache began.

A grunt broke the tableau, and a second later, the giant crashed into the table, his head hitting the wood with a sharp crack as his flailing arms sent glass and plates flying.

Starr cursed, his chair crashing backward as he jumped up to avoid the red wine, food, and shards of glass. The buzz of energy snapped away, the shock of it making me gasp softly. My gaze met Rhoan's. He raised an eyebrow, and I nodded, just enough to let him know I was okay.

For now, at least.

The giant righted himself, and with a roar, charged back into the fight. Rhoan sidestepped neatly and gave the giant a passing punch for his troubles. That punch sent the giant flailing again. I frowned, hoping like hell my brother didn't use his vampire strength too much.

"For a scrawny piece of wolf, he sure has some power in him," Merle drawled. "There's not many who could throw Middy like that."

"No." Starr wiped spots of red from his shirt, then righted his chair and sat back down. Surprisingly, no one came running to clean up all the mess. Not until Starr clicked his fingers, anyway. As the loinclothed waiters hurried to the table, Starr continued, "Hasn't he had military training, though?"

"Yeah, but I haven't seen many military men move like that wolf moves."

"And you spend a lot of time around wolves, do you?" I asked mildly.

Merle's grin was all anticipation as he briefly dragged his gaze away from the fight. "No, but I'm intending to."

My gaze slipped down his body. The fighting had aroused him—which undoubtedly meant another session of uninspired sex coming up. Oh, joy.

Though I'd take a weekend of uninspired, boring sex over spending five minutes more in Starr's company, any day.

"There are two types of males in the wolf world—those who are alphas—pack leaders or would-be pack leaders—and those who are betas—pack followers. Alphas lead not just because they are fast and strong, but because they are willing to go to extreme lengths to protect pack and kin. I'm betting that wolf there is an alpha."

"But he's not protecting pack here," Starr said.

I glanced at him. His expression might be giving little away, but his suspicion was just about drowning my "other" senses. I forced a smile. "You can protect a pack of one, you know."

"Does that mean you consider yourself an alpha female?"

I raised an eyebrow. "I've never really thought about it, but maybe I am."

"Then perhaps we should let you fight this wolf and see what happens."

I couldn't help the glance I cast Rhoan's way. Nor could I help another surge of worry and fear. Rhoan must have felt it, because he stumbled briefly—for no reason—and barely righted himself to avoid another blow. "He's military. I'm only street trained. I hardly think that's a fair match, do you?"

His grin was another one of those chill-inducing things. "One thing you have to learn, little girl, is that what I want, I get."

Most little dictators thought that—right until the moment death looked them in the eye and ripped out their stinking, rotten hearts. And more and more, I wanted to be there to see that. If not do it. I might not want to kill on a long-term basis, but on a short-term, one-off basis, yeah, I could handle it.

But why did he want to see us fight? What was the point of it, beyond seeing if we were willing to bash the crap out of each other . . . my thoughts stilled.

That was it *exactly*.

It was just another test. Just another way to check his suspicions.

Shit, shit, shit.

He clapped his hands, and the giant stopped instantly. Rhoan was a little slower on the uptake, dropping the suddenly still giant with a kick to the back of the knee. The sound of bone snapping seemed to echo around the room. The giant dropped like a stone and grabbed his leg, and though he made no sound, the look he cast Rhoan's way suggested my brother wouldn't want to go near him any-time soon.

And I very much suspected it wasn't so much that Rhoan hadn't heard the signal, but rather, had wanted to ensure the giant could play no further part in proceedings. For which I was extremely grateful. After my comments about the giant's lack of assets, I'm sure Starr would have allowed him into the fray. And that *wouldn't* have been pleasant in *any* way.

"Change of plans, gentlemen," Starr said. "The lady to my right has mentioned her interest in entering the fray."

"The lady in question said no such thing." Which Starr knew. I was just reiterating it for Rhoan's sake, lest he think me a complete moron.

"A moot point, considering it is what *I* desire. Merle, escort her to the arena, please."

Well, fuck. What the hell was I going to do now? Logically I might be able to hold my own against my brother, but I wasn't playing myself here. And Poppy was a street scrapper who wouldn't last three minutes with a fighter of Rhoan's ilk. I was going to go down, and I was going to get bloody. There was no other choice—for either of us.

And the bleakness in my brother's eyes as his gaze briefly met mine suggested he'd reached the exact same conclusion.

"Now this is going to be fun," Merle said, grabbing my arm and forcing me upright. "Nothing like a bit of blood-shed to get a man going."

I let my gaze drift down the length of him casually. "Looks as if you need it, because there certainly doesn't seem to be much happening there now."

His grip tightened and he all but tugged me off my feet

as he pulled me roughly around the table. "I'll make you eat those words later, little wolf. Be sure of it."

"Can't wait."

I forced a dry note into my voice, and he snarled—a sound that was half human, half cat, and totally unpleasant.

"Good, because you won't be waiting long. And I shall enjoy licking the blood from your skin as I fuck you."

And I'd enjoy raiding his mind and trying to get the information we needed so we could get the hell out of this insane asylum.

He all but threw me into the arena. I stumbled a few paces before catching my balance, then turned to face Rhoan. "Do your worst, wolf."

A slight smile that only I could see touched his lips. "I promise not to hurt your pretty face too much, but I give no such promises to the rest of you."

"Like I can believe any promise made in *this* place." I shifted my feet, trying to acclimatize to the reeds under my feet. It was slipperier than the sand I was used to training on, holding far less grip. I'd have to be careful.

"Five bucks on the bitch," Moss called. "And ownership for the night if she wins."

Which was an incentive to lose if ever I'd heard one.

"Done deal." Merle was standing at the sidelines, his arms crossed and expression avid. "But this blood is mine to lap, I can assure you."

"The winner is mine," Starr said quietly. "I shall find either one entertaining."

If I ever needed another reason to lose, then that was it. Starr's evil was soul-wearying enough now—I couldn't stand it one on one, for hours on end. I'd die—maybe not physically but probably psychically. I wasn't a trained empath and my growing talent was too raw, too untrained, to survive the vile outpourings from Starr's aura for very long.

Not that I wanted my brother to face him, either, but at least he wasn't psychic and he did have the advantage of years of training behind him. At the very least, he'd give away less than I would.

"Let the fight begin."

The words were barely out of Starr's mouth and my brother was attacking, a whir of arms and legs and vicious, deadly blows. I backed away, ducking and weaving and generally avoiding each attack the best I could. The force of each one blew across my skin like a cyclone, sending chills down my spine. And yet, having seen my brother in action before, I knew he was nowhere near fighting speed.

Which was scary, considering how fast he was.

My foot slipped on the reeds, and as I struggled to catch my balance, the air screamed yet another warning. I twisted away from the blow, felt a slither of pain along my side as my muscles protested the sudden movement, then yelped as a blow skimmed past my cheek, drawing blood. Even so, the blow wasn't at full wolf force. Rhoan was holding back, keeping his promise. And that was dangerous.

I dropped and spun, kicking his legs out from underneath him. As his rump hit the floor, amusement briefly lit his eyes, then he was up and at me in one smooth movement. In the following few minutes, he let me know just how much he *had* been holding back.

If I'd been me, not Poppy, I could have let rip and at least held my own. But that wasn't an option here. Poppy was part human, not part vampire, and the time had come to get bloody.

I avoided one more blow, then let his roundhouse kick hit me in the side. The force of the blow hit like a red wave, a shudder of pain that went from my hip to the end of every hair follicle. The sheer power behind it sent me flying across the arena. I stumbled, fighting to keep my balance before going down on all fours. The vibration of Rhoan's approach ran through the reeds. I grabbed a handful before twisting around and lashing out as hard as I could. The straw whipped across his chest, drawing a thin line of blood. He laughed, a cold, harsh sound I'd never heard from him before, then he bent and grabbed a handful of straw himself. I jumped to my feet and backed away. He followed, the thick slithers of golden reeds creating a whooshing sound as he whipped them back and forth.

I ducked several slashing blows, then lunged forward, attempting an inside punch at his solar plexus. It was a stupid move and we both knew it. He dropped the straw as he sidestepped, then grabbed my arm and twisted it. Hard. Bone snapped and a scream ripped up my throat. As the red tide of pain welled, another blow came, not to my body but to my chin, snapping my head back and sending me flying. Stars danced in front of my eyes, and my mind briefly flirted with unconsciousness.

Then my back hit the floor, my head something solid, and the flirtation became cold hard fact.

Chapter 12

It didn't last long enough. Awareness surfaced, drifting in and out, as if my mind was caught in a fragmented dream. My arm felt like fire, and the heat of it mingled with pain that seared deep and hard. Laughter rolled around me, through me, a pain of a different kind but just as sickening. Starr enjoying the moment, enjoying my agony.

The reeds under my back trembled with the force of approaching steps, then hands were on me, moving me. The blackness surged again, and for a while there was nothing but the peace of that void.

When consciousness surfaced again, it came with a feeling of time having passed and a deep sense of familiarity. Of having been here before, in this same situation if not the same place.

My arms were raised above my head, tied at the wrists

with something that was smooth and tight. The pins and needles in my fingers suggested they'd been that way for some time. The fierce fire and pain of the break had gone, meaning somewhere along the line I'd shifted shape and healed my arm, but the memory of it still drifted through my limbs and there was a weakness in my right arm that had nothing to do with the pins and needles. The rest of my body just ached with a tiredness that made no sense. Rhoan hadn't bashed me around that much, nor had we fought very long, so why the bone-deep weariness?

Sweat stung the air, sweat that was both mine and another's, and with it came the heady aroma of sex and lust. My back pressed against something soft, silky, my stomach against flesh as hot as the sun. Hands were on me, caressing me, their touch bruising and familiar. Heat filled me, thrusting hard and fast if not deep, but the crescendo he was reaching certainly wasn't mine.

I cracked open my eyes. It was Merle who rode me, Merle who reached for his orgasm.

Relief swept through me. Merle certainly appeared one of the saner inmates of the asylum, and at least I knew I could touch his thoughts. If I could touch them, I could control them. Maybe not for a hugely long time, but long enough to get the hell out of this place.

Maybe.

But until I knew where we were—what the odds were—I wasn't doing squat.

My gaze drifted beyond him. The sheer blandness of the room was instantly recognizable. We were back in Merle's bedroom—and had been here for some time if the aroma of sex and sweat riding the air was any indication. I drew in a deep, careful breath, testing what other scents lie in the room. There was little beyond the staleness that came with air-conditioning. I couldn't see anyone else, nor could I smell them—though that in itself didn't mean much considering Starr's DNA experiments.

Merle's body began to jerk spasmodically. I closed my eyes, keeping still as he came. He slumped against me for several minutes, his deadweight making breathing difficult, then he slowly climbed off.

I cracked my eyes open again, watching him. And noted the fresh scars down his back and barely healed scratches on his arms and side. It looked as though Merle had been a little too close when I'd changed shape to heal my wounds. Couldn't be sad about that.

And it certainly explained why I was tied up.

"Iktar," he growled. "A drink."

The spirit lizard was there almost instantly, a bottle of soda and a glass in hand. He poured the drink then offered the glass to Merle.

"Sir, Mr. Starr phoned five minutes ago and said that he will be finished by six. He wants you in the toy room at that time."

Merle glanced at his watch—which indeed was gold and gaudy. "Gives me just over an hour to play with the bitch."

It was five already? I'd been with this bastard for nearly six hours? Christ, no wonder I was achy—it wasn't from the fight, it was the pounding I was getting from Merle.

Obviously, Starr's lieutenants had nothing better to do all day than rut like dogs. Though even the worst of us dogs had a hell of a lot more class in the loving stakes than Merle did.

Iktar nodded, but as he turned, his glance fell on me. He *knew* I was awake. That was so evident in the gleam in his eyes, the slight smile touching his thin lips.

Merle came back to the bed as Iktar left. I closed my eyes, but my other senses were on high. Not that they needed to be. Merle was extraordinarily easy to track—all I had to do was listen to the soft sound of his steps and follow his sweaty, in-need-of-a-shower smell.

The bed dipped as he sat on it, then his fingers were on my breasts, plucking and pulling my nipples. It wasn't pleasant to simply lie there and take it, especially when my wolf soul wanted to rise up and rip the bastard's hand off. It was even harder when his fingers moved down, roughly exploring. I'm not sure what he was trying to achieve, but it certainly wasn't any form of foreplay I was familiar with.

After a while, his lust stirred anew and his body shifted over mine. As his cock slid inside, I carefully felt for his mind. His shields were as tight as ever, but as his body began to move, the wall wavered, became less solid. It still felt like I was pushing through thick glue, but either I was stronger than before, or Merle's recent efforts in the loving stakes had left him weaker, because this time I got through quicker.

Once past that barrier, I didn't bother with finesse, simply stormed in and took control. It was a rout in every sense—in a matter of seconds, his body and mind were mine. Now I just had to decide what to do with him.

I ordered him off, then made him lie on the bed as I searched his thoughts for any mention of the labs. But as before, there was little. Either he didn't know, or the knowledge was buried so deep it would take hours and hours to uncover. As I had neither, I called for Iktar.

The spirit lizard appeared instantly, a smile of amusement touching his lips as he walked across to the bed and undid my bindings. "And here he was, only last week, boasting he was strong enough to repel any psychic attack."

"Barring Starr, I'm guessing."

Iktar shrugged eloquently. "That is a given."

I sat up and rubbed my wrists. "Are there cameras in these rooms?"

"Only in the hall."

"No other security device we should be wary about?"

"No. Unless Merle regains enough control to hit the alarm on the panel near the bedside table."

"Good." I rose and headed for the bathroom I'd seen my last time here.

Iktar followed, watching as I soaped up and washed the blood and sweat and fluids from my skin. If he was at all aroused, it wasn't showing. "What is your plan? You cannot hope to hold him forever."

"I know." Even as I rinsed the soap away, I could feel the muted ache behind my eyes beginning to grow. I may have controlled people this completely before, but never one who was psychic. Controlling Merle took a whole lot more power—and strength—than I thought it would. "Who has access to the main security area?"

"Merle, Moss, and those guards who man it. Access is thumbprint- and key-coded and there's armed guards at the entrance and exits."

Joy. "Is there one man or two on each shift?"

"Generally three, but because of the kitchen and the loss they incurred there, they've pared it down to two so they could put a watch on the rebuilding crew until new recruits arrive."

Well, at least Nerida's action had achieved one good thing. Not that it pacified the dead. Their need for revenge still heated the air. I couldn't see them, though, and of that I was glad. Vampires were dead enough for me— I didn't need to cope with the truly dead as well. "You'd better pray that the bomb controls are in central security, because there is no way in hell I am willingly going back into Starr's rooms."

"We had an agreement—"

"Have you ever been to Starr's rooms? Have you any idea of the security he has in there? I wouldn't get two steps in and I'd be dead."

I stepped out of the shower and he handed me a towel. "If you can control Merle, maybe he—"

"Starr is a powerful telepath. He'd sense my leash on Merle the minute I got within range of him."

Iktar was silent. I asked, "What of the labs on the second floor? Would there be a key stored in security?"

He shrugged. "I would guess so."

"Are all calls to there monitored?"

"As far as I know, only outside calls are monitored and recorded."

I threw the towel in the laundry basket and finger-combed my hair. "Is it shadowed enough outside for you to disappear?"

Amusement briefly sparked in his eyes. "There only needs to be the slightest hint of dusk and I can be gone.

The spirit lizards Starr makes do not match our natural skills."

A scary thought. "So would it be possible for you to arrange for the power in this place to be temporarily shut down?"

The amusement deepened. "At what time would you like this possibility to occur?"

I blew out a breath. Merle had a six o'clock appointment, which didn't leave me a whole lot of time to play with. Especially given I had to be back in the arena by seven. "In ten minutes."

I might be able to use Merle to get me in there, but I didn't want any physical record of me actually going near the place. Which meant we had to take the cameras out.

"You realize they have maintenance on standby to cater for such problems. The main power will not be out for more than ten or fifteen minutes."

"Then maybe you need to smash up the power box a bit more, so it takes them longer to find that many replacements." I hesitated. "What about backup systems?"

"They have several emergency generators that will kick in immediately. The main one provides power to the security systems if the main source goes down. There are also smaller units in the labs and security area to provide them with lighting and electrical systems."

"And if we shut down the main backup?"

"Everything will lock down. You would not be able to get in anywhere."

"Ah. No point in doing that, then."

I rubbed my temples wearily then spun and walked back into the bedroom. Merle was still prone, his mind still caught tight. I dove deeper, taking control of his

speech and movement centers, then forced him to reach
for the phone and dial the security center.

"Security. Harris speaking."

Merle's thoughts told me Harris wasn't the main man,
security wise, just one of the plebes who watched the
cameras and monitored phone calls, and maybe that was
just as well. A man who was only there because he had to
be was a far easier target—and one more likely to stray.

"Harris, Merle."

"Evening, Mr. Merle. What can I do for you?"

"I'm sending a woman over to collect a copy of the
day's reports."

"A woman, sir?" It said a lot about Merle and Moss
that only the faintest hint of surprise showed in the
guard's voice.

"Yes, Harris. You got a problem with that?"

"No, sir."

"She'll be there in ten. Make sure the guard on entrance ten know she's coming and lets her in. I don't want
my toy harmed."

"Yes, sir."

Lances of fire were beginning to shoot through the
back of my eyes, and sweat trickled down my spine. I had
to end this quickly, before the totality of control slipped
and he became conscious enough to fight me. I made him
drop the handset, then touched his forehead with my fingertips. Though I had no idea if touching him this way
would help enforce my will, it just seemed the right thing
to do. Besides, Jack had done it the few times he'd sub-
jugated prisoners, so it had to be of some use. "You will
sleep until you are woken. When awake, you will remember nothing more than having sex all afternoon and

ordering Iktar to escort me upstairs at five before falling asleep. Go to sleep now, and sleep the sleep of the well sated."

As the orders slipped into his subconsciousness and became fact, I pulled out of his mind, carefully erasing the traces of my presence and making doubly sure he remembered nothing more than fucking the hell out of me.

As the connection fell away, a shudder ran through me. The pain behind my eyes became so fierce that for several seconds all I could see was shooting stars. I took a deep breath and swept a hand through my damp hair. What I'd really like to do right now was to take a painkiller or two and catch a few hours' sleep. But I'd given myself an hour's window to do some worthwhile investigating and maybe even some rescuing, so I couldn't waste it, no matter how much my head ached.

"Wake him just before six." I rubbed my eyes wearily and pushed to my feet. "Let's get going."

"You know where central security is?"

"Yes."

He raised an eyebrow, but didn't question my knowledge, simply led me out of the rooms to the elevator. When it was moving, I looked at him. "Ten minutes, remember. And if you don't do what I asked, I'll find those detonators and set them off myself."

"I will do as you ask."

"Good." I glanced up, saw we were almost at the ground floor. "What is the toy room you mentioned earlier?"

"A torture room on the first level."

Trust Starr to call a torture room a toy room. "What else is there?"

"An armory. Secure meeting rooms. Stuff like that."

The elevator jerked to a stop and the doors opened. I headed left, but not directly toward the security area. There was ten minutes to kill before the power outage removed the threat of the cameras, so I pushed open the nearest exit door and walked out into the coolness of the gathering evening. The sun had moved behind the mountains and trees, and shadows hunted across the ground. The scent of eucalyptus filled the air, and kookaburras were beginning their evening laugh-fest. I walked across to the nearest gum tree and squatted down on my heels. Awareness tingled across my skin, and I glanced sideways to see a guard appear a few doors down. Meaning my earlier guess that we would be watched from now on had been spot-on.

I casually touched my ear, then plucked a long blade of grass and idly fiddled with it.

"Hey, Jack," I said softly. "Any more news of Nerida and Berna?"

"And good fucking morning to you, too. Or evening, as the damn case is."

"This is the first chance I've had to report, so don't pull the heavy on me."

"It doesn't take much to flick your ear and let me hear what is going on even if you can't speak."

"Which is impossible to do when you're unconscious."

He swore loud enough to make me wince, then added, "You'd better update me."

I did. "You heard from Rhoan at all?"

"He touched the com-link briefly as he was going into the fight, but nothing since then."

"Damn. Hope he's okay."

"He's been in far worse situations. He'll be fine."

"But Starr is suspicious of us both, Jack. He's got a watch on me, even now." I flicked the blade of grass away and glanced sideways at the man in question. He was leaning, cross-armed, against the brick wall, his face raised as if he was studying something in the trees. The mere fact I'd sensed his presence when I hadn't even heard him meant he was something other than human. Which possibly meant it wasn't going to be easy to ditch him, but I had to try before I went anywhere near the security center.

"Then maybe we'd better pull you out."

Pull me, not my brother or Kade. "I'm not going anywhere just yet."

"Riley, if he does suspect, it's far too dangerous for everyone—"

"I have things to do first."

He swore again. "You can't rescue that kid—"

"We made promises to people, Jack. I'm going to try and uphold them before I run. Besides, I'm not going to leave my brother alone in this mess."

"He's got far more experience than you to fall back on."

He hadn't seemed too damn worried about my inexperience when he'd sent me in here. "Experience won't mean squat if he's outnumbered. Which he is."

Jack grunted. "At least tell me what you're planning, then."

I gave him a rough outline. He was silent for a few minutes, then said, "You know, it might be worth destroying the labs *and* security."

"What? Why?"

"Starr may be suspicious of you, but I actually doubt he realizes that you're working for the Directorate. Even if his suspicions are raised over you losing your guard, he won't suspect you being behind the destruction of security and the lab. We both know only someone with vampire speed can manage to get to those two places in a short amount of time."

"Agreed, but I'm still not seeing the point."

"It's a simple subterfuge to deflect his suspicions. Given the kitchen bombing that barely missed taking out Merle, he may suspect the cartels playing friendly are actually attempting a little double-cross."

"Which means I couldn't actually leave, even if I wanted to."

"Yes."

"Then how do I get the baby out?"

"Women," he muttered. "Look, bring the kid to the forest and I'll call in an eagle-shifter to get her out. We'll look after her until Dia is free. Okay?"

I grinned. I'd actually figured I'd have to argue a whole lot longer before Jack gave in. "Okay. And you know this means Dia will be in the Directorate's debt, don't you?"

"Oh, I'm counting on it." His voice was dry. "Just remember, kiddo, that you can't leave live evidence behind."

My grin faded. "I know."

I'd just avoided thinking about it, because it was just another step down that road, another twist in the chain Jack was wrapping around me. One kill, then two, and before I knew it, I'd be killing without thought, without regret. Or so he hoped.

"Good. Contact me when you've finished creating havoc."

"Will do."

I touched my ear to turn off the link, then rose and walked downwind. After a few minutes, the muskiness of something feline and male touched the air. The guard was following, but keeping his distance.

Good.

I walked along the outside of the building until I was at the far end of the house, close to the remains of the kitchen and well away from the security center. Then I stepped into the trees and the deeper shadows lurking within. The minute I found a path, I wrapped those shadows around my body and ran like hell around to the other side of the house. With vampire speed it only took seconds—but that was long enough to have disappeared from the guard's sight. And the whispering wind would already be scattering my scent. All I had to hope now was that he didn't go running back to Starr to report the loss. Though given the fear *that* madman induced, I figured no guard in his right mind would want to do that. But then, nothing was ever certain in this world, and fate seemed to be enjoying crapping all over me of late.

I stopped in the duskiness of several large trees and scanned the outside of the building. Lights shone in several windows, meaning the power was still on. I shifted my weight, suddenly anxious to get things moving. Tension crawled through my limbs, and an odd sense that something was wrong teased my mind. I had no idea what or why. Maybe it was just tension rising from the knowledge of what I was about to do. What I *had* to do, if we were all to keep undercover and keep safe.

I let my gaze rest on the metal doors that were the main entrance to central security. The floor plans indicated heavy fortification within that area, which included the substantial doors and a long corridor to traverse before reaching the control room.

And though it wasn't mentioned on the plan, it made sense that the center would have its own power source if all else went down. But any auxiliary source would take time to get going. I just had to make sure *my* timing was right, or they *would* catch me on camera.

The lights suddenly went out right along the building. I waited, watching for several heartbeats, then, when the lights remained out, silently thanked Iktar and walked out of the trees. The camera above the doorway didn't move, even though I was peripherally in the camera's sensor range.

I rapped on the metal. The sound seemed to echo, but for several seconds, there was no reply.

Then a gruff voice said, "Yes?"

"I've been sent here to collect some reports."

A small hatch in the middle of the door slid aside, and blue eyes stared out at me. "Lady, we just been hit by a power blackout. No one is coming in these doors until we have the generator up and running."

I shrugged casually. "Fine. I'll just tell Mr. Merle you said I couldn't have them."

I turned to go and the guard swore softly. "Fine, fine. Just wait a moment."

The hatch slammed closed, and after several seconds, the door opened enough for the armed guard to step through. He was a big man, all muscle and broad shoulders. I couldn't tell what sort of gun he held, because while I'd been trained to use them, I didn't really like them and, like any sane person, tended to avoid them whenever possible. Hence, I'd skipped all the theory stuff on makes and models.

And really, who fucking cared what brand or type it was when it was aimed at your face? *Any* gun was scary *this* close.

I slowly raised my arms and did my best at looking defenseless. Which wasn't really hard, considering the gun and the fact I was naked. Actually, it was hard to look anything else *but* helpless when sans clothes.

He held the gun steady while he looked quickly around. In reality, I could have taken him out there and then, but that would have given warning to those inside.

When he was sure there was no one hiding in the bushes, he opened the door and motioned me inside. As I moved past him, I noted not only the thin strand of wire around his neck—a sure sign that he was shielded from psychic intrusion—but the knife at his side and the second gun strapped near his shins, barely visible through his tan trousers.

"Stop," he growled, before I'd taken three steps beyond the door.

I did as he bid, lightly drawing in his scent while trying to "feel" him with my other senses. He actually smelled quite nice—a mix of sage and sharp spice. But I wasn't getting anything along the sensory lines, which meant he was human. Anything else I would have recognized.

The door slammed shut and darkness consumed us. Bolts thudded home, then the guard's hand gripped my arm with unerring accuracy. Which suggested he was one of Starr's "enhanced" humans, because there was no way in hell a normal human could see in this darkness. Hell, I could barely see, and I had wolf sight. Switching to vampire infrared solved *that* problem, but he didn't have that option.

Or maybe he did. Who knew what gene pool Starr's people had been paddling in of late?

"Walk," he said, tugging me forward.

"Damn dark in here." I forced a quavering note into my voice. Acting helpless and scared couldn't hurt.

"Don't worry, I'm not going to lead you astray." Amusement touched his voice. "Though I'm telling you, if we weren't in this place, I'd be tempted to let you lead *me* astray."

"And here I was thinking you didn't notice."

"Lady, present *any* man with a naked woman, and they're going to notice, no matter what they're doing."

How very true. Unless, of course, they were as highly trained—or as gay—as my brother. Though Rhoan *did* appreciate a good female form, even if it didn't excite him. Concern flicked through me as I thought of him, and I frowned, wishing once again he was telepathic. I needed to talk to him, needed to know that he was okay, that this vague sense of unease had nothing to do with him.

But that wasn't an option, and there was nothing I could do except concentrate on the here and now. "Well, at least I know I'm not losing my touch."

I bumped against him as I said it, and he chuckled softly. "Stop flirting, ma'am. It's appreciated, but I'm likely to end up with my balls in a sling if I try anything in this place."

"Isn't that a little harsh on you boys in here when everyone else is allowed to sample the goods?"

"Yeah. But we're better paid than them."

"Money isn't everything."

"No, but living long enough to spend it is."

Which he wouldn't, because I couldn't afford to leave witnesses. And that was a damn shame, because he actually seemed like a nice man, even if he was working for a monster. I closed my eyes briefly. I couldn't think like that. I simply couldn't.

I *had* to kill them to throw the heat off me and Rhoan. There was no other choice.

"How are they going to know?" I said.

He glanced at me. My infrared vision made his eyes glow strangely, but even so, amusement was very evident. This man might be attracted, but he wasn't about to be *distracted*. Damn.

"There's another guard in security. He'd tell."

"And here I was thinking grown men were above being tattletales."

"He values his life, just like I do."

"What if he joined in the fun? He could hardly tattle if he's guilty of the same crime."

The amusement got stronger, touching his lips. But for the first time, excitement spun through the air.

"I don't think Mr. Merle would be too pleased if we did his lady."

My snort was derogatory. "I may be his latest fuck, but I'm not his lady."

He grinned. "You sound like a woman not being satisfied."

I arched an eyebrow, and lowered my voice several

notches as I said, "And are you the man who's going to relieve that problem?"

He glanced at the door ahead, then back at me, and cleared his throat. "Probably not."

Well, this was definitely a first. A naked woman throwing herself at a man, and *him* refusing. It looked like I was going to have to use my werewolf aura, because while I could take out one well-trained, well-armed man, I wasn't sure enough of my skills to take out two. Not when I had to beat bullets as well. And given the time restraints, and the fact that even this guard was showing wariness, I just couldn't afford to play around.

We stopped at the door. The guard pressed his thumb into the scanner, keyed in a code—which I noted—then pushed the door open. The room beyond was only semi-dark, lit by a flashlight that sat on the middle desk, its bright light beaming upward and splashing across the ceiling. There was no one else in the room, but as the door clicked shut behind us, the second man came and poked his head through a doorway across the other side of the room.

"Just about to fire up the emergency generator." His gaze ran down my body and a smile tugged his lips. "You're one hell of a messenger, lady."

Though this second man wasn't as big as the first, he also wore a thin strand of wire around his neck. Obviously, in the security heart of his empire, Starr wasn't taking chances with having just the one mode of psychic protection for his men. And personal shield wires like these weren't disrupted by power blackouts. I'd have to get them off to get the information I needed. Luckily, a wolf's aura worked on a base level rather than mental, so the wires weren't going to be a hindrance.

"The papers are on my desk, Joe. I'll just finish cleaning the generator before I start her up. The maintenance boys have been damn slack."

He disappeared again. Joe had barely taken a step when I unleashed my aura, flicking it across him like a live thing, letting the heat of it overwhelm him, until the desire to take what he wanted, what he craved, was all-consuming.

I knew what it felt like. Knew the flame of it, the way it snapped control and made you need as you have never needed, because Misha had once used his aura on me. But at least I'd had the option of negating the power of it with my own aura. I could have controlled just how much it affected me.

This man, enhanced human or not, had no such choice.

His hand shot out and thrust me hard against the wall, his lips crushing mine as he ripped at his clothes with one hand and groped wildly with the other.

I kissed him back, enjoying the taste of him, the feel of him, giving him that much as I slipped my hands up his back and around his neck. My fingers found the wire's connection. The second it was undone, I slid into his mind. When he was mine, I let my aura drop and forced him to stop. He was panting heavily, his mind dazed, confused, but not fighting. He wasn't psychic, so my hold was complete.

But the little lances of fire beginning to shoot into my brain suggested I had better not push this too far or too

long. The recovery from controlling Merle was taking
longer than I'd thought.

I quickly sorted through his thoughts and memories
to find the information I needed. The controls to Iktar's
implanted bombs were indeed here, locked in a cabinet
in the main office—which I hadn't noticed but was apparently to our right. Joe didn't have the code for the cabinet. The other man, Maz, did.

That was all I could get. I made him step back, and
put my hands around his neck. His neck muscles were
tense under my fingertips, the beat of his pulse erratic.
Killing him was just a matter of applying some pressure
to the right spot, feeling his flesh and bone crack and
break under my grip.

My stomach rolled.

I couldn't do it.

I just couldn't.

Jack might want me to be a killer, he might have
trained me to be a killer, but killing so coldly, so matter-
of-factly was a state of mind, a zone you went to. Or so
Rhoan had once said. I didn't have that zone, not yet, and
I'd be damned if I'd step on the path to that dark place
unless I absolutely had to.

But I couldn't leave this guard as he was, memory
intact, either.

Sweat trickled down my cheek as I went back into his
mind and reorganized his memories. Made him remember not me, but a short, blond man with green eyes and a
bulbous nose. I had no idea if such a man actually stayed
here, but at least Starr would waste time looking for or
interrogating him. Better than me or Rhoan. I left him
remembering Merle's order for the papers—a fact Merle

and *his* memories would strenuously deny, therefore heightening the confusion. Then I added a fight and gave him bruises to prove it with a quick one-two punch to the jaw that knocked him out cold and threw him back to the floor.

His body had barely hit when the second man suddenly appeared. I saw the gun in his hand in one of those heart-stopping moments when you just *know* you're not going to get out of the way in time, and flung myself sideways anyway. The retort echoed loudly in the small room and the bullet tore through my arm rather than my heart. Pain bloomed, but I ignored it, unleashing my aura as I hit the floor, striking him with it as hard as I could.

It didn't affect him. He just stood there, gun aimed and expression fierce.

Shock rolled through me. I'd always believed, had always been told, that a werewolf's aura would devour any race. Hell, even the Government believed it, because they'd recently put in place laws that made the use of auras on humans the equivalent of rape. We could use it on each other just fine, just don't touch the precious humans or you'll find yourself thrown in prison.

So why wasn't he affected?

I didn't know, and right now, didn't have the time to wonder. I closed my eyes and forced myself to ignore the beat of pain in my arm, the sweet smell of blood seeping onto the carpet. Let my limbs go lax, as if unconscious.

For several seconds, the man didn't move. His steady breathing stirred the air, as did the scent of him, a weird mix of grease and earthy, heady pine.

I remained as I was, on the carpet and bleeding all over the place, and eventually he cautiously walked

toward me. He toed my leg several times, then carefully
bent to take my pulse. He was too ready for action, the
gun too close to my heart, to react in any way, so I simply
lay there as his fingers pressed into my neck. After several seconds, he grunted and rose. He walked across to
his partner to check him, then walked back around me to
the desk. As he reached for the phone, I kicked his legs
out from underneath him. He was spinning, the gun
swinging my way, even as he hit the floor. I launched forward, grabbed the gun with one hand and elbowed him
hard in the face with the other. Bone and cartilage shattered under the force of the blow, and blood splattered
across my face and arm. He made an odd gargling sound,
as if he suddenly couldn't breathe, but I ignored it and
knocked him unconscious with another punch.

He went limp and tension slithered from me. Instantly, pain bloomed again, becoming a red wave that
left me momentarily gasping. The bullet might have
been an ordinary one rather than silver, but it still fucking hurt. I quickly shifted shape to stop the bleeding
and start the healing. Though the pain muted, it didn't
go away.

But right now, I couldn't afford to waste more time on
another shift. I had to get the controls for Iktar and get
the hell out of here.

I swiped at the sweat on my forehead with my arm,
grabbed the gun, and shoved it on the tabletop. Then I
scrambled back, gripped his belt, and hauled him onto
his side. Blood began to soak into the carpet and his
breathing seemed a little easier. After unclipping the
wire from around his neck, I dove deep into his mind and
grabbed the code for the security cabinet that held the

controllers, then did a quick search for other usable information—which came in the form of the location of the fire exits for the subterranean levels. Surprisingly, this *wasn't* the tunnel Moss had disappeared into, so where the hell did *that* go?

The guard didn't know. Actually, he had no awareness of that particular tunnel.

The sharp spikes beginning to drive into my brain suggested I'd better get on with it before said brain exploded under the pressure. An image that made me smile even as the pain grew and my eyes started to water.

I quickly gave him the same false memories as the first man, then re-clipped the wire around his neck and rose. A quick search in the nearby office uncovered the cabinet. After the code had been entered, the drawers clicked open. Inside was what looked like game controllers, several bunches of keys, and a notebook that just happened to contain all the codes for the various areas. I found a bag and carefully shoved everything inside, then locked up and headed out. I was at the door when I remembered one vital thing—all the locks to security areas were key-*and* thumbprint-coded. I couldn't get out of this room, let alone into the labs or anywhere else, without both.

Fuck.

I glanced at the two men, then the knife the first guard had. There was no choice—and losing a thumb was infinitely better than losing his life.

I carefully lowered my haul then walked over to get the knife. A quick check told me his pulse was a little thready, but otherwise strong. Unconsciousness would hold a little longer. I stole his knife and walked across to the other guard.

The hilt seemed to grow heavier in my sweaty palm, as if the knowledge of what I was about to do weighed down the metal. I touched the second guard's neck lightly, checking his pulse yet again, then took a deep breath to fortify myself and splayed his hand on the floor, thumb well away from the rest of his fingers.

After another breath that didn't do a thing to calm my stomach, I raised the knife and sliced down as hard as I could. There was little resistance. The knife slammed through skin, muscle, and bone as easily as it did the carpet underneath, stopping only when the blade hit the concrete base. The force of the blow echoed up my arm, making my teeth ache. Blood welled from the wound, thick and rich.

My stomach rolled, then rose. Swallowing back bile, I raised his arm so that the flow was lessened, then gingerly picked up the detached digit, wrapped it in some plastic I found on the desk, and headed back to the door. Once through, I ran like hell down the tunnel for the next door. I barely got that one open when my stomach rose again, and this time there was no stopping it.

It wasn't until the very last second that I realized there was someone standing on the other side of that door.

And by then, it was too damn late.

Chapter 13

*V*omiting is never a pleasant experience, but it's even less so when you don't know if the person sidestepping the projectile is friend or foe.

I mean, how can you defend yourself when you're chucking your heart out? It's impossible. Truly impossible.

The only way I knew I was safe was the mere fact that nothing happened in the time I had my head buried in the bushes. It was only when I leaned against the wall to steady myself while I sucked in great gulps of air that I caught the odd scent of earth and air. Iktar. Neither friend nor foe, but somewhere in between.

But he wasn't the only one here. Awareness shimmered across my skin, a warmth that went deeper than mere knowledge of presence, touching me in a way so few did.

Quinn watched and I felt a whole lot safer.

"Here." I dug into the bag and retrieved the notebook, then held out the bag to Iktar. "Your controls and some keys. Knock yourself out."

"Thank you." He accepted the parcel warily, but the glow in his eyes was that of a man who finally saw the ending of a nightmare. "I am in your debt, more than you could ever know."

"No, buddy-boy, you're in the Directorate's debt, and you may live to regret that." Because I had a feeling Jack would like at least one of Iktar's mob on his "new" team—and the old one.

He shrugged. "It cannot be any worse than being held prisoner by a madman, or being killed off one by one in his insane missions."

Except that the Directorate and insane missions often went hand in hand. Hell, why else would Gautier love the job so much?

"The maintenance crews are fixing the circuit breakers as we speak," he continued softly. "You have ten minutes, if that."

"Then I'd better get my butt into gear." I pushed away from the wall and wiped a hand across my mouth. There was nothing I could do about the blinding ache becoming well and truly settled behind my eyes, but the bitter taste in my mouth was at least fixable. All I had to do was find a tap.

"Hope you get your people out safely, Iktar. And be careful with those controls."

His smile held little amusement. "We have someone who can disconnect these. We will be gone before dawn." He held out a hand. "Thank you again."

I clasped his hand and shook it. His fingers were cool against mine, his skin smooth and leathery, like a snake's. Not unpleasant, but not something I wanted to touch on a regular basis.

As he walked away, I glanced at the trees again then went in search of a garden tap. I placed my stolen thumb and notebook out of the water's way, then rinsed out my mouth and washed the blood from my skin.

Though I heard no sound, the caress of warmth told me Quinn was close. He stepped free of shadows and said, "You look a mess."

"You always say the nicest things."

My voice was dry and amusement touched his dark gaze. "Need some help?"

"Yes. I have to rescue a baby and destroy a lab." I scooped up a final mouthful and drank it, then turned off the tap and picked up my stolen goodies. "The fire exits apparently come out in the trees behind the gym."

"Lab? Not the main ones, I suppose?"

"No. How'd your tunnel hunting go?"

"Came to a dead end. Or, more precisely, a metal door." He hesitated. "I waited the day out there, but no one ventured down from either direction."

"Bugger."

His shrug was all elegance. "The bad guys do not always play the game the way we might wish."

"Well, gee, thanks for that news bulletin."

He smiled, and my hormones did their usual little jig. Annoying, but then, a werewolf's hormones didn't usually give a fig about appropriateness or timing. "There were a lot of guards entering the forest when I came out, though."

"And you didn't stay to investigate? Why?"

He glanced at me. "I felt your pain."

"Ah. Thank you."

Which seemed totally inadequate, but what else could I say? Thanks for caring, but you really should have seen what those guards were up to? I wasn't that much of a bitch. Well, technically I *was,* but not in the way humans used the word.

"Can I ask why you're gripping a bloody thumb and notebook?"

"Most secure areas around here are thumb- and number-coded. A thumb is easier to drag around than a guard."

"Hence the vomiting."

"Hence the vomiting," I agreed. And holding it, feeling the coolness beginning to creep into the severed flesh, even through the plastic, had my stomach spasming all over again.

"Would you like me to hold them?"

I didn't even have to think about it, just handed them over. "Let's go, before they get the power back on."

We shadowed and ran around the house to the gym. Every footstep sent lances of fire stabbing deeper into my brain, and I wasn't entirely sure if the moisture running down my cheeks was sweat or tears.

There were guards everywhere, even here, outside the gym. Starr obviously didn't think the power outage was chance, and was guarding assets and exits—even the exits most knew nothing about. We stopped in the midst of the trees, out of the direct line of sight of the guards. We might be shadowed, but there was no point risking that these guards weren't more of Starr's enhanced humans,

complete with vampire DNA that endowed them with a
vampire's infrared. Quinn touched my shoulder to catch
my attention, then pointed to the two guards on the left,
his arm glowing like fire under the infrared. I nodded,
and carefully made my way toward my targets, keeping
downwind and as silent as possible.

I was nearly on them when a twig snapped under my
heel. Both men spun, their guns rising fast. I froze, my
breath catching in my throat. They didn't fire, simply
scanned the darkness, their gaze slipping straight past.
They couldn't see me and didn't have infrared.

Advantage me.

I stepped close—so close that any wolf or shifter would
have smelled my scent—and lashed out with a bare heel,
hitting the first man hard in the crotch. He went down
with a wheeze of pain. The second man swung around,
his expression a mix of surprise and wariness. I dropped
low, sweeping again with my leg, knocking the second
man off his feet. I grabbed the gun off the first man,
flipped it around, and whacked the butt across the second
guard's face. His head snapped back, and he was out of it
before his head hit the ground. The first man quickly followed his partner into oblivion with just a little help from
the gun butt. I took the clips out of the guns and threw
them both deep into the trees, but the guns I left after pat-
ting both men down to ensure they didn't have any more
clips on them.

After rubbing my temples in a vague attempt to ease
the ache, I made my way back to the fire exits. Quinn
soon joined me. The bastard wasn't even breathing heavily. But then, I'd had a few more fights than him over the

last few hours, and had lost my breakfast as well. Was it any wonder I felt weak and shaky?

Though I had a sneaking suspicion the cause for the shakes was more the lurking certainty that something was wrong. That the shit was about to hit, and everything we'd achieved so far was about to go down the toilet.

I took a deep breath to calm down my nerves. I had a job to do, and I'd better start concentrating on that rather than worrying over future problems and uncertainties.

It seemed to take forever to find the hidden exit for sublevels, though I suppose in reality it was only a minute or two. It had been concealed in the remains of a tree that looked to have burned in the bushfires that had raged across these mountains years ago, though the blackened bark was in fact well-concealed concrete rather than once-living wood. Finding the actual entrance was tricky. The tree looked whole, and it was only on close inspection that the outline of a doorway could be seen. The catch was little more than a dent on one edge. On opening that, we discovered another door, this one made of steel and accompanied by the same sort of key-coders that guard the various secure areas in and around the house.

"I'm told the backup generators power these security doors, enabling them all to function normally." And if they didn't, we'd truly be up that well-known creek.

"That makes sense."

He gave me the notebook, and I punched in the code from the book while he carefully pressed the stolen thumb against the print scanner.

The red light above the keypad flicked to green. Quinn grasped the door handle and pulled it open. The air that rushed out was old and stale smelling, suggesting this tunnel hadn't been used in a long, long time. As did the thick dust that sat on the metal stairs leading down into a red-hued darkness.

Though how dust got into a sealed area, I had no idea.

"Emergency lighting is on inside," he commented.

I bent to study the tunnel. The unease was growing, and though I wasn't entirely sure why, part of me wished it would just go away. I didn't need another reason to be afraid right now.

"Do you think they have movement sensors in there?"

"Probably, though I doubt they would be one of the emergency systems running right now. Were the cameras running in security?"

"No."

"I would think the cameras and sensors are supported by the same source, so we are probably safe for the moment."

Given Starr didn't think like normal people, that statement wasn't as logical as it sounded. "We've got to get moving—we've probably only got eight minutes or so before the power is up and running again."

"I'll go first."

I nodded. He climbed down, his steps making little noise but stirring the dust into a sluggish cloud. When he reached the concrete floor, he motioned me to follow then disappeared into the red-shrouded darkness.

"Sensors in the walls and cameras in the ceiling." He pointed them out as I joined him.

"So if we aren't out by the time the power is on, they *will* be all over us like a rash."

"Yes. Let's move."

We ran down the tunnel, our footsteps an echo that rode the air easily. If there were guards ahead, they'd hear us coming.

"I cannot hear the beat of another heart beyond yours," Quinn said.

"There are things in this world that don't have heart-beats."

"Like the chameleons. Like the Fravardin."

"Yeah. But there's no Fravardin here, other than the one helping Dia." Which was strange, really. If Misha had the Fravardin at his beck and call, why wouldn't Starr have gotten his warped little hands on them? Misha had been Starr's creature to order around—up to a point, anyway.

Another metal door loomed into view. We slowed. This one looked bigger, stronger.

"Containment door," Quinn said, running his hand over the metal. "We have them in my labs. They have a high exposure rating and durability."

I got the notebook out and checked the code. "So why have one guarding a fire exit?"

He shrugged. "Why not? If the contamination is truly bad, do you really want those inside getting out?"

"Isn't the whole point of a fire exit being able to escape when something bad happens?"

He pressed the thumb against the door. "By law we have to have them. It doesn't mean they should always be used."

"Glad I don't work in your labs."

He glanced at me, dark eyes suddenly amused. "I'm glad, too. I have a no fraternizing with my employees rule."

"We're not exactly fraternizing now." Not in a physical, one-on-one sense, anyway. Well, except for our brief session in my kitchen, and later in the barn—but *that* hardly counted.

"No." He grasped the lever and hauled the huge door open. Air rushed out, brushing my skin with its musty, ancient scent. "But I intend to remedy that."

I arched an eyebrow at the certainty—even arrogance—in his voice and reached for the psi-link between us. Given we had no idea how close the labs were or how far our voices might carry, it was better not to talk aloud. Especially when we had another option. *And just how do you intend to remedy the situation when you're never around and never in Melbourne?*

He didn't answer—no surprise there—just edged around the corner. *Another corridor and door ahead.*

No guards? Which was a dumb question, really, when he was already walking forward.

Not yet. They might be on the other side of the door, though.

You know, something about the lack of security in this place just doesn't sit right. Surely the first places Starr would send troops to would be his research areas and labs . . .

I broke off suddenly.

What if he *had* sent his troops to his labs and research areas? What if he *was* protecting them?

Maybe the guards Quinn had spotted in the forest were heading in there for *that* very reason—to guard the exit or entrance to the one place Starr had to protect above everything else.

A large leap? Maybe. Except that Iktar had said that when he and his people were transferred, they didn't seem to be out of it for very long. I'd taken that he meant only a few hours, but maybe he really *did* mean minutes.

Maybe the reason it had seemed that way was because the labs that made the creatures just like him were *here,* right under our very feet.

Of course, that would also mean there was an entrance somewhere in these hills large enough to take trucks, and surely the Directorate, with all its scanning equipment and satellites, would have spotted it by now.

Maybe not. Quinn had stopped at the next door.

Why not? An entrance big enough to take trucks needs roads heavy enough to take them. Not an easy thing to conceal in a forest.

It is if it is disguised as something else. Are there any quarries or logging camps nearby, perhaps?

I have no idea.

But Jack will.

Yeah.

I keyed the code into the door then stepped back to give him access to the thumb coder. *The labs being underground would certainly explain why Jack and the Directorate have been unable to discover any suspect buildings with their satellites. But how could Starr do that much excavating without anyone taking note?*

The only thing new about these tunnels are the doors. The concrete surrounding us is old. Decades old.

The cartel has been playing around in the DNA pool for forty years.

This place is older than that. Much older.

The light above the sensors clicked from red to green. Quinn grasped the door handle and hauled it open.

And that's about the time the shit hit the fan.

Air stirred, coming at us with the velocity of a train. For a heartbeat I thought it was merely trapped air rushing out, but then I caught the smell—fetid, unripe flesh.

I reached out telepathically, trying to catch some sense of what was coming at us, but it was a total dead zone. Not dead as in mind-blind, but dead as in nothing there, just empty space. The creature wasn't there in body form, either. Its body heat barely existed, which meant that under infrared the creature was little more than a muted flame of dark, dark red that faded to black toward the extremities.

But dead, dying, or whatever, it was coming at us hard. And it was pretty much a given that it wasn't rushing to give us a great big hug.

Instinct had me throwing myself into Quinn, knocking us both out of the way. Why, I have no idea—he had infrared and would have seen the creatures the same as me. He grunted as his shoulder hit the wall, then his arms went around me as he steadied us both. A dark shape leapt through the doorway, its guttural howl seeming to echo down the tunnel as it skidded to a halt several feet away.

Or maybe it wasn't an echo we heard, because suddenly there was another one skidding to a stop beside the first one, this one slightly smaller.

Fuck, Quinn said. *Chameleons.*

Chameleons were a rare breed of nonhumans who could take on any background, and literally *become* part of that background. Charmingly, they were also flesh eaters. We'd come across a pack of them once before, and in the end, had only survived because Rhoan, Jack, and Kade had raced to the rescue.

There'd be no such rescue this time.

I pushed away from Quinn, ducked the night-dark paw the second creature flung my way, and backpedaled through the door. The room beyond at least felt bigger than the tunnel and would provide more fighting room. Which I needed, even if Quinn didn't.

The ones we met at the breeding center didn't smell this bad. I ducked another blow, then dived in close for a quick one-two punch to the creature's gut. It felt like I was hitting iron. I danced out of the way of the creature's swipe and watched it warily. This one didn't seem as fast as the first, but that didn't mean it was slow. Just that I had more of a chance against it.

No, these ones rot. Quinn was moving so fast he appeared little more than a blurring rush of flame. *It means they are very old.*

As old as these tunnels?

Older.

I ducked another blow but missed the follow-up. It hit with the force of a hammer, flinging me off my feet and deep into the darkness of the room.

I grunted as my back hit the floor beyond, and couldn't stop myself sliding along the slick tiles. Not until I hit something hard and metallic, anyway. Pain slithered up my spine, but the rush of air suggested I had more than a bruise to worry about. I scrambled upright and quickly felt behind me. A table. A *metal* table. No chance of breaking off a leg and using it as a stake, unfortunately. Not that I knew if a stake killed these things, but it would have been worth the try. That table also meant we'd reached the lab areas—but obviously a disused section, because I couldn't imagine anyone willingly working in the presence of cannibals.

The creature lunged at me again. I spun and lashed out with a heel, my kick landing high and hard. It staggered back several steps, but managed to swipe one big paw across my shin. Needle-sharp nails tore into flesh and blood welled, the sweet scent overriding the foulness of the creatures. Even as I cursed, the darkness stirred.

There were more of them hiding here.

Great. Just fucking great.

I caught my balance and backed away again. Away from the creature, away from the stirring shadows. Luckily, the room was rectangular, leaving plenty of retreat room before I got into trouble.

Quinn, there's something else in this room.

I know. He was still near the entrance, but the creature he fought seemed to be slipping into death, the deep red of its life force barely visible, almost entirely swamped by night.

They don't feel as big, but just as nasty.

They are young.

Young?

As in, a nest of young.

Oh shit. No wonder mama and papa were so pissed. They were determined to protect their kits, *not* the labs. *We need to get out of here before those youngsters decide to help out.*

It would be a better idea than fighting them all right now.

I continued to retreat, watching the creature as I groped behind me in an effort to find each table before I ran into it. Though I couldn't see an exit through the blackness, logic said there had to be one. I had an odd feeling that if we got out of the lab, the creatures might leave us alone.

Which, considering these creatures were flesh eaters, didn't exactly make a whole lot of sense. I mean, surely it wasn't an everyday occurrence that dinner walked so willingly into their lair?

My fingers touched the cold surface of another table. As I edged around it, the creature leapt. Once again I spun and kicked, spraying blood through the air in the process. Claws skittered against the tiles, drawing closer. The young were drawn by the scent of blood more than the need to help their parents.

My blow caught the creature in the gut, the force of it reverberating up my leg. It sent the creature crashing into another table and had to have left a huge dent in the surface. It shook its head and rose to its feet, then launched itself through the air again. I quickly side-stepped. The creature tried to twist around, but its claws found no purchase against the tiled surface and it slid right on by. Giving me the chance I needed to look quickly around.

The young were muted flecks of red huddled in the far left corner of the room. Beyond them was what appeared to be a large fissure in the concrete walls. The exit stood to my right and, thankfully, didn't appear print- or key-coded. As the creature picked itself up and twisted around, I ran like hell for the door and hauled it open.

Quinn, I found the exit. Get your butt over here.

He didn't answer, but I'd barely taken a breath when his hand hit my shoulder, sending me flying as he slammed the door shut behind us. There was a thump on the other side, as if a body had hit it. Hard. But the handle didn't slide downward. Maybe creatures who held no real substance couldn't open doors—though they sure as hell could cause real enough damage to flesh.

Claws might be good against flesh, concrete, and rock, but they are of little use against steel. His hand wrapped warmly against my upper arm. *Your leg bleeds profusely.*

It's not deep, and we can't afford any more delays. The words were absent as I climbed to my feet and looked around. We were in a corridor lined with doors. Given there were no aromas other than age riding the air, it was pretty safe to guess they were empty. At the end of a corridor was another containment door, but this wasn't like the others we'd passed so far. It was more the type seen in movies about ships and subs. It had a wheel lock in the center that had to be turned to open or close. As far as I knew, doors like those had been phased out decades ago, which lent weight to Quinn's earlier statement that this area was far older than the cartel's usage of it.

I am a vampire. Though Quinn's mind-voice was soft, it held a note of censure. I blinked, taking a moment to realize he was answering my earlier statement. *I control my base needs, but I am not made of steel, and I cannot forever ignore such a delicious odor.*

Call me a dolt, but I'd actually forgotten the blood would call him. I shifted shape immediately, then motioned him forward. *And here I was thinking you only took blood while making love.*

For blood as sweetly addictive as yours, I would make an exception. His gaze briefly met mine. *I have done so in the past, remember.*

Images of him licking the wound on my wrist came to

mind, and desire skittered across my skin. Who'd have thought the touch of a vampire's tongue on a non-intimate place such as a wrist had the power to make a woman orgasm like that?

Not me. And it was an experience I wouldn't mind repeating—just not here, not now.

No. He grasped the wheel and spun it. There was a soft click and the door opened, smooth as butter. *But later, most certainly.*

You're awfully certain there is going to be a "later."

If there's one thing I know about werewolves, it's that they are easily addicted to good sex. The fact of the matter is, I give good sex.

I gave a mental snort. *And a whole lot of arrogance.*

After over a thousand years of refining my technique, I have a right to the arrogance.

It's just a shame that a thousand years of living didn't also teach you tolerance of other races' beliefs and practices.

Amusement ran through my mind, as warm as a summer breeze and just as enticing. *I left the door wide open for that gibe.*

Yeah, he had. So why was he amused rather than annoyed? That didn't run with what I'd seen of him so far—though, I guess I hadn't seen a whole lot of the real Quinn. Just the "gotta avenge my friend at all costs" Quinn.

And *that* one was hard enough to resist. I'd be putty in his hands if he actually turned on the charm for a change.

Somehow, I'm doubting that.

His voice was wry and I grinned as I edged around the corner. More darkness, corridors, and labs. Only this time, the air was warm, and heavily layered with scents that were either human, organic, or chemical in origin. And accompanying the scents, voices—men and women chatting softly. There appeared to be no concern that the darkness was anything more than a simple blackout, which was good. It meant they wouldn't be as watchful as they should be.

A soft noise caught my attention. I looked at the left-hand corridor, zoning out the drone of conversation and concentrating on the noise coming only from that corridor. Again I heard it, clearer this time—the whimper of a child.

Dia's kid. Had to be.

I padded into the darkness, my bare feet making little noise on the cold white tiles.

How many hearts beat in the lab directly in front?

He paused, then said, *Three, not including the child.*

Can you hold the adults, make them see nothing, while I rescue the kid?

Doing so as I speak. Amusement filled his voice as he added, *Not that I think they'd be taking much notice of anything else but each other at the moment anyway.*

I opened the lab door and saw what he meant. The three adults—two men and one female—had obviously decided to put the darkness to good use, because they had a little ménage à trois happening. The expression on the woman's face said she was enjoying every minute, and why wouldn't she? Having every need attended to so thoroughly by several willing men was bliss—though for me, personally, the whole bum entry thing just didn't work.

I looked past them and saw the small room at the end.

Inside the solitary small crib was a tiny child whose aura was so bright it forced me to blink.

Hurry, Riley. Our time is almost up.

I hurried. But only to the doorway. Starr was sick enough to set up some sort of trap to protect his hostage on the off chance that the power went off.

I couldn't see anything out of place. I stuck an arm through the doorway, and nothing happened. No alarms, no bombs, no traps. I walked over to the cot.

The child inside was the image of her mother—white on white—except for her eyes. They were the most amazing shade of violet I'd ever seen. And not only that, the kid seemed *aware*. Like she knew why I was there, and what I intended.

There were no wires attached to the little girl, but given Dia said her daughter had been booby-trapped, I wasn't about to pick her up until I was very sure it was safe.

I gently felt her limbs and little body, trying to see if there was anything implanted, then did the same to the area surrounding the cot. It wasn't until I looked underneath that I saw the sensors.

I looked in Quinn's direction. He was looking at me rather than the free floor show, which was a little surprising given his earlier flirtation with voyeurism.

It looks like the cot is rigged with explosives or something. Can you search their minds and find out where the kill switch is?

There had to be one, simply because Dia was allowed to cuddle her child once a week.

Light switch near the door is the trip. He paused. *Lucky*

*you didn't just lift her up—it's powered by the backup gen,
same as the security doors.*

It figured. Once I'd flicked the switch, I wrapped the
child in her blanket and lifted her up. She didn't say anything, didn't do anything, not even wriggle or whimper
at being picked up by a sweaty, bloody stranger. She just
looked at me with those amazing eyes of hers.

Seeing too much, as her mother felt too much.

A shiver ran through me. Maybe Starr wasn't just
keeping this child for ransom reasons. Maybe he also
wanted to know what was going on inside her head.
Because something definitely was.

Jack wants me to blow this lab if possible.

*I've instructed one of the lovers to reset the switch as we
leave,* Quinn said. *The cot will blow instantly, and it'll give
us cover and time to escape.*

And Starr might just think someone got careless.

Perhaps.

Quinn sounded doubtful, and I can't say I blamed
him. I cradled the little girl close and walked back to
Quinn. The threesome on the floor were reaching the
heights, their moans becoming louder and louder.

People come to investigate the noise. Shadow the child.
He turned and led the way back out.

I drew the darkness over the child's body and followed
Quinn out the door. Several people had gathered at the
end of the corridor, sniggering and talking. Even as we
passed them, they began to creep forward. At least with
their attention on the threesome doing the horizontal
tango, they were less inclined to notice us. Not that
Quinn would have allowed them to, anyway.

A point he proceeded to prove by spinning open the

old door and ushering me through. Not one of those in the hall turned to look, even though some were very close. When the door had closed again, I asked, *How are we going to get back through the chameleons?*

We run like hell.

No, really.

Really.

Fuck. Chameleons were fast. I knew that, he knew that. Outrunning them hadn't been an option the first time I'd crossed paths with these creatures, and I doubted it would be now.

As we reached the door, an explosion shook the air and the walls. Dust rained down from the ceiling, and alarms began to sound. Quinn ignored it all and gripped the door handle, his fingers a flame against the cool metal. *Ready?*

No. I cradled the baby a little closer, shielding her as much as possible, then reluctantly nodded.

Quinn thrust the door open, and I ran through. The darkness howled, a sound of anger that seemed to echo off the very walls. Air stirred, a whirlwind of hate that seemed to be aimed at me more than Quinn. I didn't look back, didn't look sideways, just concentrated on getting to the door and the tunnel beyond it.

Something brushed past my hair and crashed into the wall near the door as I ran through. Bones snapped, a creature howled. Quinn, cleaning up behind me, ensuring safe passage. I fled into the tunnel, my footsteps slapping against the cold stone.

Behind me, a creature roared, the reverberations echoing through the red-tinged darkness. Though I heard no sound, Quinn grabbed my arm, pushing me forward faster. It felt like I was being run off my feet and yet didn't seem anywhere near fast enough.

Wasn't fast enough.

Even as the ladder came into sight, there was an odd click and suddenly cameras were moving, tracking us.

A heartbeat later another alarm sounded, closer and harsher than the other, a strident sound that was deafening in the tunnel confines.

The child didn't make a sound. Didn't move. She breathed—I could feel it, see the bright heat of her body—but her stillness was eerie. Hell, *I* jumped when that alarm started, but not the kid. It was almost as if she understood that she couldn't cry, that to do so would put us all in even greater danger.

Of course, she could also be doped out of her tiny mind, but somehow, that just didn't ring true.

Maybe it was me who was out of my tiny mind.

As we neared the ladder, Quinn touched my shoulder. I slowed, watching as he scrambled up. From behind came the skitter of claws on stone. He hadn't locked the security door and I cursed him—until I realized he'd given us cover. Starr just might think it was the creatures who had tripped the alarm.

I reached for the rungs and began to climb. It didn't matter if it was clear or not up top—I'd rather face six men with guns than two extremely pissed chameleons.

No matter how awkward it might have been to climb a ladder while holding a kid, let me tell you that no ladder had ever been climbed quite so fast. Quinn grabbed my hand and helped me over the final section, then slammed the door shut on my heels and closed the cover.

I leapt over the bodies of two security guards who'd obviously been patrolling nearby, and ran like hell into the thick darkness of the forest.

The thump of many footsteps against concrete suggested security were answering the alarm. I hoped my brother wasn't amongst them or, at least, wasn't the first in line to open that door.

Unease rolled through me again, and this time, I knew for sure it centered on Rhoan. I just wasn't entirely sure why. Was it simply sibling concern? Or the growing certainty that something had gone seriously wrong for him? Maybe the next thing I needed to do once I'd delivered Dia's child to safety was hunt him out—if only to see him and ensure he *was* okay.

Because the last time I'd felt anything like this, he'd been kidnapped and milked for his seed.

And then something else hit me—the realization that Starr was likely to check the whereabouts of all his people. Including the whores and us fighters. I stopped abruptly.

"What's wrong?" Quinn's voice was even, showing no hint of breathlessness despite all we'd been through. Annoying, to say the least.

"I need to get back to my room, which means I need you to do me a favor." I swiped at the sweat trickling down the side of my face. "Will you take the child to the forest and wait for the shifter to come in and collect her?"

He frowned, and gave the silent little girl a dark look. "I am not overly fond of children."

"I'm not asking you to be fond of her. I'm just asking if you'd take her to safety."

He didn't answer immediately, so I offered up the

child. Somewhat reluctantly, he took her. "When and where?"

Rather than respond, I flicked the com-link and said, "Jack?"

"Regular reports, Riley. That was in the very first lesson on proper guardian behavior."

"I think that was the one I slept through."

He swore. "Damnit, just report."

I smiled. It might not be wise to bait my boss, but damn if it didn't feel good when he bit. "We've got the kid and blown the lab, but the shit has temporarily hit the fan. Quinn's going to bring the child to the meet now. I've got to get back and act like nothing has happened."

"Everyone's cover still intact?"

"That very much depends whether the cameras in the tunnels had infrared or not." I hesitated. "Listen, those underground levels are not new. Quinn reckons they're far older than the cartel itself. You don't think this place is situated on an old military bunker, do you?"

"Maybe one named Libraska, you mean?"

"Well, it does make sense for Starr to have his most valuable asset close to hand." And it would also explain the existence of the elevator entrance to his rooms—the one no one seemed to know about.

"We've no records of *any* installation, military or not, being built in this area, but I'll get Alex to check with her Government source. Hopefully, we'll have an answer soon as to what Starr is sitting on."

Alex was Alex Hunter, the woman responsible for the birth of the Directorate, and who'd been in charge of it since its inception. Not only was she a very old vampire—far older than even Quinn—but she was also Jack's sister. Talk about job security.

Though how Jack could be several hundred years younger than Quinn, and yet still be the sibling of someone several hundred years older, was a point Jack and said sister had so far been unwilling to explain. But I very much intended to get an answer, even if I had to nag Jack to death.

"Where do you want Quinn to meet your removalist?"

"There's an old pine leaning over the fence near the south corner. We'll have people there in five." He hesitated. "Be careful. And keep in contact, Riley. I mean it."

I'm sure he meant it the first time he said it, too. It still didn't mean I'd remember. I flicked off the com-link and glanced at Quinn. "You'd better get moving."

He nodded and shifted his grip on the child, then wrapped his free hand around the back of my neck and pulled me close. His lips, when they met mine, were warm and demanding, the kiss itself unlike any other kiss from any other man. It was both a promise of intent and a declaration of feeling, and so damn right—so damn *hot*—it had me melting.

A sigh escaped when his lips left mine. He chuckled softly. "Keep that thought for when all this is over."

I opened my eyes and stared into the obsidian depths of his for several heartbeats. "Only if you accept what I am, Quinn. It wouldn't be fair to either of us, otherwise."

His smile was tinged with bitterness, though that bitterness didn't seem aimed at me but rather himself. "It has occurred to me that to win the race, I must first be in the race. I may not like a werewolf's propensity for many mates, but if sharing means I get the chance to prove that we are meant to be, then I have little other choice but to accept it."

My hormones did a happy little jig. "Meaning no more demands that I see you, and you alone? No more gibes at the werewolf culture?"

"Yes to the first, and I will try to the second."

Well, that was better than nothing. I leaned forward and kissed him gently. "Thank you."

"Even the very old can try to change if we see something worth changing for." He briefly touched my cheek with his fingertips, then stepped back. "Be very careful in that house."

I nodded. He turned and disappeared into the night, though I watched the flame of his body heat until the trees took it from sight. After which, I turned and headed back to my room.

Only Berna was there when I entered, but she wasn't asleep. Far from it. Her expression was dark, angry, like she was ready to hit someone. And her eyes, when her gaze met mine, suggested that someone was me.

I stopped cold, wondering what the hell I'd done. Other than whip their asses earlier, that is.

But before I could ask, pain hit. Deep, deep pain that struck like a hammer, smashing through my body, driving me to my knees and snatching the air from my lungs.

It wasn't my pain.

It was Rhoan's.

Chapter 14

I'd never felt anything like it before. The pain was real, and yet it wasn't. It washed fire across every nerve ending, but the agony of it didn't linger for more than a heartbeat or two. Even so, my limbs trembled with sudden weakness. It was almost as if my strength was being sucked away by the pain.

Or maybe it wasn't the pain. Maybe it was Rhoan, calling on my strength because his own was failing. It wasn't something we'd ever figured possible, because we couldn't share thoughts and, up until now, had never shared the pain of hurts. Though we certainly knew when the other was either emotionally or physically wounded, and we'd always been able to find each other—an ability that had saved us both over the last few months.

If I was feeling *this* from Rhoan now, he was in trouble. Life-or-death–type trouble.

Panic hit like a club, sucking away my breath.

I didn't know what was happening to him, but I sure as hell intended to find out. I took a deep breath and staggered to my feet. Only to have my neck caught in a vise-like grip and my back shoved violently against the wall.

"You betrayed us, didn't you?" Berna's face was inches from mine, her expression contorted with the rage that trembled through her entire body. "We trusted you not to say anything, but you did."

If she wanted a reply, she wasn't going to get it. Not when her grip was so damn tight breathing had become a sudden luxury. I reached up, grabbed her hand, and pried her fingers away from my neck before thrusting her back and away.

Surprise flickered through her eyes. Despite the fact I'd beaten them both, Berna still had no idea as to my true strength.

"What the fuck are you talking about?" I rubbed my neck and fought the urge to run, to find and rescue my brother. Something else had obviously gone wrong—something I needed to know.

"Nerida tried to kill Merle. Only he was ready for it. Waiting for it. That could only have happened if he'd been warned."

And the fact that the kitchen had been bombed then the entire power grid had gone down had absolutely nothing to do with his readiness. These two might have been good rangers, but they couldn't have been leaders. They weren't forward thinkers.

I shook my head in disgust. "Let me guess. You were treating Merle as an ordinary target, weren't you?"

"That's because he *is* a normal target, even if he is a

half-breed." She took a step forward, her huge paws clenched and ready for action.

I held up a finger in warning. "Don't even think about it, Berna, because I'll break your fucking neck. Then who will be left to rescue that stupid fox bitch?"

"In an even fight I can take you, wolf."

I snorted softly. "You have no chance, Berna, just as Nerida had no chance."

"A fox-shifter will always beat a half-breed who has not been warned. It is the way of the world. Full bloods are stronger, faster—especially when the half-breed is part human."

"That might be true if we were actually dealing with a normal half-breed. But in the case of Moss and Merle, we're not. They're genetically engineered humans who have been implanted with the DNA of several races. They aren't normal in *any* sense of the word."

She blinked. "What?"

"I warned you there was more to this. Starr is not only the leader of one of the nastiest cartels in Melbourne, he's also the head of a lab that has been playing in the DNA gene pool for several generations." Her eyes widened as the implications of my words hit her. "Did you honestly think those winged things were a product of nature? Did you really think the zoo was nothing more than a collection of misfits?"

"Well, I've seen stranger things—" She stopped. "Why should I trust anything you say?"

"Because as a former ranger, you were trained by the military to see beyond the surface. You must know things are not what they seem in this place." I shifted my stance from one foot to the other. I needed to get out there, to hunt down my brother and beat the crap out of whoever it was causing him pain. "I don't really care if you believe me or not. But I promise you, if people I care about die because of your interference, you *will* pay."

"You can't know of our military service. Our files are sealed against public perusal."

"Who said I was public?"

She blew out a breath. "We've walked into the middle of a major operation, haven't we?"

"Yeah, and might well have blown it."

"Fuck." She thrust a hand through her short hair. "What can I do?"

I held up my hand rather than answering. From down the hall came the rough voices—the guards were doing a bed check. I grabbed a blanket and wrapped it around myself to hide my bloody state. We waited in silence until our turn came, answering accordingly when our names were called out. They didn't ask about Nerida, so they obviously knew her fate.

When the guards moved away, I said, "Help me rescue my partner, then together we'll see what we can do about yours. But if we do get her free, I want you both out of here."

"Your partner has been caught?"

Caught, tortured, and on the move. But not under his own steam. "Yes. I need to get him out of here."

"How? They have guards on all exits at the moment. No one is getting in or out."

"Let's concentrate on one problem at a time."

I threw the blanket to one side, then turned on my heel and walked out. Berna followed, her larger feet slapping

heavily against the floor, drowning out any noise my foot-
falls were making. I pushed open the exit door and
stepped into the cool night air. The guard looked at us but
didn't say anything. He was human. He wouldn't have
seen or smelled the blood and sweat and fear riding my
body.

"Where'd they take Nerida?" I asked, as we moved
away.

"To the pens, wherever they are. She's slotted in as the
after-dinner entertainment."

"Against those winged things?" I followed the path
around to the left, following instinct and that tenuous,
fragile thread that linked Rhoan and me.

"Yeah. If she happens to survive that, she wins the right
to fight Merle." Berna's gaze was grim when it met mine.
"We both know that isn't going to happen, but Nerida
can't or won't see reason. Revenge has blinded her."

I opened my mouth to say it was stupid, but the truth
was, I *could* understand it. If something happened to
Rhoan, hell itself wouldn't stand a chance against my desire to get even. To make someone pay.

"Which means she won't want to leave, even if we do
rescue her."

"She'll leave. I promise you that."

It was a promise she had better keep, or Jack would
have both their heads. He didn't have much patience for
those who got in the way of Directorate operations.

We padded along the path, heading toward the front of
the house. Guards watched our progress, and, after a few
seconds, I felt the return of my watcher. This one was a
wolf, meaning he would track me better than the first one.

How the hell was I going to rescue Rhoan when I had a tail that would report all suspicious actions back to Starr?

Unless, of course, a little distraction was provided.

I stopped near the end of the house. An old green truck with canvas sides was being loaded near one of the machinery sheds. Though I couldn't see my brother, the link between us said he was there, already inside. As we watched, the last few boxes were loaded, then the back of the truck lifted and locked into place. No one got in the back. Two men got into the cab. Time to get moving.

"We have a tail," I said, as the driver started the truck's engine.

"Where?" Berna's gaze was also on the vehicle; her voice was as soft as mine.

"He's stopped near the last door."

"That's a hundred yards back." Her gaze met mine, speculation rife in her brown eyes. "A wolf shouldn't be able to scent someone that far away when the wind is blowing against them."

I wasn't actually relying on olfactory senses, but she didn't need to know that. "A moot point when *this* wolf can."

She grunted. "You want me to distract him?"

"Yes, please."

"Consider it done."

She spun and walked back. I waited until the truck lurched into action, then slipped around the corner, wrapped the night around my body, and ran like hell for the back of the truck.

It was faster than I thought it would be, forcing me to leap in a desperate effort to get on board before it got away. I hit the backboard hard enough to rattle it, hooked an arm over the edge of the tray, and hung on for grim death as the road swept by inches from my toes. Not a position I was overly enamored of, so once I'd caught my breath, I twisted, hooked a leg over the tray, and dragged myself inside. My hip caught the end of one box as I dropped down, and I bit back a yelp, barely daring to even breathe as I lay there, listening. The rumble of the engine flowed across the air, joined by the hum of the tires on the road surface. The aroma of spice and leather hung in the air, but the relief that shivered through me was tempered by the fact that Rhoan's scent was heavily interlaced with the sweet, metallic odor of blood. They'd really done a number on him.

Anger rose, anger that was all wolf, all territorial need to protect the pack. Rhoan *was* my pack, all I had, and whoever had done this to him would pay.

Oh yeah, I could more than understand Nerida's reasoning.

Underneath Rhoan's scent came the twin scents of pine and ocean. Though I could smell them, I couldn't "feel" them, meaning they were human rather than nonhuman. With the way the old truck was rattling, they wouldn't hear me creep forward. Human hearing wasn't that astute.

But I kept the shadows wrapped around my body as I edged around the first box. They might not hear me, but it would only take a glance in the rearview mirror to see me. I was naked, after all, and a naked female of *any* description tended to catch a man's attention.

Rhoan was about halfway down the truck, thrown on the floor like so much rubbish, his face as beaten and raw as his body. In fact, the only thing that *wasn't* beaten and bloody was his genitals. It actually looked as if someone had gone out of their way to avoid that area, which was extremely odd.

I dropped down beside him and gently touched his forehead, brushing the sweaty, blood-plastered strands of hair from his face. He stirred, and relief filled me. He wasn't as out of it as I feared, even if he didn't immediately open his eyes.

I lightly pressed the com-link in his ear, then leaned close and murmured, "Jack, track this signal. When we are well clear of the gates, stop the truck. Bring medical aid for Rhoan."

I couldn't hear his answer and didn't dare use my own com-link. I'd have to speak a little louder and it just wasn't worth the risk.

After a quick glance at the two humans in the front, I stretched out beside Rhoan and gently cradled him. He stirred again, then opened his eyes.

The brown was unsettling, alien. Not so his smile. "I knew you'd find me."

His voice was the barest of whispers, scratchy with pain, but to my ears it was the sweetest sound ever.

"Isn't that what little sisters are for?" I gently pressed my hand against his bruised cheek as his eyes drifted close again. "Rhoan, who did this to you?"

"Starr. Moss." He shuddered and the pain fury had been keeping at bay rushed through me like a tide. It wasn't just the pain of his injuries. It was the deadly fire of silver.

I licked my lips, trying not to panic. There was no silver knife of any kind stuck in his flesh, nor could I see a bullet wound, but that didn't mean anything. It only took a sliver embedded under the skin to kill a wolf.

"Rhoan, where is it?"

"Butt." He made a harsh sound that could have been a laugh. "Idea of a joke."

Then it was one I didn't immediately understand. I shifted, and ran my hand across his buttocks. Having been shot by silver myself, my flesh had become extremely sensitive to its presence. If it was under his skin, I'd feel it.

My fingers began to burn in the center of his left cheek. The sliver was about two inches long and needle fine. It was also too deep to drag out with my fingers.

"Take...out," he gasped. "Things going numb."

It was *then* that I understood the so-called joke. Silver killed werewolves by destroying muscle and nerves and sensation, until the body was locked in pain and the ability to move and breathe was gone, and all that was left was a lingering, horrible death by asphyxiation.

I'd been shot in the arm, and the numbness had quickly traveled down to my fingers and up my neck. The bullet had been removed before any long-term damage had been done, but even so, I'd risked the use of my arm.

Rhoan was shot in the butt, so his loss of sensation was centered around that area—the butt and genitals. He risked the loss of something far more important to a wolf than a mere arm.

It was sick, and the bastards were going to die for it.

I touched Rhoan's cheek, drawing his attention again. "I'm going to have to shift and bite."

He nodded weakly. "Do it."

I took another glance at the men up front. They still weren't paying us any attention, so I called to the wolf within. The power swept over me, through me, until I was once again wolf rather than human. I licked my brother's face—a useless gesture that undoubtedly comforted me more than him—then slid my gaze down his body. In wolf form, the heat of the silver was more intense. The glow of it seemed to leak from his skin, a beacon that pointed to the precise spot.

I didn't let myself think about what I was about to do, just bared my teeth and slashed down into his skin. The taste of flesh and blood filled my mouth, followed swiftly by the fire of silver. I closed my teeth around it and ripped. Felt Rhoan jerk, and his body stiffen. He hissed, vocalizing the pain that reverberated through every corner of my mind.

I turned away and spat out his flesh. But his taste filled my mouth and suddenly I was gagging uncontrollably.

"What the hell was that?" one of the men in the front said.

Somehow, Rhoan found the strength to wrap a hand around my nose and hold my mouth closed. Bile rose up my throat, but I managed to swallow it down. My body trembled almost as much as Rhoan's, and I wasn't entirely sure his grip on my muzzle was going to stop the tide for long.

"What was what?" The second voice was gruff, bored.

"That sound. Like someone coughing and throwing up."

"Probably our passenger. Don't worry, with all the broken bones he's got, he ain't going nowhere."

"Nowhere but the farming labs."

They both laughed. Relief slithered through me. Rhoan released my nose, and as I glanced down, the golden haze of changing began to slide over his broken body, snatching his pain from my mind even as it began healing his wounds. He didn't stay long in his wolf form—it was hard to do so when the pain and the wounds are so great—but at least in shifting back, the healing was helped along that little bit further. I shifted shape myself, then wrapped my fingers around his and waited.

I had no idea how long it was before the Directorate arrived. It was probably only a few minutes later, but it seemed like forever before the truck rattled to a stop. There was no fighting, no nothing, just a stationary truck and two silent guards.

Then the backboard opened and Jack was there. "About bloody time," I muttered.

"We couldn't stop the truck any closer to the gates. They would have seen us." He climbed into the truck and hunkered down beside me. "How is he?"

"He'll live." It was Moss and Starr who wouldn't.

"Good." Jack's gaze went to Rhoan. "Why did this happen?"

"I don't know." He coughed, a hacking sound that tore at me. "But he knew who I was."

"How?"

He shrugged, and gave a bitter laugh. "He gave me one small comfort, though. He said I was a good fuck and he'd miss me. At least I haven't lost my touch in that area."

Something inside froze.

I'd heard those words before.

In the Blue Moon, when Rhoan had been snatched for milking and I'd only just started looking for him. I'd gone there to find either of Rhoan's mates in the vague hope they might know something. Liander hadn't been there, but Davern was. He'd been sitting at a table, getting pissed because he'd broken up with some guy. When I'd asked him why it even mattered, he'd repeated that same phrase. That *exact* same phrase.

That was why Starr's bloodshot eyes had seemed so familiar. Davern's eyes that night were the image of Starr's.

Davern *was* Starr.

But if that were true, why had Misha said that the ringleader of this whole shebang didn't know who I was? Had he been primed to say that at a certain question? Misha might have skirmished from the edges and found ways to avoid some of Starr's edicts, but in the end, he couldn't totally escape the control Starr had on him. And that control had killed him.

"Riley?"

I blinked at the sharpness in my brother's voice, and glanced down. "It's Davern. Starr is Davern."

"What?" Jack and Rhoan said as one.

"Where the hell did that conclusion come from?" Jack added.

I shrugged. In truth, I probably couldn't justify the statement with facts, but intuition had gotten me out of more trouble than it had landed me in, and I wasn't about to start questioning it now. "When I met Starr for the first time, he felt familiar. There was something about his eyes I'd seen before—and now I remember where. In the Blue Moon, when I was talking to Davern and trying to find Rhoan. I thought at the time his eyes were red because of the booze, but, despite appearances, he didn't really act drunk. He said he'd just broken up with another mate and used that exact term."

"Coincidence."

I glanced at Jack. "Is it? Misha told us several times that the man behind all this was someone in my life. We'd always presumed that meant a lover of mine, but Rhoan's mates are in my life as much as his."

"He's from the Helki pack," Rhoan mused. "They're able to take on multiple human forms, so in theory, it could be possible."

"But it makes no sense that Davern would do that. He had Misha and Talon watching Riley, and Gautier at the Directorate. He didn't need to put anyone on you, much less become your lover himself."

"Maybe Gautier reported that Rhoan needed to be watched, and Davern either had no one else he trusted, or no one who was homosexual." I looked at my brother. "Did he ask you any questions while you were being tortured?"

"No."

"And why not? Because he didn't need to. He might have been suspicious about your identity before our fight, but when he took you to bed, he knew for sure." I grinned faintly. "A man's technique rarely varies, and is usually unique to himself."

"Thought there was something familiar in the way he went about business," Rhoan murmured. "But I was too busy concentrating on where all the weapons were and making sure none of them were missing."

"His bedroom is an arsenal?"

"Yeah. It also has guards, so if anyone but Starr goes near a weapon, they'd be dead in an instant."

"From what we've seen," Jack said, "Starr rarely leaves his foxhole. If that's the case, Starr cannot be Davern."

I frowned at him. "But Starr's foxhole is underground,

and we have no idea where the main exit is. So how can you say he never leaves?"

"Plus, Davern regularly disappeared on business trips." Rhoan's voice was still extremely scratchy, yet sounding stronger now that the silver had gone from his body. "It would be interesting to correlate Davern's disappearances with Starr's appearances."

"Which we can do, but not right now. Riley, you need to get back."

Rhoan grabbed my arm. "No—"

I touched a finger lightly to my brother's lips. "Yes. He might suspect who I am, but you gave him nothing to confirm his suspicions. If I leave, he will know for sure, and then neither of us will be safe until he has been taken out. This could be our only chance to stop him and shut down the labs."

"But—"

"No buts." I hesitated, grinning wryly as I added, "I've had more than enough for one night."

His short laugh ended up a groan. "God, don't make me laugh. It hurts too much right now."

I squeezed his hand and looked at Jack. "The driver said they were taking Rhoan to the farming labs. I'm betting if you let this truck continue its journey, you might just discover the missing Libraska lab."

"It's certainly worth a try." He rose, restrained excitement evident in the way he moved. "Do you need help to get back in?"

I shook my head. "I'll shadow and run right past the gate guards."

"Use the out gate," Rhoan said. "No infrared scanners."

I nodded and bent to kiss him. "You get well while I go clean up this mess."

He touched a finger to my nose. "Just keep this out of trouble. I don't want to be climbing out of a sickbed to come to your rescue."

I grinned and looked at Jack. "Are you going to be monitoring the com-link?"

"Someone will be. If you need out, just holler."

I nodded and rose. The medics climbed into the truck as I climbed out, though there wasn't much they could do that Rhoan's own body couldn't now that the silver was out—except ease the pain, which is why I had Jack call them.

I grabbed a water bottle from one of the stretcher bearers and rinsed out my mouth. Jack climbed down from the truck and walked across to where I stood.

"What are you up to?"

"Me?" I batted my eyes innocently.

He wasn't buying it. "Yeah, you. The werewolf who has a badly beaten brother lying in that truck. Give, girl."

"I don't plan to do anything until you give me the thumbs-up that you've found the lab." Which wasn't exactly true, as I planned to try and rescue Nerida.

Not that I actually thought *that* would be achievable.

"And when and if you do get the thumbs-up?"

"Then I plan to kill the bastards who did that to my brother."

He grinned and patted my arm. "That's my girl."

I shook off his touch. "It's not for you or the Directorate. It's for Rhoan and me."

"I don't care about the reasons, I just care about the kill.

You're going to be a great guardian once you fully accept your fate."

"Don't hold your breath waiting for it, boss."

"Wouldn't matter if I did. I don't actually need to breathe."

Well, yeah. I guess it was a pretty stupid statement to make to a vampire. "I'll leave the link on."

"If you start getting static, turn it off. It probably means they're catching the signal."

"Will do."

I turned on my heel, wrapped the shadows around me, and ran back to Starr's property. The dinner bell was ringing loud and clear as I neared the house. I swore under my breath and headed for my room. The window was still open, so I climbed through, grabbed my towel and wrapped it around my body to hide the blood, grime, and scratches, then headed to the bathroom for a quick shower.

A guard appeared minutes later. "Hey, you, can't you hear the dinner bell? Hurry up."

I hurried. At least there was one good thing about running around in skin—no struggle trying to pull clothes over a wet body. I finger-combed my hair as the guard hustled me along.

I expected to be led to the holding pens behind the main arena for our wrestling match, but instead was taken into the arena room itself and led to a table.

Berna was already there. I plonked down beside her and crossed my arms.

"A successful affair?" she asked, as the guard walked to the back of the room.

"Yep."

"Then how the hell are we going to rescue Nerida?"

"I don't think we really can."

Her fury swept over me, its heat blistering. "We had a deal."

"We had a deal to *try*." I waved a hand around the room. "Do you think either of us have a chance of getting her out with all the hardware and personnel in this place?"

"I can't *not* try."

There was a desperation in her voice that was more than just concern. More than just a favor owed.

Berna and Nerida, as I'd suspected earlier, were lovers as well as friends.

"We may not be able to get her out, but maybe we can give her the one thing she really wants."

"But in seeking that she may very well *die*." In the depths of her eyes, a war between fury and fear briefly raged, but the emotions were gone as quickly as they'd appeared, sucked away behind a facade of calm acceptance.

There was no "very well" about it. Nerida was going to die, and we both knew it. And the pain I'd seen so briefly in Berna's eyes only confirmed that. "Look, this is her one chance to fight Merle, and possibly kill him. Do you honestly think she'd appreciate you taking that chance away from her?"

"Probably not. But I can't—"

"You can. You have to. They'll kill us both the minute we try to make any rescue attempt, and I'm sorry, but this operation is too darn important to risk that."

And if *she* tried, I'd have to stop her. She knew too much now. If they caught her, and she blabbed . . .

My gut churned at the thought of killing Berna, but I'd come too far now to let it all fall apart at the last hurdle.

Berna made a low sound in the back of her throat. Whether it was anguish or acceptance was anyone's guess.

"If she fights Merle, maybe she can put her ghosts to rest."

"I thought you said the ghosts wanted her death?"

"The ghosts here, yeah. I meant the ghosts holding her to such a destructive path."

Berna shook her head. "There will be no pleasing them until both men are dead."

I looked at her. "And if I promise to finish what she starts?"

Berna's gaze raked me. "I think maybe they might be satisfied. I doubt she will be, though."

"Isn't one revenge better than nothing?"

"She's obsessed. Sensible thinking is not exactly her high point at the moment." She shifted, staring at me. "How do you plan to help her beat those creatures?"

"By giving her the key to their destruction."

She raised an eyebrow. "And how would you know that?"

"Because I've fought creatures very similar." Only mine had been a mix of griffon, cat, and human with arching gold and brown wings.

Berna didn't ask where, which was good, because I wasn't about to tell her.

The doors down the far end of the room opened, and with all the ceremony of a king entering his domain, Starr swept in and took his seat. But his gaze ran around the room, as if seeking something. When it stopped on me, I knew he'd found it. I was too far away to see if there was any surprise in his eyes, but the smile that touched his lips had a shiver running down my spine. I had no idea what that smile meant, but it sure as hell couldn't be good.

Waiters appeared, dropping platters of food on every table. I ate because I had to eat, because I'd need the strength, not because I actually wanted to.

As we ate, a solitary man walked into the arena. Once again the babble of voices died, and excitement rushed into the void. Starr's guests had a taste for blood sports, and that's certainly what was provided in the arena.

"Ladies and gentlemen." The bald guy's voice rang out loud and clear across the vast arena, and the soft clink of cutlery died. "There has been a change of plans tonight. We will not be offering the wrestling, as originally planned."

A disappointed murmur rolled through the crowd—though it wasn't something any of the fighters added to.

"Instead, we have the possibility of a death match. But only if the fighter survives a match with our Kayvan."

Another murmur went though the crowd, but this time it was filled with anticipation. I had to hope that Jack found the lab, because then he could get here and clean up these sickos.

"Ladies and gentlemen, tonight's fighter." He made a sweeping motion with his hand, and the far side section of the arena began to slide up. From it came two men and Nerida.

"This fighter, Nerida Smith, was caught trying to assassinate Alden Merle."

Laughter trickled around the arena. Even the announcer smiled before continuing. "She has been sentenced to death via the arena. If she survives the Kayvan, she will meet her target in a battle to the death."

It was all so very formal. All so very melodramatic. These people were basically sanctioning a murder and *no one* seemed to give a damn.

The cage came down, then the announcer said, "Release her ropes. Release her competition," before beating a hasty retreat.

Nerida rolled her shoulders, shook her arms, as the doors near Starr began to open. From out of the shadows came the thin, blue humanoids with the butterfly wings. Anticipation trembled through the air, touched with a lust that was both sexual and blood-based.

The blue things halted just past the door and lightly fanned their wings. As the lights highlighted the jewel-like colors, one of them began to fan harder and, with gentle grace, rose in the air. The other walked forward, his wings fanning slowly.

They were repeating *exactly* their actions from the first fight. Maybe that was their pattern, what they did each and every time. And if I'd noticed it, surely Nerida—who was military trained—would.

"When the fight starts," I said softly to Berna, "stand up and tell her to attack the wings."

"What?"

"Trust me. It's her only chance at beating those things."

"So why don't you tell her that?"

I looked at her. "Do you really think she'll trust anything I say?"

Berna sniffed. There was no point in answering simply because we both knew the fox-shifter would do the exact opposite of anything I suggested.

Unlike the previous woman we'd witnessed in the

arena, Nerida didn't attack, just waited as the one creature walked toward her and the second soared high.

"Now," I said to Berna.

The bear-shifter thrust to her feet. "Nerida, their wings!"

Footsteps rushed toward our table and air sighed its warning. I spun, grabbing the butt of the rifle before it cracked Berna's head open, stopping the blow in its tracks. The guard cursed me.

"Two against one hardly seems fair," I said mildly. "A little advice surely can't hurt."

The guard didn't answer, his gaze going instead to the other end of the room. I twisted, saw Starr shake his head. That smile seemed larger. The guy was a freak, no doubt about it.

The guard stepped back, though he remained within rifle-butt range. I turned and watched the fight.

The second creature flicked his wings and dove downward even as the first creature leapt into action. Nerida dropped low to avoid his blow, then swept with her foot, knocking the blue thing off his feet. With the air screaming under the force of the other creature's plummet, Nerida rolled out of his path and back to her feet in one smooth action. Claws raked the air, barely missing her stomach. As the creature soared upward again, she ran and leapt high, landing on the creature's back. It screamed—a high sound that was neither animal nor human. Nerida grabbed the base of the wings and drew her legs up underneath her, hanging on so tightly as the creature bucked and twisted that the white glow of her knuckles was evident even from where we sat.

The first creature screamed and rose into the air.

Nerida gave it a glance, then, after positioning her feet a little more, pushed up and twisted backward hard and fast.

Wings are such delicate creations. No matter how strong the body underneath, a wing can so easily be crushed. Or destroyed. I knew that from experience. These wings were no different from the ones I'd ripped apart.

With an odd sort of popping sound, the wings tore free from the blue creature's flesh. As blood and wings and screams filled the air, the creature—with Nerida still riding its back—plummeted toward the sand. As the other creature swooped to the aid of its mate, Nerida leapt. Not for the fast-approaching ground but onto the back of the remaining winged creature.

It didn't seem to notice. Maybe it was too busy trying to stall the dive of its mate. Maybe it simply wasn't bright enough to realize it, too, was about to have its flight skills clipped.

Either way, Nerida grasped the wings and tore them free a second time. Then she leapt off the creature's back, hit the ground running, and finished off what she'd started with the wings.

Very quickly, very neatly.

The crowd was silent for several heartbeats, then applauded wildly. Anticipating the bloodbath that was to come.

My gaze went to Starr. He was leaning forward in his chair, talking to Merle. After several nods, Merle rose and made his way toward the arena.

The crowd became silent again. Nerida stood in the middle of the arena, breathing a little faster than normal but seemingly otherwise unperturbed.

"Any advice on beating this one?" Berna said softly.

"I've never seen him fight. I don't know what he can do." Or what Starr had ordered him to do.

But one thing was sure—it wouldn't be a fair fight. Starr not only played dirty, he played to win. I had no doubt his lieutenants would, too.

Merle leapt over the railing and dropped onto the sand. Nerida flexed her hands, but otherwise didn't move. Merle studied her for a moment, an arrogant smile touching his lips. "You will die, little fox. You have not a hope against me."

"Vengeance is a powerful motivator against the odds," she said. "Never dismiss it out of hand."

"Oh, I won't. But vengeance should never outweigh common sense." With those words, he took out a gun from behind his back and shot her. Red bloomed across her chest, and just for a moment, shock and anger touched her features. Then she dropped like a boneless sack to the ground.

Berna surged to her feet, crying out in denial and rage. The guard behind us stepped forward, gun butt raised. I twisted, knocking him off his feet, then froze as the muzzle of another gun dug into the back of my neck. Call me strange, but I liked my brains just the way they were.

Three guards jumped on Berna. She fought them, grabbing at their weapons, trying to claim one. More guards jumped into the fray, overwhelming her with sheer weight of numbers. As she went down, I heard a click, and realized someone had tried to fire a gun. In that mass of bodies it could have been deadly. But something had gone wrong, because there was no blood, no gore, no moans of pain.

Maybe the weapon had misfired.

Or maybe it hadn't even been loaded.

A freak like Starr wouldn't want loaded weapons within easy reach of his rivals. He wouldn't take the risk. Probably the only live weapons in the room were the ones being held by Starr and his entourage.

The guards finally managed to restrain Berna. Her gaze went to the arena, to the lifeless body lying on the sand, and her shoulders drooped. There was nothing anyone could do for Nerida now. Not even save her.

Movement in the shadowed corners of the room caught my eye. Ethereal wisps stirred in that darkness. The dead were gathering to collect their revenge.

My gaze darted back to the arena. Merle had lowered the weapon and was walking across to the fox-shifter's body. Underneath her chest was an ever-growing pool of red-soaked sand. Nerida didn't appear to be breathing and yet the dead were holding themselves to the shadows.

Maybe the fox was foxing.

Merle stopped and kicked her in the side. There was no response. He did it again, harder this time. Still no response. He bent and warily pressed a finger to her neck.

"Not dead," he said, looking up at Starr. "But close to."

Starr waved a hand. "Feed her meat to the zoo carnivores. They will enjoy the sweetness for a change."

"No!" Berna's voice echoed around the room. "She's alive. You can't do that. It's not human."

"There are very few us of here who are human." Starr's dead gaze moved to me, and the chills running down my spine became a landslide. He knew. Who I was, why I was there. The knowledge was right there in his unholy gaze and in the arrogant smile stretching his thin lips. "But if there is someone who cares enough for this person, I will allow another challenge."

He was baiting me, challenging me. I didn't bite. I couldn't, not until I heard from Jack.

"What? So you can allow your coward of a lieutenant to shoot them, too?" Berna shouted, struggling against the grip of the men who held her. "I hardly call that fair."

"This is my arena, my rules. Those who disobey me or try to betray me must expect swift revenge. Justice will never enter the equation."

It was more a warning to the heads of the other cartels who were in this room than a statement to Berna. And it was one I bet everyone in that room took heed of.

I looked back to the arena as Merle walked away from Nerida, the gun held loosely in one hand by his side. His left side, the side closest to Nerida.

She came to life, lunging forward in one of those risk-all movements that only the very desperate make. She snatched the gun from Merle's hand, twisted around as she dropped back to the sand, then pulled the trigger and shot his brains out the back of his head.

Chapter 15

As bits of bone and blood and gray matter sprayed across the sand, she slumped back down and didn't move. Merle fell like a stone beside her.

A wisp that seemed little more than steam but was much, much more began to rise from her body. The dead moved in to collect their prize.

I closed my eyes against the sudden sting of tears. Nerida had her revenge—or part of it, at least. But heaven—or whatever it was that fox-shifters believed in—was now beyond her reach. Hell was her resting place. A hell that involved an eternity of torment from the ghosts of those she'd killed.

"No!" Berna's scream seemed to echo around and around the arena. No one moved, no one said anything. Not even me.

"Well, that was unexpected." Amusement rode Starr's

voice. Maybe he had other Merles in the making, so it didn't matter if he lost this one. He was still staring at me, challenging me. There was no sign of anything other than the certainty that he would get what he wanted in those soulless depths. What he wanted was me to fight. But my fate would not be death, like Nerida, but something far worse. A one-way trip to the hell of the breeding pens.

But even as I sat there, returning his arrogant, overconfident, insane gaze, the wolf within rose snarling to the surface. This bastard had beaten me, drugged me, and all but destroyed my white-picket-fence-and-babies dream. Worse still, he'd beaten my brother to a pulp. Not because he needed to, but because he *wanted* to. Because he enjoyed it.

I needed revenge. Needed it. *Now.*

I might fear the fate I saw in his eyes, and I certainly feared the man himself, but I'd be damned if I could sit here any longer cowering like a newborn pup. If I was going to fight, then I'd damn well do it my way. It might not change the outcome, but at least I'd go down fighting.

"Are there any other grievances I should know about?" he continued. "Is there anyone else who feels the need to challenge my lieutenant or myself?"

The wise remained silent.

No one would ever accuse me of being wise.

I rose to my feet. The gun barrel rested against my neck again, so cold against my skin. I twisted, punched the man holding the weapon in the balls, then grabbed the gun as he went down. A dozen other weapons were instantly aimed in my direction.

I dangled the useless weapon from a finger and smiled. "Tell them to fire, Starr. I dare you."

He didn't take up the dare. Surprise, surprise. "What do you want?"

"I challenge that loose-assed prick, otherwise known as Moss, to a fight. Knives or guns or bare knuckles, as long as we are both equally armed." My gaze went to Moss. "Or is your remaining lieutenant as scared of a girl as your first one was?"

Moss thrust angrily to his feet. Like that was a surprise. "You want a fight, you'll get one." His gaze swept me. "When I finish beating you, I shall enjoy fucking you."

"Because the only way you can get it up is by beating someone up first."

"Can I just point out," Jack said into my ear, "that this doesn't really sound like you're intending to wait for my thumbs-up?"

Moss snarled. It was an ugly, nasty sound. Starr laughed. "I shall enjoy watching this fight and its aftermath. What shall we agree to? Knives?"

"And skin." I met his gaze squarely. "No place to shove hidden weapons. Unless, of course, he's a bum lover like yourself."

Starr's smile was lazy. "And you'd know all about them, wouldn't you? Your missing flatmate is one, after all."

Flatmate, *not* brother. No matter what else Starr knew about us, he was still missing that vital bit of information.

"Why all the chatter, Starr? Giving your bum-buddy time to stick that gun up his ass? Or is it more the fact that you know what I can do, know that I can beat him, and you're just waiting for the troops to get some bullets in their guns?"

"We found the lab, Riley," Jack said. "We haven't moved in to take control yet, but we have forces at the ready. We're also surrounding the estate. Feel free to take your revenge, though from the sound of it, you intended to anyway. Just remember your training and don't die on me."

"There will be no interference from guards or guns," Starr said. "You're right, I *do* know what you can do, and you are so far beneath Moss it doesn't matter."

"Are you always prone to such errors of judgment?"

He merely smiled. "Moss, enjoy yourself."

"Oh, I will." Moss finished stripping and walked down to the arena. "Join me on the sands if you dare, little girl."

My grin was sheer anticipation. I dropped the gun and walked down to the arena gate. The sand was surprisingly warm under my feet. It was also very grainy, sucking at every step, making free-flowing movement that much harder. But what slowed me would have greater impact on Moss. He was bigger, heavier.

I walked past the bodies of Nerida and Merle. The smell of their blood twitched my nose, and my wolf soul stirred excitedly. It wanted blood. Wanted to rent and tear at flesh and muscle and bone.

I didn't often let her free. Most wolves controlled their nature simply because we had no other choice in this modern, human-governed world. Maybe that was why we put so much passion, so much energy, into the moon dances. The wildness that was so much a part of our nature had to go *somewhere*.

But tonight, the chains around my wolf would be dropped. I needed every ounce of her strength, all her ruthlessness, and most of all, her readiness to take punishment if it meant being the eventual winner. Jack might have trained me to be a guardian, but I'd been a fighter all my life. It was those skills—the skills of a scrappy street fighter combined with the hunting instincts of a wolf— that would serve me best here. I couldn't play nice because Moss or Starr certainly wouldn't.

I stopped in the center of the arena. Moss strode toward me, a knife held in each hand. I raised my gaze to his, watching his eyes, waiting for the moment he decided to throw the knife.

His smile was all confidence. Tasting his victory. Anticipating it.

He continued to walk toward me. I shifted my stance, ready to move, to fight.

Most people telegraph their intended move in their eyes a brief second before they actually do it. Moss wasn't one of those people. His hand rose in a single, blurring movement, and suddenly the knife was a glittering streak of silver aimed my way.

I stepped sideways, then reached out and caught the knife. Pain slithered up my arm as one edge of the blade sliced into my palm, but I ignored it, flipped the knife, and wrapped my fingers around the hilt.

"Thank you for the weapon."

Moss laughed. "To a good fight," he said, saluting me with the blade of his own knife.

"To the glory of your death and the ghosts who will enjoy tormenting your soul."

He raised a mocking eyebrow. "Ghosts hold no fear to me."

"Then you are a fool."

"And you are bleeding. The first cut of many."

The words were barely out of his mouth when he was coming at me, a whirlwind of power and speed and sheer, bloody force. I weaved and dodged and blocked, using every skill, every instinct. He was fast, there was no doubt about it, but he was bigger and heavier and the sand was hindering him more than it was me.

Eventually, several blows got through my defense, one nicking my left breast, the other cutting my stomach. But I was still upright, still relatively unhurt, after several minutes of heavy fighting. Best of all, I'd managed to mark Moss. It enraged him, as I'd hoped it would.

He came at me again, a blurring mass of muscle, anger, and determination. I continued to dodge and weave, but let myself be forced backward. Ever backward.

If you need help in any way, I am here, in the room. Quinn's voice swept into my mind, as comforting as a cool breeze on a hot summer day. *I found a guard with similar weight, coloring, and height.*

A guard who was undoubtedly feeding the fish in the lake as we spoke. I ducked under a sweeping slash of blade, then spun and kicked. Moss sucked in his gut, and my blow missed. Not so his knife. It sliced across my foot and damn near took off a toe. I snarled in frustration and pain and Moss laughed.

He was enjoying himself. I was happy for him. Truly. A condemned man should always enjoy his last meal.

I watched him warily, even as I said to Quinn, *You're*

in the room and not taking the chance to kill Starr yourself?
I leaned back to miss the sweep of Moss's fist, and slashed
at his arm with my knife. It missed, but at that point I
didn't really care. *Why?*

*Because there is a sharpshooter sitting in the shadows at
the opposite end of the arena from Starr. He has orders to kill
you if you win.*

I backed away, and swiped at the sweat running down
my forehead with a bloody arm. Confidence fairly oozed
from Moss's pores and yet there was annoyance in his
eyes. Which didn't make sense when he thought he was
winning... my gaze skimmed his body and saw the problem. He wasn't getting an erection. He needed fear to get
it up, and I wasn't giving it to him.

I waved the knife at his inactive bits. "Hard to rape a
girl when there's no action happening downstairs. Maybe
you really do prefer boys."

He snarled and attacked. Again and again. I dodged,
attacking him when opportunities arose, taking hits
every now and again but never truly deep ones. And all
the while, I kept backing away.

The smell of blood and death began to touch the air.
We were close to the bodies. Very close.

He lunged forward. I jumped backward. My feet hit
Merle's body, but rather than steadying myself, I went
with the momentum of the fall. Moss laughed and raised
the knife, the bloody blade glittering silver as the lights
caressed it. I twisted in the air so that I landed on my side,
then thrust an arm under Nerida's body. My hand
touched the barrel of a gun, my fingers burning with the
closeness of silver even as I gripped the handle.

As the air screamed with the force of Moss's oncoming

blow, I pulled the gun free, aimed at Starr, and shot his fucking brains out.

A second shot rang out almost simultaneously, and Moss fell backward, a small hole in the middle of his forehead.

Quinn, finishing things off.

I took a deep breath and slowly released it.

It was over. Done.

Moss was dead, Starr was dead, and pandemonium was beginning to erupt around the arena.

And like it or not, I'd just stepped over the line and become a full-fledged guardian.

Chapter 16

$\mathscr{I}$ drew together the edges of my borrowed coat
and watched the dawn color the sky with flags of red and
gold.

From where I sat near the stables, I had a full view of
what was going on. The house was a hive of activity.
Trucks lined the driveway and people were bustling back
and forth, most leading prisoners but some carrying
boxes and files.

I rubbed my forehead wearily. The sense of déjà vu
was strong, and like before, I just wanted to go home,
take a long bath, and forget this whole damn episode.

And while I *could* finally go home and be safe, forget-
ting wasn't an option. Like it or not, my actions here in
this place had changed my life forever. I had my revenge
all right, but the cost was still to be counted.

Warm awareness tingled across my skin, and I looked

around. Quinn walked out of the trees and sat down beside me.

"How are you feeling?"

"Like shit." I shrugged. "Several gallons of coffee, a long hot bath, and several days of sleep will make a serious difference, though."

His smile reached his dark eyes and my hormones reacted accordingly. "Thought that might be the case." He produced a china mug from behind his back. "It's not hazelnut, but it is hot."

"God, I think I love you." I wrapped my chilled hands around the mug and inhaled deeply. "Bliss, even if it's not hazelnut."

"I'll treat you to hazelnut when we go out this weekend."

Amusement ran through me. "When? Don't I get a say in it?"

"You can choose the day. You can choose the time. But you cannot refuse." His eyes were filled not only with determination, but a warmth that did strange things to the beat of my heart. "Because I will hunt you down, throw you over my shoulder, and forcibly abduct you to our date."

The vampire had joined the chase and fully intended to give Kellen a run for his money. Modern wolf or not, my blood raced at the thought.

"You do realize part of me is tempted to test whether you'd carry through with the threat?"

He shrugged. "I don't intend to play by the rules anymore. I'm playing to win."

"Love is not a game."

He raised an eyebrow. "Life itself is a game. Love is

the greatest prize. One I've held myself apart from for entirely too long."

Nice words, but I wasn't exactly believing them. "So why the change, Quinn? What makes me so acceptable now when I was so unacceptable four months ago? I can never change what I am."

"Unless you find your soul mate. Unless you promise yourself to the moon and him." He touched a finger to my chin, holding it still as he leaned forward and gently kissed my lips. "I intend to prove I am that man."

"You're not a wolf."

"Neither are you. Not entirely."

"But I want what all wolves want. A wolf mate. A home. Children."

"We both know some dreams are never meant to be."

"But there are still options left for me, Quinn." I freed my chin from his grip and looked away from him. "And I will not give up on my dreams until I draw my very last breath."

"Then I will have to remain by your side until those dreams turn to dust or you accept what is meant to be."

I glanced at him. "You can stay for as long as you like, but I will never play us solo. Never."

He looked away, but not before I'd seen the flicker of cold determination in his eyes. The vampire might be saying all the right things, but in the end, the result he wanted was me and him, his way, not mine.

And only time would tell which of us was the stronger.

I followed his gaze and saw Jack approaching. Bad timing in some respects, good timing in others.

As Quinn rose to his feet, I said, "You never answered my question earlier."

"What question?" But the sparkle in his dark eyes suggested he knew entirely too well what question.

"You had the chance to take your revenge on Starr but didn't grab it. Why not, when you've declared from the beginning that nothing and no one would get in the way of your revenge?"

He paused, as if searching for an answer, then said, "Because Henri would have called me all sorts of a fool for choosing revenge over matters of the heart. In the end, Starr died anyway, so what did it matter who actually pulled the trigger?"

"That decision could earn you brownie points, you know."

He grinned. "I'm counting on it." He touched a finger lightly to my shoulder, then walked away.

Jack took his place beside me. "So, how is my favorite recruit feeling?"

"I'm not making killing a full-time habit. You can't make me." I paused for impact, even though I doubted there would be any, then added, "Can I go home now?"

"Not yet." He grinned. "And killing will come in time."

I sniffed. "How goes the cleanup?"

He shrugged. "Here, fine, though we've had to bring in local cops to help handle all the arrests and documentation."

"And the lab?"

He looked at me. For the first time ever, I saw anger, true, unforgiving anger, in Jack's green eyes. "That bastard didn't deserve the easy death you gave him, Riley.

What he has done—" He blew out a breath. "I've seen some truly horrific things in my time, but this lab takes the cake."

I didn't want to know the details, I really didn't, so I changed the subject. "What about the spirit lizards?"

Iktar's people, despite his confidence, hadn't been able to free themselves from the implants as quickly and as easily as he'd boasted. They were all still here when the Directorate swept in.

"We've come to an agreement. His people I've let go. The clones will be held for study to ensure they have no Starr-implanted agendas in their subconscious."

They'd already had an agreement in place, but I didn't bother pointing that out. "And Iktar?"

He grinned. "Will be joining the Directorate's new daytime division, along with a few of his people."

"Don't you think their featureless faces are going to be a little noticeable?"

"Just because it's called a daytime division doesn't mean it'll actually be all daytime work."

"Did you come all the way up here just to give me that cheery piece of news?"

His amusement faded away. "No."

"Then what?"

"You can't go home." His gaze met mine. "Not immediately. We're arranging a new apartment for you and Rhoan."

I had no reaction to the news. I think I was simply too darn tired. "Why?"

"Gautier slipped the noose."

"Bound to happen given he was our best guardian." I

rubbed my eyes wearily. "Maybe he'll just move to another state and leave us alone."

"You don't believe that any more than I do." He
slipped a hand into his pocket and drew out his cell
phone. "You'd better read this."

He pressed a button then held the phone out. I took it
and read the message.

> *Thank you for freeing me from the restraints
> of servitude. For that, I shall give you time to re-
> cover. But not long. We have unfinished business,
> Riley, and I fully intend to make good the prom-
> ise I made in the arena.*

I handed Jack back the phone but didn't immediately
say anything. Because what was there to say?

The Directorate's best guardian had turned rogue.
The hunter had become the hunted.

And the hunted was coming after me.

I hugged my knees a little closer to my chest. "I guess
the one good thing is that bringing down Gautier will
probably be a piece of cake compared to Starr."

"If you think that, then you're not as bright as I
thought you were."

"Way to kill feeble hopes, boss." I blew out a breath.
"So what do we do now?"

He shrugged. "We wait. And when he finally shows
himself, we'll kill him."

How? I wanted to ask, *When you couldn't even contain
him when surprise was on our side? When he didn't even
know he was being watched?*

"He won't get you, Riley. I promise." Jack raised a

hand and lightly squeezed my shoulder. "There's a car waiting near the gates—why don't you go see your brother?"

"And the cleanup here?"

"Could take days yet. But there's plenty of people here to worry about it. You need to rest and recuperate."

I blew out a breath, then rose. I'd go see my brother, then get the bath and coffee I desperately craved.

After that, there was nothing I could do but wait.

And worry.

Because death was coming after me, and it was going to take every ounce of strength I had to survive him.

About the Author

KERI ARTHUR received a "perfect 10" from *Romance Reviews Today* and was nominated for Best Shapeshifter in PNR's PEARL Awards and in the Best Contemporary Paranormal category of the *Romantic Times* Reviewers' Choice Awards. She lives with her husband and daughter in Melbourne, Australia.

Four times the heat.
Four times the suspense.
Four times the sass.
Four months in a row.

This much excitement isn't normal—it's paranormal!

Now is your chance to fully immerse yourself
in the wonderful world of

Keri Arthur

Smart, sexy, and suspenseful, the Riley Jenson novels
are rapidly gaining fans worldwide. And now we are
giving you the unique opportunity to read **four** books
inside four months, as part of our exciting
new publication schedule:

Full Moon Rising
January 2007

Kissing Sin
February 2007

Tempting Evil
March 2007

Dangerous Games
April 2007

Be sure not to miss any of these exciting novels—or
this series of special previews, to give you a taste of
what is still to come or what you may have missed....

A RILEY JENSON GUARDIAN NOVEL
KERI ARTHUR
Half vampire,
half werewolf,
all trouble...
FULL MOON
RISING

FULL MOON RISING

On sale January 2007

The night was quiet.

Almost too quiet.

Though it was after midnight, it was a Friday night, and Friday nights were usually party nights— at least for those of us who were single and not working night shift. This section of Melbourne wasn't exactly excitement city, but it did possess a nightclub that catered to both humans and nonhumans. And while it wasn't a club I frequented often, I loved the music they played. Loved dancing along the street to it as I made my way home.

But tonight, there was no music. No laughter. Not even drunken revelry. The only sound on the whispering wind was the clatter of the train leaving the station and the rumble of traffic from the nearby freeway.

Of course, the club was a well-known haunt for pushers

and their prey, and as such it was regularly raided—and closed—by the cops. Maybe it had been hit again tonight.

So why was there no movement on the street? No disgruntled party-goers heading to other clubs in other areas?

And why did the wind hold the fragrance of blood?

I hitched my bag to a more comfortable position on my shoulder, then stepped from the station's half-lit platform and ran up the stairs leading to Sunshine Avenue. The lights close to the platform's exit were out and the shadows closed in the minute I stepped onto the street.

Normally, darkness didn't worry me. I am a creature of the moon and the night, after all, and well used to roaming the streets at ungodly hours. Tonight, though the moon rode toward fullness, its silvery light failed to pierce the thick cover of clouds. But the power of it shimmered through my veins—a heat that would only get worse in the coming nights.

Yet it wasn't the closeness of the full moon that had me jumpy. Nor was it the lack of life coming from the normally raucous club. It was something else, something I couldn't quite put a finger on. The night felt wrong, and I had no idea why.

But it was something I couldn't ignore.

I turned away from the street that led to the apartment I shared with my twin brother and headed for the nightclub. Maybe I was imagining the scent of blood, or the wrongness in the night. Maybe the club's silence had nothing to do with either sensation. But one thing was certain—I had to find out. It would keep me awake, otherwise.

Of course, curiosity not only killed cats, but it often took out inquisitive werewolves, too. Or, in my case, half weres. And my nose for trouble had caused me more grief over the years than I wanted to remember. Generally, my brother had been right by my side, either fighting with me or pulling me out of harm's way. But tonight, Rhoan wasn't home, and he wasn't contactable. He worked as a guardian for the Directorate of Other Races—which was a government body that sat somewhere between the cops and the military. Most humans thought the Directorate was little more than a police force specializing in capture of nonhuman criminals, and in some respects, they were right. But the Directorate, both here and overseas, was also a researcher of all things nonhuman, and its guardians didn't only capture, they had the power to be judge, jury, and executioner.

I also worked for the Directorate, but not as a guardian. I was nowhere near ruthless enough to join their ranks as anything other than a general dogs-body—though, like most of the people who worked for the Directorate in *any* capacity, I had certainly been tested. I was pretty damn happy to have failed—especially given that eighty percent of a Guardian's work involved assassination. I might be part wolf, but I wasn't a killer. Rhoan was the only one who'd inherited those particular instincts in our small family unit. If I had a talent I could claim, it would be as a finder of trouble.

Which is undoubtedly what I'd find by sticking my nose where it had no right to be. But would I let the thought of trouble stop me? Not a snowflake's chance in hell.

Grinning slightly, I shoved my hands into my coat pockets and quickened my pace. My four-inch heels clacked against the concrete, and the sound seemed to echo along the silent street. A dead giveaway if there *were* problems ahead. I stepped onto the strip of half-dead grass that divided the road from the pavement, and tried not to get the heels stuck in the dirt as I continued on.

The street curved around to the left, and the rundown houses that lined either side of the road gave way to run-down factories and warehouses. Vinnie's nightclub sat about halfway along the street, and even from here, it was obvious the place was closed. The gaudy red and green flashing signs were off, and no patrons milled around the front of the building.

But the scent of blood and the sense of wrongness were stronger than ever.

I stopped near the trunk of a gum tree and raised my nose, tasting the slight breeze, searching for odors that might give a hint as to what was happening up ahead.

Beneath the richness of blood came three other scents—excrement, sweat, and fear. For those last two to be evident from that distance, something major had to be happening.

I bit my lip and half considered calling the Directorate. I wasn't a fool—not totally, anyway—and whatever was happening in that club *smelled* big. But what would I report? That the scent of blood and shit rode the wind? That a nightclub that was usually open on a Friday night was suddenly closed? They weren't likely to send out troops for that. I needed to get closer, see what was really happening.

But the nearer I got, the more unease turned my stomach—and the more certain I became that something was very wrong inside the club. I stopped in the shadowed doorway of a warehouse almost opposite Vinnie's and studied the building. No lights shone inside, and no windows were broken. The front metal doors were closed, and thick grates protected the black-painted windows. The side gate was padlocked. For all intents and purposes, the building looked secure. Empty.

Yet something *was* inside. Something that walked quieter than a cat. Something that smelled of death. Or rather, *un*death.

A vampire.

And if the thick smell of blood and sweaty humanity that accompanied his sickly scent was anything to go by, he wasn't alone. *That* I could report. I swung my handbag around so I could grab my cell phone, but at that moment, awareness surged, prickling like fire across my skin. I no longer stood alone on the street. And the noxious scent of unwashed flesh that followed the awareness told me exactly who it was.

I turned, my gaze pinpointing the darkness crowding the middle of the road. "I know you're out there, Gautier. Show yourself."

His chuckle ran across the night, a low sound that set my teeth on edge. He walked free of the shadows and strolled toward me. Gautier was a long, mean stick of vampire who hated werewolves almost as much as he hated the humans he was paid to protect. But he was one of the Directorate's most successful guardians, and the word I'd heard was that he was headed straight for the top job.

If he did get there, I would be leaving. The man was a bastard with a capital B.

"And just what are you doing here, Riley Jenson?" His voice, like his dark hair, was smooth and oily. He'd apparently been a salesman before he'd been turned. It showed, even in death.

"I live near here. What's your excuse?"

His sudden grin revealed bloodstained canines. He'd fed, and very recently. My gaze went to the nightclub. Surely not even he could be *that* depraved. That out of control.

"I'm a guardian," he said, coming to a halt about half a dozen paces away. Which was about half a dozen paces *too* close for my liking. "We're paid to patrol the streets, to keep humanity safe."

I scrubbed a hand across my nose, and half wished— and not for the first time in my years of dealing with vampires—that my olfactory sense wasn't so keen. I'd long ago given up trying to get *them* to take a regular shower. How Rhoan coped being around them so much, I'll never know.

"You only walk the streets when you've been set loose to kill," I said, and motioned to the club. "Is that what you've been sent here to investigate?"

"No." His brown gaze bored into mine, and an odd tingling began to buzz around the edges of my thoughts. "How did you know I was there when I had shadows wrapped around my body?"

The buzzing got stronger, and I smiled. He was trying to get a mind-lock on me and force an answer— something vamps had a tendency to do when they had questions they knew wouldn't be answered willingly. Of course, mind-locks had been made illegal several years ago in the "human rights" bill that set out just what was, and wasn't, acceptable behavior from nonhuman races when dealing with humans. Or other nonhumans, for that matter. Trouble is, legalities generally mean squat to the dead.

But he didn't have a hope in hell of succeeding with me, thanks to the fact I was something that should not be—the child of a werewolf *and* a vampire. Because of my mixed heritage, I was immune to the controlling touch of vampires. And that immunity was the only reason I was working in the guardian liaisons section of the Directorate. He should have realized that, even if he didn't know the reason for the immunity.

"Hate to say this, Gautier, but you haven't exactly got the sweetest scent."

"I was downwind."

Damn. So he was. "Some scents are stronger than the wind to a wolf." I hesitated, but couldn't help adding, "You know, you may be one of the undead, but you sure as hell don't have to smell like it."

His gaze narrowed, and there was a sudden stillness about him that reminded me of a snake about to strike.

"You would do well to remember what I am."

"And you would do well to remember that I'm trained to protect myself against the likes of you."

He snorted. "Like all liaisons, you overestimate your skills."

Maybe I did, but I sure as hell wasn't going to admit it, because that's precisely what he wanted. Gautier not only loved baiting the hand that fed him, he more often bit it. Badly. Those in charge let him get away with it because he was a damn fine guardian.

"As much as I love standing here trading insults, I really want to know what's going on in that club."

His gaze went to Vinnie's, and something inside me relaxed. But only a little. When it came to Gautier, it never paid to relax too much.

"There's a vampire inside that club," he said.

"I know *that* much."

His gaze came back to me, brown eyes flat and somehow deadly. "How do you know? A werewolf has no more awareness when it comes to vampires than a human."

Werewolves mightn't, but then, I wasn't totally wolf, and it was my vampire instincts that were picking up the vamp inside the building. "I'm beginning to think the vampire population should be renamed the great unwashed. He stinks almost as much as you do."

His gaze narrowed again, and again the sensation of danger swirled around me. "One day, you'll push too far."

Probably. But with any sort of luck, it would be *after* he'd gotten the arrogance knocked out of him. I waved a hand at Vinnie's. "Are there people alive inside?"

"Yes."

"So are you going to do something about the situation or not?"

His grin was decidedly nasty. "I'm not."

I blinked. I'd expected him to say a lot of things, but certainly not that. "Why the hell not?"

"Because I hunt bigger prey tonight." His gaze swept over me, and my skin crawled. Not because it was sexual—Gautier didn't want me any more than I wanted him—but because it was the look of a predator sizing up his next meal.

His expression, when his gaze rose to meet mine

again, was challenging. "If you think you're so damn good, you go tend to it."

"I'm not a guardian. I can't—"

"You can," he cut in, "because you're a guardian liaison. By law, you can interfere when necessary."

"But—"

"There are five people alive in there," he said. "If you want to keep them that way, go rescue them. If not, call the Directorate and wait. Either way, I'm out of here."

With that, he wrapped the night around his body and disappeared from sight. My vampire and werewolf senses tracked his hidden form as he raced south. He really *was* leaving.

Fuck.

My gaze returned to Vinnie's. I couldn't hear the beating of hearts, and had no idea whether Gautier was telling the truth about people being alive inside. I might be part vampire, but I didn't drink blood, and my senses weren't tuned to the thud of life. But I could smell fear, and surely I wouldn't be smelling that if someone wasn't alive in the club.

Even if I called the Directorate, they wouldn't get there in time to rescue those people. I had to go in. I had no choice....

A RILEY JENSON GUARDIAN NOVEL

KERI ARTHUR

Between desire and
bloodlust is the
sweetest sin of all....

KISSING SIN

FROM THE AUTHOR OF *FULL MOON RISING*

KISSING SIN

On sale February 2007

All I could smell was blood.

Blood that was thick and ripe.

Blood that plastered my body, itching at my skin.

I stirred, groaning softly as I rolled onto my back. Other sensations began to creep through the fog encasing my mind. The chill of the stones that pressed against my spine. The gentle patter of moisture against bare skin. The stench of rubbish left sitting too long in the sun. And underneath it all, the aroma of raw meat.

It was a scent that filled me with foreboding, though why I had no idea.

I forced my eyes open. A concrete wall loomed ominously above me, seeming to lean inward, as if ready to fall. There were no windows in that wall, and no lights anywhere near it. For a moment I thought I was in a prison of some kind, until I remembered the rain and saw that the concrete bled into the cloud-covered night sky.

Though there was no moon visible, I didn't need to see it to know where we were in the lunar cycle. While it might be true that just as many vampire genes flowed through my bloodstream as werewolf, I was still very sensitive to the moon's presence. The full moon had passed three days ago.

Last I remembered, the full-moon phase had only just begun. Somewhere along the line, I'd lost eight days.

I frowned, staring up at the wall, trying to get my bearings, trying to remember how I'd gotten here. How I'd managed to become naked and unconscious in the cold night.

No memories rose from the fog. The only thing I was certain of was the fact that something bad had happened. Something that had stolen my memory and covered me in blood.

I wiped the rain from my face with a hand that was trembling, and looked left. The wall formed one side of a lane filled with shadows and overflowing rubbish bins. Down at the far end, a streetlight twinkled, a forlorn star in the surrounding darkness. There were no sounds to be heard beyond the rasp of my own breathing. No cars. No music. Not even a dog barking at an imaginary foe. Nothing that suggested life of any kind nearby.

Swallowing heavily, trying to ignore the bitter taste of confusion and fear, I looked to the right.

And saw the body.

A body covered in blood.

Oh God...

I couldn't have. Surely to God, I couldn't have.

Mouth dry, stomach heaving, I climbed unsteadily to my feet and staggered over.

Saw what remained of his throat and face.

Bile rose thick and fast. I spun away, not wanting to lose my dinner over the man I'd just killed. Not that he'd care anymore...

When there was nothing but dry heaves left, I wiped a hand across my mouth, then took a deep breath and turned to face what I'd done.

He was a big man, at least six four, with dark skin and darker hair. His eyes were brown, and if the expression frozen on what was left of his face was anything to go by, I'd caught him by surprise. He was also fully clothed, which meant I hadn't been in a blood lust when I'd ripped out his throat. That in itself provided no comfort, especially considering *I* was naked, and obviously *had* made love to someone sometime in the last hour.

My gaze went back to his face and my stomach rose threateningly again. Swallowing heavily, I forced my eyes away from that mangled mess and studied the rest of him. He wore what looked like brown coveralls, with shiny gold buttons and the letters D. S. E. printed on the left breast pocket. There was a taser clipped to the belt at his waist and a two-way attached to his lapel. What looked like a dart gun lay inches from his reaching right hand. His fingers had suckers, more gecko-like than human.

A chill ran across my skin. I'd seen hands like that before—just over two months ago, in a Melbourne casino car park, when I'd been attacked by a vampire and a tall, blue thing that had smelled like death.

The need to get out of this road hit like a punch to the stomach, leaving me winded and trembling. But I couldn't run, not yet. Not until I knew everything this man might be able to tell me. There were too many gaps in my memory that needed to be filled.

Not the least of which was why I'd ripped out his throat.

After taking another deep breath that did little to calm my churning stomach, I knelt next to my victim. The cobblestones were cold and hard against my shins, but the chill that crept across my flesh had nothing to do with the icy night. The urge to run was increasing, but if my senses had any idea what I should be running from, they weren't telling me. One thing was certain—this dead man was no longer a threat. Not unless he'd performed the ritual to become a vampire, anyway, and even then, it could be days before he actually turned.

I bit my lip and cautiously patted him down. There was nothing else on him. No wallet, no ID, not even the usual assortment of fluff that seemed to accumulate and thrive in pockets. His boots were leather—nondescript brown things that had no name brand. His socks provided the only surprise—they were pink. Fluorescent pink.

I blinked. My twin brother would love them, but I couldn't imagine anyone else doing so. And they seemed an odd choice for a man who was so colorless in every other way.

Something scraped the cobblestones behind me. I froze, listening. Sweat skittered across my skin and my heart raced nine to the dozen—a beat that seemed to echo through the stillness. After a few minutes, it came again—a soft click I'd never have noticed if the night wasn't so quiet.

I reached for the dart gun, then turned and studied the night-encased alley. The surrounding buildings seemed to disappear into that black well, and I could sense nothing or no one approaching.

Yet something was there, I was sure of it.

I blinked, switching to the infrared of my vampire vision. The entire lane leapt into focus—tall walls, wooden fences, and overflowing bins. Right down the far end, a hunched shape that wasn't quite human, not quite dog.

My mouth went dry.

They were hunting me.

Why I was so certain of this I couldn't say, but I wasn't about to waste time examining it. I rose, and slowly backed away from the body.

The creature raised its nose, sniffing the night air. Then it howled—a high, almost keening sound that was as grating as nails down a blackboard.

The thing down the far end was joined by another, and together they began to walk toward me.

I risked a quick glance over my shoulder. The street and the light weren't that far away, but I had a feeling the two creatures weren't going to be scared away by the presence of either.

The click of their nails against the cobblestones was sharper, a tattoo of sound that spoke of patience and controlled violence. They were taking one step for every three of mine, and yet they seemed to be going far faster.

I pressed a finger around the trigger of the dart gun, and wished I'd grabbed the taser as well.

The creatures stopped at the body, sniffing briefly before stepping over it and continuing on. This close, their shaggy, powerful forms looked more like misshapen bears than wolves or dogs, and they must have stood at least four feet at the shoulder. Their eyes were red—a luminous, scary red.

They snarled softly, revealing long, yellow teeth. The urge to run was so strong that every muscle trembled. I bit my lip, fighting instinct as I raised the dart gun and pressed the trigger twice. The darts hit the creatures square in the chest, but only seemed to infuriate them. Their soft snarls became a rumble of fury as they launched into the air. I turned and ran, heading left at the end of the alley simply because it was downhill.

The road's surface was slick with moisture, the streetlights few and far between. Had it been humans chasing me, I could have used the cloak of night to disappear from sight. But the scenting actions these creatures made when they first appeared suggested the vampire ability to fade into shadow wouldn't help me here.

Nor would shifting into wolf form, because my only real weapon in my alternate shape was teeth. Not a good option when there was more than one foe.

I raced down the middle of the wet street, passing silent shops and terraced houses. No one seemed to be home in any of them, and none of them looked familiar. In fact, all the buildings looked rather strange, almost as if they were one-dimensional.

The air behind me stirred and the sense of evil sharpened. I swore softly and dropped to the ground. A dark shape leapt over me, its sharp howl becoming a sound of frustration. I sighted the dart and fired again, then rolled onto my back, kicking with all my might at the second creature. The blow caught it in the jaw and deflected its leap. It crashed to the left of me, shaking its head, a low rumble coming from deep within its chest.

I scrambled to my feet, and fired the last of the darts at it. Movement caught my eye. The first creature had climbed to its feet and was scrambling toward me.

I threw the empty gun at its face, then jumped out of its way. It slid past, claws scrabbling against the wet road as it tried to stop. I grabbed a fistful of shaggy brown hair and swung onto its back, wrapping an arm around its throat and squeezing tight. I had the power of wolf *and* vampire behind me, which meant I was more than capable of crushing the larynx of any normal creature in an instant. Trouble was, this creature *wasn't* normal.

It roared—a harsh, strangled sound—then began to buck and twist violently. I wrapped my legs around its body, hanging on tight as I continued my attempts to strangle it.

The other creature came out of nowhere and hit me side-on, knocking me off its companion. I hit the road with enough force to see stars, but the scrape of approaching claws got me moving. I rolled upright, and scrambled away on all fours.

Claws raked my side, drawing blood. I twisted, grabbed the creature's paw, and pulled it forward hard. The creature sailed past and landed with a crash on its back, hard up against a shop wall. A wall that shook under the impact.

I frowned, but the second creature gave me no time to wonder why the wall had moved. I spun around, sweeping with my foot, battering the hairy beastie off its feet. It roared in frustration and lashed out. Sharp claws caught my thigh, tearing flesh even as the blow sent me staggering. The creature was up almost instantly, nasty sharp teeth gleaming yellow in the cold, dark night.

I faked a blow to its head, then spun and kicked at its chest, embedding the darts even farther. The ends of the darts hurt my bare foot, but the blow obviously hurt the creature more, because it howled in fury and leapt. I dropped and spun. Then, as the creature's leap took it high above me, I kicked it as hard as I could in the goolies. It grunted, dropped to the road, and didn't move.

For a moment, I simply remained where I was, the wet road cold against my shins as I battled to get some air into my lungs. When the world finally stopped threatening to go black, I called to the wolf that prowled within.

Power swept around me, through me, blurring my vision, blurring the pain. Limbs shortened, shifted, rearranged, until what was sitting on the road was wolf not woman. I had no desire to stay too long in my alternate form. There might be more of those things prowling the night, and meeting two or more in *this* shape could be deadly.

But in shifting, I'd helped accelerate the healing process. The cells in a werewolf's body retained data on body makeup, which was why wolves were so long-lived. In changing, damaged cells were repaired. Wounds were healed. And while it generally took more than one shift to heal deep wounds, one would at least stem the bleeding and begin the healing process.

I shifted back to human form and climbed slowly to my feet. The first creature still lay in a heap at the base of the shop front. Obviously, whatever had been in those two darts had finally taken effect. I walked over to the second creature, grabbed it by the scruff of the neck, and dragged it off the road. Then I went to the window and peered inside.

It wasn't a shop, just a front. Beyond the window there was only framework and rubbish. The next shop was much the same, as was the house next to that. Only there were wooden people inside it as well.

It looked an awful lot like one of those police or military weapons training grounds, only *this* training ground had warped-looking creatures patrolling its perimeter.

That bad feeling I'd woken with began to get a whole lot worse. I had to get out of here, before anything or anyone else discovered I was free...

A RILEY JENSON GUARDIAN NOVEL

KERI ARTHUR

Desire. Temptation.
Seduction.
Let the night begin....

DANGEROUS
GAMES

FROM THE AUTHOR OF *TEMPTING EVIL*

DANGEROUS GAMES

On sale April 2007

I stood in the shadows and watched the dead man.

The night was bitterly cold, and rain fell in a heavy, constant stream. Water sluiced down the vampire's long causeway of a nose, leaping to the square thrust of his jaw before joining the mad rush down the front of his yellow raincoat. The puddle around his bare feet had reached his ankles and was slowly beginning to creep up his hairy legs.

Like most of the newly risen, he was little more than flesh stretched tautly over bone. But his skin possessed a rosy glow that suggested he'd eaten well and often. Even if his pale eyes were sunken. Haunted.

Which in itself wasn't really surprising. Thanks to the willingness of both Hollywood and literature to romanticize vampirism, far too many humans seemed to think that by becoming a vampire they'd instantly gain all the power, sex, and wealth they could ever want. It wasn't until after the change that they began to realize that being undead wasn't the fun time often depicted. That wealth, sex, and popularity might come, but only if they survived the horrendous first few years, when a vampire was all instinct and blood need. And of course, if they did survive, they then learned that endless loneliness, never feeling the full warmth of the sun again, never being able to savor the taste of food, and being feared or ostracized by a good percentage of the population was also part of the equation.

Yeah, there were laws in place to stop discrimination against vampires and other nonhumans, but the laws were only a recent development. And while there might now be vampire groupies, they were also a recent phenomenon and only a small portion of the population. Hatred and fear of vamps had been around for centuries, and I had no doubt it would take centuries for it to abate. If it ever did.

And the bloody rampages of vamps like the one ahead weren't helping the cause any.

A total of twelve people had disappeared over the last month, and we were pretty sure this vamp was responsible for nine of them. But there were enough differences in method of killing between this vamp's nine and the remaining three to suggest we had a second psycho on the loose. For a start, nine had met their death as a result of a vamp feeding frenzy. The other three had been meticulously sliced open neck to knee with a knife and their innards carefully removed—not something the newly turned were generally capable of. When presented with the opportunity for a feed, they fed. There was nothing neat or meticulous about it.

Then there were the multiple, barely healed scars marring the backs of the three anomalous women, the missing pinky on their left hands, and the odd, almost satisfied smiles that seemed frozen on their dead lips. Women who were the victims of a vamp's frenzy didn't die with *that* sort of smile, as the souls of the dead nine could probably attest if they were still hanging about.

And I seriously hoped that they *weren't*. I'd seen more than enough souls rising in recent times—I certainly didn't want to make a habit of it.

But dealing with two psychos on top of coping with the usual Guardian patrols had the Directorate stretched to the limit, and that meant everyone had been pulling extra shifts. Which explained why Rhoan and I were out hunting rogue suckers on this bitch of a night after working all day trying to find some leads on what Jack—our boss, and the vamp who ran the whole guardian division at the Directorate of Other Races—charmingly called The Cleaver.

I yawned and leaned a shoulder against the concrete wall lining one side of the small alleyway I was hiding in. The wall, which was part of the massive factory complex that dominated a good part of the old West Footscray area, protected me from the worst of the wind, but it didn't do a whole lot against the goddamn rain.

If the vamp felt any discomfort about standing in a pothole in the middle of a storm-drenched night, he certainly wasn't showing it. But then, the dead rarely cared about such things.

I might have vampire blood running through my veins, but I wasn't dead and I hated it.

Winter in Melbourne was never a joy, but this year we'd had so much rain I was beginning to forget what sunshine looked like. Most wolves were immune to the cold, but I was a half-breed and obviously lacked that particular gene. My feet were icy and I was beginning to lose feeling in several toes. And this despite the fact I was wearing two pairs of thick woolen socks underneath my rubber-heeled shoes. Which were not waterproof, no matter what the makers claimed.

I should have worn stilettos. My feet would have been no worse off, and I would have felt more at home. And hey, if he happened to spot me, I could have pretended to be nothing more than a bedraggled, desperate hooker. But Jack—my boss, and the vamp who ran the whole guardian division at the Directorate of Other Races—kept insisting high heels and my job just didn't go together.

Personally, I think he was a little afraid of my shoes. Not so much because of the color—which, admittedly, was often outrageous—but because of the nifty wooden heels. Wood and vamps were never an easy mix.

I flicked up the collar of my leather jacket and tried to ignore the fat drops of water dribbling down my spine. What I really needed—more than decent-looking shoes—was a hot bath, a seriously large cup of coffee, and a thick steak sandwich. Preferably with lashings of onions and ketchup, but skip the tomato and green shit, please. God, my mouth was salivating just thinking about it. Of course, given we were in the middle of this ghost town of factories, none of those things were likely to appear in my immediate future.

I thrust wet hair out of my eyes, and wished, for the umpteenth time that night, that he would just get on with it. Whatever it was.

Following him might be part of my job as a guardian, but that didn't mean I had to be happy about it. I'd never had much choice about joining the guardian ranks, thanks to the experimental drugs several lunatics had forced into my system and the psychic talents that were developing as a result. It was either stay with the Directorate as a guardian so my growing abilities could be monitored and harnessed, or be shipped off to the military with the other unfortunates who had received similar doses of the ARC1-23 drug. I might not have wanted to be a guardian, but I sure as hell didn't want to be sent to the military. Give me the devil I know any day.

I shifted weight from one foot to the other again. What the hell was this piece of dead meat waiting for? He couldn't have sensed me—I was far enough away that he wouldn't hear the beat of my heart or the rush of blood through my veins. He hadn't looked over his shoulder at any time, so he couldn't have spotted me with the infrared of his vampire vision, and blood suckers generally didn't have a very keen olfactory sense.

So why stand in a puddle in the middle of this abandoned factory complex looking like a little lost soul?

Part of me itched to shoot the bastard and just get the whole ordeal over with. But we needed to follow this baby vamp home to discover if he had any nasty surprises hidden in his nest. Like other victims, or perhaps even his maker.

Because it was unusual for one of the newly turned to survive nine rogue kills without getting himself caught or killed. Not without help, anyway.

The vampire suddenly stepped out of the puddle and began walking down the slight incline, his bare feet slapping noisily against the broken road. The shadows and the night hovered all around him, but he didn't bother cloaking his form. Given the whiteness of his hairy legs and the brightness of his yellow raincoat, that was strange. Though we were in the middle of nowhere. Maybe he figured he was safe.

I stepped out of the alleyway. The wind hit full force, pushing me sideways for several steps before I regained my balance. I padded across the road and stopped in the shadows again. The rain beat a tattoo against my back and the water seeping through my coat became a river, making me feel colder than I'd ever dreamed possible. Forget the coffee and the sandwich. What I wanted more than anything right now was to get warm.

I pressed the small com-link button that had been inserted into my earlobe just over four months ago. It doubled as a two-way communicator and a tracker, and Jack had insisted not only that I keep it but that all guardians were to have them from now on. He wanted to be able to find his people at all times, even when not on duty.

Which smacked of "big-brother" syndrome to me even if I could understand his reasoning. Guardians didn't grow on trees—finding vamps with just the right mix of killing instinct and moral sensibilities was difficult, which was why guardian numbers at the Directorate still hadn't fully recovered from the eleven we'd lost ten months ago.

One of those eleven had been a friend of mine, and on my worst nights I still dreamed of her death, even though the only thing I'd ever witnessed was the bloody patch of sand that had contained her DNA. Like most of the other guardians who had gone missing, her remains had never been found.

Of course, the tracking measures had come too late not only for those eleven, but for one other—Gautier. Not that he was dead, however much I might wish otherwise. Four months ago he'd been the Directorate's top guardian. Now he was rogue and on top of the Directorate's hit list. So far he'd escaped every search, every trap. Meaning he was still out there, waiting and watching and plotting his revenge.

On me.

Goose bumps traveled down my spine and, just for a second, I'd swear his dead scent teased my nostrils. Whether it was real or just imagination and fear I couldn't say, because the gusting wind snatched it away.

Even if it wasn't real, it was a reminder that I had to be extra careful. Gautier had never really functioned on the same sane field as the rest of us. Worse still, he liked playing with his prey. Liked watching the pain and fear grow before he killed.

He might now consider me his mouse, but he'd yet to try any of his games on me. But something told me that tonight, that would all change.

I grimaced and did my best to ignore the insight. Clairvoyance might have been okay if it had come in a truly usable form—like clear glimpses of future scenes and happenings—but oh no, that was apparently asking too much of fate. Instead, I just got these weird feelings of upcoming doom that were frustratingly vague on any sort of concrete detail. And training something like that was nigh on impossible—not that that stopped Jack from getting his people to at least try.

Whether the illusiveness would change as the talent became more settled was anyone's guess. Personally, I just wished it would go back to being latent. I knew Gautier was out there somewhere. Knew he was coming after me. I didn't need some half-assed talent sending me spooky little half warnings every other day.

Still, even though I knew Gautier probably wasn't out here tonight, I couldn't help looking around and checking all the shadows as I said, "Brother dearest, I hate this fucking job."

Rhoan's soft laughter ran into my ear. Just hearing it made me feel better. Safer. "Nights like this are a bitch, aren't they?"

"Understatement of the year." I quickly peeked around the corner and saw the vampire turning left. I padded after him, keeping to the wall and well away from the puddles. Though given the state of my feet, it really wouldn't have mattered. "And I feel obligated to point out that I didn't sign up for night work."

Rhoan chuckled softly. "And I feel obliged to point out that you weren't actually signed up, but forcibly drafted. Therefore, you can bitch all you want, but it isn't going to make a damn difference."

Wasn't that the truth. "Where are you?"

"West side, near the old biscuit factory."

Which was practically opposite my position. Between the two of us we had him penned. Hopefully, it meant we wouldn't lose him.

I stopped as I neared the corner and carefully peered around. The wind slapped against my face, and the rain on my skin seemed to turn to ice. The vamp had stopped near the far end of the building and was looking around. I ducked back as he looked my way, barely daring to breathe even though common sense suggested there was no way he could have seen me. Not only did I have vampire genes, but I had many of their skills as well. Like the ability to cloak under the shadow of night, the infrared vision, and their faster-than-a-blink speed.

The creak of a door carried past. I risked another look. A metal door stood ajar and the vamp was nowhere in sight.

An invitation or a trap?

I didn't know, but I sure as hell wasn't going to take a chance. Not alone, anyway.

"Rhoan, he's gone inside building number four. Rear entrance, right-hand side."

"Wait for me to get there before you go in."

"I'm foolhardy, but I'm not stupid."

He chuckled again. I slipped around the corner and crept toward the door. The wind caught the edge of it and flung it back against the brick wall, the crash echoing across the night. It was an oddly lonely sound.

I froze and concentrated, using the keenness of my wolf hearing to sort through the noises running with the wind. But the howl of it was just too strong, overriding everything else.

Nor could I smell anything more than ice, age, and abandonment. If there were such smells and it wasn't just my overactive imagination.

Yet a feeling of wrongness was growing deep inside. I rubbed my leather-covered arms and hoped like hell my brother got here fast.